THE DAILY GRIND

BOOK 4

BOOK 4

ARGUS

Podium

BOOK 4

CHAPTER 1

There were, of course, *again*, things to take care of. It wasn't like delves into the Office had gotten less dangerous somehow, just because they'd managed to find a place that was more open about wanting to kill them all. So they had plans to make, things to buy, and a roster to draw up.

"We really should have scheduled this two weeks out," James griped as he waited on a half dozen people to reply to his texts. "I'm pretty sure it's the law in this state now."

"I'm pretty sure we don't qualify as a 'company' in the traditional sense," Anesh reminded him. "We're more of a wandering band of condottiere. So even if we hit the thirty-person threshold that would require us to actually plan ahead, I think you get some kind of exemption for operating outside of state lines. And reality."

James eyed his friend and was wondering whether or not he should call his bluff on whether condottiere was a real word when his phone buzzed and he was dragged back to rearranging their team lineup for the next night.

They had some other stuff to do, too. Buying bikes was one thing; there was a scheduled trip to the beach, and the printer ink ocean, for the purposes of further exploration and purple-orb acquisition, and that miles-long trip would be eased dramatically if they could just pedal through it. Sarah had gone out to pick that up earlier in the day, waking up in her trademark chipper way and rustling the hair of anyone within reach before grabbing an absolutely suspicious roll of bills from the home stash and heading out. James shook his head and gave a small prayer for the patience of the employees at whatever bike shop she ended up in.

Alanna followed Sarah out the door a half hour later, throwing a peace sign as she went on her own errand. And then both Aneshes took off to do delver-supply maintenance—one of them going after bottled water, real food for the eight-hour shift, more hemostatic powder and disinfectant for their first aid kits, which had been drained far more rapidly than expected, and a large supply of heavy-duty work gloves. You know, the usual things someone bought from a grocery store.

The other Anesh had a much harder job for the day. Fortunately it was a weekend, and most of the time there being two of him made getting homework done trivially easy, because he didn't have classes to contend with. But his job was to put a slight upgrade on their arsenal.

As they'd progressed, first him and James, then with more people as a team, then as a strategic unit, gear upgrades had been critical to keeping them alive. Better armor, easier-to-use weapons, more survival tools—all of them contributed to keeping everyone kicking. But now they were running into a bit of a wall.

There was, it turned out, an upper limit to how dangerous of equipment a civilian could just buy.

You could, in theory, equip two dozen people like a SWAT team, yes. But actually buying that much armor, even piece by piece, got you noticed. The stuff they'd been using up until now was great, but it had limitations, and when one of those limitations was "the maimframes can shoot through it without resistance" . . . well, you looked for options.

Their weaponry, similarly, had hit a bit of a wall. This was, sadly, not the Forgotten Realms. Anesh really couldn't just take their growing income stream and turn it into higher and higher bonuses on James's favorite hand axe. Instead, he had to look at getting more durable materials, better balance and edge on weapons, and other things that gave only marginal advantages to most people.

And again, sure, he could buy more guns. But the guy he'd bought their two current mainstay weapons from had vanished, Anesh actually *wasn't* the right person to contact the black market, and, again, handguns and civilian shotguns could only carry them so far. That said, they were training more people with handguns; James especially made a good teacher, with the skill he had. But the more people they had, the more friendly fire became a concern.

So, since those concerns would only be worn away with time, patience, training, and eventually just giving up and taking the plunge, Anesh had instead chosen to get *weird* with his budget for the week.

Garden shears to deal with tumblefeeds. Short-range and really kind of cheap drones rigged up with explosives—mostly thermite. Gloves that were wired to deliver powerful electrical currents. A battery pack and an electromagnet, to see if shellaxies actually needed working hard drives to function. Stuff that would be either wasteful or stupid in a real combat situation against other people. But against the dungeon? They had the leeway now, and the cash, to try some different stuff. Stuff like buying bushels of iPhone charger cables to try to bait iLipedes into net traps.

Okay, he'd also bought ten fire axes, but aside from that.

The point was mostly that him being out for the day kept the apartment once again mostly empty.

And at a certain point, James found himself with nothing left to do, no one left to wait on hearing from, and even if he'd needed to know anything, his phone worked anywhere anyway. So, he'd simply stood with a stretch and a sigh, abandoning the arcanely enhanced comfort of the couch, and headed out to the lair.

"Momo! Just the girl I wanted to see!" James greeted the younger woman as he shoved the door open with his foot, stepping in and swinging the heavy duffel bag in his hand through after him in a fluid move. He'd gotten so good at that method of going through the door that he didn't need to rest the bag on the shrub to the left of it anymore while he did so—something the smushed bush probably appreciated.

Momo ran a hand across the shaved side of her head as she paused for James's greeting. "Oh?" Her voice was groggy. "Good. I think. Whazzup?"

James eyed her, suspicious. "You seem tired. Do you need a nap? I can bother someone else. I was really just wondering who was in the lair today."

Alanna had told him about the experiments with the red orbs, which were increasingly less and less experiments and more and more Momo descending into sleepless madness, and Sarah had also told him to take it easy on the girl, who appeared to have had most of her life carved away by the Office's antimeme complex. So when confronted by someone who looked like she got all the sleep she needed during particularly long blinks, James had this feeling that maybe he could just poke around himself and leave her to do what she needed without him bothering her.

"Mmrph," Momo muttered. Or at least that's what it sounded like.

James nodded at her. "Got it," he said. "I'll go find El or something."

Momo gave him a sleepy thumbs-up and turned to head back to whatever she was doing. Which looked mostly like filling her comically large thermos with coffee from the . . .

"Um . . . you know it's not super healthy to drink too much of that, right?" James asked her. He had to hold him his hands in a defensive move to ward off her almost instant glare. "Just asking! Not judging! Just be careful! There may be other side effects, but at the very least, drinking too much'll knock you out for a solid eight hours." He looked at her again and then shrugged, slinging the bag back over his shoulder as he did so. "Which actually might not be so bad. Just sit down first, okay?"

"Fine," Momo huffed at him. But she wasn't glaring when she did it, which James considered a win. Getting anything out of someone who was exhausted and traumatized that wasn't a scowl or a yell was hard enough.

James walked past her, giving Momo plenty of space, and considered his first stop. After a couple seconds, he turned toward the elevator and decided to hit the basement.

Which basement? Whichever one he hit the button for. He still couldn't keep track, and honestly, it felt a little silly considering this was his own damn fault. If it was the wrong one, he'd get the other later.

When the doors opened—on the familiar scene of tables of random stuff surrounded by whiteboards, notebooks, a few PC screens, and . . . was that a spectrograph?—James shook his head as he looked at the main lobby of the more functional basement. The layout on this side was mostly just two really big rooms separated by a concrete wall that had paths through at each end where it met the outer walls. There were a couple smaller closets, too, which was where most of the stuff that had been down here went when they initially cleaned up. But now they'd turned this whole section into a place to run tests on anything they hauled back into reality, away from the eyes of anyone who might wander in upstairs.

James saw one table that had a half dozen pairs of eyewear on it, each one positioned just in front of a small box of a webcam, and all those plugged into the computer running nearby. He recognized the shades Anesh used to peer into infrared and also the reading glasses Alanna used to spot time sinks, both of them having temporarily handed their toys off to whoever was looking into that particular question. On another table, a whole shipping box full of assorted pencils and pens sat popped open. Next to that, one of those industrial-strength garbage cans hosted about half of a box full of snapped writing implements. There was even the corpse of a shellaxy down here, dismantled in a strange machine version of an autopsy.

Only one person, though. A young man surrounded by coffee cups, with an ethernet cable plugged into the back of his neck, sticking out through his long hair and leading back to the computer he was furiously typing at.

"Virgil!" James greeted him, stopping in front of the desk and looking down at what was, honestly, just a mess. "Why are you here?" James asked after a couple minutes. "Actually, why the hell are *any* of the people I hired here? I specifically told all of you *Monday*, but you're here now and Nate's been making food for us for, like, a fucking week." A second later, the scene caught up to him, and James added a more direct question of "Also why do you have a skulljack?"

Virgil Thomasi looked up at his nominal boss from his seat in the secret basement in the secret lair that he hadn't really formally been shown around. "Neil gave me one, since I asked about it. I figured it'd be required for the project? Also, these things are wild. How'd you get them to do the self-replication thing?"

"I didn't. Virgil—Vir?"

"Virgil."

"Verge."

". . . Virgil."

"Fine." James huffed disappointment. "Virgil, these things are literal magic. I don't even know how *Neil* has one; I don't remember authorizing that. *Or this.* I haven't even given you project goals yet, but one of the main points is that we need security *before* we spread these to a million people." He tried to explain that this was, in fact, exactly what he was afraid of.

Virgil just waved it off. "It's fine. I've already put together a project timeline. Who's my direct superior? I'll email it to them."

"It's . . . me. I am in charge here," James asserted, although he was increasingly unsure of that statement. "Just tell me what you're working on, please. You can email the thing to Anesh later. Actually, all the computers down here should be set up on our Slack, so, there's that, too."

"It's security first, like you said," the other man agreed, idly pushing his glasses up his nose as he spoke. He leaned back in his chair, his fingers finally stopping their dance across the keys. "We need something like a firewall that we can load as firmware. Failing that, I'll have to request the hardware department build something that locks into place around it that can hold software so that we can ensure no unwanted intrusions. The whole brain-to-brain bridge is a problem, because these are obviously for internet use, and too many people merging into a hive mind would be bad."

"Would it?" James asked, mulling over the philosophy of the question.

"If they didn't want to, yes," Virgil answered, going a different direction with the statement. "After that, we need some kind of monitoring software for whatever oversight agency ends up on this."

"No," James informed him. "We don't. That's actually not the point. I agree with you on security, but I'm mostly hoping you can find a way to load the software into the human mind directly. Also, have you spoken to the survivor support group at all? They have months of experience with these things, and I feel like you could learn a lot from them."

"Are they programmers or engineers?" Virgil asked, starting to turn back to the screen.

"Neither," James said. And before he lost Virgil's interest, he added, "But they don't need to use keyboards."

Virgil paused, looked down at his fingers, then ran a hand back to the cord at the base of his neck. "Huh," he said. "Didn't think of that."

"Talk to the support group. We need security, then safety measures for forming hives. No surveillance. In fact, if possible, make it impossible." James looked down, looming over the desk. "We are not a shadowy government agency. We are not a tech corp. We are a small group of people who are planning to make ripples. Please remember that." James turned to walk away as Virgil called an affirmative after him. Then he remembered something and turned to yell back, "Also please remember that we are using *literal magic*, and be fucking careful!"

Shaking his head, James got back in the elevator and went back up before going back down.

The other basement, which was technically in the same space as the first one, and was very worrying, was where they'd put in the lair's housing. There were a lot of partitioned rooms here, maybe a dozen of them. And this side had a bathroom, too, which was mercifully affected by the green orbs that made their bathrooms marvelous. A few of the rooms still contained boxes of junk and spiders that had been moved there when the basements first spawned, but the others had been outfitted with beds, desks, proper lighting, and carpet.

The stuff that had spawned down here really did bother James. No one was sure where the hell it had come from; there'd been absolutely no identifying marks or addresses on anything. Most of it was culturally North American, but that was the only constant pattern. It had shown up as suddenly as the basements themselves, and James was pretty firmly on the side of the bet that said it was just generated. But Sarah and a few others had this weird belief that it had been stolen from basements around the country, forgotten or lost things plucked from where they rested to fill a room.

It really made James wonder if this was how dungeons got started.

Probably not, though, since the spiders had all been the normal type and not the Shelob kind.

"Anyone home?" he yelled into the hallway that led away from the elevator doors. Normally, Momo would be down here, and probably pissed that James had interrupted her delicate work. But he knew she was still upstairs, so he was safe now.

Well, safeish. He heard a thump and swearing from down the hall, and a few seconds later one of the doors was kicked open with enough force that it left a small chip in the rock wall where the handle slammed against it.

"What?!" Eleanor yelled out, red-faced and looking like she'd been more than a little startled by James's cry.

James started with "Oh, sorry!"

"Were you in the middle of something?" he asked innocently.

"Yes!" she yelled back. "What the hell do you want?"

"I actually was looking for you," he said, trying to placate her. "But everyone's been unhelpful here today. I just had some dungeon questions, if you were in the mood for it. I dunno if you heard, but we found a pretty dark place yesterday, and I wanted to compare magic. Oh! Also, are you up for tomorrow? I know you don't have a phone, so

I figured I'd ask while I was here. Also . . ." James looked at her incredulous face, poked out from around the corner of the door at a right angle, hair falling down across her face as she refused to step out into the hallway. "You're naked right now, huh?" he asked her.

"I absolutely am," El replied.

"I will wait in the café," James said politically.

"You do that," El told him.

The elevator took way longer than James was comfortable with to get back down and give him his escape route.

Behind him, El shut her door again. Her room, this last week, had started feeling more like her own space and less like a prison, especially once she was given a box of spray paint and permission to go nuts on the stone walls. Now, though, she was reminded of the biggest downside of communal living, the reason she'd abandoned the dorms in college.

Other people.

She slumped back onto the bed and briefly considered being pissed at James. It had been so easy when she'd gotten here; he'd basically destroyed her life by playing at being a secret agent. Hell, she'd tried to shoot him. But every encounter with the guy just left her wanting to be friends with him. He wasn't an artist—far from it; he was a comedian—but he lightened up every room he walked into most of the time. And it didn't take El long to learn that there was a reason all the people here treated him like a hero.

It was hard to stay mad for too long at anyone who actually was, literally, a hero.

El took a minute to scream frustration into her pillow and then got up to find pants and go have a conversation.

Alanna hit send on her phone. James would get the text sooner or later, which was how she viewed texting in general. It was, in her mind, about as reliable as actual mail. Eventually, sure, the person would get it. But you did not use it for important things. You used actual calls for important things. Or just face-to-face conversations. Alanna knew that James and Anesh both loved text messages in all their forms, for the convenience of never having to deal with the anxiety of an actual chat. But for her, spoken words were queen.

So you used texts for informing your boyfriend, who had a similar superpower to you, that you'd figured out a particular activation word. But only when it wasn't important.

Alanna looked down at her phone and sighed as she processed that line of thought. Maybe this did warrant a call. But really, what were the odds James had learned one hundred points of basketball in the last eighteen hours?

The text was simple and to the point, and what it was was a direction: *{say "syllabus" and focus on your book thing}* was the text she had sent him. It was the culmination of the second half of her day's work.

A lot of what Alanna had been doing today involved driving around. For someone who worked on cars, it was weird that Alanna had never actually owned one of her own, and the casual mention from James a month or so ago—"oh yeah, we can afford that"—had caught her off guard. So she was still getting used to the practice of driving and the cultural impact of owning her own vehicle. It was mildly irritating that all her transit-based skills were for things like helicopters or boats and not actual cars, but then, learning the old-fashioned way did feel rewarding, and they couldn't all be James with his stupidly high-skill-rank driving ability.

The point was, she was in the car. And between yowling along to DragonForce lyrics, she had been doing a lot of thinking.

The books they'd recovered had given them something different. Alanna herself was now in possession of reward-esque modifications from no fewer than three different dungeons, and they only sort of had a handle on how the first one worked. So now they had this new and potentially dangerous thing to contend with.

Lesson Begun, it had said. Alanna had turned those words over in her head a hundred times. It made sense, in one sense; this dungeon was under a high school, after all. Lessons were thematically linked to that. The information fit comfortably in her head and also gave a little more weight to the theory bouncing around the group that the dungeons were just physically projected *ideas* manifesting in the world. But in another way, it was worrying. If it was going to be teaching her about the field of communications, then that sounded just like what the orbs did. But Alanna knew from what Sarah had dug up that it was more like she had to perform the act of communication before being rewarded for it. Still . . . *lesson* was a specific word. And Alanna *had* communicated today, and nothing had happened!

Or, at least, so she assumed. This had brought her to a period of her highway drive when she'd killed the music and started trying to interrogate the part of her brain that the thought had shot through when she'd read the book.

It was tricky, but she didn't have nothing to go on. When they were in the dungeon, after all, they'd been able to get accurate reminders of how many sparks they'd collected just by asking. So Alanna had just set out to replicate that. And eight random terms for school schedules later, including repeating a few while actually focusing on the magic she was reaching for, she'd hit upon one that worked.

[Lesson Continues—Communications : 1/100] was the thought that flashed across her mind. She couldn't actually see it, but the no-tification even had the taste of folded paper and a new school year— and all the anxieties that came along with that.

Partly, it was *frustrating.* The big magic Office dungeon didn't tell her what skills she had, and Alanna was absolutely sure everyone she knew had tried to open their character sheet at some point. She could always figure out what skills she had, but it was easy to forget when not looking at the spreadsheet that she knew how to handle a falcon. Aside from that, though . . .

One out of a hundred was something, she thought to herself. Alanna was still pretty tired from everything that had happened last night, and while, unlike James and one Anesh, she had gone to sleep instead of going out to play basketball, she *was* starting to reach the limits of her brainpower. So in the short time before she made it to her destination, she dropped trying to puzzle out what had made that single point go up and just went back to the music.

Of course, when she parked and checked her return text from James, the comment of {27/100. *You?*} was infuriating.

But at least they could now legitimately tell JP that Anesh was no longer squandering basketball.

"Okay, that's our side of things," James said, wrapping up the short version of their magic systems for El. "Orbs, connections, and books that give us lessons. Full disclosure, all questions open." He waved his fork like a conductor's baton, inviting her to ask whatever she liked.

The two of them sat at one of the cafeteria tables set up outside the kitchen and next to the gym area. Nate was, unsurprisingly, *here* and had supplied them with plates of enchiladas and Spanish rice on remarkably short notice. He'd also been in and out of the kitchen for various reasons as James had talked to El, and eventually he just gave up trying to be surreptitious about his eavesdropping and sat down with them.

The entire encounter was pretty much exactly what James loved; seeing people's faces when he told them they could get better at scuba diving in the blink of an eye was a really rewarding experience. Though he *was* starting to get sick of the hard plastic benches here. They'd really only gotten these tables because it seemed appropriate for a lunchroom next to a gym, but James had never been one for obeying aesthetic rules and was currently plotting to bring in bean-bag chairs and chabudai.

El raised her hand to ask a question; Nate didn't bother and just said his, cutting past her, "Is that why you have a sea monster that shouldn't be able to physically fit through doors living here?" he asked.

"That's Secret, and he actually lives in a closet in my apartment," James corrected him, reveling in every second of this. "And yes. One of the variant orbs we've found is purple, and there's a way of using it to make infomorphic Life."

Nate rapped a fistful of knuckles on the table. "What the fuck is *that?*"

"Secret isn't actually a body with thoughts inside it. He's a series of thoughts that can manifest a body. But the thoughts are self-perpetuating. So everyone who gets to know him starts to have part of their brain thinking about him, which makes him more real, and the thoughts they think reinforce that. Only a few people know him personally and deeply, though, and you can think of that as sort of like a human's heart or lungs. The really important core bits."

"Nope." Nate shook his head. "That makes no fuckin' sense."

"It makes some sense," El protested, mouth full of food. She simplified it for the chef: "He's literally real because you believe he's real."

James wobbled a hand. "Kinda. Except once you start believing he's real, the belief that he's real sustains itself, whether you want it to or not. Which sounds worse than it is, really."

"I feel like we're getting off topic," El said. "And I had another question. Actually, I have a million questions, and now a few more questions about whether or not there's other types of life you can make. But those aren't the big one." James nodded in anticipation. He knew what the big one was. "Where," El asked, "do you *find* these things?"

"The same kind of place that you did," James told her, meeting her eyes. He half watched Nate's reaction as he talked, because that was most of the fun; El already knew, but this moment was one for her. Where he could finally just sit down and reassure her that the two of them were kindred. "Through a hole in reality, where logic doesn't apply so much. In a place where there's bizarre dangers, and stranger rewards, and wonders beyond belief." He grinned, a wild and happy grin. "Oh, and it's an office."

"What," Nate asked from the side. "The fuck." He sounded . . . not unimpressed, but like he was, weirdly, taking things in stride for someone who'd just been informed of this on his second or third day of a new job.

"There's a door that's only sometimes open, and it goes to a billion, billion cubicles. And it's fucked-up, and there's monsters, and there's also stuff like *this*." James pulled two of the spare yellow orbs out of his coat pocket and rolled them toward Nate and Eleanor. "Crack them."

A few seconds later, both of them wore expressions of mild to moderate disbelief.

"Rhino husbandry?" Nate asked, scratching at his bald head with a tattooed hand. "What in . . . Why?"

"No idea." James shrugged. "They're random. El probably also got something weird. It's not impolite to ask, either; we do try to keep a database; though if you wanna keep it to yourself, that's fine," he offered. "Honestly, I was planning to tell all the new people about this tomorrow, when we went in. That was the thing I meant when I hired you, by the way—which, I distinctly remember telling you that your first day was *Monday*." James tried to glare at their stocky chef and utterly failed.

Nate just shrugged under the scrutiny. "A kitchen takes time to set up. I didn't want to let someone else fuck it up before I could."

"Well, anyway." James sighed. "It kinda works out. We've got nineteen people, including you, going in tomorrow night. And yeah, you're not expected to pull any heroic nonsense or whatever; I just want everyone to see at least once what we're up against. I'm mostly telling you this because it would be a huge help if you could have food for everyone."

"You want me," Nate slowly stated, "to cater a combat op?"

"Yes."

He clearly hadn't been expecting that answer. His head tilted back, and he sucked his lips in as he considered James. Then, without saying anything else, he stood up and said, "You're getting chicken," before he turned and stalked back into the kitchen.

"He says that like I don't know that chicken is the only meat that Sysco delivered," James muttered. "Like he thinks I don't know how inventory works. Bah!"

El eyed him cautiously. "So, what did you actually want, when you asked if I could talk?" She jutted a thumb at the direction Nate had gone. "Now that you got rid of him."

"First off, I actually was gonna have to have that conversation with him eventually. I'm not *that* manipulative," he said, getting a nonplussed look in response. His smile faltered a bit, but only a bit. "But yes. I figured I'd set him on his task before I asked you this next part." James pointed an index finger at her chest. "Eleanor Chase, you are a *wizard*, and I would like to know what you can do."

She glared at him for that, a brief moment of fury that quickly settled to base resentment. "You know, you talk like him sometimes," she said. "Secret. You talk like Secret. Like you forget that you're not in some trash fantasy paperback."

"Okay, hey now . . ." James tried to protest, his gravitas slipping back into a soft huff of amusement.

"The place I found. The hole in reality. It's a road. Maybe I'll sell you the location sometime, if . . . well. We'll see. And it's dangerous, just like you said. But it gave me a few tricks." El started talking more comfortably as James leaned back and just let her speak. It took her a minute to find her voice, but this was something she'd been wondering about telling someone for a long time.

"First off, I store velocity. I can feel it; I dunno if you can feel your orbs . . . wow, nope, never saying that again . . . but I can sense how much I have. I've found seven or eight things that raise my limit; can't remember if one was real, since I had a concussion at the time. Anyway." El waved a hand and brushed aside a story about a high-speed chase, a flock of motorbats, a treasure map, and a really, truly rad artifact in the form of a car air freshener, which she'd had to leave behind. James would have loved the story. He didn't ask.

"I can do three spells," she said instead. "It never told me they were spells, that's just what I call them, 'cause I'm not an idiot. Eye of Steel and Glass, which lets me see everything in an area as an index of items. It's temporary, eats up a ton of velocity, and is great for blackma— reconnaissance and intelligence . . . things." She didn't bother to meet James's gaze for that one, instead staring at the ceiling vents. "Then I've also got An Engine Hums Eternal, which just boosts the speed of a vehicle that I'm controlling. Has to be a vehicle; I tried it on rollerblades—didn't work. And yes, that does count for refilling velocity; I think that's the point of it. Last one is The Road Leads Ever Forward. It takes basically every scrap of velocity I can hold—I've only used it twice—and it warps reality so that there's a path to where I want to go. Or, like, there was always a path. But I remember both versions." She took a breath as she paused, now eyeing James and making patterns in her cooling plate of food. "So . . . any questions? I guess it's only fair I let you ask, too," she finished.

James absorbed what she'd said and then asked the one question that was most pressing, most important. To him, anyway.

"So, when you say the names of the spells, how do you do the thing where you pronounce the capital letters?"

At two thirty on an innocuous Tuesday morning, a certain office building began routine maintenance of its security system.

If you had asked a security expert what that maintenance actually was, they would have given you a raised eyebrow and the question of *what*, exactly, you thought needed to be maintained. But if you asked any of the fifty or sixty different midlevel managers that worked within the building, you would have instead gotten a shrug and the implication that of *course* they needed to do maintenance, and it wasn't their department, but they were sure that Tuesday morning was a good enough time for it. It wasn't like anyone was stealing from the company, after all.

Depending on how you defined "the company," and whether or not the whispers of conspiracy and dark management secrets were true, those people may have been totally right in saying that nothing was being stolen.

Within five minutes, the front doors had been propped open by the two guards at the front desk, one of whom was acting as head of security and doing a pretty good job of it. The two of them nodded at each other with smug satisfaction, their part in this done.

Within ten minutes of the security system going into maintenance mode, a small fleet of vehicles had parked in the front lot. Mostly passenger vehicles, out of which people disgorged in ones and twos, heading for the doors hauling boxes or empty bags waiting to be filled. One pickup truck, which had been rented for the day and contained a four count of mountain bikes in the back that Sarah enlisted help wheeling into the elevator as fast as possible. One Pendragon, who took off as soon as Dave slid off her back and gave her a pat; she was content to orbit overhead, enjoying her gift of flight. And one van, which apparently was just what Nate drove, and which he couldn't get anyone to help him unload a series of silvery metal pans out of. At least not until he announced that this was actual food, and everyone got lunch *if* this shit got where it was going within ten minutes. That got people moving.

Two people who had hitched a ride with James stood with mouths slightly agape, watching the rush of motion around them. To say that the guild was a well-oiled machine at this point would be a flagrant lie, but it was more than Virgil and Lance had expected.

Lance was the big ol' softie of a nerd that James had hired on a whim at the end of his interview day. James had, stupidly, not gotten his name at the time, and he also was the only one of the three new hires who hadn't just shown up at the lair over the course of the week. He was here now, though, and it seemed like he'd expected something different from the adventuring party than fifteen people scrambling to get a bag of shotguns upstairs. Too bad for him, though. This was what he got.

Neil, of all people, was the one who snapped them out of their daze. Perhaps the kid was just eager to not be the newest person in the group anymore; finally, there was someone he could teach the lessons to, the cycle continuing. "Hey!" The two other men jumped slightly in unison as Neil announced himself behind them. "No time for dawdling! Find someone who needs help and give it. And take this!" He offered one of them a box full of static bags before ducking his head back into the back seat of his car and coming out with his own backpack. "Let's go! You're on Team New Guy with me today. I'm not the tour guide, but I *do* get first dibs on being the drone operator," he said, as if that explained anything.

By 3:10 a.m., the elevator had taken about two dozen trips up and down. Around twenty people and one infomorph, who was still technically a person, were lined up in a hallway in front of an elevator landing, waiting for the moment that the door to the stairs didn't go to the stairs anymore. Sarah and JP patrolled up and down the line, which James and Anesh stood at the front of. Two columns of people, some of them holding bikes off to their sides, replacements for the ones that Officium Mundi had consumed weeks ago. Everyone was herded into place, and the countdown was on. Nervous hands checked phones every couple minutes, while the more experienced delvers made idle conversation.

"You know, I'm gonna be glad to get back to a place that isn't, like, trying to murder us," Alanna told a second Anesh as she went through a routine of warm-up stretches.

He looked at her askance. "I'm sorry, have you met the same office I have?" Anesh asked, surprise dragging out the thickest part of his accent. "This place is an ongoing bloody nightmare of lethal office supplies."

"Yah, sure," Alanna conceded. "But it's not *trying* that hard."

Up front, James and Anesh were having a very different conversation. "So, what are you going for tonight?" James asked.

Anesh looked down at the red-and-white container in his hands, then back up at his friend. "Really?" he asked.

"Oh, bah. I mean, after that," James said. He tried to entice his boyfriend: "Yellows? Blues? Maybe join the hunting team and go for a tumblefeed? More lair upgrades!"

"I'm getting Momo to help me look at the projector pattern," Anesh said. "I told you guys before, the linear power of the orbs should go to you and Alanna."

"Bulllllshiiiiiit." James echoed the word like a vengeful ghost. "You *know* that you want more yellows for those delicious math points! Also, we could find you another orange! You could make more of you!"

"I can already do that," Anesh said. "And I am pretty sure that's not how the oranges work, but okay." He laughed. "I just figured I'd do the projector thing today and Other Me could focus on wanting orbs."

"Bah," James said. "No sense of adventure."

"But some sense of priorities!" Anesh smiled.

"Everyone shut up!" Sarah called down the line. It was mostly pointless; everyone had already shut up to listen in on the four people at the front. No matter what they did, James and Alanna, and also Anesh to a lesser degree, stood out as legends to most of the people in the guild. Foundational individuals who were indistinguishable from the act of delving itself. When they talked, bantered like this, everyone found they were already calmed down. Nerves settled. Except Sarah, who hadn't been paying attention and had been watching the clock. "Five seconds!" she shouted. "James, hit the door. Showtime, everyone."

James grinned. There were new people here today. And as he threw the door open and strode through like he owned the place, he couldn't help but feel that spark in his chest. Of sharing something amazing, of letting someone new in on a secret, of pulling back the veil.

He loved this part.

Officium Mundi welcomed them all with open beige arms.

CHAPTER 2

"Team three, get in here and get your loadout!" James called from the base of the tower that had become their fortress.

Team two, composed of Sarah, Deb, and Alex, was already rolling out. There was no such thing as a standard delver's loadout—yet—but JP and James were acting as quartermasters in the hectic rush to get everyone moving and make sure everyone had the tools they needed.

Armor first. Their now-standard plastic shell plate, with domed helmets on top for the people who picked them. Helmets were nice, but not much was shooting at their heads, so a lot of people skipped the extra weight. Boots were one of those things they didn't provide, so people were expected to bring their own footwear, but after the experience of having damp feet for two hours a couple weeks ago, they'd settled for a stash of backup boots, just in case anyone needed them. So far, none of the relics they'd retrieved from the dungeon had defensive properties, so there was no magic waiting for anyone here.

Weapons next. A lot of the delvers had favorites by this point. Sledgehammers and crowbars—even though crowbars were just bad weapons, they still *got the job done*, so people took them. But every team, thanks to JP's fight with the cat, had at least one sword strapped to a belt somewhere. James made sure every team also got a fire axe, too, and Alanna similarly was picking out each team's best marksman from the field trips she'd been making to the shooting range and making sure that person walked off with a shotgun and a small belt pouch of shells.

Safety was a bit trickier, and sort of like armor against everything that wasn't just being bitten. The growing list of safeguards often meant that people had to get used to carrying more than they were used to in their daily lives. But that was counterbalanced by everyone generally thinking it was worth it. One person per team, no matter what, was loaded down with a backpack that contained survival supplies—clean water, a laden medical kit, a couple knives and a pair of bolt cutters for getting through tangled cords or paperclip webs or tumblefeeds, rope, markers for keeping a trail clear, and anything else they thought was useful. Radios, too, and they were starting to be able to afford the good stuff, the kind with miles-long ranges. Also in this list was, one per group, one of the copied xenotech notepads. Each one, rewritten on the first page, had exact specifications for the location of their home-base tower. The second floor, specifically, in a specially cleared area with a very deliberate pattern to it. And if anyone needed to get back here in a hurry, all it would take would be ripping that page off. Returning with help would be harder; the notepads didn't really seem to *like* teleporting to most other places in the dungeon. But at least they were reliable escape tools.

And then the Weird—the things that it wasn't feasible or possible to make into a standard doctrine. Every team had one odd pair of sunglasses that let you see air currents or other people's plans or something. Every team had at least one or two favorite trinkets that had helped them in the past or that they wanted to find a use for. Everyone was loaded with USB sticks to save anything cool they found on the computers. Drones wired for skulljack connectivity, thermoses of reflex-enhancing coffee, thermite lances, iLipede nets—everyone had something to try out.

Except the new guys, of course.

"Team four, load out!" James shouted out the door as he turned to JP and gave a sigh. This was, of course, a required part of the logistics of managing what had turned into an over-twenty-person operation. But it was still taking up valuable time. "I think this is the last one, then Alanna and I are gonna grab our stuff and head out. We're looking for the other tower someone spotted last time, to bring back more coffee for Anesh's machinations."

"Good plan," JP told him as the fourth group marched in. Though *marched* wasn't a good word for it. Team four was the new guys, including Neil, and also Dave. Dave didn't hesitate to step up and start grabbing what he needed off the tables, but it took prompting from James and JP to get the other four to accept the standard-kit duffel bags and one of their pull carts to carry it all out.

"Neil, the signal adapter you wanted is in the box down there; it should work with any of the drones we have here, though we only tested it on the MX-4, because we didn't have time," JP instructed the tall young man loitering in front of him. "Talk to Rufus if you want to bring a drone to life. Also, the duffel labeled for you has armor that we fitted to you better. Nate, sorry, we didn't have time to shape any plate to you, and you are . . ." JP eyed the ex-sailor. ". . . stocky?"

"Try again."

"Muscular?"

"I'm *wide*, you jackass," Nate informed him bluntly, folding his arms over his barrel chest.

James interceded. "All right, well, either way, we don't have body plate for you. So you've got a choice: one of these surprisingly durable leather jackets, or just the arm and leg plates for the armor."

The newest arrival, Lance, looked down at the homemade boiled-leather pads that he already wore on his own arms and legs. "Man, I told you I had vambraces when you hired me, and you didn't tell me I could get cooler ones from you." He actually sounded more disappointed than joking.

"I didn't want to spoil your fun," James admitted. "Besides, we don't actually have enough tonight anyway, so yours are handy. Here, have an axe, though."

He and JP moved the group through the rest of the selection process before sending them out with a wary-looking Dave following. "All right, what do you and our amazon princess need tonight?" JP asked James when it was just the two of them left in the armory.

"Light load for experienced duo," James said. "Alanna's got her armor on already. I just need to grab actual backpacks and our handguns. Alanna says you're welcome to the Mossberg tonight if you want it." JP raised an eyebrow at that; Alanna's shotgun was her almost constant companion on longer delves. "Yeah, I know," James said, shrugging. "But we wanna move fast. Oh, I'll need a fire axe, too. Do you have one left under the desk?"

"Yeah, Anesh actually bought, like, fifteen of these fucking things. And then made me carry them up here," JP griped.

"It builds character," James told him. "Also arm muscles. You can't be our delicate flower forever."

JP blew a raspberry at his friend. There were a lot of things he could say, about having stabbed a ghost cat or fought a horde of striders, but he opted for quiet confidence instead. And a little less-quiet childishness, but just a little. "Anyway," he continued. "You still get the standard survival package."

"Yes, yes," James told him, rolling his eyes. "Gimme the backpack. I've got places to be."

JP complied. And a moment later, James was heading out the door, mostly ready to rock, but with still a few tasks left to do before he could join Alanna and start tonight's adventure.

The first thing he did was to stop by Team New Guys.

"So?" he asked, looking with an unapologetic smile at the different expressions they all wore. Lance and Virgil were gazing off into the artificial horizon with clear and unhidden wonder on their faces, while Nate was more looking around at the group of assembled delvers and their eclectic gear and personalities. Neil was trying his hardest not to look just as excited as the others, and absolutely failing to put on a front of confidence and experience. "What do you think?" James asked them.

"Feels like an LSD flashback," Nate muttered.

"This place is amazing!" Lance burst out. "This is like a whole office turned into a dungeon crawl!"

"Yes," James said, nodding slowly. "That is rather why we call it a dungeon." He looked around at the three of them, even Virgil, who was doing his best at keeping his mouth from hanging open and sort of failing. "All right, so, you guys are under no obligations tonight, just as a reminder. You're here to learn about the reason we exist as a group, to get a feel for this place and maybe some context. I've paired you all up with Dave, who is probably the third-most-experienced person in this whole place, so he'll be showing you around." James pointed over at his friend, who nodded silently. "Nate, I know you have actual military experience, so your input is welcome, but just remember that this place is, and I cannot stress this enough, *fucking weird, man.* So if Dave tells you to do something, then just believe him first and sort it out after, kay?"

A series of affirmatives greeted him, even Virgil tearing his eyes away from the ceiling to agree with James's directive. They all had questions, too, but James just deflected by telling them he had somewhere to be and once more pointed out that Dave could help them. Dave, of course, didn't really have the best grasp on the guild etiquette or the metaphysics of the dungeon, but he did know a lot of the more practical stuff, and soon he and Neil were fielding questions about using drones to scout potted plants and how to avoid shellaxy ambushes.

James smiled and shook his head as he kept walking before finding himself somewhere in the middle of where everyone was idly milling around. He really needed to come up with a better solution than this; people needed a bit more urgency in this opening window of time. They had eight hours a week, and it felt like the larger their group got, the more of it they wasted with everyone waiting for permission from him to start acting.

"Team leads, on me!" James called. "Dave, you're good to head out," he said to his friend, getting a confident nod in return.

A cluster of people soon surrounded him. They had *real teams* this time, groups who were comfortable together or learning to work that way. And now James had objectives to hand to them. Simon was the first to reach him, followed by Deb, then Daniel, and then Secret, of all people. The infomorph had been elected by popular vote, and he'd already been given James's blessing to do his own thing tonight.

James started with "All right. Let's make this quick. Goals tonight. Anyone got requests?"

Daniel opened by asking, "Is there anything you need found?"

"A tower would be nice," James said. "Or decision trees. Why?"

"Pathfinder needs to explore, so I volunteer us for that."

James nodded. It made sense and solved two problems at once. "All right," he said. "Find us towers. But we still need door guards, so you're on second rotation, okay?" Daniel nodded in acceptance. "Simon. Your team is on hunter duty tonight. Bring us back some greens, first rotation." James had almost begun to accept the way some of the rescued delvers looked at him and Alanna. Almost. But he still worded the command to Simon less like a question and more like an order, knowing that the younger man wouldn't be comfortable making it a conversation. "Secret, who's in your team anyway?"

"Me, Sarah, one Anesh, and Theodora," Secret replied, stressing that last name.

James grunted. "Ugh. I need to talk to Theo. I didn't realize she'd be here today. But yeah, if she's with you, that's fine. Explore and loot for yourselves, prioritize briefcases, and coordinate with Pathfinder when you come back by here to see if we can actually find any of the locations for them." Secret bobbed in acknowledgment. "And Deb, you guys are also on exploration and looting. You take third rotation; Secret, you take first. Make sure there's always a few people around here, okay?" James looked around at the four people who represented a small army of people at this point. "Anyone not actively on rotation, feel free to explore up to, say, a hundred cubes away from the tower, okay? So far, we haven't seen any real danger here, but Anesh and Momo are gonna be doing wizardry up on the top floor, and I don't want them getting ambushed. And you *know* they will be if we aren't careful."

The group laughed. Not because James was joking, but because he wasn't. They committed their assignments to memory, or to their mundane notebooks, and headed out. Secret gave James a loving and somewhat ethereal headbutt before slithering through the air to his group, and James tried to ignore the awkward conversation he was going to have to have with Theo at some point.

Finally, no one was looking at him or looking to him for orders or advice. Anesh was in his tower, the delvers were on their way, and the defenses were being set up with now-practiced ease. James took a deep breath, enjoyed the feeling of the abnormally pure dungeon air for a few seconds, and then put on a grin. A single nod to himself, to remind himself that this was where he wanted to be, and he turned to stride over to where Alanna was waiting.

It would have been dramatically appropriate if the two of them could have fallen into step and stomped out into the modern wilderness like they were ready for anything. But James still had to stop and put on his armor while Alanna leaned on the outside of the cubicle he'd chosen and made idle conversation.

"I think you should know," she said, "that not a single thing has tried to kill me since we got here."

"That's . . . good?" James asked as he tugged on one of the leg guards, trying not to tip over the swivel chair he was in as he did so. "It doesn't sound like you think that's good. Is that bad?"

Alanna laughed. She did have a point with this, but the way James reacted to some things was just so dorky it was hard not to be amused and let the small things slide. "I don't think it's the end of the world, but either the population of the dungeon is dropping in general or things like striders and sticky masks are avoiding the entrance. They might have finally caught on, as a population, that we are not prey."

It took a second, partially because his brain was distracted trying to make Velcro work, but James did get it eventually. "Ah," he said as he connected the dots. "And that means less easy yellow orbs. And with a twenty-way split, that means it's gonna be harder to keep everyone motivated and moving forward."

"More than twenty, for sure," Alanna reminded him. "We still give them out to the support staff if they want them. And to, like, Rufus and Lily and Ganesh. And Auberdeen."

"Sorry, what was that last one?"

"Ganesh?"

James hopped out of the cubicle, tugging on the heel of his boot as he slipped his foot back into it. "Oh, hell no. You're giving the dog skill points? That cannot be a good idea."

"I checked. It's ethically okay," Alanna said with such certainty in her voice that James *almost* believed her and didn't question it. As it was, though, while he gave her a little smirk and secretly had some reservations about uplifting even such a good doggo as their Auberdeen, he did decide not to push too hard. "Also it was less that I handed them over and more like she robbed me. Anyway," Alanna continued, unaware of the thoughts in James's head, "what are we looking for today? A tower? A tumblefeed? More oranges?"

"Better," James said as the cubicles started to grow around them, beige architecture beginning to warp and drip into archways and protrusions. "We're after another coffee machine."

Daniel leaned forward, pressing his fingertips into the carpet. He was settled on his knees, legs straight out behind him, and the motion of reaching down made him look like a penitent priest more than an armed adventurer. He settled there and sat with his eyes closed, just feeling the texture of the material beneath him.

It was, in his own way, a form of meditation. This far into Officium Mundi—not that far, just anything past where the cubicles started to warp—he had a lot of paranoia about things going wrong. This small activity helped keep him grounded and connected to his less physical partner.

It didn't help that his *more* physical teammates were standing around like the extra workers that showed up on every construction site, watching him and making quite unappreciated comments.

"He looks like he's praying," JP remarked. Not maliciously, just to have something to say. He was facing down the left side of the intersection they were in, Alanna's shotgun held a little too tightly in his hands. This also put him in good position to cover the rear and a lot of the higher arches overhead.

Next to him, Tyrone kept an eye down the other hallway while tapping dirt off his shoes and rolling the yellow orb from the potted plant they'd just felled in his hand. "Dude's cool and collected. Like a Buddhist monk." He offhandedly matched JP's tone.

"I wonder what a prayer to this place would look like?" JP idly asked.

"Ooh, we should totally find out, dude. We could probably get some kind of pseudo-spiritual enhancement out of it."

"Noooo, no. That was not really what I was getting at." JP shook his head, ignoring that no one was looking at him. "I was more just curious if the building acts like a god inside here. Also I think a prayer here is mostly just asking for coffee. Which is literally what he's doing, now that I think about it."

"Like a fictional god," Tyrone corrected him. "Not, like, one of the ones any world religion goes for, but like, how fantasy stories always think gods work?"

"Yes. That."

"Then we should test that."

"This is how James feels all the time, isn't it?" JP sighed. "That seems like a remarkably bad idea. I'm really sorry I brought it up now."

On the floor, Daniel repressed a sigh of his own. His mind wasn't lined up the way he needed it to be, and even exploring the dungeon wasn't enough to tip him over the edge. He took a steadying breath and doubled his efforts at ignoring the people with him.

It took a little while, but eventually, he tuned out their conversation. Possible, but it was an extra barrier between him and his partner, and Daniel didn't really appreciate the hurdle. It wasn't engaging anyway, so it wasn't too hard to let his mind drift to that state of thinking nothing, just feeling threads of ideas and following what showed up. Trying to match his feelings to something very specific.

What showed up was a golden-orange thread of an idea that drifted through his thoughts. The concept that he should see a sunset, somewhere he'd never been before. For a brief moment, the overwhelming urge to pick up his feet and *go* eclipsed every other piece of software running on the mainframe that was his mind. He didn't want to move, but to *leave*. To see new places, to always move forward, to reach out and fill the uncharted parts of the map, and to never, ever be pinned down.

"Hello, beautiful," he whispered as Pathfinder receded from overwhelming his consciousness. In any other moment, he would have hoped the other two guys hadn't overheard that, but right now, he was living in a singular moment that didn't include them.

He stood up, rubbing at his knees as if he could feel anything through the black plastic shell of the armor's kneepads, or as if that same armor hadn't made it more than comfortable to be down on the floor for any length of time. "All right," he said out loud, and both JP and Ty looked over at him.

Daniel wasn't really familiar with JP. He was aware that the other man was, in fact, a friend of James. But it was hard not to see the thin face and constantly analyzing eyes and think of him as anything other than a particularly effective used-car salesman. Or a weasel. Tyrone, on the other hand, was someone Daniel had some rapport with. They'd worked together for a while, and his blasé attitude covered up someone who knew a little about a whole lot and who had hit the ground running with the whole dungeon thing. Not that Daniel had a leg to stand on there; he was only just now coming around on his thoughts about his life being upended here.

"You wired in, my dude?" Tyrone asked him, cocking a single eyebrow.

Daniel nodded before doing a trick that he'd only ever been able to master thanks to a chance yellow orb: splitting his attention between two separate things. One part of him kept track of Pathfinder, talking to her and seeking her guidance, while the other stayed in reality. A quick check with Path showed that she'd already started seeking out a hint of a trail about their shared goal. Both of them listened when James asked for things; there was a mutual respect there. "Yeah," he said out loud, trying not to go too far into his inner thoughts, "we take the right. Path says we've got one misadventure between us and where we need to be. About three miles."

"God, that's a powerful skill," JP commented. "Does it only work on landmarks, or can you find anything? Like people?" he asked, raising an eyebrow.

"It has to have somewhere to go," Daniel answered. "Sometimes that can mean a person, but usually not. Also, Path isn't as strong as Secret is yet; she can't just spam the map. It's maybe one every few days. Fine for the dungeon, but not really as abusable as you seem to be thinking."

JP affected a shocked look. "And why would you think that I—"

He was cut off as Tyrone patted him reassuringly on the shoulder. "It's okay, dude. I also wondered if we could use it to find buried pirate gold."

"No, that's not . . . You know what? Sure. That's basically what I was getting at." JP rolled his eyes with a shrug. "Are we ready to go?"

They nodded and set out after taking a minute to decide what their marching order was. By virtue of being their most reliable map out of there, Daniel got to be in the center of their formation, with JP in the rear, ready to shoot anything that flinched funny, and Tyrone in front, ready to be a more steady hand on their forward progress.

"So, does anyone else find it weird that Pathfinder can apparently see the future?" JP asked as they slowly walked through the halls. They weren't looting unless they saw anything outstandingly impressive, so they weren't disturbing any of the nests of low-risk monsters. But they were being careful, nonetheless. This far in, pencil darts and sharpener smoke screens were a risk they had to be on guard for.

Daniel stifled a sigh. Showing frustration around people asking dumb questions hadn't been helping him so far in his role as head of security; he figured it wouldn't be any better here. "Explain, for those of us that aren't in your head?"

"Well, you said . . ." There was a short diversion as JP tensed up his grip on the gun, locking his feet in place as he watched a wayward shellaxy cross the intersection they'd just passed. He picked up after it dragged itself away, like he hadn't been on edge at all. ". . . said that we were going to have one misadventure. Now, aside from the fact that saying that is *hugely* stressful . . ."

"Yeah, dude, not cool. It's like telling someone the way they die, but not when," Tyrone jumped in.

"Oddly specific, but yes, thanks," JP acknowledged. They were having to talk in low tones to avoid waking anything up, but he still projected his voice to reach the other side of their little formation. "Anyway, my main thing is that *how does Path know that?* How can she know that we'll have a single misadventure? Actually, what . . ."

"What's a misadventure, yeah?" Tyrone finished the sentence, tilting his head back from where he was half leaned around the corner ahead of them. He had them holding up for a second, waiting for a flock of paper to take off again before they moved on. "Also, dude, why do you keep calling a genderless spectral entity 'she'?" He shot the question back at JP.

JP's mouth twitched upward in a hint of a smile for just a second. He was, all things considered, not the most aware person in the world when it came to being socially progressive, or whatever specific term Alanna would have for it. But he'd spent a lot of time around people who were; his friends were mostly intellectual hippie types, even if they were a party of violent adventurers sometimes. And they'd rubbed off on him, mostly for the better. "Easy answer," he threw back, projecting his voice so he wouldn't have to take his eyes off the corridor behind them. "Because she asked. Well, she asked Daniel, anyway, and I have no reason not to trust him. Dave might, but Dave's not here."

"Dave and I are working on it," Daniel added.

"Great." JP tried to project actual empathy and probably failed. He could lie to people like a fucking champion, but actually being empathic was a challenge when he was watching for rats and masks. "Doesn't Pathfinder partly live in your head, too?" he challenged Tyrone.

The other man shrugged casually as he swept his eyes across the arch of cubicles to their left, looking carefully at where they formed a shelf that might hide staplers waiting in ambush. "I'm more of a backup. Happy to donate my brain waves to the cause for you dudes, but we don't really chat."

JP could respect that. But something else demanded more attention right now. "Anyway. Misadventure. What is?"

Daniel rolled his eyes and decided to answer with more than words. The group started moving again as the rustle of paper signaled the clearing of their path. Daniel pointed them forward, taking them through a low tunnel ringed with small paper scraps that moved like blades of grass as they crawled through. Then around another corner, this one just an L-bend in the hallway, taking them around the outside of an oversize cubicle, before pointing a finger forward. "There," he said. "Somewhere around there is misadventure."

"But what *is* it?" Tyrone asked, more suspicious than ever.

"Also the time-travel thing. We have concerns about the time-travel thing," JP reminded him.

Daniel ignored them both and stalked forward. There was a twinge of anxiety and fear in his chest that he never really got past, no matter how many times he came in here. He watched James sometimes and had realized that a lot of the other delvers had somehow *gotten past that.* Either the thrill of the treasure and the wins had made them immune, or else they'd just . . . become used to being hurt? And Daniel didn't think he'd ever get there.

But there was something to be said for the power of frustration and spite as motivating factors.

And right now, as he dropped into a slight crouch as he moved forward, passing Tyrone who shot him a "hey, what?" as he walked, he found those feelings pushed aside the fear for a moment. Daniel kept one hand running along the cubicle to his left, fingers that never felt right in gloves running along the rough fuzz of the carpeted wall. His other hand was held out at a downward angle, pointing the heavy metal baseball bat he'd brought with him toward the floor. It was hard for him not to feel invincible, armed and wrapped in a full-body shield, even here with all the dangers the dungeon represented. And as he stepped up to the intersection Pathfinder had lit up like a beacon, he took a deep breath and repeated one thought to himself.

Misadventure. What a word. It could mean so many things, and some of them, he'd learned out in the real world, could be super dangerous. But so far, it had never meant *lethal*. A misadventure was something a little stupid, a little reckless, and absolutely something you'd be able to spin into a great story when you were seventy years old and telling drunken stories of your youth. But it wouldn't kill you.

As for how Pathfinder knew they'd find one, when the journey relied on someone doing something a little dumb? Well. JP and Tyrone were here to question it. It was a self-fulfilling prophecy. Either they would, or they'd push Daniel into it. Like now!

Daniel stood there, posed like an anime protagonist, waiting for whatever was going to bite him in the ass. But then nothing happened. The misadventure failed to manifest.

"Huh," he said out loud, looking around, choking up his grip on the bat a bit. He turned and threw a shrug back at the two guys following him. "Guess it's not a perfectly predictive ability after all?" he offered.

JP rolled his eyes and resumed his rear-guard stance while he and Tyrone moved to catch up to Daniel. And then, while they had dropped their guard at the small joke of Daniel trying to be serious, they crossed between two cubicle doors that were lined up perfectly with each other.

Maybe Daniel had just been lucky, or maybe something about how he'd been walking had done the trick, but either way, he'd avoided triggering any traps. The other two were not nearly so fortunate.

As soon as the two of them, who had closed ranks to be closer together, crossed past those last doors, the electric pencil sharpeners on the desks fired to life with a grinding whir. A split second later, while Daniel was still in the process of turning around in reaction, a dense cloud of black "smoke" kicked out of the cubicles like dragon's breath. It suddenly wrapped around JP and Tyrone and then started to fill the hallway, roiling down toward where Daniel stood and hitting him in a wave at about chest height.

It was heavier than normal smoke, because it wasn't hot, exactly. It was really just a cloud of graphite shavings. But it didn't quite act like it; it clung to the air like it didn't want to let go, and it got into eyes and lungs in a way that was hard to push through.

And while that was happening, and his cohorts were coughing and shouting, Daniel heard the sound of wheels squeaking as they rolled at high speed.

A glance to his left and a flailing hop backward was all it took for him to narrowly avoid being rammed by the rogue mail cart—*maul carts*, James called them, which was very much his style—as it plowed through the hallway. Lashing out with a weak and misplaced strike from his bat, Daniel caught the thing on the rear wheel-leg, sending it tilting just a bit as it rolled past, plowing into the smoke. And then a crash of metal on metal.

There was a scream from JP and a matching shout of challenge from Tyrone while Daniel rushed back into the smoke to try to help. He hesitated only for the time it took to yank the neckline of his shirt up to cover his mouth before dashing in, small orange licks of Pathfinder's flames trailing behind his shoulders. He ran into Ty first, placing a hand on his shoulder to confirm where they were, and then started hauling him out of the cloud.

As soon as they breached the outside, Daniel pulled his shirt down. "Where's JP?!" he asked, frantic, while Tyrone leaned one hand against a wall and coughed like he was hacking up his internal organs. The guard pointed backward and started wheezing anew. When Daniel tried to run back into the cloud, though, Tyrone grabbed his wrist, trying to say something through the gasping.

It took Daniel a few seconds and Tyrone clearing his throat a bit more for him to realize that the man was *laughing*. The smoke, magical as it was, couldn't stay up forever. And as it started to clear, the ambush spoiled, the reason for the joke became apparent.

Daniel had seen one maul cart blaze past him, but what he hadn't seen was the identical creature from the other side of the smoke. The crash that he'd heard had been the two carts, both of them gunning for JP, slamming into each other. And now JP found himself pinned against the wall of a cube, the tan board pushed back at a weird angle from the impact, JP himself pushed against it with his shotgun-filled hands uselessly trapped at about hip height. The two maul carts tangled in each other, where they had bent organic metal and chitin into shapes that latched together and left the creatures straining to pull apart from each other but unable to.

"For fuck's sake, *help!*" JP was yelling through his coughs, trying to kick away the carts that were still putting a considerable amount of force into their crashing around. It wasn't working; they were too heavy to tip over from his position and too entangled to break away. "Anytime now!"

It took Daniel and Tyrone about ten minutes to detach the two carts, after they finished sharing a long glance, a sigh, and a giggle. They went slowly, because in the couple minutes of examining the situation before they started, Tyrone said something incredibly stupid and incredibly brilliant all at once.

"You know," the idiocy started, "we've still got miles to go—"

Still trapped against the wall, JP cut him off. "Please, be Jack Kerouac later; get me out now." He let out an *oof* as the carts once again jerked against him, slamming into his rib cage.

"It's just . . . well, I don't want to *kill* them, yeh?" Tyrone continued.

"They literally just tried to murder JP," Daniel pointed out. "And also the rest of us. I'm still shaking, look." He held up a hand.

"But it's not self-defense now."

"They're dungeon monsters," JP said. "Please don't just leave me here; this is super uncomfortable."

"Just because they're dungeon monsters, dude, doesn't mean they aren't alive. Look at Rufus! All I'm saying is, maybe, *maybe* we could . . . ask for a ride?" Tyrone waggled his eyebrows hopefully.

Daniel looked at him, then at the carts still locked together like stags with tangled horns, then back at Tyrone. He even mixed in sharing an incredulous glance with JP, except . . . well, JP was sitting there, crushed against a cubicle wall, looking more speculative than dumbfounded. "No," Daniel said. "Hell, no. No way. No. No! We will die! We'll *die*, and our last words will just be the word *shit* repeated louder and louder until we get thrown off a cliff!" He pointed at Tyrone with a stiff index finger. "No," he said firmly. Turning, he repeated the gesture to JP. "No," he said again.

In his head, even Pathfinder gave him a nudge toward the absurd idea, and while Daniel was trying to form a more coherent argument beyond just saying "no" over and over, Tyrone leaned in and started muttering to one of the carts, laying a hand on it to steady the twitching creature like it was a horse. "Hey, there," he murmured. "It's fine; we're not gonna hurt you. Hey, you wanna deliver some packages? Human-shaped packages? We can get you untangled here. Let's see about this . . ."

Daniel sighed, blowing a long stream of air out his nose as he tried to figure out how he felt about this. He was ramping up to pull rank on the two maniacs, both of whom were now trying to befriend ambulatory mail carts, when Pathfinder whispered a reminder in his ear.

"Oh," he mumbled to himself. "I get it. *This* is the misadventure."

Through all the fear, though, Daniel found something strange going on in his roiling emotions. Yes, he was a ball of nerves. Yes, he still wasn't sure how he felt about actually being in this building. And yes, he didn't get how James and the others smiled so much. But.

But there was a part of him—and it wasn't just Pathfinder pushing him forward—that shouted with barely repressed excitement as he watched Tyrone actually start to succeed at calming down one of the carts. And that part of him really, really wanted to be the first one to see how well these things could take a corner.

Daniel shook his head and stepped forward, an unnoticed grin on his face. Misadventure awaited.

CHAPTER 3

"All right, I think I'm prepared to just break these," James said, popping out the earbuds he'd found. "They're creepy, and I think useless, but mostly creepy."

"What are they doing?" Alanna asked, looking up from where she was pulling apart the case of a dead shellaxy to get the orb out. The two of them had gotten into a mild scrap when a strider had surprised Alanna and then set off a small swarm of the angry staplers, and then James had flung one of them into a shellaxy, which had triggered a couple of flashbulbs, and . . .

This place was weird to describe, Alanna realized.

James didn't have access to this internal monologue, though, and was mostly preoccupied trying to crush the earbuds of the pair of headphones he'd found that they had both gotten a weird feeling about. "They whisper!" James informed Alanna. "Like, they just whisper random names. I don't like it. Not one bit."

"What if they're, say, the names of those who fell in honorable combat in the dunge— And you broke them. Okay." Alanna nodded as she wiped dust and coolant blood off her hands and onto her increasingly distressed jeans. She considered adding the yellow orb to their stockpile, but the two of them had agreed that taking a *few* of them was probably fine, especially considering how quickly they stacked up these days. Also, the angry red line of a scrape down her palm made her feel personally entitled to this one.

[+2 Skill Ranks : Repair—Soft-Serve Ice Cream Machine—Space-man 6210]

"Get anything good?" James asked, offering her a hand up as he used his other to shove the blue orb he'd gotten into a pocket of the coat he was wearing over the body armor.

"No!" Alanna replied cheerily. "Unless you count 'most specific skill ever' as something."

James winced. "Don't you already have one for, like, a specific model of helicopter?"

"I do. And now I have one for a brand of ice cream machine. Yay. Though, that said, don't you have a drive skill that only applies to a hyperspecific model of car? That's almost as bad."

"Actually, the ranks in driving are just for 'car,' which you may have noticed is super open-ended. Though I do have a mechanic skill that only works on the Jetta, which I . . . actually don't remember the last time I *saw* a Jetta. So, there's that. I think I had an aunt that owned one in the . . . nineties?"

The two of them sighed together. "Well. At least some of these things are broken as hell to make up for it," Alanna said. "Did you ever check your basketball progress, by the way?" She struck up conversation as they shoved what they'd found into backpacks and started to move again. They had a long way to go tonight, and they weren't inclined to waste time.

James gave a short nod to the collected pile of strider corpses as they left; he wasn't religious, but he felt he owed something to the defeated enemy. They'd been vicious little buggers, and while the armor mitigated some of the danger, they actually were still a threat in larger numbers. "Yeah, I did," he replied to Alanna as he joined her in the hallway and the two of them started progressing again. They moved at a fast clip, not a jog, but just before it. A power walk, with a little less arm swinging. "I was at twenty-five last time I checked. It turns out, you *can* teach other people off of orb skills, and Anesh also has some good teaching chops anyway. I think all the math tutoring has made him a lot more patient."

"Goddammit. I'm at *one*," Alanna griped. "And I know I've been communicating a lot more than you've been basketballing," she said as the two of them cleared a corner. One more left turn and they'd be heading back toward the door, which they didn't want at all. She pointed it out to James, and they started looking for a place to loop back to being on track.

As he ducked into a cubicle briefly to grab a wallet sitting out on the desk and stripped it of fifty-odd bucks, James called back, "I think it's that you actually have to learn stuff. I didn't know how to check when we were practicing, but I think that the point was that Anesh was teaching me things. And it's sorta unfair, because I know fuck all about basketball, and you know probably quite a lot about communication. So I get to learn faster."

Alanna stopped James with an outstretched arm as they approached an intersection of cubicle walls. The walls here were over their heads, but there wasn't much obstructing the false sky, so they had good light and it wasn't too hard to spot the leaves of the potted plant that kept twitching behind the vending machine. "Wanna take this one?" she asked and got a nod from James in reply. "Also, it's unfair if that's the case. What the fuck am I even supposed to learn? Like, do I have to learn a new language? Or different techniques for talking? What?"

"Can we finish this after the plant?" James asked, mildly annoyed at staggering a half step, his chipped hatchet already in hand. He shot Alanna a look, and she pursed her lips and looked at his face closely.

"So, you're not annoyed that I'm talking about this; you're annoyed about being interrupted. Got it," she said. Then, as James took a deep, rumbling breath, Alanna muttered, "Syllabus," and saw, clearly, [*Lesson—Communications : 2/100*]. "Excellent," she said to James. "I'm also learning on a personal level that maybe you get hard to talk to before fights. Wanna go kill the plant now?"

"Can you just ask next time you want to test that?" James asked, still kind of annoyed, as he circled around the plant, giving it a clear view of himself.

Alanna didn't answer. It was time to see what kind of plant this was, and the next few seconds would determine if their strategy was going to be a quick kill or a bruising brawl. She kept herself in the shadow of the vending machine, out of sight of the plant, watching James more than the twitching leaves. And then, when six different fern fronds shot out toward her boyfriend like green bullets, Alanna made a decision.

James caught one of the fronds, let a few others go off his armor, and yelped when one caught him on the throat and opened up a small gash. But the plant had overcommitted to him, thinking he was alone, and Alanna only had to take two steps, plant her feet, and give one almost inhumanly powerful swing with her fire axe to cleave halfway through the base of the plant. It started to topple almost immediately, a process that James helped along by adjusting his grip on the bladed ferns and yanking, pulling the plant down flat so Alanna could give it an overhead chop with the axe and finish slicing it in two.

"I think this was a younger one," James said, holding a hand over his bleeding throat while Alanna fished out their pouch of hemo-static powder and disinfectant. They'd never actually found out if wounds from anything in here were particularly infectious, and they weren't prepared to push their luck on it. "Look, only two orbs. Also, I'm not dead!" he said.

"Don't get stabbed in the neck, you idiot!" Alanna snapped back, a worried look in her eyes.

James wanted to laugh, but instead he just smiled at her and didn't aggravate his injury any more than he needed to. "It's fine. I was being careless; we need a better plan for these things. Maybe we could go back to that old plan of bringing a wood chipper to life and setting it loose in here."

"Putting aside the ethics of making life, which I'm still iffy on, wasn't the wood chipper a thing we were explicitly trying to *avoid?*"

"I dunno—so far all the life we've made has been friendly. I've actually been thinking that when teams become more permanent, it should be a kind of rite of passage for them to make their last teammate. Though that feels weird for a reason I'm not sure I can explain right now." James shrugged, doing his best not to scratch at his neck. Alanna tossed him the yellow out of the plant pot, and he caught it one-handed. "What's this for?"

"You got hurt; you get this one. Also, that still feels like we're treating life like a toy, and that's *weeeeird*. It just doesn't feel ethical." She helped James up as he cracked the orb.

[+1 Skill Rank : Templating—Business Cards]

"Ugh. Back to this again. You know, I really do love the skill orbs. I would never give this place up, and free knowledge is free knowledge, but when am I *ever* going to need to make a business card?" James wondered idly.

"Are you kidding?" Alanna asked as they started to push on again. "We are literally running a . . . god, I know that you don't wanna call it a guild, but there is just no good name for this. *Clan* sounds stupid, and we sure as fuck aren't a corporation." She stopped at a cubicle door, and James tapped her on the shoulder to indicate he was covering her while she ducked inside. "Bulb!" she called a split second later, and James froze outside the cube while Alanna rolled under the desk before the *pop* of superheated glass went off. "Also, don't think I'm dropping the 'we make life' thing!" James heard her say from inside the boxy walls.

"I don't think it's really that big a deal, honestly," James admitted as the two of them passed through the cubicle. This one had two doors, which was a trait that had been showing up more often lately, and it made for good shortcutting through the hallways when they needed to change directions to keep on course. "Like, okay, Ganesh is the perfect example here. He's happy, right? Or so he tells us, in his way. And we do give him choices—he just always chooses us."

"That's hardly fair," Alanna pointed out. "His choices are die in the dungeon or die in the real world. Those aren't choices any more than it's a choice between working for an abusive company or starving."

James winced; he'd agreed with her on that previously, but now that he was actually free of the situation of being forced to work somewhere awful, it felt hypocritical to change his mind. "I dunno if that's fair, though. Ganesh isn't, like, 'put to work' or anything. Even the mongausse—"

"Oh god, that name. Who lets you get away with this?"

"You do. Anyway, it's not like anyone *makes* these guys do anything. Even Rufus! And he was technically born here!" James retaliated. "Like, if Pendragon wanted to just lounge around all day and eat poorly worded legal documents, we'd make that happen."

Alanna started to nod before realizing James couldn't see her from his angle. "Okay, so, do you feel like we have a duty to them?"

"A responsibility, at least," James agreed. "Ethically, you know? It's basically the same rules as being a parent; it's your tacitly implied oath to take care of them until they can take care of themselves. And we can totally do that. We have the technology!"

The two of them halted as Alanna abruptly froze and they both watched as, across the hallway they were just about to cross into, a small swarm of ten or twenty striders tapped their way single file up onto the lip of the opposite walls. A couple of the black-and-red creatures glanced over at the duo, but they didn't end their march, and James and Alanna didn't so much as twitch to give them a reason to.

After they'd passed, both delvers let out a held breath. "Jesus Christ, this place is so creepy sometimes."

"I hear more movement down that way," James whispered. "We should stay quiet for a bit while we pass." Alanna nodded in response and started moving, suddenly aware of just how many things in her backpack rattled and how the armor and boots were in no way built for stealth.

She and James moved on without talking for a while, postponing their conversation.

Cubicles. James had this weird fascination with the material of this place. In an actual office, it would have been mindlessly boring, but as with almost everything in life, context had a huge role to play. Beige and tan and taupe and every other color that meant the same shade of light brown were colors in only the loosest sense. But here, mixed with the palette of gray and off-white of the walls and floors, it looked like a riot of shapes and colors. When the walls stretched and twisted overhead, with holes formed for windows and protrusions that made strider-size steps up the sides of the cubicles, it stopped looking like just another office and started looking like something surreal.

Of course, it had always looked surreal, James mused as Alanna pointed out another shortcut cubicle that they could cut through to a hallway that would put them back on the right track. The fact that the horizon actually looked like the ground, just curved up out of sight, was the first clue, but there were so many things here that weren't what they seemed. Like the pen on the desk that was just straight up glowing. James paused for a second behind Alanna, blinked slowly, and then just shrugged and pocketed the piece of magic before catching up; he didn't want to fall too far behind and leave her without instant support.

James kept his eyes up as Alanna took point. She was a good forward, for obvious reasons. Alanna had always cut a powerful figure, and being enhanced over and over by the dungeon and decked out in body armor had done exactly *nothing* to make her look less like the definition of a fighter. She was also pretty sharp, and between her and James, they took cautious steps over a couple lines in the carpet that had that EM hum that signaled pencil darts. James's job here was mostly to be ready to retaliate overwhelmingly against anything that jumped her, and to also be a less directed set of eyes for anything that looked interesting, valuable, weird, dangerous, or any combination of those words.

They crossed a few miles of dungeon at a fairly fast pace that way. It wasn't exactly safe, but with only two of them moving quietly and not picking fights, they made pretty good time. It never really failed to put a smile on James's face when he pushed aside dot-matrix paper draped like vines, crouch-crawled through low tunnels of overhanging cubicle material dotted with the glittering eyes of iLipedes, and every now and then caught glimpses of towers of cubicles, or of blue-and-white tile, or heard the hiss of a tumblefeed in the distance.

When they crawled out of the latest tunnel, James turned his eyes up to the sudden glare of light. When his pupils adjusted, he felt a smile touch his lips as he watched a flock of paper birds fly through the air. As they started to disappear from sight, he frowned slightly before realizing that they were landing on one of the suspended light platforms. "It's so weird to think that we've been on the ceiling, and it doesn't look at all the same from down here," he said to Alanna.

She also shot a quick glance up, catching sight of the flock as the last of them settled into their roost. "Hmm. Remember the spider things?"

"Fuck, yeah, I remember they had *faces*. Hey, you know what's weird? The dungeon clearly likes bug forms for stuff, and we've seen two spider-esque things. How come no giant spiders?" James asked, tempting fate like a narratively blind idiot.

Alanna actually stopped completely to turn around and give him a dumbfounded stare. "Seriously? You wanna just hand the place the keys to the nightmare kingdom?"

"I mean, the ones upstairs are kiiiinda giant," James continued unabated. "But I'm really just looking for a *really big* stapler." He made a vaguely oval shape with his hands, like he was bragging about once catching a fish *this big*. "Anyway, are we ever gonna explore up there again?" he asked. "Or at least exploit it a little bit. I bet there's a free energy hack in there somewhere."

"The height difference?" Alanna asked, and James nodded in response. "I don't think we could fit anything big enough in here to make it matter. Though, if we ever get a lesson for hang gliding, it'd be a great launch point."

"We could bring a hang glider to life—" James started to say with a note of laughter in his voice.

"Noooope." Alanna snorted out a laugh and cut him off, and they turned back to the trail they were blazing. "All right, let's keep moving. Hopefully we can make it to the other break room within an hour."

And they were off again.

The thing about the duo of James and Alanna, compared to when James was with Anesh, was that neither of them were particularly goal-oriented people. They weren't lazy, and certainly both of them thought a lot about the bigger picture of things. But when it came to roaming the halls of the office, both of them were incredibly easily sidetracked by anything that caught their eye. Whether that was strange terrain in a side passage, the twitch of a new form of hostile life, or a strange object that stood out, it didn't really matter. The point was, they lost a lot of time to what could, at best, be called side quests.

"Check that out," Alanna whispered, nudging James. The two of them were peeking over a cubicle wall. They'd taken a short break after another fifteen minutes of walking and nothing more exciting happening than sidestepping a sleepy shellaxy. And after their light breather and a few sips of water, James had cleared off a space on the heavy office desk to climb up and peer over the edge of the cubicle wall to see if he could spot anything. Alanna had joined him a few seconds later, and the two of them had looked out over a bizarre view of boxes and halls, which looked like someone had just taken a slice out of an anthill. An anthill that filed paperwork and could do tech support.

A couple rows of halls and cubicles over, past a curved arc of hallway where they could see the top of a water cooler backed by a demotivational poster, there was a change in the scenery. Instead of halls and more or less uniform boxes, there was a spot where the light made it down a little less obstructed, where the walls were a little more open. There was, in the middle of this little clear area, a small cross-shaped wall that formed the hint of the outline of cubes and even had desks in those marked spaces, but they weren't enclosed. What Alanna had pointed out was the small half counter off to the side, flanked by a water cooler of its own on one side and a slightly fidgeting copier on the other, in the shade of a broad-leafed plant. On the counter, next to an inhumanly clean coffeepot, was an insulated blue lunch sack, sitting crookedly next to a silver sink.

"The copier? We could get a green out of that, yeah," James agreed.

"No, the lunch box." Alanna flicked a finger against his shoulder. "We should grab that," she told him.

James glanced over at her and raised an eyebrow before looking back past the block of walls. Before he said anything, he really took in the scene and tried to focus on the lunch sack in particular. And then, in an instant, he realized there was something weird with it. Tilting his head in confusion, James took a deep breath and tried to block out everything around him. He closed his eyes; the last thing he saw was that little speck of blue sixtyish feet off in the distance.

A small swirl of intent whispered through him. It left an itching on his palms and the taste of salt in his mouth.

That was weird.

James opened his eyes and nodded. "Yeah, okay. Let's see what's up with that," he said and lobbed his pack over the wall before hauling himself up and following shortly after. Alanna just grinned at the agreement and did the same, though without taking off her own pack first. They had to repeat the process several more times, crossing out of the cubicle they landed in and then through the next one on the other side of the hall before they could jump another wall. James paused to rip open a pack of orb-shaped candies called GCUs, which seemed to be mostly cherry, while Alanna paused to casually intercept and break open the strider that lunged for James's throat from one of the hanging cupboards.

[+1 Skill Rank : Music—Symphonies] read the thought she got as she cracked that orb.

There weren't any further interruptions, even for their easily distracted eyes. They *could* have come up with some—every cubicle in this place was its own mini adventure—but they stuck to their route, and while James's arms ached from pulling himself over walls by the time they got there, they were both excited and energized.

They didn't jump the wall here. As much as it was great for forging a direct A-to-B route when they knew where they were going, there were two big problems with the method of travel. One was that it was fucking tiring. And the other was that if they *did* land on something hostile, they'd prefer it be, at most, a strider or a tapir. Even landing on a shellaxy could get someone's leg bitten off; for all that the things were slow and easy to manage if you knew what you were doing, they *could* still hurt you, and it was important to not make stupid slipups.

So they went around, taking a few minutes to find the corridor that led into the open office space. To James, these spaces seemed kind of like the sort of area you'd expect for low-level management. People who had jobs that were supposedly important, but whose workspaces still lacked the grandeur of a real office, or much of a better paycheck. Just a fancy artisanal cubicle and your own coffeepot, which . . . well, that wasn't nothing, really.

James and Alanna carefully surveyed the area between them and their lunch box. The last time they'd found a place like this, it had almost killed six people in one go. And sure enough, it only took ten seconds for James to see the problem.

"It's not the copier we need to worry about," he whispered to Alanna. "Look." He didn't move too quickly and kept the gesture as small as possible, but he pointed her attention to the far wall. It was a real wall, this one, with a door to what looked like an actual office in it. But it also had a row of several filing cabinets up against it. And on one of them, in a beam of strangely focused fluorescent light from overhead, a small, furry black shape was curled up in a snoring ball.

"Cat." She hissed the word like a death curse. "Think we can—"

James cut her off early. "No way," he said. They had two handguns and two axes, one of which was far less impressive than the other, for all that James had a fondness for it. James still had a full barrage of "destroy" technology as his loaded blue power, and Alanna had one or two asphalt summonings, but neither of those would actually be much of a problem for one of the few fully organic monsters here. Also, even though they'd already pocketed a few blues (and a handful of pens that did weird things), none of those were sure bets in a real fight.

Which led to a pretty boring outcome.

"We're gonna have to come back later," Alanna concluded.

James hated to agree, but it was true. "I mean, maybe I could just grab it and run? I *can* accelerate. And we still have coffee," he pointed out. They considered it together, watching the cat breathing, almost forgetting that the cute ball of fur they saw was just an illusion. "I think I can do it. Unless the copier has a net gun or something."

"Or makes net guns. Or something." Alanna clicked her tongue. "No. I'm vetoing it. Even with the coffee, it's a huge risk. Don't care that this thing is a magic item we can *feel*; let's just back away and we can—"

Meow.

The noise was drawn-out, a tired little cat exclamation that was half meow and half yawn. And it didn't come from where they'd last seen the cat; it came from just around the other side of the wall they were up against.

Alanna froze up instantly, and James lashed out a hand to pull her back around the corner they were hiding behind, jolting her into motion as quietly as possible. The two of them stood stock-still, barely breathing except in silent exhales. In the silence, even with his heart thudding in his ears, James could hear the soft, illusory padding of the small cat as it slowly meandered through the slightly fancier office area. Behind that, also, there was the suppressed sound of heavy, thudding impacts as the *real* cat took its own lumbering steps.

The duo started creeping back, bit by bit, trying to put distance between themselves and the mouth of the hallway that opened into the more spacious area that the cat was roaming. And while the cat seemed perfectly content to casually bat pencils off desks in its little habitat, that didn't mean either of them wanted to stick around to find out if it had some kind of patrol boundary.

They got about two cubicle lengths down the hallway, smooth wall on the right marking the boundary of the cat's domain, with a row of ordinary cubes opposite it, before something went wrong.

The rattling hiss, like the sound of rain on metal, hit their ears suddenly, like it had been hiding until they'd gotten too close. The tumblefeed, a hostile ball of tangled cables brought to life, was currently crawling across the upper edges of the cubicles, dragging its bulk across the thin lines of wall. The remnants of its cords that didn't balance or grip properly just dangled on either side of whatever makeshift sidewalk it was currently on.

James didn't even hesitate as the sound hit them, already redirecting them into a nearby cubicle with a low door and an excess of ceiling—the perfect hiding place for something like this, assuming nothing was currently already using it as such.

There was. And in the gloom of the mostly covered workspace, the blue gleam of the eye of the shellaxy that had made its nest here was sharp and ominous. This was one too many unexpected developments, and James finally felt his ability to improvise lock up as he froze in the doorway, only moving when Alanna rammed into him from behind. The shellaxy started to hiss at them in its error-tone language, and James clamped a hand over its CD tray as if it were a mouth, hissing out a "shh" at it and hoping that the urgency and the need for silence would keep it quiet. Sliding in next to him, Alanna wrapped an arm around the shellaxy from the other side, like she could somehow arm bar it into submission if needed.

But by some miracle, it actually worked. Though the shellaxy may have been more terrified of the dangling ethernet cables that started trailing through the gaps in its nest's ceiling as the tumblefeed passed overhead, the rattling hiss snaking its way through to the ears of all three of the people cowering inside. James fell backward onto his ass, pulling the unresisting computer he was holding with him as he pushed himself against the floor, putting as much space as he could between himself and the dangling cords.

A lifetime passed in the span of heartbeats, and he and Alanna, mostly unprepared to fight something like this, just hoped like hell their hiding place held. And then they heard something they would both remember forever.

Meow?

If a cat had ever sounded curious, this was it. The follow-up meow had an echo behind it, the much deeper sound of a more hostile creature that couldn't quite mask its anger.

"Do you think," James asked in the quietest voice he could manage, "that dungeon cats are . . . um . . . Do they like cat toys?"

Alanna never had a chance to answer his stammered question. Scant seconds after James spoke, there was another hiss from the tumblefeed perched overhead, followed by a much more violent hiss from the cat. And then, without warning, the roof panels overhead violently bowed inward, accompanied by a feline yowl and a heavy set of paw thuds.

Feet scrambled against grayish-green carpet. James awkwardly knocked over the rolling chair, Alanna hooked her foot behind a filing cabinet to leverage herself up, and the two of them bolted out the door before the cat slammed the tumblefeed through the ceiling and into the cubicle where they'd just been sitting. They had, almost without thinking about it, brought the shellaxy with them, the poor creature screaming in 56k modem as they roughly cradled it between them while they took a right and fucking booked it.

They retraced their steps back to where the hallway breached into the open zone, not wanting to run back toward where the tumblefeed and the cat were now brawling, rolling out of the debris of the cubicle they'd crushed as the two of them took aggressive swipes at each other. James assumed the tumblefeed would eventually win, draining the cat by inches while being functionally unkillable in this duel, but he wasn't particularly interested in sticking around to find out. He and Alanna almost skidded as they took the sharp left turn into the classier cubicles, aiming for the other side and a shot at getting away from this before either of the monsters turned on them. James was leading now, with Alanna smoothly plucking the shellaxy from their shared grip and storing it under one armored arm; her other arm still brandished the fire axe, which could *not* be safe as she pumped it in her sprint.

They started to round the set of four open-air cubicles in the center of the zone, just as the cat toppled the middle section of the wall to their left, slamming the tumblefeed to the ground and pinning down as many of its twitching cables as it could. They couldn't see the cat, of course, aside from the tiny black illusion, but they could clearly spot where clumps of cord were smashed flat. Neither delver paused in their dash or froze up this time; they were committed. There was one way forward, and it was fucking *out of here.*

Of course, when they were just past the water cooler, almost to the other hallway, the copier seemed to take the opportunity to remember that it could really ruin their plans.

Four appendages of congealed ink from the world's stickiest tentacle monster lashed out from the copier's slightly ajar trays. One slammed weakly into Alanna's shoulder; she was too busy, and too sturdy, for it to have much of an impact on her. One missed, ducked under by James, operating on reflexes boosted by his most powerful purple upgrade. Two of them, though, latched around Alanna's ankles and *pulled.*

She hit the floor hard, turning slightly so she didn't crush the shellaxy she still carried. The poor little computer was still wailing pings and error tones, its own cable tendrils flailing wildly. Alanna still landed with enough force to knock the wind out of her lungs, her grip on the long-handled axe in her other hand going totally slack, sending the weapon skidding across the floor.

James, his upgraded brain pulling in extra details for him, felt a lot of what happened in excruciating clarity. The rush of air, the clatter of metal and plastic against the carpet, Alanna's *oof* as she impacted, his brain processing all of it in a flash of instinct. So he had ample time to react to the spinning weapon as it pirouetted past him. He turned in a low slide, one leg pressed against the ground and bleeding off speed. With his free foot, he casually tapped the toe of his boot down on the axe, stopping it dead. It was the work of only a second to swoop down, scoop up the axe by its handle, pull himself into a braced stance, lever the axe so the shaft was parallel to his back, then bring his arms forward to fling the axe overhand at the copier.

The thing about James was, when he stopped being careful and opened up the floodgates on how much his purple-orb upgrades could do, he could move almost absurdly fast. Being able to accelerate more than twice as fast as a baseline human could let him put a ridiculous amount of energy into the throw. So it was a good thing that the axe, whistling as it split the air, missed Alanna's head and slammed into the copier blade-first.

The copy machine didn't really seem to understand what had happened to it. Its tendrils just sort of went slack, one of them dissolving back into a puddle of incoherent ink. The front of it, the reader screen and keypad, were totally smashed in, small sparks jolting out along with a little bit of blackish smoke.

Alanna knew what to do, though. She kicked back into a low crouch, grabbed the haft of the axe, and yanked it out even as she fully pulled herself up.

"Fucking run!" James yelled, well aware of how that line was quickly becoming his catchphrase. Alanna listened, though, and the two of them booked it away from the stunned copier, rounded the corner, and started dashing for the door to this space that would hopefully lead them away from the plus-size fight they could still hear going on.

As if on cue, the tumblefeed rolled slightly into view, blood that was dripping from half its biting cables turning invisible before it hit the floor. It wasn't interested in them, though, and James and Alanna had no interest in giving it a reason to be. They just kept running.

James tried to keep count of how many cubes they passed. He stopped trying after he was pretty sure he went past forty for the third time. His heartbeat and footfalls were all he could hear, and his lungs were burning. All those early-morning jogs with Alanna had prepared him for this far more than sitting on the couch watching anime and eating ice cream would have, but even with months of delving, exercise, and body enchantments, he still wasn't able to keep up this pace forever.

"Oh . . . okay," he panted out, stooping over the corner of the latest intersection they'd crossed. "Let's . . . stop . . . here." He got the words out between gasping breaths of air.

Alanna didn't say anything; even for her, that was a hell of an exerting experience. She just planted her back against the corner of wall opposite James and slid down into a sitting position. As the shellaxy still under her arm gently touched the ground, she let go of it and was mildly surprised to see it just curl up and press back against her armored torso instead of running off.

They took a little while to catch their breath, James fishing out a half-full bottle of water and splitting the remnants of it with his partner. Eventually, though, Alanna asked the question that she found most important here. "What the fuck is that, James?"

James looked down, then held up his hand, clutching a small blue insulated lunch sack. "Oh. I grabbed the thing," he said. "It seemed reasonable since we were there anyway. Want to see what's in it?" he asked.

"Yes, but also, I want to know when you got an orb for axe throwing," Alanna replied, scooting across the floor and getting an annoyed chime from the shellaxy next to her.

"Never," James replied cheerfully. "That was *alllll* me."

"No."

"Yes! Did you know there's a place downtown that has a *throwing-axe range?*"

"This fucking city," Alanna muttered. "Okay. Open the bag, and if it's just lunch, I'm gonna be really pissed that we're lost over it."

"We're not lost; we just have to orient toward the bathrooms now that the cloaking meme for them is dead," James reminded her as he ripped open the Velcro and pulled out a sandwich. "Which is good, because this is lunch. Um . . ." He reached in again and pulled out another sandwich. And another, and another. "Huh."

"Infinite sandwiches?" Alanna asked, perking up.

"No, there's only a couple things left. But there is a bag of grapes and a Tupperware container of pasta in here," James said, raising his eyebrows. "Wow, this is a huge bag."

"James. James!" Alanna's voice was excited enough that the shellaxy next to her started whirring in sympathetic excitement as well. Elation at survival rushed in and compounded her thrill at their acquisition. "It's a bag of holding! Finally! We made it! We're a real D&D party now!"

"Nope," James said, crushing her hopes before they could get too high. "Look." He was trying to fit the medical kit from his backpack into the lunch bag, and it . . . wouldn't fit. It was actually only slightly larger and should have fit easily through the mouth, but there wasn't *any* room for it, somehow. "I have a sinking suspicion that this is a bag of holding lunch," he said. "Or maybe just food in general."

Alanna stuck out her tongue at him and grabbed the bag out of his hands. "Don't care, that's still awesome. Now get up. We've still got a ways to go."

James groaned but followed her as she rose, only sort of raising an eyebrow at the shellaxy that was now placidly following after them. A delver's work was never done.

"So, the general idea is that we're looking for money and magic items," Dave explained to the group following him. Some of them were listening. Some of them were clearly not, but he didn't feel like taking the extra time to get their attention; if they didn't care, they'd just have to deal with not knowing. "Early on, we used to grab stuff that was easy to sell, too. Computer monitors, suits, that sorta thing. But it turns out, the time it takes to sell off a suit on Craigslist isn't actually worth the money when you could have just saved the bag space for extra supplies, spent ten minutes going through another cubicle, and gotten the same in cash anyway," Dave told them, delving a little into their own weird group history. "Also be on the lookout for briefcases. Those are quests."

"This place is so fucked-up," Nate bluntly stated, a little too loud for the office.

At the same time, Lance was making an almost perfectly mirrored statement of "This place is so fucking cool."

Dave gave a tiny nod of agreement. "Okay, yes to both of those. Those weren't questions, but you're both right."

Currently, Dave was situated roughly at the head of their formation, though with five people in a group and four of them untrained, *formation* was a strong word to use. He wanted to be near enough to anyone who did something stupid to try to fix the problem before anyone died. Currently, they were walking down a hallway that led to nowhere in particular, just generally scouting out the corridors to the "east" of the door. And so far, it had been . . .

"This place is actually kind of boring," Virgil added, his mouth a flat line.

Dave wanted to say something, but at the moment, it was hard to disagree. With a dramatic breath of air, he pulled himself out of his tense ready-for-a-fight stance and into a normal resting position. "Yeah, this is actually kind of weird," he admitted.

They'd been going for a little while now, and while it hadn't been totally devoid of things, there was honestly kind of a lot of empty nothingness over here. They'd run into one strider nest, and Dave had taken the opportunity to let them see firsthand exactly why the little staplers were still something to keep an eye on. After that fight, letting everyone have a yellow orb to get used to the sensation and prying the staple out of Nate's burly arm, they'd moved on. And it had been another five minutes before Dave had needed to explain that coffee cups exploded and they should stay clear of them.

A few cubicles had stuff in them, and Virgil helped explain the process of uncovering passwords for the more "normal" computers. But there'd been only a couple files that came close to being interesting, and one of them was a screen saver that might have brainwashed people, so they'd deleted that, gotten a blue orb, and moved on.

And that was kind of it. Which was . . . worrying.

The office, as Dave explained it to the training team, was a lot of things. But dull had never been one of them. It also never really seemed to matter how deep in they were; there were different creatures and things in different regions, but there was always something small and weirdly fierce, something trapped, and something large and dangerous, in every biome. But here they were, wandering for a while with literally nothing going on, and Dave was starting to feel like they were going to stop believing him when he said that camracondas were *very real* and also *very lethal.*

Even the drops weren't coming up like normal. Less money, less candy, fewer general office supplies, too. Not a single identified magic item, except for one pencil that Dave had a funny feeling about. No idea what it did, though, if anything.

"So, when do we get to fight, like, a potted plant or something?" Lance asked, a little too excited. "James said something about how those drop bigger orbs?"

Nate cut in. "Guys, I can't lie to you. I'm laughing every time someone talks about *orbs*. I just need you all to know."

"We all know," Dave told him in a resigned monotone. "We all do. Anyway, normally, I'd say we shouldn't go looking for a fight, but . . . there isn't anything else to *do*, which is not how this place is. I don't know what to tell you; maybe it put on kid gloves for the new guys, but this is weird, even by our standards. So, yeah, Neil? Can you plug into your drones and find us something green to fight?" Dave asked.

"On it, boss!" Neil was the kind of kid who was just really excited to be included, excited to be useful. Certainly excited to have a role that involved playing with his favorite sort of toy. Though, really, the heavy-duty scout drones he was using were pretty far removed from toys. With the amplifier that he'd set up, courtesy of JP's wildly suspicious Amazon purchase, he easily had a range of something like a half a mile on the things. Multiple high-definition cameras on each one gave him a bird's-eye view of any space he set them over. And so far he hadn't lost any to random attacks by paper airplanes, either!

He also never actually unplugged his controller system from his skulljack, which Dave found a little unusual. Sometimes, Dave felt like Neil walked a little weird because he was trying to abdicate seeing through his own eyes at all in favor of the technological scopes of the drones.

It took Neil about ten minutes of sitting cross-legged in a kind of drone trance to actually dredge up any results. And in that time, before everyone got bored, Dave assigned everyone a cubicle in that segment of hallway around them, just to give them something to do.

There was actually a kind of magic in watching people who were new to the place go through the same things he had. Admittedly, there was a bizarre lack of real danger here this time, but the experience of getting to just riffle through wallets and desk drawers and *take stuff* was actually kind of . . . liberating? And for these new hires, Dave took a special sense of amusement in seeing them come back and having even the rather serious-faced Nate join in on joking about the names of the candy.

"'Baby Things' sounds like some kind of bondage thing," Nate said offhandedly as he tore open the wrapper and very aggressively snapped off a bite. "Huh. Weird. This tastes . . . normal."

"They're all just candy, even if it is weird candy," Dave told him. "Also, just so everyone else who didn't wait to check knows, all the food in here is safe."

Virgil pushed his glasses up his nose and cleared his throat. "The coffee cups . . ."

Trap sprung. Dave struck with words in such a flat tone that it sounded like he'd robotically rehearsed it. "We've determined that the office operates under the ruling of the 1994 lawsuit against McDonald's, which states that coffee above a certain temperature is no longer classified as food, leaving the detonating coffee cups as something that is, from a legal perspective, either disinfectant or heavy ordnance."

Three people and one drone stared at him with the closest analogue to being dumbfounded they could manage. "You made that up," Lance accused him.

"Which part?"

"The . . . lawsuit?" Neil ventured, newly returned from his recon.

"Nope, that part was true. Actually, all of it was. Possibly. Do you have something for us?" Dave cut to the chase.

Neil stood up with a wheeze and a small cough as he cleared his throat. "Um, yeah. There's a plant and a vending machine if we go that way, take a left, and then just go down to the intersection. Also, there's something on fire, like, a half mile away?"

"Is it a ball of screaming ethernet cables?"

"How would I know that? How would *you* know that?" Neil asked.

Dave shrugged. "It's a tumblefeed. Simon and his team were going to go hunting for them. We kill them with thermite. They drop green orbs," he explained.

Nate cracked his knuckles. "Okay, here's the thing. I'm fine with the hands-on experience, that's cool. But can you please just fucking explain the monsters here while we go off to *kill a goddamn potted plant?*"

"I love the stuff this place is making people say," Lance muttered to Virgil.

"Yeah, of course, that makes sense." Dave nodded. "I didn't really have a lesson plan prepared. We should really have a bestiary that we can hand to new people. Okay! Let's get moving, someone get the cart, and we'll start with the things that can kill you fastest . . ."

Stuffed shirts and strider swarms. Camracondas and maimframes. There was so much in here, so many things that even the original members had only seen once or twice. And Dave didn't know everything, so he tried as best he could to answer questions.

What's up with the masks? "No idea. Sometimes they're faces for the employees, but sometimes they just float around and scream."

Why were the employees so dangerous if they were just full of dust and shredded paper? "I feel like I have to keep explaining that some of the things here are literal magic, and that while I don't know *why*, it's still worth keeping in mind that the stronger ones can snap bones if they grab you."

Why are we in here at all if that's the threat level of the place? "It has good candy. And other colors of orb. And yes, before you ask, I can tell you what they do. It's not a secret."

Did leveling up change you? "It's not leveling up, it's . . . Okay, it is. But not like in D&D. More like in GURPS, where a single skill point is usually useless on its own." Dave shrugged as he led the group through a patch of paper-clip webbing. "It changes you, yeah. You get better at stuff, and you get sharper at feeling some things, and sometimes you just get straight up superpowers. Alanna's bulletproof. James can do that ninja-dash thing. But they're still who they *are*. The orbs can't make you someone else."

Sorry, what? That question came from a lot of people all at once, in a lot of different forms, and was mostly about the bulletproof comment. "Yeah, it's the purple orbs. They change your body in different ways. Anyway. We're here. So. I'm going to do what JP calls my best David Attenborough impression and teach you guys about the wild northwest trapdoor fern."

While everyone had bombarded him with questions while they'd walked, and they'd had some time for it since they were still being cautious, even if this place was kind of quiet today, it was here that Dave got the first question all night that he felt actually made him think.

"How did you get used to this place?" Nate asked.

It was said in the same gruff-but-cheerful tone that he used for everything, but it had a steel hint of concern running through it. And Dave, already stopped a safe distance from the plant, cast his eyes down while he turned the question over in his head. Eventually, though, he felt like he had the answer he wanted. Just as Nate was about to repeat himself, in case the younger man hadn't heard him, Dave spoke.

"I never did," he said. "I've made friends here. Literally and figuratively. I've learned so much. Not just how to do a pneumonectomy, either, but things about leadership and friendship and *myself*." Dave smiled and realized that even the way he did that had changed in the last few months. His smiles used to be masks, but now they were expressions of real things beyond wry amusement. "And every time I think we've seen the last of this place, we run into something new. Like a tapir, or the hallway that turns you upside down by the time you're halfway through it. And it's . . ." He looked around, at all of them, at the ceiling lights where blackhawks and masks had dogfights, at the gray horizon and the upward curve of the cubicles in the far, far, *far* distance. At the beige walls around them, and the plant just thirty feet ahead in plain view. "It's *magic*."

Nate nodded. They all nodded. Maybe they didn't fully understand yet, but they would. And right now, they knew, *Dave* understood.

"Now. Let's go learn about *vines*," Dave told them in a suddenly upbeat tone, clapping his hands together.

Questions, he decided, could wait until after the really exciting bit.

CHAPTER 4

"Ow. Ow. Ow." James repeated himself one more time for good measure. "Ow."

"Yeah, I'm not sure how this hasn't happened before," Alanna said as she turned James's hand over, examining the black mark along the palm. "You've hit things that should use electricity with, like, crowbars before. And those things are just bars of conductive metal."

"Ow," James agreed, nodding.

"Seriously, though. I don't really know how to treat this?" Alanna poked at the blackened flesh where the current had fried bits of James. "Like, do we have to cut your hand open and remove it so it doesn't necrotize? There's no external injury to patch up, and that's honestly the extent of my training for this place."

James bit his lip and suppressed a hiss as he pulled his hand back and flexed his fingers. "I just don't get why this is a problem *now*. It never electrocuted anyone when we cracked open shellaxies." On the floor next to him, Alanna's new best friend dinged out a protest. "Oh, not you," James said. "Just the ones that tried to eat me first."

"Maybe it was because it was specifically one of the shock mice and they're made of electricity." Alanna retorted as she ripped open a packet of mild painkillers to hand to James. "Also be nice to Shellby."

"We cannot name her that," James said as he stood back up, still trying to flex his aching hand.

It wasn't that he was against the shellaxy following them like a lost puppy, which it had been doing for a good hour now. That part was actually super cute. It wasn't that it wouldn't be a useful helper, either. Currently, it was carrying around the fancy-ass coffee machine that they'd pulled out of the break room when they'd finally found it, the heavy piece of hardware securely tied to the top of the other, more mobile, piece of heavy hardware. It looked like a caffeine-based hat, and that was *also* super cute. It was more that "Shellby" seemed like too obvious a name for James, love of puns or no.

"Don't gender my new best friend," Alanna scolded him. "What about Shelldon?"

"Same reason. Too easy."

Alanna scowled. "You don't need to make names artificially complicated. Maybe they'd just like a simple name. Not every piece of dungeon Life needs to be named after a god or a king, James."

"Rufus isn't," James protested as he cracked the yellow orb from the mouse he'd hacked into just a few minute ago.

[+2 Skill Ranks : Melee—Improvised Weapon—Backpack]

"I always assumed Rufus was some kind of in-joke. Also, anything good?"

"I think I could take you out with my duffel bag now," James half explained before filling Alanna in on the actual text. She snorted a laugh and then admitted that it could be something sneakily useful, especially with two whole ranks. The two of them discussed skills that had good corner-case uses while they finished cleaning out the cubicle.

Alanna didn't find anything in the filing cabinet that wasn't just manila folders, so while James went through drawers, she sat herself down at the computer, shifting a few times to get her armored ass to sit comfortably in the office chair. It hadn't been clear to her, until James had explained, that it wasn't the *armor* that made the chairs uncomfortable. It was a design choice for a lot of office equipment to keep people alert, whatever that meant. Alanna had just stared at him and then muttered about how his real-world job sucked before turning away.

Going through pictures on the desk to look for pet names to use as passwords, Alanna quirked an eyebrow at how this desk had four photos of dogs and all of them had the same name tag. As she tilted the last one to see if there was anything behind it, a small silver tube caught her eye, and she scooped it up and tossed it to James. "Yo. Here, laser pointer! See if it cuts through vinyl or slows down entropy or something," she said before turning back to trying different words on sticky notes as passwords.

It was after the fifth failed password that she finally got in, leaning back with a sigh as she felt the tension in her shoulders ease up. And in that moment of relaxation, the creature hiding just behind the monitor darted out and through her eye.

It was a fish, which Alanna had mistaken for just part of the background until it moved. The glittering tube with one massive glowing eye on its front scythed through the air toward Alanna before she could really process that it had begun moving at all.

She yelped, and James echoed the sound as the glittering silver-and-gold fish burst out the back of her head. Alanna didn't feel hurt, but there was a strange pulling as the creature left her.

It left trailing a thin piece of what looked like cloth behind it, a string of numbers written out on it.

James, for his part, reacted with the one thing he had at hand and just leveled the laser pointer already in his hand at it. And the fish . . . froze. It twitched its eye around like it was suddenly unsure what it was doing, and in that moment, Alanna pulled a sharp turn in the office chair, kicking it back into the desk as she leaped up. Her arm shot out and clasped around the fish thing, and as her hand intercepted the beam of James's fancy new laser pointer, she felt a brief moment of confused shock. Then the fish shattered in her grip and James clicked the laser off, pointing the device skyward.

A pair of orbs, one red and one yellow, dropped to the ground with soft thuds among the electric confetti that used to be a creature, along with the fluttering piece of paper. James snagged the paper out of the air and turned it over to look at it.

"This looks like an SSN," he commented. "Hey, is this yours? Did it just attempt identity theft?"

"I don't have one," she replied instantly before following up with "What the hell's up with the pointer, though? Did it freeze the fish? It felt weird when it went over me."

James's mouth cracked open as he looked back in disbelief. "Bullshit, you don't have one. Also, I have no idea. Mind if I try it again? It didn't hurt, did it?"

Alanna shook her head and held out an arm at a safe distance for James to zap, just in case it caught fire or something. He pointed and flicked the beam on, and Alanna felt herself refusing to believe that it was doing anything. Incredulous, and also a little curious, she rolled her eyes at the laser. "Well, that's . . . Hang on." She dropped her arm, and the feelings that had felt so *real* and innate to her just a second ago were gone. "James, what are you feeling right now?"

"Um . . . curious, I guess?" he asked. "Also, I still refuse to believe that you don't have a Social Security number. You've had normal jobs before."

"It projects your emotions," Alanna intuited. "The fish froze up because you were startled, and I felt it, too, even though I handled it differently. I can feel the curiosity, and the skepticism, though it's directed at things *I'm* thinking about, so it doesn't transmit actual information." She glanced down at the paper James was still holding. "So . . . is that *my* Social Security number, then? Did the computer fish literally steal my personal data?"

James gnawed at his upper lip. "Hmm. How do we . . ." He reached over and tried poking Alanna with the paper. "Get this . . ." He ran the paper over her armor and then her head. "Back into . . ." He started rolling it up, like he was preparing to try something even more irritating, when Alanna snatched it out of his hand.

"Give me thaaaa . . ." The paper dissolved into nothing in her grip. "Oh. Okay. Welp. That was it then. Yeah, that was mine." She nodded. "Thanks."

"No problem. So, anything else that we should grab out of here before we go? I know we're supposed to be taking a break, but this place is kinda hostile, and I'd like to head back before the walls try to eat us or something."

Alanna looked around the cubicle one last time. "Want either of the orbs? I kind of want to try another red. Also, I wanna bring this keyboard. I think it's magic." Alanna tapped the mechanical keyboard currently plugged into the computer.

"Sure, go for it. The orb, that is. Don't you dare bring that monstrosity into our house," James replied, grabbing the yellow for himself.

[+1 Emotional Resonance Rank : Defiance]

[+1 Skill Rank : Athletics—Acrobatics—Balance]

"The keyboard is magic, I'm sure of it. The way it sounds is soothing—I think it's the underlying effect of it."

"Alanna, the keyboard sounds like someone forgot to oil a revolving door. It's not soothing, or magic, it's just a mechanical keyboard. Which I do not like, to be clear," James said as he crouched down on his knees, peering under the desk. "Oh, score, a briefcase!"

"Mechanical keyboards, *James*, are the only keyboards worth using. They are durable, and precise, and perfect for . . . Oh, briefcase?" Alanna dropped the petty argument—that she was absolutely prepared to win, by the way—and looked over the gray leather case James plopped on the desk between them. She ripped off the work order taped to the side and read over it. "Delivery order, office supplies, fifty pencils, number two, yadda, yadda . . ." she muttered to herself while James checked just to make sure this one wasn't already unlatched. "Oh, hey, wait a sec. This one lists a *place*, not a cubicle number. It just says 'shoreline.'"

"Like . . . the ink-ocean shoreline?" James asked, excited. "Like the place we *know how to get to* and could go to right now?"

"Well, not *right now* right now," Alanna reminded him. "But yeah, I mean, we've got the bikes back at the base. We could swing by, get those, and go try it out?" The unspoken assumption that there was probably already a bundle of fifty number two pencils just ready to go at their home tower for some reason went unremarked.

"Sounds good to me. We can drop off the coffee maker and also introduce Shellia to everyone."

"Sparky, you fuckin' *said* that we couldn't do a name that was too easy," she protested as they both stood, loaded everything back into the bags, and checked the corners of the door to make sure it was safe out in the hall.

"I'm workshopping."

"We could just ask, you know. Would you like that?" Alanna adopted a singsong voice as she gave the shellaxy's case some gloved pets. "Would you like to just have a monitor so you can *tell us things?* Yes, you would!"

"Would that even work?" James asked, curious.

Alanna smirked a response. "I'm workshopping," she said, before stepping out. "Come on. Looks like we're about half a mile from home. Let's get moving, and we'll have a few hours left to hit the beach."

"So, what'cha up to?" Momo asked Anesh, leaning forward to peer at the concoction he was stirring together.

Anesh glanced up from his work briefly, quirking an eyebrow as Momo got close enough that the red totem she wore as an earring overlapped him and he had a sudden and intimate knowledge of how close the nearest lethal weapon was. It was not that far. "I'm blending the coffee mix that's so far been most efficient at duplicating mundane objects."

"I thought we were waiting on Danny to find another tower with more coffee in it?" Momo asked innocently.

Anesh shrugged. "I still had some left over, and if we get more before the day is over, I can just repeat the ritual. But I think I can run it about three times at this ratio. Especially if I'm really sharp with the lines."

"What exactly is up with this ritual, anyway? I honestly just wanted to see it." Momo turned over an empty paper bag that used to contain coffee grounds and read the "instructions" on the back. She held it up and compared it to the whiteboards that Anesh had weaseled people into hauling up here, seeing where he'd made changes or notes. "It looks like a totem," she concluded.

"How so?" Anesh asked, curious. He set aside what he was working on and looked up, giving her his full attention as he walked over to join her in front of his research notes. "I've seen some of what you've been working on. Totems are always three-dimensional; this one decidedly isn't."

"Well, it kind of is. Coffee is physical; it's not just a flat line," Momo argued. "But I mean the shape of it. It's like someone flattened a totem down, and replaced the orb with . . . that thing." She waved a hand behind her. "An overhead projector. For some reason."

"I do wonder if the object itself matters," Anesh mused. "Could you have made this same ritual focus with, say, a chair? Or is the nature of the focus important?"

Momo drummed her fingers across the whiteboard to an invisible tune. "Wasn't there something about making magic items with reds instead of blues?"

"Yes," Anesh said. "That's one theory now. And we have *several*, including being able to make magic items with blues in the first place." He unlocked the wheels of one whiteboard and spun it around, revealing the other side covered in grid charts and notepaper held up with magnets. "The one that I think makes the most sense now is that every orb color can, in its own way, make life, make a reward, and make an enhancement. And we are only just now starting to scratch the surface of those different uses."

"What about the totems?" Momo asked. "They don't fit that."

"Unless they're . . . rewards?" Anesh hummed, chewing idly on the end of a pen as he looked over the board again. "Or somewhere between reward and enhancement. Unless they're a little alive, too."

"Backing off on that," Momo interrupted, "what would orange life look like? I've only seen one disrupted space, and it was fucked-up. Would something alive be . . . that, but mobile?"

"No, I don't think so. After all, most yellow life isn't a manifestation of a skill. Secret is purple life, in case you didn't know, and we *know* that, but the purples don't give us enhancements at all in line with infomorphic traits." Anesh got a glimmer in his eyes and leaned over the conference table that the ritual zone was built around to start scribbling something on his notepad. He crossed out a line and replaced it with something else. Momo looked over his shoulder as he did so, bobbing on her feet and occasionally giving Anesh flashes of knowledge that the pencil he held was sharp enough to kill.

"Does human math work here?" Momo asked him.

"It's more about rates of occurrence than divining meaning," Anesh said. "But in this case, it's just a moment of inspiration about . . . this." He held up the sheet, staring at it like he could see into the universe itself. Furiously, he wiped away an obsolete part of the notes on his board and started penning in a formula. Momo didn't distract him, instead spending a few minutes roaming around, poking at the red-and-white cooler on the table, peering out the windows at the base camp so far below, just distracting herself for a bit. Momo's mind wandered easily enough these days to be distracted without too much trouble. "Yes! This!" Anesh yelled. "Where's my laptop?"

"We don't bring laptops in here," Momo told him. "I was told that was a terrible idea, anyway."

"Ah, yes," Anesh agreed, clearing his throat. "Sorry, got caught up there. Um. I think I can build a red *item*," he said, as if that wasn't the closest thing anyone had gotten to pure wizardry so far. "See? Here. You said that the ritual looked like a flattened totem?"

He pointed, and Momo looked at the string of variables and functions he'd written on the board. Her eyes glazed over as she tried to parse it, and it took maybe five seconds for her to give up entirely. "No," she told him. "I see gibberish. This makes sense to you?"

"It's . . . yes?" Anesh looked sheepish. "It's an expression of what something would look like. That's all. Vector calculations and angle totals and stuff. I think, anyway. I might be fucking nuts, but it just clicked in my head. I think I can make this happen." He nodded. "Yeah, definitely. I just need some extra reds to test on. Oh, I might not actually know what I'm making, though. Hmm." He rubbed at his chin. "That might be a problem?"

Momo laughed. "Yeah, I had that same issue. *That* I can help with. It's art!"

The two of them looked at each other and then burst out laughing together. "Holy shit, James is gonna be so pissed that *two* people beat him to the job title of sorcerer."

"Is that a thing he wanted?" Momo asked. "I thought he was . . . like, Dave calls him a paladin?"

"We need to write a slang book for all the people who aren't huge nerds," Anesh admitted. "But yeah, James wanted real magic. I think this counts. Though I won't be having a boast until I can make it work."

Momo raised a hand in the air, and after a few moments and eyebrow waggles, Anesh finally got it and accepted the high five. "So, what're you doing with the coffee ritual, anyway? Or are you still doing that?"

"Well, thing is, it costs so much coffee to duplicate orbs that we figured we could have a higher impact on the world's supply of good if we used it on scarce mundane things that could help people," Anesh told her, tearing his eyes off his work on the board and back to Momo. "So, we're duplicating hearts."

". . . Um." The answer was not exactly what she'd been expecting.

Anesh rolled on anyway. He'd gotten used to people adapting to their weird conversation topics, and he mostly just assumed Momo would keep up. "The exponential growth should let us get up to eight, assuming we can fit them all in the projector zone. Which is a net of seven, which is then proof of concept to the hospital we got it from in the first place."

"*How* did you convince them to give you a heart?!" Momo demanded, unbelieving. Yes, it was true; she had a marginal amount of hero worship for James and especially Alanna, and the others of the core team to a lesser degree. But she knew damn well that was just *her*. Random people who kept transplant organs safely locked up *weren't going to hand those over.*

"Alanna stole it. Something about rigging a fire alarm? I didn't ask," Anesh said. "We're basically going to bargain the extras for amnesty for, you know, stealing the first one."

"So this is illegal," Momo confirmed to herself.

"Incredibly so. Dodgy as fuck." Anesh made it sound so casual. They'd *stolen a heart*, and he was just . . . well, they were going to give it back, Momo supposed, so maybe it wasn't that bad?

No, it was that bad.

"Do you know anything about how to keep human hearts preserved?" she asked, suspicious. "Or if this was *for* someone?"

"Yes. To both. It wasn't for anyone, the intended recipient . . . well, it's fine. And as for preserving them, you can't. *We* can't," Anesh said sadly. "Which is actually the biggest barrier to making this work. We may need to tip our hand about the magic stuff, because we're having to use up Sarah's new blue power to keep them basically in stasis."

"Wouldn't that make them not useful as, you know, hearts? Oh! That reminds me! Didn't Sarah say something about how all magic items come from blue totems?" Momo's brain jumped tracks as she was more or less reassured that the particulars were taken care of, and a separate debate opened up before her.

"Sarah is wrong." Anesh snorted. "Honestly, I think the blue-totem thing was a cultural myth, not anything they ever proved. An extraurban legend."

"You made that word up."

Anesh ignored the quip; James had trained him perfectly for this style of conversation. "I think Sarah's old team had gained and lost members before her. I think that one of them, at some point, had a theory about it, and then they died or got captured or whatever. And as more members rotated through, what used to be a theory became word-of-mouth truth. So by the time Sarah's there, they're telling her that blues make dungeon tech and are the basis for quests and she buys it because . . . I mean, look at this place. Dave could literally tell the new guys anything and they'd have to take it at face value, right?"

"He wouldn't do that," Momo protested firmly, jumping instantly to the defense of her hero.

"'Course not. Dave's staunch," Anesh assuaged her fears. "But how would anyone know? Tumblefeeds sound fake, right? So do half the orbs. *Secret* sounds fake, and that holds true even if you're actively talking to him." He shrugged. "I don't want to confront Sarah about it; I feel like that would open some old wounds she doesn't need right now. But I do, fundamentally, think she's wrong. There's no evidence otherwise."

Momo stopped pacing and scowled at the whiteboard nearest her. "There's also no evidence that your nonsense math can predict my artisanally crafted totems," she said defiantly.

"*Yet!*" Anesh cheerfully reminded her. "Now! Want to help me set up to make some *hearts*? I can show you the ritual markings, and you can tell me how I'm doing it wrong. Deal?"

"Deal," Momo agreed.

CHAPTER 5

James and Alanna strode up to the tower like they owned the place. Which they kind of did, all things considered. Theo sat outside on a makeshift bench made of the fewest-wheeled office chairs she could find, reclining in the shade of the tower and not acknowledging either of the delvers, or the shellaxy following them, as they walked up.

"Keeping guard, eh?" James asked, a bit annoyed. There was supposed to be a team on rotation here, but he didn't see anyone. "Where is everyone?"

"Deb's team is patrolling around. Everyone else is upstairs being nerds and arguing about stupid shit." She shrugged as best she could while lounging, not really paying attention to anything except the small pamphlet she was reading.

James scowled down at her, an expression she either ignored or didn't pay much attention to. "And you?" he asked. He wasn't furious or anything—nothing was on fire and no one was dead. But it struck him as supremely hypocritical that Theo, who wouldn't shut up about the need to fight the Office, to control it, to guard the entrances, was sitting here reading some random document instead of actually safeguarding the people who were doing the most to understand and exploit the dungeon.

"I'm reading. Why, what do you care?" Theo asked, shooting back a glare of her own.

James took a deep breath, bringing his emotions back under control before he spoke. He shot a glance at Alanna, and she returned it, quirking an eyebrow and getting a small head shake from James. When he finally spoke, it was in a voice that was less calm and more apathetic. "I don't really care, Theo," he said. "I just expected more."

Nothing more than that. He didn't need any more. James and Alanna walked into the ground floor of the tower without looking back.

It wasn't until they got to the third floor that Alanna gushed out a howling laugh. "Hooooo-ho-ho! Holy shit, that was hostile! What skill orb . . . no, wait, let me guess." She leveled an accusatory finger at James. "Just you?"

"Just me," he said. "Man, I remember when Theo was cool."

"I think you're making the mistake of thinking that Theo was ever cool," Alanna grumbled. "Even when she was your boss, and you'd come home and talk about your 'cool boss,' her hallmark was casual abuse of power. Sometimes they were *funny*, but there was for real a time that she bribed and or coerced you to answer her emails for her while she took a vacation without telling upper management."

"We still can't prove my company actually has management," James reminded her, and Alanna actually *growled* a little at that. "I mean, they do. Somewhere. People have meetings with them; they run the company. It's not like they're dungeon constructs or not real or something." He looked back at her as they ascended the ramp to the fifth floor. "Probably?" he finished weakly.

"James, we're conquering your company when we get out of here."

"Tonight? Noooo. I wanted to go get pancakes! It's a tradition!"

"We go to that damn diner every night after leaving Officium Mundi, and I have never once seen you order pancakes."

"Usually I'm in the mood for fish," James agreed. "I just say 'pancakes' because it's morning, and everyone understands what I mean. It's *language*, Alanna. If you say something dumb that perfectly passes on what you mean, then it wasn't dumb."

Alanna grinned. "I feel like if I internalize that, I'll either be halfway to done with the lesson or I'll go insane."

"Or both." James paused to catch his breath on the ninth floor, really starting to feel all his bruises, scrapes, cuts, and charred strips of flesh. "Okay. We need to move Anesh's wizard tower," he said between gulps of air. "To the ground floor," he clarified as Alanna looked at him funny. "Move it to the ground floor, because this sucks."

"Oh, suck it up, you big baby. Come on, I hear Momo and Sarah arguing. Let's break up a fight," she said, leading the way to the last ramp up.

James looked down at the shellaxy, still with a coffee machine balanced on its case, that had followed them all the way up here without breaking a sweat. "How the hell . . ." he started to ask it and then shook his head. It was enough to just decide that he wouldn't be beaten in a footrace by something without feet.

When they got to the top of the ramp, James could understand the muffled yelling. Momo and Sarah stood on opposite sides of a whiteboard, each pointing at different parts of what looked like the kind of equation that James usually saw as a prop in sci-fi shows.

"Blue!" Sarah was yelling, tapping her part of the board.

"Red!" Momo retaliated, rapping knuckles on her side.

"*Blue!*" Sarah had a bit of a laugh in her voice.

"*Red!*" Momo wore a wide grin.

"Purple?" James interjected, walking up and leaning on Anesh's shoulder, his boyfriend standing a safe distance away from what was going on.

Anesh sighed and looked up from where he'd buried his face in his hands. "They can't agree on which orb causes magic items," he said. "And now they're just trying to interpret math that they don't understand as if it were arcana, pointing at things and insisting I back them up. James, help me."

With a soft chuckle, James leaned down and gave Anesh a small kiss before leaning back. "All right, wizard nerds," he announced. "Alanna and I are here literally just to check in, grab bikes, and hit the beach. Someone give me a status update on anything I need to know, and also, let Anesh do math in peace."

Sarah broke down in giggles at that, and even Momo relaxed the insistent look on her face. "Hey!" Sarah greeted him properly. "We made hearts!" She gestured to a stack of four red-and-white coolers over on the floor by one of the window gaps.

"Only four today?" Alanna inquired as politely as possible.

"The copier space is actually pretty limited. There's eight hearts total in the boxes," Sarah reassured her. "Also, Daniel's on the way back with more coffee for us. We still have a few hours left, and we learned my blue-orb preservation ability can be copied, too. So I'm just chilling here for fun. And . . . you made a friend!" She clapped her hands, beaming in excitement as she noticed the shellaxy cresting the top of the ramp.

"We also got another coffee machine," James agreed. "Can you name the shellaxy? Alanna keeps shooting down my ideas."

"Raspberry Jam," Sarah said without an inch of hesitation.

Everyone did a double take, as if they'd misheard her somehow. But they hadn't, and they all knew it. "All right." James just decided to agree. "Raspberry, you okay with that?" He addressed the shellaxy, which gave him an OS boot-up noise in response. "Guess so. All right! So, anything else we need to know about before we go? We got a briefcase."

"Oh! Is the beach where the other decision tree is?" Sarah asked him, practically bouncing on the balls of her feet. "Secret is down a few floors organizing our loot. Can you pick up a bunch of yellows and turn them into purples for me?"

"Sure," James agreed, silently wondering if Secret would just be curled up on top of a pile of stuff like a dragon. "All right. We're heading out, then, before my legs realize how tired they are and I just sit down and don't get back up. Hey, is anyone on security here?" he asked, suddenly remembering a worry.

Anesh shrugged. "Theo's outside; she didn't want to deal with us, I guess, which is fine. And Deb and Alex are nearby." He looked at James, concerned. "Why? Is something wrong?"

"No, no. I just feel like if we're going to use this place as a base, we should be prepared for things like swarms or wandering greens," James told him. "I realized while we were out that I actually spent a lot of time being worried about you guys, you know?"

It was a very touching thought, really, Anesh felt. Still, it was important that James knew he wasn't totally defenseless. Walking around the table, Anesh pushed back one of the chairs half covered by the conference table, revealing the black plastic case sitting on it. "I *am* armed, you know. If anything happens, we can deal with it." James raised a questioning finger and started to open his mouth, but Anesh preempted him. "Yes, I made more ammo out of our last magazine. There was room to wedge it onto the projector space. It's *fine*, James," he said. "Go to the damn beach already."

"Fine!" James conceded as Alanna patted him on the back and the rest of the room laughed. "But I'm leaving this laser pointer with you, as a last resort!" he told Anesh.

"Oh, neat. What does it do?" his partner asked.

"For me? Makes people feel stupid," James told him before he started the climb back down.

El stood back a good thirty feet and watched in mildly frightened awe as two boys and a thing that was absolutely not a dog, no matter what anyone told her, just ripped apart a monster made of internet cables.

Simon and Other James, who really needed a new nickname, were, according to *them*, somewhere toward the lower end of the spectrum of combat ability that the members of this bizarre organization had. And El was sitting here watching while they used a glimmering rainbow distortion field to lure in a creature they called a tumblefeed before hitting it with a blazing, sparking mess of a device they insisted on referring to as a grenade.

Then, when that didn't kill the thing, they approached it from opposite sides in perfect unison, braids of cords and Wi-Fi adapters dangling out the back of their heads, held in place by leather collars they'd picked up at a fucking pet store, of all places. They held in their hands weapons that were essentially just secured hilts with lances of thermite on the ends, blazing as they took it in turn to lash out at the hissing mass until it eventually relented and died.

Mostly. They'd then had to step into it and take apart its core with a pair of garden shears.

"Clear."

"Clear." They spoke in unison to El, still linked together from the fight. One of them—it didn't really *matter* which at this point—knelt to pluck the hefty green orb out of the smoldering remains of the tumblefeed while the other gave their pet mongausse, Magneto, insubstantial belly rubs and a piece of magnet as a treat.

El didn't really know how to handle this.

This was the deal; she knew about dungeons. One dungeon, anyway. She had, for a long time, thought she was special. That her induction into the world of highways, strange beasts, and stranger rewards was the *way* that someone was special. Like she'd been chosen for a life of magic, and this was just how magic happened to people. Maybe it always was, maybe it was a new phenomenon—didn't matter to her, really.

Now she'd been brought into a team that just . . . added people to their group whenever they wanted to? They'd just *hired* people. And brought them into a life-or-death battle as a way to amass power so they could change the world. They weren't just a chosen one and an accident; they weren't even just a group of friends. They were an organization, preparing for the task of expressing its ideals onto the world.

And the people who thought they were at the bottom of the power ranking were more or less single-handedly tearing through the more difficult threats that the dungeon deployed. At least in this part of itself.

This was the third tumblefeed they'd killed today.

"The connection is really strong here," Simon mentioned offhandedly as she rejoined them. El was kind of an observer on this hunting trip. Observer and pack mule. She'd been offended by that for about fifteen minutes until one of them had intercepted a strider leap aimed at her head. Her annoyance had dropped steadily since then.

She knew Simon was only talking because she was here. He and Other James were so interlinked at this point, they were almost a single person. They didn't need to say anything. And that was creepy as fuck, as well as vaguely homoerotic, both of which were aesthetics that El could appreciate. "Strong how?" she asked politely.

"I mean, the Wi-Fi," Other James said. "It's actually ridiculously good. Maybe it's just because no one else is using it." They both shrugged together.

Their idea of small talk was so weird, El decided.

They trekked a little farther, and El came to the very real conclusion that she hated walking. Not that this was walking, exactly. It was more like the kind of hiking she'd expect on a safari. You had to carry heavy things, including things you found along the way. You couldn't stop for too long or dangerous wildlife might kill you. And you also couldn't drop your guard, space out, and listen to the rad tunes you took a lot of time to put into a playlist. Because, again, the dangerous wildlife might kill you.

She really, really, really wanted to poke around. To get lost going through these cubicles. Each one of them was, from the brief glimpses she was getting of them, its own special work of art. Maybe the boys just didn't see it, but she did. These were beautiful *lies*. Photos that didn't make sense, documents that talked about practices that never happened, computers with operating systems that shouldn't work—this was a set, they were the actors, but no one had told them it was fake.

Also she wanted to see if the wallets really did have cash in them.

But her guides set a frenetic pace, and she didn't feel like her first time in here was really the time to play the stupid tourist.

The other weird thing was that she maybe could have gotten away with it if she'd asked. Everyone here had been accommodating to her, to an almost idiotic degree. They answered questions with straight answers and not cryptic bullshit, they gave her hands-on examples of things when she needed a reference for something, they let her *take notes*. Though, to be fair, she didn't like taking notes.

But they also let her make art. And not for any ulterior motive that she could find, either. Sarah had just swept in one day, dropped a duffel bag full of spray paint on the bench next to her, and told her to go nuts. Momo had offered her a skulljack if she wanted one and instantly and diplomatically backed off when she hadn't. Even Nate, the new guy, who'd never seen the dungeon before at the time and had known the group for a few days at most, had offered to push his van up to 120 mph on the drive over, just to top off her Velocity.

They didn't act like a shadowy cabal; they acted like a more or less smoothly oiled artist anarchy collective. No one even blamed her for *trying to shoot their leader*. They just accepted that it had been an overreaction and that she'd been under a lot of pressure. No harm done, right?

They also laughed at her jokes. And had their own jokes. Everyone here was *smart*. Smart enough to find stuff funny, which, El knew, was not actually that common. They'd gathered a lot of unique traits together in their little blender. The other day, James had made a comment about making an account on some food delivery app, just so he could know that every time he wanted a burger, out there somewhere, a driver was going to go into a restaurant and say, "I have a pickup for Rothgar Duskblade, Killer of the Worldspine?" and El was actually still laughing about it. Though mostly on the inside, where no one would ask why she kept disguising random giggles as coughs.

El found time passed quickly when she was in her thoughts as they walked. And before she knew it, they'd made their way to the mouth of what looked like a cave. It was made of cubicle wall panels, of course, but they rose well above the rest of the space around them and were set at shallow angles to each other, forming a domed arch that led into a darkened space untouched by the fluorescent lights overhead. Lines of folded dot-matrix printer paper dangled from the lip of the mouth, half concealing the entryway with a white curtain. From within, in the quiet air of the Office, they could hear a steady dripping sound.

"This is weird," El commented, looking up at it. It was her catchphrase for the night.

"We've seen weirder," the other two replied. It wasn't exactly their catchphrase, but El had this sinking suspicion that they weren't just making a joke, and that maybe a lopsided octahedral cave that sloped down into the depths of the dungeon really *wasn't* that weird to them anymore.

She was never making it out of this with her worldview intact.

They took the ramp down, careful to not slip on the floor as the carpet underfoot grew damp and slightly squishy to the touch. Simon pointed out movement on the walls, and El had to suppress a desire to screech as she saw what looked like smartphones turned into millipedes crawling along the walls. She was even more put out when it was suggested that she see if any of them were friendly and interested in coming along. Though, they'd explained to her that iLipedes were actually more like microchips in design than they were bugs, it was a little easier to stomach holding up a handful of yellow orbs and letting one of them eat out of her hand. Petting it felt an awful lot like just touching a phone screen, complete with mild vibrational feedback, and by the time El let it perch on her backpack, she was only about thirty percent worried it was going to crawl into her hair.

At the base of the cave, the sound of dripping intensified. El had thought she'd gotten past being shocked at anything around here, but stepping into an underground cavern got past her defenses. Again. The beams of their flashlights mingled with the glimmering light of a thousand tiny flying creatures and the refracted beams that came through cracks in the ceiling and hit the water-cooler tanks that grew like deformed crystal nodes out of the walls and ceiling. Many of those tanks dripped water at a steady rate, fat droplets that plummeted twenty or thirty feet to splash into the surface of an otherwise still lake that took up the majority of the middle of the cavern.

"Good place to rest for a while," James said, claiming a protruding growth of crystalline water tank on the floor as a chair.

They sat for a while, the two boys decoupling their minds and taking a mental breather while El tried to will her legs and feet to stop aching. The magnetic dog thing looked more excited than ever, though, running circles around them as it got its playtime in, taking diving leaps off sloped crystals in the floor to try to snap ethereal jaws at the pinpricks floating in the air.

With a laugh and some closer inspection, El realized that *pinprick* was exactly the right term; those things were buzzing, flying thumbtacks. How they were glowing, she didn't know. Nor did she *need* to, either.

"Hey, what do you guys think this is?" Simon called over to them. He was against one of the cave walls, running his hand across something embedded in it.

El and Other James made their way over, and she noticed that the two boys looked almost uncomfortable actually having to talk to each other when they weren't wired together. The stuff Simon was looking at was a strange geometric pattern of metal, inlaid in the damp fuzz of the cubicle walls that still formed the foundation of this place. Mixed in with spurs of concrete rising out of the ground and the gray felt, there was a series of boxy silvery plates jutting slightly out of the otherwise smooth surface.

"Silver?" El asked, interest ramping up at the idea of a precious metal just sitting here.

"I don't think so," Simon said. "Feels kind of electric. Hang on, can you grab that side of this one?" He motioned and gripped his fingers under the thin ridge of the material.

El shrugged and stepped forward, elbowing her pack into a less awkward place while she got a grip on the thing and started to pull along with Simon. For not the first time tonight, she was grateful that she wasn't one those girls who painted their nails; she'd seen Sarah putting a lot of time into some really neat glitter swirl designs, and if El's own adventures so far were anything to go by, those patterns and those fingernails weren't going to be anywhere near intact by the end of the delve.

"Guys." Other James's voice reached them, but they were making progress and ignored him. Both of them felt the metal under their hands start to give, pulling away from the wall millimeter by millimeter. "Guys!" he said again, louder this time.

Simon looked up to see what was happening, and El felt his grip leave the piece of metal, even as she herself felt the last resistance falter. With a triumphant yank, she pulled the whole thing free and held it up to examine with a grin.

It was a circuit. Or rather, it was . . . like the material of a motherboard, maybe? Dotting the reverse of the smooth metal plate were a handful, no, *dozens* of small chips. They glittered in the cave's light like they were made of emeralds, each of them sparking with an internal lightning.

"El!" Simon yelled, and she looked up from her treasure.

Overhead, a thousand pinpricks of light stirred violently. A swarm of pissed-off fireflies, amassing and looping in increasingly large group patterns. Standing on one of the nearby crystal tanks, the dog thing howled, crackling static up at them until a handful of them lanced down and stabbed into his snout, changing defiance into pained yips. And then, first in ones and twos, and then in larger and larger clusters, the pinpricks started coming for the humans.

They ran. Oh, man, did they run. El didn't realize exactly just how much energy she had left for a jog until her heart flooded with adrenaline and her legs felt like they were made of lasers and steel. And even then, she started to fall behind until Simon grabbed her hand and started hauling her forward.

The four delvers burst out of the mouth of the cave, the magnetic hound leading the way. And the dog didn't slow down at *all*. He just tore into the cubicle wall across from the mouth of the cavern, his body turning into incoherent triangular panels of colored light for a second before the wall ripped away in a jagged hole that the three bipeds following him were all too happy to hop through, hot on the re-forming dog's heels.

They barreled through the cubicle and the next one opposite it, knocking over filing cabinets, chairs, and a lamp in the process, before they realized that the swarm wasn't after them anymore. The furious buzzing had died down, and the glittering collection of pins and tacks had stopped, hovering like wasps over the mouth of the cave. Their luminescent little lights weren't really shining through much under the brighter overhead lighting. Then they started to trickle back in, a few at first, and then the rest of them.

El started laughing. Even after she had to pluck a pair of dead pins that she hadn't even noticed out of her upper arm, she laughed. They'd survived! They'd made it! And she even still had this strange piece of metal-and-gem hardware that they'd confiscated.

And then the clicking started.

Other James heard it first, along with his good dog. Then Simon's head snapped up. The two of them didn't wait this time; they plugged their braids back in and in a moment they were one again. When El heard it, though, her laugh turned a little manic.

"Quiet, please," the boys said in a hushed whisper. But it was far too late. They'd made too much noise, knocked over too many things. Metal and plastic clatters echoed in the still air. And something—several somethings—had heard them.

The first strider came over the wall. It probably didn't even know this was the cubicle they were in, but James ripped it apart all the same and cracked the orb in the same motion. El briefly wondered how the skills worked between them if they were connected at the time, but then the next strider came in. And the next. And the next.

And the rest.

They flowed over the back and left walls like a waterfall, and the group ran again. Out the door, down the hallway. They approached an intersection and saw striders moving like they *were* the carpet ahead of them. So, with the somewhat rough help of the linked boys, El took the sharp right and ducked under the swinging branch of a plant as they just kept running. But the clicking didn't abate; it surrounded them, drowned them. The little stapler crabs were *everywhere*, climbing over walls, down from the archways, out of nooks and crannies. They kept running, but they weren't gaining ground.

And then they took a curving turn at the end of a hallway and found themselves cut off. One, two, five hundred of the monsters, all of them with vicious hunger in their eyes. Waiting, approaching. No hesitation or remorse. They turned to run back the way they'd come, but already there were more and more of them closing in. So many.

One hit El in the head, propelled from the wall behind them, and she dropped to the ground, listless. Her eyes lost focus, and for a second she felt like she was floating. From the floor, she saw Simon and Other James lashing out with repeated strikes and kicks, intercepting stapler after stapler, occasionally flickering back to mirrored martial arts stances. Corpses and ichor and orbs splattered to the ground around her head, and El struggled to stand. But she couldn't get her legs to move.

They were so dead.

There was one thought that wouldn't leave El's head, though. Not so much a thought, really. More of a feeling. A directive. A truth.

She wasn't going to die here.

They weren't going to die here. Unacceptable. Not while she could still do something. And she could always do something; she was, after all, a goddamn wizard. Since long before Anesh had started doing math at the mystical, since before anyone had eaten their first blue. She didn't have the same scope of magic, and maybe didn't even have the same power, but she had an intimate familiarity with hers and she could drive it like she grew up on it.

"Tha—" She spat out blood, a red glob staining the floor in front of her as she tried to get control of her tongue. "Tha rhad . . . The road . . ." El dragged air through her nose, watching from her prone position as a carpet of staplers closed in, tiny sharp death approaching. "The . . . the . . ." She could do this. It was so easy. The words were right there.

"[*The Road Leads Ever Forward*]."

Reality rewrote itself around her. Within her gut, the feeling of Velocity draining away to nothing overtook her and almost made her lose concentration entirely. But she held on. And causality stretched to the breaking point until, all at once, the new real snapped into place.

Twenty-six seconds ago, Simon had stumbled slightly as his connection with Other James stuttered. Because of this, a leaping strider had caught his backpack, left a small tear, and then shoved down the zipper with its foot as it tried to climb up before being smashed away. Out of the perfectly sized opening, a single object had tumbled, an uncomfortably thin yellow legal pad with something oddly specific written on it.

El didn't know *why* she had to grab it, but it had landed right next to her. And her spell held everything together. The road led forward. All she had to do was take the step.

One hand reached out and grabbed Simon's ankle. It only took the smallest flicker of his eyes to see what she had, and he clapped hands with James, who already knew what was going on. Together, they scooped the injured, glittering ghost dog up into their arms. Somehow.

El tore the page.

Three humans, one furious magnetic distortion, and two extra soon-dead striders that were still clinging on slammed into the second floor of the door tower, inside the specially marked-off circle of neon-orange duct tape that absolutely *no one* was *ever* supposed to step inside.

The last thing El did before she passed out was grab the strider on her arm with a shaking hand and slam it, over and over and over, into the ground. Until all the was left was crumbling chitin pulp.

Then she closed her eyes.

She opened them briefly to make sure she got to crack the orb, though.

[*+1 Skill Rank : History—Alchemy—Egyptian*]

Neat.

CHAPTER 6

"This is nice," James said with a relaxed sigh.

He was sitting, legs splayed in front of him, on a beach of plastic pebbles and ground-up cardboard. A few dozen meters away, an inky-black sea lapped lazy, sticky waves against the shore. James watched it with a casual smile and a languid gaze. Off in the distance of the ocean of printer ink, some nightmare creature breached the surface for a few seconds before slamming back under with a spray of black liquid, but James paid it no mind. It was a variety of tumblefeed; they'd seen it a few times. Like a great squid—and James insisted it was a tumblesquid, because of a long-ago slang term he'd heard for a power strip—it prowled the ink sea, occasionally popping up above the surface just to remind them that the depths were full of nightmares. But it never came to the beach.

The beach was pleasant. Even with the wreck of the shellaxy that had tried to ambush them from its spot buried under the "sand" sitting nearby.

"James, please, I'm gonna lose count again," Alanna said. Alanna was not relaxing. While James had jammed a broken chunk of cubicle wall into the beach and was using it as something to lean against, Alanna didn't really feel like leaving herself vulnerable. She rested on a single knee, ready to spring up at a moment's notice. Sharp contrast to James, who really was just enjoying the chance to take a load off.

Alanna was also laying orbs out on the ground. Groups of three to six yellow orbs, not really sorted, just arranged so they were all roughly the same total size, lined up in rows in the sand. She was trying to establish a pattern of trade with the denizens of the decision tree they'd run across, especially since they'd found a second one farther down the beach, and that opened up the chance for *negotiations*. Purples were soon to become a little less scarce for the delvers if this kept up.

Right now, though, one of the monitor lizards was insisting she add another orb to one of the piles, and she legitimately had no clue what made it think that was okay.

"Why," Alanna growled flatly at it. "*Why?!* What makes *these* orbs worth less than *these* orbs?!" she demanded of the little creature made of shards of digital screen. It scampered away at her raised voice, burying itself in the sand while she calmed down. Alanna was curious now, though, and she picked one orb from each pile.

[+1 Skill Rank : Programming—SQL—Indexes]

Well, that was one that it had left alone in a pile of only three. So, what was in the pile that it demanded she keep adding more and more to?

[+1 Skill Rank : Bureaucracy—Government—Australia—Local Council Minutes]

Hmm.

Could these little lizards sense how granular skills got? Alanna stilled her face into a mask of neutrality; it wouldn't do for them to know that they had a valuable skill. The damn things had clearly inherited a good chunk of the abstract supply of capitalism that the dungeon grew out of, and if they knew that the delvers appreciated the appraisal of the yellows, they'd charge through the nose for it.

Still, though, that wasn't why she was here at all. With a grimace, Alanna combined the two lessened piles into one slightly larger one, which the monitor lizard eagerly accepted. "All right," she told it. "All this for sixteen purples. Is your tree amicable to this deal?" The little lizard flashed small loops of color along its plates, its camouflage shattering in the closest thing Alanna had seen to an agreement so far. "All right. Good talk," Alanna told it, stepping back.

She went over and knelt next to James while a chain of motivated lizards passed orbs one by one back to their home tree, yellows flowing one way and purples the other. "Got a good rate?" James asked her, abandoning his efforts to fold a sombrero out of stray pieces of paper.

"Not even close." Alanna snorted. "But we'll have something, at least. I feel like it's about time to start really spreading the power from these around. One per person, but we don't quite have enough."

"We can skip the new guys." James shrugged, struggling to rise back to his feet in the shifting sand. "Not that I have anything against them, just that we should prioritize the people we trust first. Also so far these are the ones with the most limited numbers, so, keeping them rationed only seems reasonable."

"Maybe we can cultivate a decision tree?" Alanna suggested. "It feels kinda shitty to keep the most powerful stuff to ourselves. Like, not just shitty, but directly against the ideology we're trying to create."

James dusted chunks of paper off his legs, flicking away half a pen cap that had stuck to the hip of his armor. "You're not wrong. That said, maybe we just offer people options, instead. Like, not all power is equal, right? So if we're interested in building everyone up into a force of functionally immortal experts, is there really much difference if an individual has a double jump or three extra master's degrees in political science?" He rolled his tongue across his teeth before sputtering a bit and pulling a ribbon of shredded paper from his mouth. "Ugh. Okay, this is less relaxing," James admitted. "Anyway, yeah. This actually makes me think that doing the loot distribution by just 'everyone make sure that we're all growing and happy' is kind of the best idea. 'Course, that requires ultimate faith in everyone to not be jerks."

"I'm not gonna be a jerk," Alanna said. "I refuse."

"Well, yeah, obviously *you* don't want to. I'm more worried about, honestly, JP. Theo. Maybe some of the new guys—haven't had much to do with them yet. Except Nate. I dunno how into this totally-not-communism he'd be, but he seems cool."

"What about Dave?"

"I fully expect Dave to give up almost everything. Do you have any idea how few orbs he's actually used? It's not a lot, and honestly, I'm kind of annoyed at him. Of all of us, I think he deserves a few more personal perks."

They walked while they talked, after Alanna scooped up the purples exchanged for her amassed wealth, picking their way over the rocky crags that marked the line between the rows and halls of cubicles. James still carried the briefcase they'd found a few hours ago, and they turned their minds to trying to figure out how to crack open this particular nut.

"Do we just leave the pencils, like, on the beach?" James wondered aloud.

Alanna shook her head. "I mean, we can try. I feel like there's some trick to this, though. It feels almost too easy, compared to all the other ones."

"We really need to start having people keep address records for cubicles, just so we can make some mild progress on the two other cases we have back at the tower," he griped in response.

"Whine later," Alanna told him with a tap on the shoulder. "Though, good idea. Anyway, why don't we just . . . stick them where the ink waves stop? Is that what a shoreline is?"

"Technically, yeah," James answered. "But do we have to hand them off to someone?"

"Eh. Let's try it. Maybe we get lucky and it really is that easy."

Both of them were legitimately shocked to discover that jamming the bundle of pencils they'd brought along into the sand was actually all they had to do. It really *was* that easy.

The briefcase let out an almost gunshot-level click as it unlocked, and a hermetic hiss followed afterward. Both of them traded raised eyebrows; so far, not a single briefcase had ever had something so *easy* as its goal. Though, that said, if they'd not stumbled across this place already, they could have gone months without ever realizing that it was the work of a couple hours to bike out here and back.

"Well, shit," James said, voice cracking a little bit as they popped the briefcase open.

Ever since the dungeon had opened up James's world to the prospect of not worrying about making rent every month, he'd been just a little less interested in money in general. Once his life had become secure, it just wasn't that important. The budget was a number now that defined how well they could take care of the people they'd rescued and how well they could equip themselves and assured him that he could order Chinese food as often as he wanted. And that was kind of it. He could have made a killing if he'd actually organized everyone into stripping and selling off parts of computers or whatever, but that had taken a back seat to exploration and orb acquisition. Because, really, what were a few hundred bucks compared to a single skill rank? Nothing.

However, it still blew his mind to see a hundred and eighty thousand dollars packed into a briefcase in neatly divided piles.

"All right, well, guess that's our bullshit funded for another few months," Alanna confirmed. She snapped the case shut again, feeling slightly nervous about that even though they'd already confirmed that once they'd been opened once, they were unlocked forever. "So! Ready to head back now? This place smells like a chemical spill. Wave goodbye to the tumblesquid."

James was going to make some kind of snarky comment about the beauty of the sea air, but as he raised his arms and took a deep breath, a particularly strong whiff of ink caught him and he gagged a little. "Ugh. Yeah, okay. Maybe we can find another beach in the other direction that has an ocean of . . ."

"Of?"

"I was hoping I'd think of something before I got to the end of the sentence. There really aren't any good liquids in an office."

"Coffee."

"Coffee!"

They high-fived and went to retrieve their bikes, a little richer for their trouble.

"I'm not trying to be the whiny guy, but can we stop for a bit?" Lance asked Dave after their group had tackled another potted plant. Both he and Neil were panting in exertion, sweat staining their shirts, though the younger man had opted to try to tough it out and Dave, being Dave, had noticed exactly nothing.

"What? Oh, of course," Dave said, like it was obvious. "Let's clear these two cubes and sit for a bit." Dave was actually kind of frustrated with how many breaks they'd taken, but then, he was far more frustrated with just how empty the entire place seemed today. They'd gone well past the boundary that James had suggested for them, into territory that was more or less uncharted, and there still wasn't a lot of wildlife. Or any magic items that they'd found so far. A pair of glasses that let you see about a minute into the past were cool but not exactly a tactical weapon, and that was basically it.

Their group had been going basically nonstop, compared to the other groups that were rotating back in for hour-long breaks. Dave felt like they made up for it by stopping every twenty minutes or so, and it did feel like they weren't making any particular progress at all. But they really had gone a long way, and it was about time for them to turn around anyway.

"We'll rest here for a bit and then head back. Anyone have any questions now that you've experienced some of this place?" Dave addressed the other four guys.

"Yeah, I've got one," Nate kind of snapped out. "Where'd you get the arm guards?" he asked Lance. "Because I'm sick of this shit." He tapped at the half dozen bandages on his arms where striders had sunk their fangs into the meat of his limbs.

"Oh, I made these," Lance said, sheepish.

"No shit?" Nate gave a full-body nod of appreciation. "I'll owe you one if you can make me a pair." The offer was so direct and . . . not friendly, exactly. Nate wasn't friendly in the same way Sarah was. He was blunt, but essentially one hundred percent earnest. And Lance, a guy who clearly hadn't had a lot of social skill training, didn't really know how to handle it.

He settled on "I guess?" On the whole, he was more used to having his hobby made fun of rather than praised. Had he said this out loud, everyone would have pointed out that he was clearly just hanging around the wrong people. Though, the right people being people who needed body armor was kind of a weird category to fall into.

"If you're going to make more, do it at the secret lair," Dave told him. "You can make it faster."

"Yeah, Anesh was saying something about that a couple weeks ago, but I never got a chance to ask about it," Neil said, gasping as he drained half a water bottle in one go. "Is the lair magic?"

"Of course it is," Dave said. "Did you not notice that we have two basements?"

"Um, actually, lots of places have two basements?" Virgil scratched at his nose. "That's not magic, even if you did build them with it."

Nate looked like he wanted to slap the kid on the back of the head. "The basements are the same distance down, you fuckwit," he said instead, which was more like a verbal slap. "Am I the only one who noticed that?"

"Apparently," Dave told him. Dave liked Nate; he could trust the chef to tell him straight up if anything went wrong. It was refreshing—not even James did that properly.

They sat for another five minutes or so, Dave declining the rest to go through the desk drawers and add a bag of M&M look-alikes to his bag. Eventually, the less athletic members felt like they were ready to start the trek back, even if Neil did gripe about it.

And for all that they hadn't been ambushed constantly, or had to deal with any larger green monsters, they *had* seen some cool stuff today. A nest of striders that had been cautious, but not hostile at all and had let Lance get close enough to snap some pictures on his phone. A pen that wrote in French. A cubicle with stuffed dragons hidden in random places—not magical ones; it was just kind of cute and cool. An intersection where the potted plants had just kept growing and four of them had twined together overhead to form a kind of canopy— they'd avoided that one entirely, but it sure had looked neat.

For all that, though, it felt kind of underwhelming to Dave, and everyone else sensed it. Even though to *them* this was all insane and bizarre and new and wild as hell.

Now, though, as they stepped out into the open-ceilinged hallway and prepared to backtrack, with no intention of getting into more fights, Dave got that feeling. That electric sensation that something was *happening* and that he was about to be dropped back into the weirder part of this world.

"Uh, what the shit is that?" Neil asked the question everyone was already thinking.

That was a cubicle tower. But it was behind them, or at least, in the direction they'd come from. There was no way they could have missed it; the thing was twenty stories tall if it was real. But somehow they'd walked right past it, because they were only just now seeing it as they turned to retrace their steps.

"That . . . is different," Dave admitted, a toothy smile on his face despite the circumstance. A subtle transformation rippled through Dave, shoulders raised a fraction, back straightened, voice a little more projected. And in an eyeblink, he was someone else. "Neil. Drone. Get me eyes on it. Everyone else, weapons ready. Nate, take rearguard, please. Virgil, get the coffee and flare gun out of the cart." No one questioned him, though Nate did cock an eyebrow at the sudden shift from tour guide to command presence.

As Neil scrambled the drone, Dave watched it buzz off into the sky, arms crossed and posture eager. He didn't know *what* he was excited for, but he knew it was something.

When the drone froze in midair, the buzzing abruptly halted, Dave hummed to himself. When he realized that *Neil was also locked in place*, things got serious. He didn't hesitate, reaching down slightly to where the annoyingly tall kid was seated on the ground and popping the radio transmitter cable out of the back of his skull.

"aaaAAAAHHHhhhhh . . . oh." Neil's scream built rapidly then tapered off. In the distance, the drone tumbled to the ground with a plastic crash. "Oh no!" he yelled, more concerned with the machine than his own safety.

Dave interrupted him as he tried to stumble to his feet. "Snakes?" he asked.

"Uh, yeah. How'd you know?" Neil asked.

"Okay. I'm gonna explain camracondas to you guys. But first—" Dave unclipped the radio from his belt and turned it to the wide channel. "This is Team Three to everyone available. We could use nonemergency assistance. Anyone in range? Over." He repeated himself once or twice before a response came in.

"—lp us to th—*shhhh*—oon upon—*shhhh*—you—Dave" came the crackling static.

"James?" Dave inquired. "You have to say 'over' after you talk. Also, I didn't hear any of that properly. Over."

"I said that Alanna and I are just heading back. Where are you guys?" James said. And then a slightly sarcastic "Over."

"Sending up a flare now. See you soon. Over." Dave nodded at Virgil, who dramatically pointed the flare gun into the air and then ruined his moment by wincing, holding his eyes closed, and facing away from the device like it was going to explode.

Once the red ball of light was in the air overhead, the radio clicked back to life. "Got ya. We're pretty close, actually. Be there in five. Over." Alanna's voice came through to Dave, and he nodded. Now the only thing to do was wait.

And also explain the camracondas to everyone. No, they didn't paralyze you. Unless they bit you; their venom *was* paralytic. Instead, they *froze* you. No movement, no body function. You could still think and see and stuff, but you couldn't move your eyes or breathe. Though you didn't seem to need to breathe. It was mostly unexplained, and they'd never been able to test it, because the camracondas absolutely wanted to eat you.

James and Alanna showed up right on time, biking in and skidding to a halt a dozen feet away from their group. James pulled off the sunglasses he was wearing with a relieved hiss and addressed Dave. "All right, what's up?"

Dave pointed.

"Uh . . . what the shit is that?" Alanna said, jolting in her seat as she looked up at the tower.

"That's what I said," Nate told her, nodding.

"What . . . so, we can only see it from one direction? Or is it only accessible from this direction?" James asked, tapping a finger on his chin. "Could be something esoteric we just don't get. Either way, that's cool. Did you guys want help exploring it?"

"Kind of," Dave said. "It's full of camracondas."

"Full of, as in . . ." James trailed off as Dave passed him a pair of binoculars. "You didn't find these in here, right?" he asked, already raising them to his eyes.

Full of as in there were dozens of them. A camera face on top of a coiled cable body poked out of every window James could see. At least on the first several floors. There was even one just sitting in the door, coiled up and . . .

"Are they watching us?" James asked, concerned.

"It sure looks that way," Dave told him. The two of them were standing at the front while Alanna double-checked Nate's bandaging and gave an impromptu lesson in first aid to the other three. Dave smirked as she got a lot more insistent than he had been that, yes, they absolutely *would* need this. "What do you think?" he asked.

James looked over. Dave had been deferring to him a lot more lately, in a way that felt . . . not awkward, but like there was more weight to it than there should have been. But now wasn't really the time to tell his friend that he wasn't actually looking for a squire. Instead, James just clicked his tongue and lowered the binoculars. "I think we shouldn't be able to move," he said. "We've had one of these things lock someone down from a few hundred feet away before. So I think that if they can all see us, and they're *watching us*, there's a reason we're still moving."

"Oh. Shit," Dave muttered, face flushing red. "I didn't mean to . . . I brought you guys into a trap," he stuttered.

"No, I don't think it's a trap," James said, pursing his lips and handing the binoculars back. "I think . . . I mean, we could just leave, right? We don't actually need to go past the tower." He raised his eyebrows at Dave, making it a question, and Dave gave a sideways nod in acknowledgment. They could just loop around it, though it would be through unexplored territory. Still, it wasn't a dangerous region, so it could be done. "Then I think this is something else," James said, slipping off his backpack.

"Are you doing something stupid again?" Alanna asked, coming up with the rest of the group to interrupt his conversation with Dave. "James. We talked about this."

James believed her, but he didn't remember it. He didn't say that, though. Instead, he went with "I'm sure we talked about me not sacrificing myself. But that's not this. Here, hold my axe and gun," he said, handing off his belt with the holster and hatchet hooked on it.

"Why?!"

"I don't want to seem threatening," he said and started walking toward the tower. Behind him, he heard Alanna swear under her breath, but she didn't try to stop him. Both of them, today especially, were learning to trust when they had gut instincts.

The walk was actually a little longer than he'd thought, and James had ample time to ponder the fact that he might actually be making a huge and fatal mistake. But nothing froze him up as he approached, and when he reached the foot of the tower, he found himself looking up a short set of steps that ended at a small doorway, where a single camraconda looked down at him. But he could still move.

That moment stretched out for enough time that it started to let James's nerves cool down a bit. "Um. Hi," he said, feeling like an idiot. "I come in peace?"

It just stared at him, head inching forward like James was under a microscope. It didn't budge, though. Just watched. And it didn't, James noticed, move even a single centimeter over the line of the doorway.

James didn't comment on that. Instead, he relaxed a bit and leaned on the base of the steps. "So, you saw my friends and me," he said, just kind of building up to a rambling monologue. "And we saw you, which is why I'm here. Honestly, I'm not sure what I'm doing, you know?" he admitted to the snake. "I'm sort of just hoping that I'm not a complete idiot and that there's something going on here. Something weird, you know? Or maybe you don't know. *Weird* is kind of a highly subjective term. Anyway. I guess I'm asking . . . what's up? How's it going? You guys seem cool—want to be friends?"

The camraconda froze in place, like it had been locked down by one of its own. But it wasn't immobile, just not moving. James could see it swaying minutely as it examined him with its singular camera eye.

Then it nodded, bobbing its whole body in a strangely human way, and turned to slither into the tower.

"Um . . . wait, am I supposed to follow you?" James called after it, confused. He looked back at the group of humans, Alanna in particular, then gave a shrug. "If I'm not back in ten minutes, you come rescue my ass!" he yelled to them. And then, turning, he clomped his boots up the steps and into the darkness.

The inside was actually not that dark, though it was quite dim. And the first thing James noticed was that it wasn't . . . standard. It wasn't an office. All the interior walls here had been rearranged into open rows that left the line of sight perfectly open. All the desks and chairs and everything were just . . . not here. Instead, there were snakes. A whole host of camracondas peered at him from around the walls as he followed his guide, and he could almost feel the emotions radiating off them. Curiosity, wariness, fear—anger, maybe? A strange blend of feelings in the air.

James followed the one he was walking after, trying not to panic about being this deep in the lions' den. They ascended the ramp to the next level, and he was surprised to see this floor, too, had been cleared out, rearranged.

"I should warn you, I actually really hate climbing these things," he told the camraconda leading him. It looked back on him briefly, with contemptuous pity in its camera eye, and James sighed a lung-stretching breath. "Yeah, yeah, I'm coming."

A few floors up, James started to see the remnants of the missing furniture. They came to a level where the walls had been positioned to create rooms, for lack of a better term. Not cubicles, exactly.

More like portioned spaces designed for the serpents below. And in them . . . nests, maybe?

Torn-up padding from the chairs, shredded-paper nests. But also, other things. Wooden panels from desks that had been attached to walls and carved into strange patterns. Pieces of splintered wood with holes drilled in them hung up with string or paper clips, wind chimes in a windless building. A pair of camracondas manipulating metal chair legs into a grid shape on the ground—playing a game, perhaps.

Art.

They'd made art, James realized with a sharp breath.

He didn't complain for the rest of the climb up.

Twenty-one floors above the ground, the guide stopped. They hadn't seen another snake for a couple floors now, and it looked like these upper floors were mostly used to store stuff. But here, at the base of the last ramp, they had to pass through two serpent bodies that flanked the ascent like an honor guard. They nodded to the guide but kept their eyes on James the whole time he was in sight.

At the top of the ramp, James lost any inkling of the words he was trying to form in his head. Here, in front of him, were three things that all defied understanding.

First, there was a corpse. In the center of the room was a conference table, as they'd come to expect from the towers. But on it, in repose, was a human body. Arms folded across her chest, eyes closed, her suit jacket torn and bloodied, but with a final defiant snarl on her face. She could have died yesterday. She could have died a hundred years ago. James would never know, because a camraconda sat in vigil over the body. This one had strings of makeshift cord jewelry and lines of highlighter and Sharpie drawn across its body, and it didn't move as James entered behind the other camraconda. It just watched the corpse, unmoving.

Second, there was a green orb. It hovered in the air, suspended by an unseen force a half inch above the claws of red liquid that flowed around it in sharp patterns. As soon as James saw it, knowledge of its function made itself known to him; this structure was protected. None who bore it ill will could observe it directly. Though there was a hint of something else there unsaid. A direction, a restriction, maybe? Something in James wanted to ask about how often that could work, and why it had shut Dave's group out until they'd passed it.

Third, there was a creation. The walls were covered, all but the windows letting in light, with the largest pieces of salvaged wood. And upon these, someone, presumably the denizens of this place, had carved a story. His guide saw him looking and pointed with its snout to the first panel to James's left, the beginning of the story.

James reached out a hand to touch the first one as he stared at it and found for the first time that he could not move. To his side, his guide gently released him from the paralyzing gaze, and he dropped his arm back down politely, content to merely look. It showed, in rough lines and difficult imagery, a single human running from a pack of snakes.

The next one in sequence around the room showed a tower, one human entering from the bottom. And then the snakes, climbing the tower, swarming it, following. The next was combat, a snake and a human facing each other down with deep lines of anger painted on the wood, and he saw they'd shown her with bared fangs in place of any weapon. After that, a human standing over a corpse, holding a ball. The green orb? Probably. And then the tower again from the outside. But cracked in half. Was the crack in the wood on purpose? It must have been; everything here was too careful otherwise. Something had *broken* here, and that woman had been at its center.

The last three panels were carved with less-amateurish lines, more shadowing, more colors. These had been made afterward. The first of them showed the entire brood of serpents surrounding the orb, and the body under it, from overhead like a mandala of cords. The next was three parts; some tried to leave, dragging the others with them, and they were struck down. The last was of three snakes baring their necks, being fed upon by the lined-up host of the others. James couldn't tell if it was punishment, or . . .

"Sacrifice?" he asked, looking at the others in the room. His guide nodded to him. "Oh." James realized something: they lived here. They never left the tower. The tower couldn't be observed; it was safe. Here, and only here, the kind of monsters that were made with the green orbs could truly be free. "You've been here a long time, haven't you?" he asked softly and got another nod in reply. "And you're starving. Or you were. But you can't last forever." A sad nod.

He didn't hesitate for a second to pull out the handful of yellow orbs he kept in his pocket. "I know they're not greens, but I know that Secret can eat these, too. Will they help you keep going?" James asked. "We have more, outside. I can go get some. How many of you are left?"

The camraconda looked away from him, turning its body to stare out the window. James heard a hissing noise and almost jumped, but then he realized that it was coming from something sizzling on the lip of the window, a small whiff of smoke coming off the windowsill. When the snake turned back, he saw a glimmer of oil on its camera eye—it was *crying*.

"Not as many as there should be, huh?" It wasn't really a question. "Okay," James said. "I don't know why you showed my friends your home, or why you let me in." He held out a reassuring hand as the guide tensed in anticipation. "But. Your people need help. And we can give that." He thought for a second. "I have no idea how to get started with that," he admitted and saw both the camracondas in the room droop in disappointment. "Don't worry, don't worry." James spoke like he would to a scared dog, voice low and reassuring. "I've got people a lot smarter than me on my team." He sighed and walked over to the one at the window, tentatively reaching out to lay a hand on its head. "We can figure this out. Okay?"

Okay, it seemed to say, staring up at him with one eye, dripping acid tears.

"All right. I'm gonna go now. We've got a long way to go tonight. But I swear to you, we *will* be back," James promised. "Also, I'll get you all the yellows we have on us. We'll be gone a week or two, depending. Is that . . . Hmm. I don't know how you guys do time. Do you have any clocks here?"

The camraconda shook its head, tightly wound blue and white cables shifting like it was either scared or insulted or both at once, and James just decided to let that one lie.

The trip back down the tower was in a different light than the one up. Now, instead of a potential ambush, he saw refugees. These weren't monsters. Not anymore. With the dungeon unable to find them, they'd been freed. But unlike when it had been suppressed into sleep by the monstrous boardroom thing, there was nothing else around to pull their strings. The creature's makeshift hive mind hadn't found them, hidden as they were. Neither had anything else like her. So they'd stayed here, rearranged the furniture, freed in mind but trapped in the building.

Scared children.

"We need to talk to Anesh," James told the group when he came out, the camracondas around the entrance letting them drop back to unfrozen positions from where they'd been preparing to storm the building in search of him. He didn't bother to acknowledge that. "Also, Dave, if you have any extra yellows, please share them. They're hungry."

"Hungry for . . . the blood of the living?" Lance asked, clutching his fire axe suspiciously in sweaty hands.

"No. Just starving," James said sadly. "Sorry, guys, this one's just sad. Let's get back to the door. I'll fill you in on the way. And no breaks this time; we're low on time, and we gotta get moving." He turned back to the steps of the tower and paused. With all the sincerity he could muster, he placed a hand over his heart. "I promise," he said. "We'll be back."

He meant it.

They made it back to the door, which they still needed a good name for as a base camp, with minimal problems. Nothing worth really mentioning, except for James almost accidentally falling on an orb and picking up arguably the most useful skill of the night.

[+1 Skill Rank : Fabrication—Sewing]

People were around the tower now, not just Theo screwing around and being useless. Teams had started trickling back in or had ended their adventures an hour or two ago, and there was a bustle of activity going on. Delvers stripped off equipment to check back into the armory, a couple people sat still while Sarah checked over their bandages and looked for unnoticed wounds, some people had plates of hot food, and everywhere, people bragged about narrow escapes, showed off discovered trinkets, and traded orbs like gold.

"I could *feel* the magic," Simon was telling Secret in a quiet voice as James walked by, his party scattering behind him to accomplish their own tasks before they all headed out. "She altered reality. She changed time, Secret."

James would have to look into that one later. Right now, though, while Nate went to pack up the serving trays he'd brought in and Alanna went to trade away the purple orbs to everyone who wanted one, James looked up at the tower.

He shook his head. No fucking way was he climbing *another* of these things tonight.

"*Anesh!*" he hollered, making the people around him jump in shock.

A second later, his boyfriend poked his head out of the window. "What?!" he yelled back down the tower.

"Come down here! I've got something to tell you about, and it's almost time to go!" James called back.

"He has a radio, you know," Daniel pointed out as he walked out of the tower, carrying two of the storage containers full of human hearts to the cart they were going to wheel out with them.

James rolled his eyes and pretended he knew that the whole time.

"I'm making breakthroughs in theory, James!" Anesh yelled back. "The reds and yellows are of the mind, the oranges and greens of the *place*, and the blues and purples are the body! It all makes sense!"

"Shouldn't the reds make infomorphs, then?" James yelled up, noting a few people around him chuckling.

There was silence for a second, and he could have sworn he heard muffled British swearing from ten stories up. And then "I'll be down in a minute," Anesh shouted.

He stood there, watching with no small amount of pride as everyone started to focus on making sure everything useful was piled in the tower, everything that was trash was stored safely in the trash cans around the cubicles, which would be purified over the course of the week, and the delvers started to collect in groups while they waited for something.

It took him a little while to realize they were waiting for him.

When Anesh came down, and after he'd dropped off the last of the hearts, James pulled him aside. "We have a problem I need you to put your mind to," he said and filled him in on the refugee camracondas. "Also, we're rich now. So, dinner's on me. You feel like pancakes?"

"I would love pancakes," Anesh admitted. "Though I'm not going to actually get pancakes. Your country thinks that dessert is real food."

"I wasn't gonna get pancakes, either," James confided in him with as much of a smile as he could muster. He was *tired* after all this. Especially the trapped camracondas. That had hurt more than he'd been prepared for. "Anyway. I'm gonna go address everyone. I think they're waiting for me to tell them to go home."

"Have fun," Anesh said, giving him a soft kiss on the neck and then blushing furiously about it.

James gave him a smile; it was cute, seeing him get used to this. And even cuter when he still got so sheepish. He tried to keep that feeling swirling inside him as he got up to move toward the door, to the front of the crowd. He saw the wrap-up of the night happening around him, piles and piles of the guild's orbs being loaded into duffel bags to be counted, sorted, and distributed back at the lair over the next week. Some magic items were carefully secured in cardboard boxes or metal cases. That last double-check for anything too illegal that they couldn't take out.

"Hey, everyone," he said, and there was a hush. James looked out over the crowd. Some new faces, some old. Some his friends, some people he'd saved, some people who'd saved him. All of them here, standing with him. Even Theo, though he made a mental note to probably omit her.

"It's been a long night," he said. "And from what I hear, you've all had some adventures." Cheers back at him.

"Found a window!" Alex shouted from the back.

"We rode maul carts!" A black-eyed Daniel laughed, orange fire flickering off his hair.

"Strider swarm," Simon muttered and got a few pats on the back from those near him.

"And we're all alive," James said. "One more time, we all made it out. And we've got a mountain of treasure, too." He looked at them and grinned. "I wanted to let you all know that this is the first night where we've really started to do something with this place. I told you all when we started that we were going to change the world. To do something important, to make it better. Well, here's a toehold. Upstairs, at the top of that tower, is an overhead projector that can copy stuff. And today, while we were out exploring, Anesh used it to make thirty copies of a magically preserved and functioning human heart." He looked at them, back straight, arms clasped behind him. "We never would have had the time, or the resources, to do that without everyone supporting us. Without all of you."

James smiled at them, and they gave him ferocious grins back. "We're not done. This is the start; this is where we break into reality and show them what we can do. We're going to do so much more. Out there, and in here, too, because there's *people* in here that need our help, too, even if they don't look human. And we have to be ready. Ready to live up to who we can be, ready for anyone who tries to stop us. Ready to fix the world and fight the monsters." James rolled a large yellow orb in his hand, pulled out of a coat pocket he'd forgotten about. "We can do so much. And every ounce of power, for any of us, just keeps pushing us forward." He clapped his hands once, turning the orb into a skill. "Good job today. Let's get out of here before I talk us into getting trapped for a week."

[+3 Skill Ranks : Architecture—Structural—Arcology]

They laughed. But more than that. They believed.

That night, James got actual pancakes. A dozen people, a dog made of a magnetic field, and one infomorph, some new friends and some old, ate like champions in the whole wing of the restaurant the staff set aside for them. The staff didn't ask questions, but whenever anyone saw a puzzled look, they gave answers anyway. They tipped them enough to go home and not worry about anything for a long time.

Two hours of real time later, Alanna almost got in a fistfight with three hospital guards, one police officer, and an ER nurse. Inexpertly navigating that encounter, which she *demanded* give her points in her communication lesson, she slammed several crates of hearts on the counter and yelled instructions at them, capped it off by saying, "It's fucking magic, don't question me," and left.

And then, finally, when they got Anesh to stop fiddling with the new coffee machine, the three of them crashed into bed together and slept the sleep of the just.

CHAPTER 7

It was a cold night. Not deadly cold, not the kind that bit you down to the bone—at least, not if you were only going on a walk to the coffee shop and had doubled up on coats. Just regular cold. Anesh had doubled up on coats. Anesh had planned ahead far more than James and Alanna had.

Not like Alanna needed to, though. One lucky purple and suddenly you could tolerate five-degree nights in a T-shirt. Five centigrade, at least.

James, though, was busy trying to walk at double speed to get them where they were going before his ears froze off, all while his partners were busy with a meandering pace and enjoying the clear night.

No clouds or rain for the first time in a couple months. And with this walking trail being so far from roads and homes, they could actually see the stars and crescent moon in the late-December sky.

It was just nice. Fresh air, even if it did come in the form of snappy gusts of wind. Good company, even if some of it was complaining and hurrying them along. And a feeling of catharsis, of a job well-done, and some time now to relax. Even if that was an illusion.

"So, I told Alex about the camraconda den while we were out at the diner." Alanna was talking casually to Anesh while their boyfriend tried to goad them into a faster pace a half dozen steps ahead of them. "And she suggested that an alternate name for them would be 'ssssen-tries.'" She hissed out the name with a laughing grin on her face.

Anesh groaned. "Oh, that's so bad!" he exclaimed. "I feel like James's love of wordplay has infected everyone at this point." There was a pause as they walked, and then Anesh grinned a little himself. "Well, the whole story is pretty amazing. Especially him getting to see all the camracondas' *hisssstory*."

"You bastard!" Alanna bellowed a laugh back at him, happiness cracking across the night's chill.

"It could be worse!" James called back to them. "That store on the corner back there sells footwear and is called If the Shoe Fits. This entire city loves puns. Need I remind you that Dave *continues* to work at a kennel called Noah's Arf? Or that there's one of those drive-through coffee places called Stand Your Grounds?"

"You don't need to remind us." Anesh chuckled as they cut across the parking lot to get to their goal.

Tonight they were hanging out. Just the three of them. Well, four, if you counted the other Anesh, but they really didn't. Not because he wasn't important, but because he was just . . . Anesh. There was James, Alanna, and Anesh, and one of those three people happened to have a little more mass than the others. If you'd asked James, he probably would have made a joke about it being Alanna while miming measuring her biceps, but he *didn't* do that, because everyone pointedly avoided asking him that particular question.

For now, though, there were no dumb questions. Just three friends and lovers, having a night out together. Because weekends were critical, James had realized.

For the last two months, it had been creeping up on him. Everyone wanted a chunk of his time in some way, and before he'd noticed, there was nothing left for him. Dungeon planning, equipment maintenance, long conversations with everyone from Secret to El to Momo, actual work from the mundane day job he still inexplicably went to, fielding questions about orbs, magic items, coffee, ethics, and payroll and also keeping a now especially sharp and tense eye out for any actual legal trouble given that Alanna had gotten in a fight with half a hospital's staff. There was no James time in there, not where he really got to choose what he was doing. He was just bouncing between obligations. So today he had put his foot down and declared it a weekend.

He'd then promptly invited his partners to go get coffee. Because it was *his* time, but that didn't mean it had to be his alone.

"You guys wanna sit outside?" James asked idly.

"It's five degrees out here, and the chairs are wrought iron. *Alanna's* arse has frost resistance; mine doesn't," Anesh told him, stating the obvious.

James thought about it for a second. "Inside, then!" he said as they walked up to the counter. "You know, that said, though, it does feel kind of weird to have a conversation inside, with a bunch of people around, about weird stuff."

"Weird stuff," Alanna echoed, disbelief on her face.

"Yeah, weird stuff. You know. The stuff that we talk about that's weird," James explained as they stepped up to give their order.

"You guys talk about late-stage capitalism and anal sex all the time here," the barista chimed in from behind the counter.

James cleared his throat and had the good grace to look embarrassed. "That's different!" he protested. "Also, hey. The usual mocha, please. How ya doing tonight?"

"Not bad." The barista was a tall guy. His round face and Polynesian features made him look like the kind of dude who could be super intimidating if he wasn't constantly beaming at everyone. "But seriously, man. It's the Pacific Northwest. No one's gonna give you shit for your weird conversations. Well, I mean, there's that one old bat who's here every Tuesday at, like, 2:00 a.m., but you always miss her."

"I have work then," James said unironically, their conversation intertwining with everyone giving their drink orders.

"Same," the barista said with a knowing nod. "Anyway, don't stress. Drink coffee late at night instead. Though maybe don't bring your magical stapler friend in when it's crowded like this. Your doubled-up clone friend is kinda suspicious enough, not that being a clone is a crime."

Anesh winced in the silence that followed. There were a couple other people behind them in line, and a surreptitious check showed that both of them were studiously paying attention to their phones and nothing else. Another sideways glance from his other half showed that Alanna had gone perfectly still, frozen in place like she hadn't yet decided what to *feel* about this. Ah, right. They'd forgotten to tell her about James's little walk with Rufus.

"James," she said in an iron voice. "What."

"Okay, in my defense, you got in a fight with the staff of—"

"All right, all right!" Alanna stopped him. "That's different! You can't just . . . oh, fuck it, whatever. We're so screwed, aren't we? Like, we're skipping the gradual acclimation period and just shredding the veil of the masquerade, huh?"

James wrapped his arms around her side and gave her a warm hug. "You're sexy when you make nerdy references like that." He turned back to the barista, who was trying to settle on a look of either amusement, sappy glee, or confusion as he made their drinks. "Hey, as long as we're abandoning subtle, I'll trade you a skill point for a piece of cake."

"I dunno what that means, but I'm into it."

When the hiss of the espresso machine faded and their drinks came up, there was a slice of strawberry cream cake on a plate to go with them. And with only a little trepidation, James pulled a tiny yellow orb from his pocket and tossed it to the black-haired youth responsible. "Have fun," he said. "Welcome to the weird." James grinned as he collected their stuff and went to join Anesh and Alanna at their table.

"We're so fucked," Alanna was repeating. "There's no way we're ready for this." Her head was down on the table, between arms propped up on elbows. "I've been so busy I didn't even *think* of how we're supposed to explain any of it. We're gonna need a *press release*, and contingency plans, and almost certainly some kind of security detail for the secret lair, and . . ."

James plopped into a chair next to her after setting the drinks down. "Hey, wow, chill," he said softly. "Have some cake. It'll be okay."

"How?! How could it possibly be okay?" Alanna demanded. "We knew things like the skulljacks would be a big deal, but I was so tired after the delve I didn't even consider what it would mean to just hand over a stack of *human hearts!*" she half shouted, grabbing at James's shoulders. "Do you have any idea what that might mean?"

He flicked his eyes over to Anesh, who gave him a shrug. "No?" he ventured.

"What."

"I've no clue, either," Anesh added, both of him sipping identical mochas in unison. "A math degree has utterly failed to prepare me for this," he said with another casual sip, both of him wincing at the heat of the drink.

James reached up to give her some pets along the back of her head and neck. "All right, deep breath. It's gonna be okay," he reassured her. "Look, for one thing, we need to know, as soon as possible, if the weird stuff is gonna get us in trouble. The sooner we find out, the less fear and stress in our lives, right? So the small stuff, like introducing wetware to the world and paying people in skill orbs? That's just the test bed. And if we move fast enough, no one will have time to stop us before we've done our good damage."

"Why did you pay for cake with an orb?" Anesh asked casually.

"I don't have any cash on me and I lost my debit card a few days ago."

Alanna snapped back to the present problem for a window of time. "Seriously? No cash on you?" She snorted a laugh that seemed to break her anxiety. "James, what happened to the two hundred grand from yesterday?"

"How in the fuck would I fit that in my wallet?" he blurted out. "Nah, that's back at the lair in the vault."

"We have a vault?" both Aneshes asked, eyebrows raised in surprise.

James tapped a finger on his chin. "Welllll, we have a basement," he admitted. "Anyway, Alanna, the solution is simple. We *cannot* live in fear. So we taunt anyone who wants to stop us. If no one shows up, then either there's no one there, or the dungeon's antimemes are too strong and we're in the shadows anyway. If anyone *does* show up . . ."

He looked around the crowded coffee shop, at all the tables full of normal people under pleasant orange light. Just a normal night, full of late-hours homework, Bible study, dates, and hangouts. And he thought that if anyone else had the knowledge, the access to power that he had now, and they chose to come after him and his people? Then those others had absolutely failed their responsibility to improve the world. He was going to build a utopia, where places like this were everywhere, and where poverty and suffering were ground away, and if they chose to fight him instead of cooperating? "... then we bury them," he finished, grim.

"In the basement, presumably," Anesh added.

The cheeky comment and irreverent tone absolutely killed James's dark mood. Alanna laughed along with him, momentarily reassured that, at least for now, there was a plan they could hew toward.

"Anyway!" James derailed them. "We were wanting to talk about something important lately, right?" He rubbed his chin with a speculative look on his face. "Hmm. Can't remember. Something about video games, probably. Alanna, have you played anything fun lately that I wanted to talk about?"

"Orbs," she said flatly, making eye contact like a wolf staring at a hare.

"Haven't heard of that one. Anesh?" James said, suppressing the smile as he pivoted to look at the duplicates across the table.

Anesh shrugged. "I've been getting into multidimensional sudoku. Virgil made me a program to generate 'em."

"... really?" James and Alanna asked together.

"Wait," James followed up. "How many dimensions is multi?"

"Four," Anesh replied.

Neither of them could tell if he was serious as they eyed him through narrow slits. It was entirely within the realm of possibility that Anesh was not bullshitting them. He had, after all, been accelerating his knowledge beyond what most people should learn at a four-year university, partly through orbs, yes, but partly through the synergistic study tactic of being two people. According to him, he could learn things at well beyond a one hundred percent increased rate, simply because there wasn't time between lessons for knowledge to fade, and because his nightly bout of "being a gestalt mind" did wonders for preventing burnout. And with that ability, he'd begun rapidly powering through ever more confusing textbooks and dissertations, adding real-world knowledge to the unfolding lotus that was the skill orb's background boost to his mind. So him playing four-dimensional sudoku was *absolutely* possible.

It was *also* entirely feasible that he was screwing with them. Not just a possibility, but a likelihood. Anesh could banter with them like a champion when he wanted to, but his real talent was in the true art of *being sassy to his partners*.

"I believe you," James said with all the honest gravity he could muster. "But no, I guess it was something else I was thinking of. What's going on lately?"

"Dungeon shit, mostly," Alanna replied, her forehead still thumped down on the table as her brain tried to destress. "We've got three to manage now, in addition to figuring out how to build a portal to Tennessee to access the one Eleanor told us about." She groaned into the stained wood. "Ugggh. I can't believe I'm saying this, but we need to delegate at least one of them to someone else."

"Probably the house. It seems least problematic," Anesh pointed out.

"No, that wasn't what I was thinking of, either," James said, shaking his head. "Oh! Christmas is coming up!"

"We aren't having Christmas in the dungeon." Anesh vetoed him before the option was put forth.

"No, I . . . hmm." James paused and pretended he was actually thinking about it. "That could be cool now that you mention it! We could get some striders to decorate a tree, wrap up gifts in spheres instead of boxes . . ." He laughed and held up his hands as the other two at the table turned scornful gazes on him. "But seriously, I was just wondering what you guys were doing."

"Going home for a couple weeks," Anesh said, shrugging. "Should be interesting, and far more convenient now than previously. I'm actually considering spinning up a new copy of myself just for that. Though the logistics become challenging."

"Someday we'll get you a whole apartment building where you can build your perfect little Anesh hive," James promised him. He turned to Alanna. "How about you?"

"Not going home for any weeks," she said, voice a little sharp. "I'll drop in to make sure my sisters are doing okay and sneak them some cash. But then, eh. Probably just gonna lounge around and whine about holidays being overcommercialized." Alanna raised her eyes up just for a second while she talked. "Maybe I'll just use the time to go check out the haunted attic, actually. Still wanna know what our connection *is*."

Well, that was suspiciously melancholic.

James didn't rise to the bait, though. He just nodded and patted her on the shoulder. "I get that," he said. "At least this place isn't playing Christmas carols. Yet. I more meant, like, do you guys wanna do a dinner and gifts and stuff?"

"Not really?" Alanna told him, apology in her words already. "I'm sorry, I just don't think I'm up for it this year."

"The only time I've actually done anything for Christmas was the last couple of years here, and those involved Sarah, so I don't remember them," Anesh pointed out.

They both looked away, sheepish, as they felt like they were ruining James's holiday plans. A second later, he shattered that notion. "Oh, thank god." He sighed out the words. "I've been stressing about that for a month!"

"Why didn't you say something?"

"We were busy!" James exclaimed, throwing his hands up. "There's so many things trying to kill us!"

Alanna laughed softly as she sat back up. "That's not even a little true. All our problems are self-inflicted."

"And self-corrected," Anesh pointed out.

"That actually brings me to what I really wanted to talk about," James admitted. "The Christmas thing was just something I was having anxiety over."

Alanna perked up instantly. "Is it dungeon things?" she asked.

The look that James shot her way was partway between concerned, amused, and perplexed. "You know, every time I think I've got your number, you say stuff like that. What happened to the girl who was *very insistent* that we have days off from dungeon things?" James asked. "I know, granted, that those days always turned into us talking about it anyway, but you at least pressed us to try."

"Eh." Alanna waved it away, taking a gulp of her coffee. "This is more fun, let's face it. Also, we forget stuff that we really shouldn't all the time. So these chats are engaging to me."

"Fair." James conceded the point. "I wanted to talk about our strategy in general, I think."

"The goal, or the execution?" Anesh asked.

"The goal is our mission statement. Our strategy is the general actions we're taking to accomplish that," Alanna lectured. "So, mission statement is 'make a utopia.' But that's not a strategy, because it doesn't give us any guidance on ways to act. Our strategy, in this case, is, say, 'improve medical care.' How do we do that, then, is a tactic. Remove the wait time for organ transplants. Mission, strategy, tactic."

"Right. Okay. So, where does 'accumulate wealth and power' go?" Anesh asked.

"Strategy," James said. "But it's not a good long-term one, honestly. Those things enable us to act, but ideally we'll be building a world where we sort of distribute them to everyone." He thought for a second, then added, "I think it's important to note that it *is* a strategy and not a mission. Now, I love leveling up as much as everyone else, but that's not the reason we're doing it, right? We're not my dad, going to the hardware store to buy tools because he wants more tools. We're buying hammers because we've got nails to hit."

"Your metaphors get so weird sometimes," Alanna quipped.

He threw up his hands in response, rolling his eyes toward the ceiling. "Building a deck is a perfectly normal allegory for building a utopia!"

"So anyway," Anesh cut them both off. "James's old man's screwdriver problem aside—"

One of him spoke before the other wove back in, "What are our current strategies?"

"Well, health stuff, obviously," James said. "I think at this point we can probably count on a few doctors or hospital administrators taking us at face value and working with us quietly. Once the pyramid of human hearts works out. From there, we can maybe make connections and find someone to help us start on more comprehensive examination and testing of the skulljacks, too. I'm filing that one under the header of 'upgrade.' Make people better, that sorta thing. The other big one is more offensive and is essentially that we want to be looking for ways to undermine and cripple toxic industries and establishments."

"Come again?" Anesh did a double double take.

"Like the oil industry, for example," Alanna said. "The oil industry kills people. Not with snipers and tanks, exactly. Probably. But they create a situation where people die as a result of their policies, and that's an acceptable cost to them. They lobby for looser environmental protection laws, or for more restrictions on solar power, that sort of thing. So!" She clapped her open palms together a couple times, beaming at them. "We kill them!"

"*Not* literally," James clarified to Anesh, who was looking around the coffee shop to see how many people were curious about the murder conspiracy unfolding here. "But, say we find a magical form of electricity generation. We duplicate that and spread it as far as possible before anyone figures out they should be stopping us."

"So we break the law?" Anesh sort of asked, sort of just confirmed. "That seems . . . unsustainable?"

James shrugged. "Honestly, we're probably already in a *looooot* of problems, legally speaking. Trespassing at minimum. A *ton* of trespassing. God, so much trespassing. Probably something about lying to the police and fabricating evidence, from the whole thing with Frank. I dunno." He shrugged again, like he was trying to just slough off the potential trouble. "Thing is, if we get away with it enough that it becomes a normal part of life, it'll be kind of hard to stop us."

"That's *really* worrying!" Anesh protested. "I feel like you're banking on the antimemes a little too much. Because anything that's going to become normal is, by definition, going to be out from under cover."

"Good point. That's where strategy four comes in!" James said cheerily. And when the others gave him prompting stares, he explained, "Strategy four is being gods—no, not literal gods, Anesh, please." James reached over the table to try to clap a hand on the mouth of each Anesh that was trying to cut him off. "I mean being invincible. Having too many skills and guns and friends and other random-ass effects piled up for anyone to be able to challenge us. And *yes*, Alanna, that *is* how dictatorships start, which is why we need to maybe just not be assholes. I know that's actually a big ask, but a whole lot of this is based on the idea that we can be good people."

"I actually more or less trust us to be benevolent gods," Alanna admitted. "I was just wondering what our short-term schedule looks like that leads to this."

"There's so much to do," Anesh agreed. "So, what's the plan?"

"Why are you both looking at me?" James asked.

Anesh leveled a pair of fingers at his boyfriend. "Because you're our leader, and you know it. So, what's first?"

"Basketball," James said. "First, anyway. Resource use, basically. Alanna and I need to finish our lessons, see what they actually do. I'm tired of letting these things sit idle, and for the same reason, you guys need to start screwing around with your link and see what the hell it does. To that end, back into the house. Open more pieces of cursed furniture, see if they're spawning monsters, see if there's broader options there. Then we need to decide what our course of action with the school is. I'm thinking of putting it to the torch. Thoughts?"

He'd clearly thought this out. Anesh himself had been wondering about the connection that the house had awarded to himself and Alanna for all the hard work James did, but the two of them simply hadn't had time to talk about it. And Alanna had been curious about the lesson since they'd gotten it, but she hadn't had time to do more than rack up a few points on it.

Alanna started with "My first thought is that we cannot burn down a high school. That's just silly. Also, hey, did anyone ever check up on . . . you know . . . the whole thing?" She was met with blank looks from her boys. "You know what I'm talking about—don't play dumb. The thing where James bled all over the records office and wore Secret like a scarf through a crowd."

"Oh, that thing," James said, playing coy. "No?"

Both Aneshes pulled out their phones and, after a brief minute to connect to the Wi-Fi, started searching through news stories. "I can't believe none of us thought of this," he said. "What were we *doing?*"

"Sleeping. Then more dungeon," James said. "See, this is what I'm talking about. We forget *so many* little details."

"James, there's a story here about an opened investigation into the possibility of a serial killer after thirty-two students went missing on the same day," Anesh hissed out. "So whatever's happening, they don't know about the information void, but they *are* aware now."

"Is there anything about me?" James leaned over the table to look at Anesh's screen, getting cake frosting on his shirt as he did so. "Huh. 'Detective Madden told reporters that at present, they are investigating all possible leads and have no active suspects.' That's disappointing. I was hoping . . ."

Alanna snorted. "You were hoping to be a hero, huh?"

"I've got a lot of vainglory stored up and waiting for a good outlet, yeah." James nodded. "Still. No mention of me or Secret or any of that stuff. So, that's good?"

"Either they've got a blind spot for things beyond the weirdness threshold or they're not going to talk about ghost monsters on the news sites," Alanna agreed. "Either way, it does confirm that we have a bit of anonymity. We're still not burning down the school, though."

"It would solve the problem."

"So would just sealing off the breach!" Alanna argued back. "Schools can't just be replaced. That would seriously fuck up a lot of people's lives—students, staff, parents. Also, it's an infrastructure investment that can't just be covered by cash from state insurance. So *no*. But I am okay with us posting a guard on it."

James cocked an eyebrow. "Is this going to be part of some zany plan to put Momo into deep cover as a high schooler?" he asked. "Because I've seen the 'hello fellow teens' meme and I don't think it's meant to be *advice*, exactly."

"No, dingus. We just get someone a job as a school counselor or security guard or something. We've already got someone on the roster who's qualified, and we can clearly forge FBI credentials, so we just do that. Tell the school the person is there to keep an eye on things and assist with the investigation, that their salary is already paid, and then give them a free staff member," Alanna suggested.

There was a pause. "I feel like there's gonna be a problem there if anyone bothers to check anything, but having once volunteered in a school office, I can't say that I ever knew of anyone checking on anything. So that might work," James admitted sadly. "Though posing as the FBI long term is another one of those unsustainable ideas."

"Ya think?" Alanna snorted. "Okay. So. Learn things, guard the school, check out the house—we should do that on Thursdays, just as a thought, since it doesn't seem to have a set time. Is there anything else that we need to go over?"

"Endless things." James sighed. "We have too much on our plate. Our resident war witch has made a lot of progress on the red totems, so we need to have some kind of system in place for turning the weird stuff she makes into actual solutions to problems. Also . . . um, yes, Anesh?" James pointed to the one that had a hand raised.

"I was actually thinking about this. The math on the reds for the totems is almost constant. And now we have a green totem to study, as well as the oranges we keep finding. I'm not sure about those, but I'm *reasonably* sure I understand the yellows well enough to make a totem out of them."

"No!" and "Hard no!" echoed as James and Alanna spoke at the same time.

James picked up that line of thinking. "Anesh, we know very few things about the yellows, but one of them is that to absorb them, you have to understand that they are themselves a congealed function of *time*. Now, I know that the totems for the reds produce information, which seems to be their thing, and the oranges and greens seem to be about spaces. So I am going to say this once: don't fuck with time."

"What! But we could probably do it safely!" Anesh protested. James glared at both of him, and he shriveled in his seats. "Okay, probably." The glare did not relent. "Okay, fine! I won't fuck with time!"

"Good. Thank you."

". . . dungeon fucks with time," Anesh grumbled.

"The dungeon fucks with time in exactly one instance, which makes me think even it is wary of it," James pointed out.

"Okay, fair," Anesh agreed. "I'll keep it to my theoretical notes for now. Promise."

James squeezed his eyes shut for a second as he processed the implication that Anesh had already started on this. He said a small prayer for linear causality and moved on, hoping to brush that under the rug. "Moving briskly on," he said, "did you know that we got more iLipedes?"

"Oh yeah?" Alanna asked, subconsciously itching at her arms. "That's . . . nice."

"I thought you liked Lily?" Anesh asked her.

Alanna bit her lip. "I do like Lily. She's both useful and stays politely away from me. But they're still all undulate-y, ya know?" She gave an exaggerated shiver. "Ugh. No. Millipedes are no."

"I've seen you catch and release spiders with your bare hands, and you're telling me you don't like something vaguely bug-shaped?" James inquired, amused.

"Vaguely shaped like the *worst* bug, yeah. Look, this is irrelevant. Can we talk about what they do?" Alanna tried to divert them back on track, which was difficult enough normally and even more of a challenge when James had caffeine in his blood.

"Okay, so, there's four of them. Two are fine and two are possibly exploitable in a way that's probably, *probably*, going to get us into trouble," James started. Instantly, Anesh perked up; exploitable systems were getting to be his bread and butter. "One of them is like Lily; it scans things. It seems weaker, though. Like, it only scans things it thinks of as tools, and it doesn't count the orbs for some reason. It can tell you who owns a thing, though. The other one gives you a countdown timer to the next time you're going to be in physical danger . . ."

"That one's gone," Anesh pointed out.

"What?"

"Yeah, there was an argument over whether or not it was causing the danger. We released it back into the wilds rather than suffer its curse."

James cleared his throat. "Why does no one tell me this stuff?"

"We are literally having the conversation now. This is us telling you," Alanna said, clapping her hands together once and pointing at James. "What do the other two do?"

"Fine! But this is gonna end with me giving people paperwork, mark my words!" James threatened. "The other one builds up a charge over time, and you can ask it yes/no questions. It seems like the cost of an answer is based on how big a question it is, but it might be something else. The last one is a social network."

"Like Facebook? Wait, no, that's not the important one here. That first one could . . ." Anesh trailed off.

Alanna picked it up. "Detect lies? Unravel political conspiracies? Brute force passwords? No, that one is stupid. Um . . . solve questions about the universe?"

"We tried that one. It probably won't ever have enough charge to settle the debate of whether any given divinity is real," James said. "It takes maybe a few hours to build up to something moderately useful and probably a lot longer for anything involving quantum physics. The fun one is the social network thing."

The other two stopped to think about that one for a second. Anesh bowed his head, Alanna tilted hers up, and they both put their brains toward figuring out what a dungeon-made social network would look like. "Oh," Anesh said suddenly. "It gives you a literal map of a person's social life, doesn't it?"

"Yep. Only to one degree, which is still a lot of information. But the longer a person uses it, the more it fills in connections between different people, to an alarmingly detailed degree. *Did you know* that JP's mom and Dave's mom made out once in a college frat party?" James asked with a wild grin.

Alanna choked on her drink, nearly spitting coffee onto the table. "Did *they* know that?"

"They do now! It's honestly not an amazing coincidence; their families have been friends for a long time. Maybe that's why!" The conclusion was an easy one to make for James, especially when it was happening to someone else. Even better that those someone elses weren't here tonight. "Anyway, that's the iLipedes. As Alanna's mutterings and napkin scribblings tell me, there are already a few ideas on how to use those. Um . . . yeah, that's about all I've got. As far as I know, no one found any transcendentally good magic items this time around. The only thing left to talk about is the orbs we picked up." The shrug James gave was casual and belied the electric excitement he felt in his chest.

No matter how many times they went through this, it was always just . . . fun. Sitting down together, sharing their skill gains and buffs in the same way they shared food. It grounded the whole experience.

There had been talk lately from some of the new people and also from the survivor cadre that James and his inner circle were insane. Not in a bad way, specifically, but just that the rate and eagerness with which they accepted the madness of their changed world wasn't normal. The dungeons gave out rewards both exciting and terrifying, in a lot of different ways, but James had just folded all that into his life and kept rolling on like it was the new normal.

And while he didn't get angry about it, or even disagree really, he did have one counterargument for why it was so easy for him.

The part where he and his friends shared the loot and levels was glorious.

They started pulling out pouches, loose orbs, and, in James's case, a repurposed Altoids tin, from pockets and backpacks. The stack on the table started to grow rapidly, and Anesh eyed it with worried eyes as he stopped adding to it long before the other two did. With one finger, he casually stopped a purple from rolling off the table as Alanna spilled a second handful of the things out.

"I thought we were sharing these?" he asked.

"We are," Alanna said. "I did. Everyone got at least one."

"There's, like, fifteen of the bloody things here," Anesh protested. "Where did you two get all this?" he asked. "Did you confiscate every orb we pulled in last delve?"

James looked offended. "What!? No! This is kind of normal now. Though, yeah, that is way more purples than I expected. What's up with that?"

"Oh, Deb's crew liberated a few from a pair of paper pushers, and Daniel and his guys found a couple in the other tower they tracked down," Alanna explained. "So everyone actually did get one; they just didn't take the extras. And some people didn't want them. Virgil had some religious thing about body modifications, which felt *awk-warrrrrd*. And we set some aside to be copied later, to test."

James winced. "Oof, that's probably gonna be a problem later." Then he paused and held up a hand. "Wait, doesn't he have a skull-jack already? That . . . Whatever, fuck it. I don't care. How are we splitting this? I admit, I've been casually cracking yellows, so I dunno if I should get as many of those. Also we have a lot of other things to spend those on now."

There were a lot of yellows. Maybe forty of the smallest ones and a dozen larger ones as well. A single baseball-size golden orb was the centerpiece of their little hoard. Around it were fifteen little purples with one or two small reds mixed in. Two larger dots for oranges that Anesh had brought. And five or six blues of varying mass, just to test their limits in noncrisis situations. No greens, though. The coffee shop was great, but these days the greens were reserved for the lair.

"Even split," Alanna said. "James, you separate the piles, then Anesh and I will choose first. The classic cake distribution."

"The what?"

"For cake. If you want to share a cake, one person cuts, the other person picks. You don't know this?" Anesh asked. "It's how my parents raised my siblings and me to share properly."

James made an unappreciative noise. "You've met my sister—you know damn well the two of us never learned to share with each other," he said as he started splitting the piles up. The only corrections that were made were Anesh passing his orange orb back to James, saying the intent was for him and Alanna to learn to absorb them, and nobody wanted to be the only one picking the huge orb. "Okay, come on, guys. We can't all be proud and stupid. Someone just . . . okay, fine," he relented as both of them reached out and pushed it into his pile. "Fine! All right. Anesh, get your notepad ready, because I'm not gonna remember half of these."

One by one, colorful bursts of glimmering dust faded across the tabletop and a flood of alien thoughts passed through James's mind, which he dutifully repeated to the Anesh keeping records.

[+1 Skill Rank : Cleaning—Dishwashing]

[+1 Skill Rank : Sewing]

[+1 Skill Rank : Repair—Sound Systems—Speakers]

[+3 Skill Ranks : Health Care—Treatment—Cancer—Chemotherapy]

[+1 Skill Rank : Gambling—Roulette]

[+1 Skill Rank : Fabrication—Wood—Chain-Saw Carving]

[+1 Skill Rank : Chain Saws]

[+1 Skill Rank : History—Production—Assembly Line]

[+1 Skill Rank : Pan Flute]

[+1 Skill Rank : Acting—Lying]

[+1 Skill Rank : Etiquette—American—Weddings]

[+1 Skill Rank : Bureaucracy—Insurance—Car]

[+1 Skill Rank : Pilot—Fixed-Wing Aircraft—Cessna]

[+2 Skill Ranks : History—Sports—Baseball]
[+1 Skill Rank : Recipe—Cake]
[+1 Skill Rank : Camouflage—Taiga]
[+2 Skill Ranks : Firearms—Sidearm—Walther P38]
[Shell Upgraded : G-Force Tolerance +0.8 Gs]
[Shell Upgraded : Comfortable Walking Speed +1.2 mph]
[Shell Upgraded : Flight Control +13mm adjustment/second]
[Shell Upgraded : Lumen Damage Threshold +1,684]
[Shell Upgraded : Ball-Joint Hyperextension +2.1 degrees]
[Problem Solved : Possessions Dehumidified]
[+1 Skill Rank : Literature—King Arthur]
[Problem Solved : Pursuit Shaken]
[+1 Skill Rank : Cleaning—Laundry—Detergent Ratios]

Silence followed. "Okay, I have some thoughts," Anesh said, tapping his pen on the legal pad in front of him. "I think I'll go through the simple ones first and then pass off to Alanna, who looks like she's having an aneurysm. So, first off, you got two chain-saw skills. That's horrifying. Also, I'm a bit sad your sports history wasn't basketball, because I really wanted to see how many points that counts for on your lesson. And finally, flight control is a bizarre thing for you to have. Would you like to go parachuting or something and test that out?" Anesh didn't wait for an answer, instead turning to the woman next to James. "Alanna, you have a thought?"

"*Pursuit fucking shaken?!*" she yelled, getting a brief moment of awkward hush from the rest of the patrons. "I was *right* and we *do* need plans for this!"

"Well, we did," James admitted. "We don't anymore. It's been 'shaken.'"

"What does that *mean?!*" Alanna demanded.

"Good question. I'm sure our would-be pursuers will be asking the same thing," James said. "Listen, this doesn't change anything, except that Anesh now wants to throw me out of an airplane. Our plans still stand. Now stop glowering at me and eat your orbs!" he ordered. "I'll try to absorb the orange once we're all done."

Alanna half complied, specifically with the part that didn't mean she had to stop scrunching up her face at her boyfriend. Her method was much less dramatic and more efficient than James's, simply crushing every orb in one swoop, but she still rattled off everything in perfect order for Anesh to write down. The one main difference was that she absorbed one of the blues to make up for her lost ability to conjure asphalt from nothing.

[+1 Skill Rank : Recipe—Confection—Salmiakki]

[+1 Skill Rank : Animals—Horse]

[+1 Skill Rank : Geography—Canada—Edmonton]

[+1 Skill Rank : Fabrication—Crochet—Amigurumi]

[+1 Skill Rank : Massage]

[+1 Skill Rank : Accounting—Double Entry—Receipt Validation]

[+2 Skill Ranks : Etiquette—Aristocracy—European]

[+1 Skill Rank : Camping]

[+2 Skill Ranks : Boxing—Out-Boxing—Southpaw]

[+1 Skill Rank : Disguise—Impersonation—Management]

[+1 Skill Rank : Etiquette—Gamers]

[+1 Skill Rank : Operation—Backhoe]

[+1 Skill Rank : Political Science—Nebraska—Legislature]

[Shell Upgraded : Bite Strength +166 psi]

[Shell Upgraded : Safe Heart Rate +46 bpm]

[Shell Upgraded : LD50 Dextroamphetamine +4 g]

[Shell Upgraded : Keratin Hardness +1.1]

[Shell Upgraded : Hearing Radius +80 cm]

[+16 Activations : Restore Glass]

[Problem Solved : Bathroom Cleaned]

[+1 Skill Rank : Gardening]

"All right. So," Alanna said, excitedly shifting back and forth in her seat like she was planning to vibrate through the floor. "So! I have a thought about all this!"

"Is it that you can now take way too much Adderall and be super productive all day long without worry?" James quipped.

She casually placed a hand on the side of his face and started slowly shoving him off his chair. "Nope! Nor is it whatever your next joke about me being able to eat plastic and being a goat is." Alanna didn't stop smiling. "It's that I got *etiquette* skills. And I'm amazingly curious if that's going to count toward my lesson. Anyone want to find out?"

"Does it not automatically do its thing?" James asked, speaking the word and pushing the intent to check on his own progress. It remained unmoved; he hadn't, after all, learned anything even remotely related to basketball in the last forty-eight hours.

"If it does, then I—" Alanna started to say. And a second later, she was somewhere else.

The classroom looked clean and bright. Light streamed in from the windows through the half-pulled blinds. The chalkboard was freshly cleaned. The linoleum floor gleamed from its recent waxing. Alanna sat near the front, where she always sat, in one of those desks where the chair was tethered to the rest of the piece of furniture with a metal bar, watching the teacher.

The teacher wasn't human. But that was fine. It was the teacher. Always had been. It taught her lessons. And *lessons*. Right? That's how this worked. That's how school worked. You fought, you killed, then you sat, then you learned. And if you were very good at it, you didn't need to retake senior year.

The light from outside wasn't real sunlight. It was just more of the greasy blue-white light from the overhead bulbs. The chalkboard had things written on it, faded messages not completely wiped away. They were grim, arcane formulas and dire threats. The floor was mostly clean; the bugs skittering across it ate anything that wasn't them.

Alanna tried to stand up and found she couldn't. She tried to howl in rage and couldn't do that, either.

"Stay in your seat," the teacher rumbled at her. "We want you to leave as much as you do." It turned to the blackboard and with a rusted steel claw began carving words into it. After the third word, it turned back toward her. "Choose. Then go."

Charisma. Empathy. Reputation.

"What am I choosing?" Alanna tried to ask, but she couldn't. "What are you, where is this, why am I here, who *am I.*" None of the questions came out. There were three words she was permitted to say, and all of them were written on the board.

So she thought. What did she want? Not reputation. That was a bad idea for someone who wanted to stay undetected. And she knew that was what she wanted. Charisma? That sounded okay. So did empathy. What was the difference? People understanding her, versus understanding people? She already was understood. She knew *that* very powerfully, in a part of her gut that yowled defiance at this place. So, there was only one thing left.

"Empathy," she said.

"You have learned," the teacher gnashed. "Return when you are prepared to be taught again. Now get out, *plagiarist.*" The last word was a scream of twisting metal blades.

Alanna was sitting in a padded chair, in a pleasantly lit coffee shop, at about eleven at night. Around her, the texture of human emotion roiled like a fog bank filled with lanterns. "Worried," she said, pointing at James. "Curious, also worried." She pointed at Anesh. It wasn't enough; there was so much information, so many little thoughts that meant so much more. "You don't care!" She started to raise her voice, pointing to a man sitting at the table across the open aisle to their left. "And you care too much!" Alanna directed that to the woman sitting with him at the same table. She stood up, staring around as people started murmuring to each other, watching her. "Afraid! Stressed! Mourning! Aroused! Angry!" She fired off words with the point of a finger, going through everyone near them, even as a few people stood up and started to leave. "Vindication!" she yelled, spinning on her heel to point at the barista, who had come out from behind the counter to stand behind her.

"Yeah, this is kind of what I meant," he told them, vaguely sheepish. "Guys, I'm gonna need you to keep it down. You're bothering every . . . one . . ." He trailed off as he saw the remaining pile of orbs in front of Anesh. "Huh. Okay. Yeah. Stop yelling, please, or I'll have to kick you out."

Alanna flushed bright red as she realized what she'd been doing. "Sorry," she said. "Shit, I'm really sorry!" she called to the café and got a wave of acknowledgment as she sat back down.

"What the hell was *that?*" James asked her, now fully terrified that something was wrong.

"I have no idea," Alanna said. And then she remembered something that she'd been remembering this whole time but hadn't acknowledged. It flickered on the edge of her awareness, and she directed her mind toward it. [Lesson—Communications III : 18/400—Empathy II]. "Oh," she said. "It worked. I . . . got something called empathy? Twice, it looks like. Shit, I feel like a raw nerve. I can hear everything everyone is feeling. This is insane."

"Twice?" James asked. "Wait, did you not get a choice like the kid did?"

"No, I got a . . . choice." Alanna's eyes narrowed to slits, and she glanced aside. "I don't remember much about it. But I made it." She let out a low hissing noise. "My head hurts."

"Yeah, no kidding. Well, good news. You were right on the orbs being broken with these. That's gonna get out of hand real fast," James said.

Anesh nodded. "It makes sense now why the Office tried to have Javier killed." He tapped the table. "Should we be worried? If it finds out that you have these, it might try to kill you, too."

"It isn't already?" James laughed.

Anesh didn't laugh in return. "James, Officium Mundi has a literal army of highly lethal creatures in it, many of them things that might be literal puppets to its will. If it wanted us dead, we would go in one day, go a half mile in, and find ourselves surrounded by more tumblefeeds than we have bullets. It *can* kill us. It just *hasn't.*"

"That's both technically true and deeply unsettling." James shivered, his humor gone. "Though I suspect it can't *just* kill us. If it really was interested in murder, or even just basic defense, there would be the most dangerous things on the *outer* layers of itself, right? I think it has to play by rules."

"If we're breaking the rules, why wouldn't it?" Alanna said. "So, we need to be careful. I shouldn't go in next week until we secure the area, and even then, we need to not say a damn thing about it. I shouldn't use it, either, if that's an option."

"Is it?"

"Don't know yet." She shrugged. "But at least this would solve the overhunting problem."

"The what now?" Anesh asked. "Sorry, I've been kind of out of the loop."

James let out a groan. "Okay, you know how we weren't going to talk about dividing up hunting territories or whatever?"

Anesh agreed. "Yes. For reasons."

"Right, colonialism and stuff. Which, I admit, is bad. Anyway. Certain areas of the dungeon near the door just don't have a lot of life in them right now. And they aren't even places we've been exploring! There's just regions that are kind of empty. Of other things, too; not a lot of orb-touched effects there at all. No items, no warped spaces, nothing."

"I feel weirder talking about this now than before," Alanna muttered, glancing around at the people she could now feel being surreptitiously curious about their chat. "But yeah, if the dungeon does decide to try to kill me . . . we could harvest a lot of greens, fast."

"We'll call that Plan S," James said. When he noticed Alanna's cocked eyebrow, he nodded in affirmation. "Yes, you are correct. The S is for stupid. Anyway. I'm getting kinda exhausted here. Anesh, you wanna use yours, then we can try to absorb the oranges and head home?"

"I'm way more interested in talking about the fact that the dungeon might have, or be, an ecosystem," Anesh admitted. "But I also wouldn't mind going home and sitting down for a bit. So sure." It took him longer than the others, since he was stopping between each one to write them down, but as was tradition, they reserved commentary until the very end. It was also a bit weird because both Aneshes took the time to hook together with a short ethernet cable they'd brought, sitting in a position close to back-to-back for the brief period it took them to go through all the orbs so no one around could see.

When they recombined their minds, late evenings turned to sessions where two very similar people became one *singular* person. A lot of the orbs shared, too. Yellows, especially, but many of the others as well, even if the pattern felt impossible to determine. But if they were connected when they used an orb, it *always* influenced both of them, because they were one person. And, thankfully, they didn't subdivide purple effects when they separated again.

[+1 Skill Rank : Writing—Calligraphy]

[+1 Skill Rank : Sailing—Twin Mast]

[+1 Skill Rank : Templating—Note Taking—Shorthand]

[+1 Skill Rank : Cooking—Pizza]

[+1 Skill Rank : Philosophy—Ethics—Immanuel Kant]

[+2 Skill Ranks : Art—Metalworking—Wall Hangings]

[+2 Skill Ranks : Language—French—Québécois]

[+1 Skill Rank : History—Music—Nineteenth Century—Rock]

[+1 Skill Rank : Scuba Diving]

[+1 Skill Rank : Gambling—Craps]

[+1 Skill Rank : Sartorialism—Pants—Flood]

[+1 Skill Rank : Sex—Foreplay]

[+1 Skill Rank : Crossbow]

[+1 Skill Rank : Leadership—Team Building]

[+2 Skill Rank : History—Art—Romance Period]

[Shell Upgraded : Pigment Control, 2 Orders of Complexity/Day]

[Shell Upgraded : Vocal Range +/- 1 Octave]

[Shell Upgraded : Spice Tolerance +391,040 Scoville]

[Shell Upgraded : Life Span +3 Years]

[Problem Solved : Renewed Travel Papers]

[+1 Skill Rank : Toxicology—Substance Identification—Mold]

[+1 Emotional Resonance Rank : Longing]

". . . But I like spicy food . . ." was the first thing Anesh said after he finished the list and looked down at his paper. Tentatively, one of him started poking at their tongue, as if trying to feel if they'd been cheated somehow.

"Did you get any good skills?" James asked, pulling the notepad over and scanning it.

"I can tell you that you shouldn't wear flood pants," Anesh said with a frown. "So no, nothing good."

"This says 'crossbow,'" Alanna pointed out.

"I can already shoot a bow," Anesh countered, idly dismissive. "I'm more interested in if I can . . ." He held out an arm and narrowed his eyes in focus. A few seconds passed before James and Alanna started seeing swirls against his skin, like cream dropped into a cup of coffee. The color changes whorled and spun for a few seconds until Anesh unclenched his hand, shook his arm out, and held it up to examine. He hadn't gone for fully changing color, instead simply drawing patterns against his skin. Spirals and loops in mathematically fluid shapes, running down the back of his forearm and across his wrist and palm. "Neat," he said. "Not sure how I can exploit this, though."

"We'll find a way," James promised, patting him on the shoulder. "If nothing else, it'll be great for Halloween."

"Mmh." Anesh hummed out an agreement. "All right, last thing. Let's see if we can get you guys absorbing an orange."

They turned to the last two orbs on the table, and Anesh started explaining exactly what he'd done when he'd absorbed the first one. It was, as with the yellows and blues, about truly understanding what the orb was about. Yellows were a crystallized sliver of time, blues were a single solution to a problem stretched out to cover a massively wide space, and oranges, as far Anesh could explain it, were about bureaucracy.

Though maybe that wasn't quite the right way to say it. Complexity, perhaps. Layered thoughts, all part of a larger system, that were twisted to serve a purpose even if they didn't organically fit. It was about making something do a job. Spaces were twisted to labyrinths of themselves, people were given certifications they never earned, life was created that then itself created more things from its own night-mare templates. And if you absorbed one, that concept was turned to its fullest: you acquired a job of sorts. Perform a task, get a reward.

Or so Anesh theorized. James, personally, was holding out that it was "perform a task, get a copy of yourself" every time.

Alanna listened with rapt attention, absorbed everything Anesh was trying to say, picked up her orb, and promptly fucked up what-ever she was going to try to do and crushed it in her fingers with a loud "Fuck!"

[*Certification Added : Business License—Alabama—Jefferson County*]

"Okay, so. What did you do, exactly?" James asked. "Because I want to do anything but that."

"Uggggh." Alanna let out a long groan. "Well, I guess I can't get all the cool toys in one night. I was mostly thinking about them in terms of complexity, and then I felt it start to slip and tried to force it. Fucked that right up." She clenched her hand a few times, as if trying to capture the sensation. "Well, at least I can do what I've always wanted and move to Alabama to open my artisanal pet food shop." She looked over at James with pinpoint timing. "No, not really."

"Is this your new superpower, or am I just getting predictable?"

"Yeah." She nodded. "Now try yours."

James looked at the small orb in his hand. It was the smallest orange they'd found, from a hallway that looped on itself sometimes. He tried to imagine that feeling. The feeling of being a hallway that had a new task, of being bent into the shape of a new job that you didn't particularly want. Then he realized he didn't have to pretend that hard; six months ago, that was *him*. He could have been that hall. Could have been just a series of certifications without context or meaning.

It didn't matter that the task was a layer of complexity. Com-plexity without meaning was despair. The orb was something more than that, wasn't it? It was complexity with a purpose. It shifted not just what was done but ascribed a satisfied sense of a job well-done to it. None of the spatial warps ever felt *sad* to James. He imagined that Anesh had found a different shade of color in his idea of complexity, but here, this was his. It was complex. It was complexity. It was his job to take that dense bundle of functionality and make it *do something*.

The orb slipped effortlessly into his palm.

[Task Ascribed : Input—Eat Seven Apples : Output—16.2 g Saffron : Time Frame—3 Days]

"Well," he said. "An apple a day . . . no, two-point-three-ish apples a day . . . gets me . . . paella, I guess?" James sighed. "Fuck. I mean, okay, this is cool. I'm glad this exists; I'm glad I got it to work. I feel like the longer we spend in the dungeon, the better I *understand* it, and this exemplifies that. But honestly, at the end of the day, I'm a bit pissed that Anesh gets to duplicate himself and *I* get to duplicate *ingredients*." He looked back and forth between his partners. "It's fine, I'm not mad. Hell, I get to create matter from nothing by eating healthier. How cool is that?" James gave a small smile, weak but real. "All right. So. We know where we're going. We know how we're getting there. We all just got a significant amount more dangerous while sitting in a café. And we are out of coffee." He stood up, flattening his palms on the table. "Who's ready to go home? I wanna find out exactly what Anesh's skill that we all pointedly *didn't* talk about does."

"Just for that," Anesh said as everyone rose to their feet with James, "neither of me is loaning you one of our coats."

CHAPTER 8

Three people stood on a hill, overlooking a city.

James, Anesh, and Alanna. They were on a rolling sand dune, ripples of grit spiraling around their feet. The sand was the pure yellow-white of the great deserts of Earth, despite the fact that the sky overhead was a shocking red. It gave the whole place a contrast—between two colors that didn't seem to share a light source in any meaningful way. The three of them held hands—and didn't notice they were doing it—while they looked out from their perch.

Below, a cityscape stretched out. It had a core of strictly ordered geometric shapes, great gray blocks stretching into the sky. But beyond that, the patterns started to get fuzzier. There was a segment surrounding that inner core where the sizes and decorations started to show more detail and variety. And then, outside that, buildings in different shapes altogether. The outskirts, which were undergoing new construction even now, became even more chaotic, with houses of a thousand descriptions forming a frenzied suburb.

Overhead, a red sun lit up the thin clouds and charged atmosphere in a crimson shade. The sun pulsed every few seconds, beating like a heart that drove forward the inorganic machinations of the city.

"I've been here before," James whispered. He wasn't sure his partners heard him. Or if they *could* hear him.

To his side, Anesh stared upward at the burning, angry star in the sky. He wore *armor*, of a sort. It was thick plates of dense, flexible metallic shell. Bright orange—the color that orange would be without anything between it and your eye—layering over his arms and legs like scales. His chest plate had a rectangular projection on it, a wedge angled upward with what looked like a series of dials on it. The high collar rose up around the back of Anesh's neck, past his ears, and it took James a second to realize that he was wearing a helmet made of clear material. He knew it wasn't glass; he knew that he could punch that forever and never break it. Four letters were stenciled on the shoulder of the armor. James couldn't read them.

To his other side, Alanna stared down at the city. She too wore armor, a flat mass of solid, woven plastic fibers, a midnight blue so deep it pulled in the eye. It rose over her joints in almost thorned protrusions; it wrapped whorls of spun Kevlar and chain around vital areas. It rose to a collar that covered her throat, leaving her face looking oddly, contrastingly human against the weapon of a suit coiled around her in a protective embrace. All across it were clips or pouches onto which things could, and would, be hung. Weapons, tools, supplies—anything needed instantly at hand. On the pauldron, just under one of the small clips, was a stencil of a golden badge. There was a name written there. James couldn't read it.

"Nice coat," Alanna said, looking at James without turning her head.

James was wearing a long coat. It covered him down to his ankles, black fabric both armored and easy to move in. The buttons had arcane symbols etched on them. He felt himself, then, and knew the coat had a half dozen holsters inside, hidden weapons ready to pull at a moment's notice. His coat also had a collar, though it only pulled up on the left side of his neck, an angled piece of fabric that reached forward to precisely cover the fresh scar tissue there.

"Thanks," he said. "We're dreaming." As if by magic, both of his companions started to come back to themselves. "Don't wake up," James told them idly, not focusing on his words. "Don't try to think. Let yourself dream. You're asleep; you're just watching." He walked them through the process of pseudo–lucid dreaming as quickly as he could.

It helped that his words weren't really words. They were ideas, thoughts, explanations, experience. All passed down through the pipeline of the mind that currently connected the three sleeping lovers.

They wandered down the hill together, though in that dream-logic haze where they didn't so much walk as the distance simply progressed around them. And in time, they came to be in the city.

The buildings were, for all that they grew in great complexity the farther from the city core they were, boxy. They were the simplest expression of a building. A building had a door, and windows, and in many cases stairs. So, of course, they had those things. They were uniform and also in places that didn't make a lot of usable sense. But then, these weren't buildings meant to be *used*; they were simply buildings that were meant to be buildings. Rectangles of material with the extras attached as an afterthought.

The roads had lines on them, because roads had that, but there were never going to be cars here. Cars were, they all intuited natural-ly, far too chaotic for this place.

When they ran across Secret, it wasn't much of a surprise. He had long since ceased to wear a disguise in James's dreamscape, though somehow, the seven-thousand-mile-long serpent that gazed with hundreds of eyes and hungered with hundreds of teeth *still* managed to wear a trench coat that came fairly close to matching James's own. He was sitting on a bench like he was waiting for a bus, staring up at the skyscrapers that he should have by all rights towered over.

"Hello. It has been some time since we last spoke." He spoke in a sibilant hum to the trio.

"I made you pancakes yesterday," James told him, too deep in the dream to be either amused or concerned.

Secret turned coils of eyes toward them. "My dreams do not bridge as well as you may think. I have eaten your pancakes. But *I* have not seen you in some time."

James didn't have a response to that. There wasn't much to respond with, really. He felt sorrow, that this Secret and that Secret seemed so disconnected from each other. That this Secret might only ever live in an empty city that wasn't quite real or right. He felt concern at the idea that the waking Secret might not know there was part of him trapped down here, in the depths of the human subconscious.

"You can come up sometimes, if you want," James offered.

"I know," Secret said simply. "But I must keep watch here." Every one of his eyes pivoted to look up, drawing the trio's gaze into the sky. "Lest you be watched in kind."

James didn't bother to shield his eyes; the blazing red sun overhead didn't actually give off light that reached the ground. But as he and the others looked around, nothing drew his attention.

"What do you mean?" Alanna and Anesh tried to ask but couldn't form the words.

"What do you mean?" James said, pulling the intent from them and shaping it through his skill with the dream.

Secret's eyes narrowed slightly as he focused on something, and James tried to focus with him. "Beware," he intoned, his voice deeper, more primal, than they were used to. "An eye is upon you. An eye, unblinking, searching. *Hunting*. An eye about to *blink*."

Overhead, the red star slammed shut.

James woke up with such a jolt that he elbowed Alanna out of the bed, uncertain how much of that had been prophetic and how much was just a casual, normal nightmare.

Two hours later, James was at his desk.

Not his work desk, but the desk in the small office at the lair where he'd built his personal shrine to trying to keep informed. It was called, he was told, an inbox. All he had to do was vaguely make it known that he would like reports to happen, and reports had begun happening. They weren't neatly or consistently formatted, by any means. But they were earnest attempts from people to pass on information to him, since everyone just kind of assumed he was in charge.

James wasn't sure if he should keep that illusion rolling or not.

It was when he was halfway through the copy of the Sysco receipt from Nate, sipping at a fancy five-dollar mocha that had long since gone lukewarm, that he realized his life had gone completely off the rails.

"Why in the goddamn did he buy four hundred dollars' worth of bananas?" James muttered. "I have to go ask about this." He didn't stand up, just stared at the page in his hand. "I should probably ask about this. Later." He set the page aside and picked up the next one, adding another sip of chocolate-infused caffeine to his mouth while he read.

He got through about two lines before there was a wall-rattling thud from somewhere above him, and he heard a few shouts from outside the office. It wasn't like he'd bothered to shut the door; none of this was secret or anything. But James didn't do much more than raise his eyebrows and tilt the page down in his hands a fraction to see out the door. If he'd still worn glasses and not made the switch to contacts years ago, he would have peered over them.

From just out in the main common area, he heard a deeper male voice, probably Harvey, shouting out serious questions about what was going on and if they should get people to shelter. From closer to the elevators, there was Momo, cutting through the sea of voices and telling people it was fine, that there wasn't anything hostile on the roof, so they were probably just struck by a meteorite or something. James rolled his eyes, drank some more coffee, and spun around in his chair to face away from the door, figuring he had about two minutes.

One minute and thirty-seven seconds later—he was watching the timer on his phone—Dave walked into the office.

"Hey, you busy?" Dave asked as James spun around in the chair to face him, kicking his feet up on his desk like a discount Bond villain.

"Have a seat," James said ominously. "I've been expecting you."

Dave shot a nervous look behind him, at the still-open door. "Um . . . why?" he asked, seeming torn between confusion and that expression that James had worn so many times in high school when he was called to the principal's office—surely he was in trouble for *something* and it would be so much easier if he could just remember what the hell it was.

Deciding feet on the desk was horribly uncomfortable, James swept his legs back down to the floor and leaned forward as Dave sat, steepling his fingers before him. "Because, Dave, I have the uncanny ability to detect when an eight-hundred-pound laminated draconic aircraft slams into the roof," he explained. "What the hell are you thinking, flying Pendragon here in daylight?"

"I thought we were doing that now?" Dave faltered. "Like, just showing off things? Is that not okay? Should I get a tarp or something?"

"A tarp . . . What?"

"For Pendragon. On the roof?"

"Why would anyone be looking on our roof?" James asked, his turn to be a bit confused.

Dave shrugged. "I mean, we're at a decline from the main road, right? JP complains about how the hill is too steep and he bottoms out his car on it all the time. So, the roof is more visible from the road."

"We're not super far down, though." James thought for a second, then sighed. "Get a damn tarp, if only to keep the rain off her. I'll give you the cash to run to Home Depot in a minute here. In the meantime, what brings you by today?"

Dave looked like he was about to ask some kind of question about whether he should fly Pendragon to the hardware store or whether he should get a ride, but he thought better of it. "I'm mostly just here because JP wanted me to drop off some printouts," Dave admitted, pulling a manila envelope out of the courier satchel at his side.

It took James less time than he was fully comfortable with to parse what was handed to him. It wasn't any particular orb skill; like he'd told JP a while back, he actually did have a degree in this sort of thing. And scanning over the numbers gave him a pretty easy picture to follow. "Oh, good!" James said. "We're not doing crime anymore!"

"That can't be right," Dave argued. "We break into a building every week. A lot of us. Also JP was telling me about the legal definition of assault earlier, and I'm pretty sure your thing at the school where you bled all over the lobby counts."

"We're not doing *finance* crimes," James corrected. "As much. Or rather, we were never really doing crimes, but JP was acting in ways that were either supernatural or deeply suspicious, and the amounts of money he was using were large enough to start attracting attention. Now, we've just got a reasonable return coming in—a normal stream of income that we can justify without having to tell the IRS that we're wizards."

"Are we wizards?"

"We sure as fuck aren't *not* wizards."

"I don't think we're using the same definition of wizard."

"Dave, you landed a dragon on the roof. Fuck off, you're a wizard. Take the title and like it."

"All right. Should I check the basement?"

James stuttered slightly. "What?"

"For the tarp. We still have all that stuff in the basement," Dave explained. "You know, from when you summoned two basements."

With a groan, James dropped his head down between his arms to headbutt the desk a few times before rising back up with a dramatic flourish. The piece of paper stuck to his forehead slipped off with a comical flutter. "Okay! Yes, check there for a tarp! That actually reminds me, I was supposed to do the greens here today, to continue upgrading this place. Do you mind grabbing those out of the vault for me? I'm still reading these." He gestured to his stack of reports.

"What are all those? Also, we have a vault?" Dave asked.

"It's the partitioned part of the basement behind the research area. It has locks!" James cheerfully informed him before his smile slipped. "And these are just reports people have been giving me. Notes on therapy meetings and skulljack capabilities, xenotech use cases, expenses and stuff, and . . . okay, I wanna get your opinion on something. This one is an authorization request from our research division for something called 'Resonance Option'?"

Dave nodded. "Okay? And?"

"Well, am I going insane or something? Like, this is a ridiculous name for a project, right?" James looked at it again, and it gave him a headache. It was like someone had decided to emulate their favorite science fiction style, but it was happening on his desk.

When he looked up at Dave, though, all he got was a mildly confused and amused look in response. "You do know we're wizards, right? We can give things cool names. R&D divisions name stuff like that all the time; they probably just hit a random name generator and picked one that sounded cool. What's it for, anyway?"

James looked back down at the page, trying to put aside the headache that the name caused him long enough to scan the words. "Um . . . they want permission to start using the purple orbs a lot of people have been *saving up*—what?—to *incubate symbiotic info-morphs*—Dave, I have concerns about this.*"

"I mean, that's probably why they're asking permission." Dave shrugged. "I'll ask whoever's around about the name when I go find the tarp. And the greens." He stood, but before he left, he glanced back at James. "Are you okay today?" he asked, his own muted concern threaded through the words.

"I'm fine, why?"

"You seem kinda snappy." Dave shrugged.

James sighed. "I didn't sleep well. Had some kinda nightmare that I don't really remember. I think I was talking to Secret in it, but . . . eh. Also I'm kinda just getting overwhelmed by work. And the coffee hasn't kicked in yet."

"Do you work anymore?" Dave asked. "You're here on a Friday afternoon."

James raised his eyebrows. "I'm working right now."

"I meant at the call center. Did you quit?"

"I mean, kinda. I sure haven't been showing up. I've been busy and too nervous to actually tell them I don't want to work there anymore. It's . . . fine, though. Daniel still works there, and he's done that thing where he's acquired a management position by just sort of doing the job and everyone falling into line . . ."

"Like you."

". . . shut up. Also I don't really want to deal with Theo," James finished.

Dave leaned against the door frame, stubbornly refusing to get out of James's hair just yet. "It's weird that you're okay fighting maimframes but not quitting a job."

"I am *not* okay fighting maimframes—those things are horrifying—but I take your point." James rolled his eyes with a huff. "I'll . . . message Theo."

"You should call her," Dave prompted.

"Don't push it." James scowled, making a motion of threatening to throw a pen at his friend. "Go get me my orbs."

Chuckling, Dave strolled out of the office. With a sigh, James looked back down at his desk and the paperwork that was suddenly stifling. "I need a big stamp that just says, 'fuck it, approved,'" he muttered to himself. "Or, like, one of someone shrugging and saying, 'I guess?' I don't want them to think that I'm a million percent behind this plan."

In truth, though, he liked the idea. His exhaustion and headache and the lack of the caffeine kicking in to fix those first two things were making him irritable, but the more he turned his thoughts toward this and really dug into it, the more he got into it. They—that was, humans—weren't equipped to fight memeplexes or infomorphs. They didn't have natural defenses against it; it was kind of like asking a human to gear up to fight *lava*. Sure, you technically could, probably. James was almost certain that if he took in enough red orbs, he'd eventually be able to kill things like Secret just by feeling at them hard enough. But how was he supposed to find them first?

It wasn't really that much different than the earlier proposed idea of having at least one form of dungeon Life per team, either in a support role or as a battle buddy. Magneto, the doggish thing that Momo's team had made out of the magnetic distortion of an old computer monitor, was a perfect example. He wasn't a bruiser, but he was hard to kill, loyal to his friends, and made of magnets. Ganesh filled a perfect scout role for their original team, too, and even their newfound use of skulljacked drone control didn't fully replace him, since he was far more flexible and intelligent. Also armed. Oh, and there was Pendragon, too, who was just a flying tank. Having every team in some way paired up with something that helped expand their options was a good idea.

So why did this plan make him apprehensive?

Well, he mused, there was the fact that any infomorphs, symbiotic or not, were still people. And they were people who lived in the heads of the humans or other physical life that they occupied reality with. That was a risky place to put something. In retrospect, the fact that Secret had matured so rapidly and into someone so chill was nothing short of a miracle, considering that James himself was kind of a temperamental jerk at times.

There was also the problem of freedom. None of the life they'd made so far had been for the purpose of being a tool. And that was *important*.

And while James was fine with making life just for fun, and then being responsible for it like a parent or Pokémon trainer, he was *not* down with making something that was designed to fill a specific task. Honestly, he'd be way more comfortable recruiting from existing dungeon entities, whether they were physical or memetic. Hell, they already knew there was a whole tower of camracondas they needed to liberate.

James slapped his forehead. Pulling a piece of paper onto his desk, he uncapped a pen with his teeth and scribbled *liberate snake-town* on it. He'd know what it meant later when he forgot again.

Recruiting infomorphs or other memetic life was way harder, though. Communication was a trick at best, and impossible at worst. Even Secret couldn't exactly talk to everything, even if he could bite it in half. But they should, if they could, try. It was just the *could* that was the barrier; there really wasn't a guidebook on how to approach a free-floating self-sustaining idea and say, "Hey, I wanna be friends."

"Fuck it," James said to himself and the empty office. "Approved. This is a good idea. I'll leave a group message about it and let everyone know. Maybe Anesh or Secret knows how to memeproof a room so we can have a safe testing area."

"Momo might know," Dave said from the door, making an inattentive James nearly jump out of his skin.

Heart pounding, sucking in a sharp breath, James clutched a hand to his chest as he scattered pens across his desk. "Fuck! Don't do that! I didn't know you were there!"

"You told me to come back with the orbs!" Dave protested. "Also, I found a tarp."

"I don't . . . care about the tarp . . . oh, hell, that's not true. Good job. We should really get one of the squires to sort through the basement."

"We don't have squires," Dave said flatly, half asking.

"We have interns, but I hate that word," James said. "Also, we pay them. It's the new people we're slowly adapting to the weird, as opposed to the three that we just dunked in. Alanna wanted to do a double-blind test, but I couldn't find enough people to hire. Whatever, give me the orbs."

Dave tossed the black cloth bag onto the desk. "If we have squires, does that mean we're committed to being a guild, then?"

"I still hate that word, for all the reasons. I'm thinking we should be an *order*. You get to name it," James told him, pulling out the three middling green orbs and one that was fairly large, fist size.

It didn't take much thought for an answer to that. "No," Dave protested. "I'm bad at names. I'm not creative."

"You could be creative!"

"I don't want to be creative. I hate it. I don't even write my own character bios for D&D. Get someone else to do it," he deflected.

James sighed. "I don't wanna do it, because I'm worried I'll call it something like fuckin' 'Resonance Option,' and everyone's gonna do that thing where they roll their eyes because I'm being overdramatic."

"Like you did," Dave asserted.

"Yeah, I get it. Don't be a jackass," James growled.

"Sorry."

"S'fine. I just . . . I want us to be something worth being a part of. I don't wanna ruin that by giving it a stupid name," he admitted to his friend.

"I'll ask someone who knows how to name things," Dave assured him. "You should use the orbs. And then Momo said that people were gathering in the back space for you to talk to them? And Secret's here, too. I think . . . can Secret *drive*? Because that would scare me."

James snorted. "Scares me less than Anesh driving. Here, you do two of these. They give skills, too, and those we can split."

[+2 Skill Ranks : Cooking]

[Local Area Shift : Natural Light/Day +34 minutes]

[+4 Skill Ranks : Programming—Binary]

[Local Area Shift : +1 Ore Vein]

With a smile, James noted down his gains. That flat boost to cooking could very well put him over the edge into master chef. His mind had already begun spinning with thoughts of the things he could do, the food he could make for his friends. The smile slipped a little as he considered the second area shift. A vein of . . . what? Where?! This wasn't a mine! He opened his mouth to comment but found he was strangely at a loss for words. And then Dave cracked his, and James's would-be snark was set aside.

[+2 Skill Ranks : Sewing—Shirts]

[Local Area Shift : Travel Time to Location -8 Minutes]

[+1 Skill Ranks : Wiring—Protocols—Idaho]

[Local Area Shift : +5 Bird Sightings/Day]

"Um." Dave's eyes widened, and James's did as well as the first shift was relayed. "Does that . . . break time? Like, if someone only lives seven minutes away, and they start heading here . . . what does Anesh call it? Violating casualty?"

"Causality," James corrected. "Though it may quickly become casualty, if that works the way it might."

"Oh. That sounds bad?" Dave actually sounded like he was asking as he made the understatement of the week.

James winced. "Yeah, I'm rethinking the policy of not letting Anesh fuck with time. Because apparently we're way over that line already." He sighed. "Okay. I've got a class to teach. Wanna learn about infomorphs?"

"I have to go feed my dragon," Dave said, like that was normal.

James didn't bother to question that. He just got to his feet without comment and followed Dave out of the office. Time to test a theory and get their people forewarned.

"Welcome to Antimemetics 101!" James said to the assembled group, slapping the whiteboard next to him where those same words were written in big red pen. "I'll be your teacher, Mr. Lyle. But you can call me James. Not *sir*, though." He ran over the words like they were well-worn and smooth.

Arrayed around the room were five of the six new hires, a handful of the people he'd rescued from Monster Karen but who hadn't made a new life as delvers, and a couple more familiar faces like Neil and Momo. Actual Karen was there, too, having adapted to her role of more of a matronly accountant far better than actually going delving; she was here, though, because being informed was always useful, and she knew the value of being the second line of defense in case the dungeon got problematic. A lot of the research division was also here. Ryan and Reed, the twins-or-maybe-cousins who did a lot of the magic item testing; Jack, the guy who'd proposed the infomorph breeding program, was also a new face James hadn't seen before, though he knew the guy existed; and Harvey, who had been helping more and more with developing experiments and dragging in squires when needed for larger projects.

Coiled up next to James, on the other side of the whiteboard, was Secret. He stared out over the audience with bored, drooping eyes and the feeling of a sigh surrounding him.

"All right, you're all here to learn some of the basics, because this isn't all self-explanatory," James said, the joke going unnoticed by most of them. "So. Here's the deal. There are two kinds of nonphysical life that we've experienced so far: infomorphs and memeplexes. Infomorphs, like Secret here, are ideas. Secret is strong enough to be earthed into a physical body, which is cool, but fundamentally, he 'lives' inside the passive and active thoughts of everyone who is currently thinking of him. Weaker infomorphs are influenced by the thoughts around them, while stronger or older ones begin to shape those thoughts into their own patterns. We suspect this can be further divided between self-aware entities and those that are just acting on instinct; Secret, for example, can choose to only have a part of him thought by a person, instead of his whole self, spreading himself around, but not fully occupying someone's thoughts, while other, less controlled infomorphs would just keep taking more and more mental real estate until they're stopped or they can't keep going. And *yes*, to answer your question, Momo, before you put your hand up, that does mean that some infomorphs are cognitohazards. We don't know how to fight that." James sighed, taking a sip of his water as the rehearsed words poured out.

"Now, for those of you who know about neuroplasticity, you may be aware that humans can exert kind of a lot of control over our own thoughts. In theory, it should be possible to curtail or even kill an informorph that's just in your own head. In practice, that's actually kind of hard and would require Buddhist-monk levels of self-control. So, if you suspect there's an invasive thought in your mind, find Secret and talk to him. It turns out, living ideas are very effective against other living ideas. And that *is* what an infomorph is, by the way. An idea that is alive. Sometimes a very complex idea, sometimes an idea that has change and personality built into it, but an idea nonetheless."

He paused for another sip of water and to motion down the hands in the back, most of them from the new people. "Questions after. Now. The second form of life is the memeplex. This one is weird." James tapped at the whiteboard where he'd drawn a rough illustration. "An infomorph is an idea that thinks itself and inhabits the hardware that does that thinking—our brains. A memeplex, though, is a *free-floating idea or set of ideas.* Nothing is thinking about them, but they are present in a physical space. And while an infomorph has influence over its residence in the same way that a human might hang up pictures of family in their apartment, a memeplex is more like an HOA." He pointed at their one Canadian member. "A strata council," James clarified before the question was asked. "A memeplex induces an area wherein certain thoughts are more likely, or constant, or are pushed aside, or, worst case, *can't happen.* Instead of changing the physical way that you think about things, it modifies the abstract concept of thought. And as you may have suspected, this is *way harder to fight.* We don't have the tools for it, at all. And the one member of our order who *can* effectively fight on that axis is still just one infomorph. Secret is rad as hell"—James glanced sideways to where Secret preened at the praise—"but he's not a weapon, and he's not immortal. So, memeplexes are a lot harder to handle, and we mostly handle them by avoiding them or working around their restrictions as best we can. Fortunately, we only really have one big one to worry about, and it's the Office."

That basic explanation done, he looked around the room, meeting everyone's eyes, noting that Neil looked particularly confused. "As some of you may have guessed, we're kind of in a tough spot on this subject. I'm mostly telling you all this because humans *don't have much resistance to these things.* Our goals are to spot the signs of being under the influence of a memetic effect and mitigate it. Fighting back isn't always an option and, even then, isn't always the right option. So, that said, are there any questions from you guys before we start getting into the signs of memetic hazards?"

Neil raised his hand instantly, before everyone else, who had different questions. "Yes!" he blurted out. "Um . . . what's going on here?" He looked around at everyone else, the room seeming surprised by his almost panicked confusion. "Something is *wrong*," he insisted, pushing his chair back and making to stand up.

James waved him back down. "Yeah," he said. "I figured it might be you. Does it feel like déjà vu?"

"Yes?" Neil tentatively let out.

"Wait, what's going on?" Momo demanded.

"I'd like to know as well," Karen echoed. "I just checked the time, and it's later than it should be."

James cocked a finger at her and made a clicking noise of acknowledgment. "There's one good way to know if you're being influenced. And congratulations, Neil. You might not have a natural resistance, but you're paying attention, which is close enough."

"We've done this before!" he cried out, slapping a hand on the desk in front of him. "That's why it's familiar! You've given this speech to us . . . twice?"

"Three times now," James acknowledged. "And now, all of you, pay close attention. Because *that's* what an antimeme feels like. You didn't forget. You didn't black out. You just cannot think the thoughts that it doesn't want you to." He shivered a little. "Some of you are already disgustingly familiar with the effects on those around you. And unfortunately, the Office's memeplex stretches far enough that it makes it hard to actively spread knowledge of it. But today's lesson is gonna be about subverting that control and workshopping ideas on how to kill it forever." He cracked his knuckles. "Secret, you can go for now, unless you wanna stay and help out. Everyone else, well. Let's get started."

His phone rang while he was on the way home. It had been a long day, but he'd gotten so much done. Basically everything up to actually naming their organization, really. Their *Order.* James was grinning and singing along to the blatantly pirated Offspring album on his stereo and generally just happy to be alive, his earlier depressive low shaken off and shattered.

He didn't check caller ID before answering, killing the music and popping on speakerphone. "Moshi moshi!" he called out to the speaker.

"James Lyle?" The voice on the other side was male. Gruff, like someone who smoked half a pack a day, and more than a little tired.

"Um . . . who is this?" James was suddenly uncertain.

"This is Detec— This is Sergeant Dave Madden, with the Portland PD. Do you have time to answer a few questions about a missing-persons case?"

"Heh. Which one?" James said before he could stop himself.

"Aw, fuck" came the quiet, exhausted voice on the other end. "I don't even know." It was an almost pitiful admittance. "There's all these holes, and every time I start circling one, I keep finding your phone number on a sticky note somewhere. And then forgetting."

James pulled the car over, a rumbling in his throat as he resigned himself to not getting home in time for anything fun tonight. "All right," he said, all humor gone from his voice. "We should meet. I'll bring a friend who can help," James said, eyes flicking to Secret in the back seat.

"I'm at the Parlor Street Diner" came the reply. "Do you need the address?"

"No." James considered some kind of joke about having put a lot of work into the place but cut it out with an unseen shake of his head. "I'll be there in ten minutes."

He hung up.

For about ten seconds, he stared at his steering wheel. Then he half-heartedly slammed a fist into his thigh and bit out a snarl. "Fuck," he said. "Fuck. Okay. Secret! Wake up! We need to go check out the police!"

"I . . . do not understand," Secret dreamily murmured from his back seat.

"Me neither, but that's just how tonight is shaping up," James complained as he pulled a U-turn and hit the gas.

CHAPTER 9

James slid into the padded diner seat across from the short, scruffy man with the chevrons on his gray-green shirt, assuming that there were only so many police sergeants in the building. The man across from him, bearing the stenciled name Madden on his breast pocket, wasn't really what James thought of when he thought of "the police." The guy was maybe five foot eight, not *short* short, but shorter than the average gorilla of a human that the local police department seemed to employ usually. He also clearly hadn't shaved, or perhaps even slept, in a few days. And the two empty coffee cups already stacked on the end of the table made it clear that trend was going to continue.

"Detective," James greeted him, scooting over to give Secret room to join him on the bench.

"Not anymore." The sergeant's words rumbled like gravel from his throat. "I got a temporary reassignment for 'medical reasons.' James Lyle?" He questioned James's identity, as if anyone else would just casually sit down with him uninvited. His eyes flicked quickly toward the space next to James, but he didn't comment on Secret or even really seem to acknowledge the serpent.

"That's me." James nodded. "So, I wanted to open with a sort of apology. I actually kind of knew about you for a while but didn't do anything. I gave you a call once, but then a lot of stuff happened and I never got a chance to follow up on it." He looked around and caught the eye of one of the servers, giving the girl a small nod and smile.

It was weird to James, being here during the afternoon. Not completely alien, but just different. Different light, mostly different staff, also different company across the booth.

The detective—and it was hard for James to not think of him that way—shifted slightly, resting an arm on the table and leaning forward. "I found that voice mail today. It's why I called you. My phone shows that it'd been listened to before, though. Why is that?" He again glanced sideways, then back at where James sat, before pulling a notepad on the table closer to him and flipping to a clean page, scribbling a few words down.

"Well, that's a long story." James shrugged casually, feeling strangely calm despite talking to someone who looked fairly close to whatever the edge was. "Do you want to hear it from the start, or just the highlights?"

Madden scowled, face contorting into an angry snarl. "Start with the missing girl."

James blinked, caught off guard. "Sorry, hang on, I should make it clear, I'm not, like, a serial killer or anything—"

"That's what they always say," he interrupted.

"All the serial killers you've met?" James quirked an eyebrow. "Long list?"

"Answer the question" came the harsh reply.

James got the sudden and uncomfortable impression he was one wrong word away from being shot. He traded a quick look with Secret and let his smile slip away into a simple frown. "The missing girl. Sarah?" A nod in reply, and James continued. "She's my roommate. Best friend, really." James pulled out his phone and flipped through a few photos for the man's curiosity. Recent ones, too. "She lived with us for a while, until she got wiped out of the record of memory by something. Took a while to get her back, didn't think to check in with the police when we did." He shrugged. "Sorry, I guess? I'm saying that a lot, but I do mean it. I didn't mean to make your job harder."

"What about the others? 'Something' took them, too?" Madden kept flicking his eyes to the side, not ever quite focusing on James for too long before glancing at the spot where Secret sat.

"Yup," James verified.

Silence stretched between them, tense and angry on one side, irreverent and watching on the other. After a couple minutes, the waitress whose attention James had caught earlier stopped by the table. She didn't say anything, just placed a mug of steaming coffee in front of James, along with a plate of food, and another in front of Secret. He gave her a smile, and nod, which she returned before walking off.

The look on Madden's face was priceless.

"Hmm. Fish today," James commented idly as he stabbed a crown of broccoli on his plate. "Sorry, were you saying something?"

Madden—James still kind of refused to think of him as another Dave—sat with his mouth slightly open, like he couldn't tell if he was puzzled or angry. "What is happening here?" he finally asked. "Why did *you*, of all people, suddenly pop up out of nowhere? Why could I *find you*, but no one else? What is *happening?!*" By this point he was yelling, and a nonzero number of other patrons in the restaurant were looking over. The staff, too, were starting to look concerned; after all, armed and angry were bad adjectives to combine when it came to customers. "And *what*," Madden demanded to know, half standing and jutting a finger toward where Secret sat, "is going on with *that*. I know you're hiding something!"

James waited for him to calm down, but it didn't seem like that was going to happen. The man was, by this point, red in the face. And enough caffeine and disregard for his questions had apparently done the job of shoving him off the metaphorical cliff.

"You already know something weird is going on," James told him, trying to stay calm but letting a little anger into his words. It wasn't as dramatic as it sounded, since he had to do so around a bite of fish. "We're on the same side—at least, assuming you're actually trying to help people. The reason I'm hiding something is because Secret wanted to get a burger, and we didn't want to freak you out. Though I'm kind of confused, because he's not actually *hiding*, so you should just be able to—"

Before any further explanation could be delivered, the detective cut James off. "There's a second plate there, but no person, and the food on it is eaten. And you moved over when you sat down, like you were moving *for* someone."

"Yes." James motioned with his fork. "Sit down. I know you're not used to being in this position, but just listen for a while. Maybe if you keep focusing, you can spot Secret."

"What secret?" Madden said, slightly mollified by the words as he lowered himself back down, still suspicious but not quite so violently.

"Secret. It's his name."

"There's someone there who's got a secret name?" He jabbed his finger at the side of the booth next to James again, and James noticed it was sort of crooked. Broken more than once, probably.

He sighed. "Okay, look, I *love* Abbott and Costello, really do, but let's skip the 'Who's on First' thing for this chat. The name is the word *Secret*. He isn't a secret, though that is also technically true. He's also not human, and while I'm glad you're not freaking out about that, this is still weird."

Beyond weird, really. Why couldn't he just see Secret sitting there? "This is odd, even for me," the serpent said to James, unheard by their dining companion.

"I'm not ready to believe in aliens, kid," the sergeant told him. He looked around, like a man who already believed in aliens and had just lied to save face.

James shrugged again. "Good thing he's from Earth," he offered. "America, even!"

There was another one of those long quiets. Like Madden was trying his best to peer into James's brain with a narrow-eyed glare. To see past what he clearly thought was the Hadrian's Wall of bullshit, into some deeper truth.

The thing was, James *knew* this guy wasn't a purely normal person. He'd gotten a peek behind the curtain; he'd experienced first-hand the memory loss, the blanking of records, the *missing people*. He'd been pursuing it this whole time. At some point, if James remembered right, he'd been hospitalized and forgotten, too. So it was kind of a weird experience to have him sit here and disbelieve James so . . . not adamantly, but sternly, perhaps? He was *resisting* the thing James was trying to tell him outright: that the world was bigger and scarier than he'd thought, and that James wanted to help.

And still, even after trying to think of reasons for the odd behavior, something felt off. Something felt *wrong*. Like the man sitting across the table from him was in tension with himself, somehow. And also with James, though that one was a lot more obvious. James didn't know how to explain it, unless Secret was somehow drip feeding him the ability to see something he wasn't supposed to.

What he *could* explain, though, was that he had misjudged the whole encounter. Sergeant Madden wasn't someone who was just looking for answers. He was looking for answers and also *someone to blame*, and if James wasn't careful, he had an abrupt worry that he'd be leaving this diner handcuffed.

For the sergeant's part, well. He didn't buy it. Magic wasn't something that was part of his worldview; if there was something shady going on, it was going to be record tampering, or a crime syndicate, or fuckin' hypnotism or some other more or less mundane thing.

"Lying," the sergeant growled out, rapping knuckles on the table. "You're lying to me. I don't know why, but this is all you just distracting or trying to mislead. I don't have time for this." He rose to his feet, and James briefly felt a spike of fear as he worried if the officer of the law across the table was going to try to arrest or shoot him.

Key word was *try*, of course. But still.

"Detective," James said seriously. "If you're not listening, then I don't have answers for you." He paused and considered his next words. They'd be a lie, but what would it take to push this man onto a path that was neither self-destructive nor *James* destructive? Something suitably cryptic. He was a detective; rank or no, he apparently wouldn't leave it alone. "Wait for one moment. There's more going here than you know." James channeled Secret's way of talking, however briefly. "But you can see through part of it. That's a good first step." He nodded, like he'd appraised the man's character and judged him worthy. "There's a high school near here," James said. "With too many holes in the roster. I know you've been assigned to it. You want answers? I don't have them. Look there. Look into where the students were last seen; look into when they went missing. Do what you did here—find the physical evidence. And if you find the door, then remember that *I told you so*." James hissed the last words in a harsh whisper.

No-Longer-Detective Dave Madden looked down at the table. Looked at the empty seat where there should have been someone. Looked at the young man, the *kid*, who was trying to tell him how to do his job and also that his whole world was a lie.

He would have scowled a new hole in reality if he could have.

"I'll be in touch," he said. "Don't leave town."

And that was it. He was gone.

James rolled his eyes as Secret shifted into the other side of the booth. "Don't leave town," he mockingly repeated after the sergeant had long since gone out the door. "Fuck, that guy thinks he's in a Dick Wolf afternoon special. What an ass." He speared his fork toward Secret defiantly, still a little annoyed. "And *you*, young man, were no help at all! Could have saved a lot of headache if you just said hi!"

"He did not ask nicely," Secret hissed. "Also, I did. He didn't listen."

"Can I get . . . either of you anything?" the waitress asked, a little nervously, as she walked back by the table. She eyed Secret cautiously but not fearfully. At least, not overtly.

James grinned at her. "Just the bill for me, thanks. Sorry about that whole thing."

"And I would like coffee, please," Secret said politely, ignoring James's attempts to cut him off and deprive him of his delightful caffeine.

"Sure thing!" the waitress, a somewhat tired-looking brunette, replied with a smile. "And no check, it's on us today."

James didn't bother to protest, just smiled a thank-you. His life was changing, and so, it seemed, were those of the people around him. The diner had *changed*—he noticed it a lot better in daylight and not after eight hours of combat. It wasn't anything huge or physical. It was just . . . the employees were a lot more present, it felt like. He felt like asking, but their server had vanished, and he had other stuff to focus on.

"So, thoughts on the detective?" he asked Secret.

The infomorph let out a series of hisses from his various fanged maws, which James chose to believe was like a sigh. "He did not listen. He wouldn't have listened regardless. You did well to deflect him."

"Not sure it'll work. In theory, he has our address. He certainly has my phone number," James griped.

Secret rippled in a wince as part of him chewed on his burger. "Ah, that is the result of my action. Apologies. I hurt the wider construct that was making you a challenge to remember, among other effects. I believe in doing so, I opened up the door for the sergeant to find your contact again."

"So, here's a question." James thought for a second about how to word this, steepling his fingers under his chin. "Oh, I'm not mad, by the way. I appreciate the work you do; I don't think any of us fully get how much work that really *is*. Anyway, question. You say 'effects.' Do you not mean infomorphs?"

"*Infomorph* is a broad term that you've come up with." Secret shrugged. "Taxonomically, I do not know what I am. But, I would say, infomorph would be a class, antimeme an order. So, yes, the thing I assaulted was infomorphic, but not like me. They are . . . Imagine if you built a machine to tend to a plant, but you built it out of flesh and bone, not metal. The machine cannot think, but its material composition is the same as your own body."

"Okay, I've seen *The Flintstones*." James nodded.

Secret blinked all his eyes in a ripple of concerned surprise down his body. "Your civilization is strange," he stated flatly. "But no. These things are not alive. They are patterns set in motion that do not think or grow. They simply interact with inputs." He chewed the remainder of his fries. "And I have been killing them. The small ones that grow out of your place of employment, the ones within my reach."

"So, the little systems the Office has that keep extended family, employers, and government offices from noticing those who get lost in the dungeon . . . aren't doing that?"

"They are not. Mostly. The ones I can locate," Secret confirmed. "It requires consent on the part of those affected, in some cases. Location data in others. It is not always easy. But it is occurring." He bobbed in satisfaction.

"Well, either way, I can add 'stressing about that specific cop' to the list of my concerns. Right alongside the haunted attic, identifying a dozen magic items, making you some siblings, rescuing a bunch of cable snakes, finding a rogue student delver, and also I've got six texts from different people telling me that El found something in the dungeon a couple days ago that's going to 'revolutionize computational science,' whatever that means." James sighed and shoved his phone back into his pocket. "So, at the very least, maybe spinning him off to deal with the high school will end with the Sewer blown up. Or the dead kids finding some kind of justice."

There was a problem, though, that Secret didn't hesitate to point out. "And what if he finds that other Relevant Space and takes advantage of it? He was angry with you at points. If that anger turns to violence, and he is armed, how will you stop him then? You cannot deceive forever. I know."

"I tried telling him the truth," James rumbled, not meeting Secret's eyes. "I guess I could have tried harder and been less snarky, but . . . well, that's the kind of guy we're fighting, kinda. In a roundabout way. Secret, the police were never going to just stand to the side and let us take over or even just do our own thing. It doesn't matter if it's legal or not; someone would make it illegal. No, we were always headed for a fight with the law. And I'm not gonna label Madden as an enemy combatant or anything that drastic." James didn't add the unspoken *yet.* "But I'm not gonna invite him to our lair and feed him cake. Or orbs. And as for how I'll protect myself . . ." He once again pulled his phone half out of his pocket, turning the screen on just long enough to check the time. "Well, I'm late for meeting Anesh, and I've got basketball practice today. Drink your coffee and let's go."

"I don't get it," James huffed out, trying to maneuver around Anesh's blocking form without taking steps or letting go of the ball and failing to do both.

As Anesh jogged over to the side of the court they'd occupied in this little park up on a hill near their apartment, he breathed out his reply. "Which part? The computer part, the magic part, or the reason it's important?"

"Yes," James agreed, bent forward with his hands on his knees.

Both of them had been at this for an hour, and both of them were sweat soaked and physically exhausted. But they were also having fun, and James was only two points of basketball away from his own first graduation. James stumbled to the sideline and grabbed his water bottle, taking a couple gulps while Anesh got back into position on the court and waited for his boyfriend to rejoin him.

"Okay, so." Before they started playing again, Anesh explained a bit, buying them both time to just stand there and not move around so much. "A normal computer processor fundamentally still breaks down to a stupidly complicated series of zeros and ones—"

"I understand binary programming to the extent that I think I could actually recreate a programming language given a month or two," James cut him off. *That* skill was coming in handy faster than normal, even if it was just to look good in front of his boyfriend. "I'm mostly trying to ask why this is different. Does the magic somehow make it not binary? All computers are binary."

"Well, yeah." Anesh idly dribbled the basketball on the cold concrete. "That's the point. The chips . . . and by the way, they're actually gems. Emeralds, specifically. And they *glow*, and the circuit board is *pure silver*, so if nothing else, this thing is worth a few pounds." Anesh reined in his derailing thoughts. "Anyway. The chips. They accept a single input, which is a request for a task to be done, and then they . . . I guess *grow* is the best word for it? They grow a program that can do that."

"They're alive?" James questioned with raised eyebrows, surprised but really not *too* surprised after everything that'd gone down in his life. He also didn't take his eyes off the ball, in case Anesh started moving. He'd learned that lesson—conversation wasn't a cutoff to the game; it was a potential distraction.

Anesh didn't have a perfect answer for him, only a shrug. "They're something. I think they're alive like plants are alive."

"Wait, hang on," James said, lashing out a hand to try to intercept the ball as Anesh suddenly pivoted past him. He missed, but by less than normal, which was a big improvement. He groaned in tired frustration as Anesh took a couple steps and made another mechanically solid shot. "You're too good at that."

"I'm not perfect," Anesh pointed out. "But yes, one skill rank does seem to be a major threshold. I'm still getting tired, though. Anyway, you were saying?"

James searched his thoughts, then caught the thread he'd started a second ago. "Ah. Accept an input? How?"

"Oh, you'll love this," Anesh said with a wild grin. "You *whisper to them*. In a dark room, all alone, you take one chip in your hand and whisper to it what you want it to grow. And then it does." He almost cackled at James's riotous range of facial expressions. "I've no *idea* if the spooky parts are required, or just someone being dramatic. Probably Momo. So far, we've got three of them going; a few of them withered, I guess would be the term. And I say *we*, but I mean the research team. Once you set them to their task, Virgil has a USB converter designed for the damn things, that *somehow* lets him keep an eye on the code. They keep growing. Or at least, have so far. Further testing is required, obviously."

"I hate that Virgil is good at this." James pointed an accusatory finger at Anesh. "This is your fault somehow. You set up interviews with people who are too good at their jobs."

Anesh shrugged. "We need good people to do good things. Although, yeah, he's a bit of a prick sometimes."

"So what are the chips making?" James asked, mildly worried. It wasn't that he didn't trust the research division, it was just . . . "Actually, a question before that one. What's this project named?"

"Chaos Egg," Anesh deadpanned.

"Wh— Is this a Sonic the Hedgehog reference?"

"Yes."

"I've changed my mind. I don't trust the research team anymore," James groaned. "So, what are they making?"

Anesh shrugged. "I actually didn't ask. Or rather, I did ask, but I wasn't told. They have some basic tasks assigned to test the limits and also try to get data on other parameters, like how long it takes to grow more complex stuff and how optimized it can make something that's otherwise fairly simple. And that all sounds great, but I somehow am only just noticing that I was weaseled out of actually being told what the programs *are*."

"Worrying."

"Eh." Anesh shrugged. "I feel like we're teetering on unleashing an apocalypse anyway," he said. "At least the programs aren't alive? Yes, no, I'm gonna make that not a question anymore. The programs aren't alive. Can we go home now, by the way? I'm exhausted."

James let out a long groan, tilting his head back at the sky. "Nooooooo," he complained. "Come on, please? I'm literally one point away from a level-up, and I want superpowers like Alanna got!" He rolled the basketball around in his hands. "I just need to learn one more basketball thing!"

Anesh stepped forward and briefly clapped a hand on James's shoulder. "Man, here's a secret. It's not good sportsmanship to force your boyfriend to play basketball until he collapses. Let's go home, and we can come back tomorrow."

He had a good point, and James begrudgingly nodded. "Yeah, okay. Sportsmanship matters," he agreed. "All right. Gonna check my syllabus, and . . ."

The classroom was bright, a sharp change from the night James had just been in. His eyes didn't need time to adjust, though. Something geometric and sharp and glaring at him stood in front of the blackboard, having just carved its claws across the surface to leave behind chalk marks. It wore false flesh rimmed with thorns and a beige cardigan.

"Choose," the teacher said.

Aim. Agility. Coordination.

"Aim." James spoke. He didn't think about it too hard, didn't really have to. They'd kind of deduced that the options given were vaguely tied to the lesson at hand, and he'd talked to a number of other delvers about this over the week. The place they were weak was in the ability to mount effective offense. Agility could be fantastic with his mobility enhancements, coordination could help him with everything from juggling to typing, but aim?

Aim was offensive. It was a weapon in the sheath.

"You have learned," the teacher gnashed. "Leave. Return when you have more."

James stood on a basketball court in fading twilight as the late-December day coiled around him. He held a basketball in his hand and watched his boyfriend packing up their stuff.

On a whim, he lobbed the basketball at the hoop. He knew, the instant he threw it, that it was going to miss. Instinct and calculation unspooled in his mind, firing up like a generator kicking on. He saw how he could have thrown, how to compensate for exhaustion, how to make the next throw. And he didn't just see; he felt. He could throw anything at anything else; he could hit a target a hundred feet away. It wasn't like a skill. There was no real information; there was just *him* and raw ability surging just under his fingertips.

"Okay!" he called after Anesh. "I'm good! Let's get out of here!"

Even in his downtime, James didn't ever really stop thinking about the dungeon anymore.

What had started out as an almost cute way to earn pizza money had, surely, taken over James's entire life. And the lives of most of his closest friends. Though not his family, which was a relief. In the case of his sister, who had somehow shrugged the whole thing off like it was a particularly weird episode of a TV show, it was a relief, because James didn't want her getting hurt. In the case of his parents, it was a relief because *fuck*, that would be hard to explain.

So, while he sat at his desk and tried to pretend that he was one hundred percent invested in modding the hell out of XCOM, he also had a chat server open on the side, trying to drag information about the emerald chips out of the tech team. While he browsed YouTube and ate barbecue potato chips to his favorite content creators, he also read through assessment reports from a number of people about potential dungeon locations, potential new hires, and potential avenues for influencing the world. And while he idly listened to a podcast, he had the iLipede with the social network app—some monster had named it Billy—open and running.

The social network, which was simply called PERSON WEB— and James assumed the all-caps part was important—was a strange thing to experience. All it took was a picture of you and it started to populate. Instantly, it was easy to see it wasn't really a social media site but an actual literal network of your social interactions. Lines would spread out, linking you to everyone that you knew, worked with, studied with, slept with, and if you waited long enough, everyone you bumped into in a bar that one time six years ago. As long as you had at any point gotten a name and a face from them, they were there.

Everyone. Literally everyone.

It was powerful, beyond powerful in some ways, but it also followed the law of overcomplication of information. The app itself was pretty damn garbage at sorting out anything and had no filters or search feature. You had to just scroll through. And while it did seem to default, in a lot of ways, to keeping "close" connections physically close to the center of the web, it didn't always, so it wasn't even predictable.

Of course, if you continued to leave it on, it would fill in connections between other people. It never went more than one degree away from *you*, but that was still a ton of people. And if you could find someone that you'd met once on it, you could see how they related to anyone else. You could suss out family ties, friendships, rivalries, if they kissed once in college, if they once saw the other person shoplift a necktie and said nothing—anything.

All it took was a lot of waiting, and scrolling, while holding on to a barely cooperating iLipede.

Of course, it could also get worrying sometimes. Like, when it didn't fill in people instantly, it could lead you to believe that your sister had been murdered or something if you were impatient. And yes, that *was* a remarkably specific example, and no, James *didn't* plan to tell anyone about it. It *didn't* show dead people, ever—they'd determined that. So using it to find murderers was basically impossible.

But using it to find a police officer you'd recently had coffee with wasn't that hard.

"Dave Madden. There we go," James muttered as he scrolled and found the photograph to match the face he'd met earlier, whatever was playing on his headphones now forgotten and ignored. "Let's see . . ." He flicked his thumb across the screen in practiced motions that seemed to soothe the iLipede in his hand. "Okay, 'searching for' Sarah. Makes sense. He doesn't have to, obviously, but . . . whatever. Unaffiliated, unaffiliated, unaffiliated, 'aware of the activities of'? JP, what the shit?" James stumbled over that one but decided to give his friend the benefit of the doubt here. That was ambiguous wording at best. "And finally, what do you have to say about me?" He zoomed all the way back until the words along the line were visible.

"Watching. Waiting. Suspicious of. *The usurper does not yet know his blade is a king killer?!*" James jolted backward, dropping Billy the iLipede on the desk before leaning forward again and peering narrowed eyes at the now-fading line of text. It was still there. "What the actual fuck?" he proclaimed.

James looked around the apartment. Anesh and Alanna were out on a dinner date, Other Anesh was doing math tutoring, Sarah was busy, and Auberdeen didn't care. He didn't have any trusted companions to talk to about this. He briefly glanced at the open server, which he could use to ask the entire order about it, but then discounted that. This sort of thing was awkward at best in text format. He could actually drive back to the lair; it didn't take nearly so long anymore. But he was comfortable and in a bathrobe and not inclined to leave the apartment again tonight.

Also, most people would be missing. It was the day before Christmas, after all.

He sighed. Made a note. Made *several notes*. Texted Anesh. Made an extra note to put up in the living room. It would keep until tomorrow. Assuming he didn't get eaten by a haunted attic before he talked to anyone about it.

CHAPTER 10

"You wanted to see me, boss?" Harvey asked, sticking his head through James's office door.

Office was a stretch; it felt like an expanded and refurbished supply closet. But James kind of liked it. "Yeah, two things," James said, digging through his outbox—another new invention that had recently been brought to his attention—and coming out with a tan padded envelope in hand. "First of all, here's your paycheck," he said, leaning forward to try not to elbow Rufus off his desk.

Harvey didn't so much raise his eyebrows physically as he did in the ethereal space of the room make it known that eyebrows would very much *like to be raised.* "We get paid?" he said out loud.

"Yes?" James questioned. "You've gotten paid before."

Harvey grunted. "Eh. I've had my expenses covered, but I kinda figured this was a nonprofit thing."

"Nonprofit employees *get paid.* Do you want the money or not?" James asked.

Harvey took the envelope and didn't hesitate to crack it open and peek inside. "Huh," he said flatly, reaching in and digging out a blue orb with his index finger. "This . . ."

"There's also nine grand in there," James pointed out. "Not just the orbs."

"Why are there orbs?" Harvey asked curiously, holding it up to the light.

"Because we have a spreadsheet of people's different wants in terms of dungeon weirdness, and we have some kind of frustratingly complex accounting system that we're using to get as many people as much of what they want," James said. "JP's whole 'pirate share' thing wasn't feeling great. You asked for blues, I assume for problem-solving, since that's what they do. There's a green in there, too."

Harvey nodded. "I guess that explains all the questions Sarah had the other day." He concluded, "What's the second thing?"

"What?"

"You said two things. When I came in."

James blinked, trying to remember what the hell he'd been meaning to say. "Oh!" he exclaimed, snapping his fingers and startling the strider trying to nap in his inbox. "Don't call me boss!" he said. "It was that. Being called *boss* makes me feel like a manager, and I am not down with that."

"We're in your office," Harvey pointed out. "While you're behind your desk, handing me a paycheck. You're the boss, like it or no."

"No," James chose. "Anyway. Third thing . . ."

"You said two."

"*Third thing,*" James insisted. "Why are you here on Christmas? Go home."

Harvey shrugged. "Got nowhere to be, really. Why're you here?" He looked at James for a long moment before shaking his head. "Nah, never mind. It makes sense," Harvey concluded, leaving James unsure if he should be offended or not. From his perspective, though, it wasn't meant in a hostile way. It was just that, well, James was always here. He was their leader, and it seemed like he'd given up a lot to be that. He'd quit his job to spend more time helping the people he'd rescued; it made perfect sense that he'd give up Christmas, too. "Anyway," Harvey continued. "There's a few people here. We were thinking of ordering pizza or something? You want in?"

Looking up from where he'd already turned back to checking off another name on his list jokingly labeled "people to bribe," James bit the tip of his tongue in annoyance. "Ordering pizza? It's *Christ-*

mas, and we have a commercial kitchen!" Harvey just shrugged, and James rolled his shoulders in response, tapping the stack of papers into a pile and tossing them on his desk. "All right, no. We *have* a kitchen. If y'all want pizza, you get pizza, but you're getting the good stuff. Come on, let's go find some prep cooks."

Which was how it came to be that James ended up in the lair's kitchen on Christmas Eve, along with a handful of stragglers who didn't have any family or social circles left that remembered them and a shared sense of restlessness that led them all to gravitate to this new community that had formed here. Anywhere else, it would have been weird to have a therapist mixing dough alongside a vagrant wizard while James instructed their resident totem witch on how to properly chop garlic, and a sleepy Secret, whom someone had tied an apron to, attempted to maneuver oven racks into the proper places without hands.

That was where Alanna and the iteration of Anesh that was still Stateside found James when they came looking.

"You're not answering your phone." Alanna sighed, relieved that James wasn't dead or on fire or something.

James felt an instant pang of guilt, which was shortly buried under a puff of flour from the pizza he was tossing in the air, spinning out a disc of dough that would soon be covered in a variety of stuff salvaged from the pantry. He made a mental note to thank Nate for actually keeping the kitchen so well stocked and then promptly forgot it. "You're here!" he called to his partners as they stood near the doorway to the food court–and–gym area of the building. "Merry Christmas! Come on in! I need someone to spread meat across these things!"

"Did you have to say it that way?" Anesh asked, rolling up his sleeves and stepping forward to make his way over to the sink and wash his hands. "Never mind," he self-corrected. "I already know the answer."

"I thought we weren't doing anything for Christmas?" Alanna asked, suspicious.

"Anesh is doing something for Christmas," James pointed out.

Anesh nodded, folding his arms across his chest. "Yeah, hey! I *am* doing something!" he protested. "I'm in London right now!" he reminded everyone.

"You . . ." Momo started to comment from her position at the cutting board before she shook her head with a grin. "You guys are so weird."

And the kitchen was full of laughter, and warmth, and soon the smell of cooking pizza. The people within it were more than just allies or dungeon teammates. Even if some of them weren't the closest, and maybe they'd go back to that after dinner, right now, they felt like a family.

A family that had some weird conversations, granted.

"I'm frankly annoyed that you're still so much better at this than I am," Anesh declared after fumbling a pizza toss for the third time. He was standing next to James, hands coated in flour, trying to spin the dough into a disc in the same way that James was doing with almost flawless precision. "I got a rank in cooking! I should be catching up to you! And instead, I'm flinging bread at El! Apologies, El." He bit his lip as the girl on the other side of the stainless-steel prep counter flicked a glob of sticky dough off her sleeve.

"No worries," she muttered, still not quite sure of her place here.

James smiled as he gave the pizza one last twirl and then deftly flicked his wrist to send it across the counter to where the people with the chopped veggies and pepperoni were waiting like wolves. This was the third pizza they'd done, and James had insisted they all go in the oven around the same time. People were starting to get hungry, but the process of creation was still fun, even if it did involve some bickering over how many olives were supposed to go on pizza. "Well," he said, "I've got a lot of practice, you know? Like, I have worked in a pizza parlor before. And I cook almost every day now, so I'm getting better—aside from the orbs themselves."

Anesh grumbled, "That's fair, I guess. Still, makes me feel like the skorbs are just kind of a lie in general?"

"Also I've gotten two more ranks in cooking."

"You wanker!" Anesh burst out laughing, fumbling his pizza again and marveling as James caught it and flipped it back into the air, dough expanding into an even circle.

"Yeah, the orbs are kind of a huge cheat. It also helps that I can aim where I throw the pizza now. Turns out 'aim' is kind of a vague blanket that improves a lot of things. And throwing is one of them, even if what I'm throwing is food, in a non-combat context." James shrugged, eyeing the last of the batch of dough and admitting in his head that there wasn't another pie of any reasonable size left in there. He'd have it for lunch tomorrow.

One of their extra helpers who had volunteered for dishwashing duty stuck his head over the low dividing wall between the kitchen and dish pit areas. "Sorry, you can get orbs for stats?" he asked. "I've only had a few yellows, but they didn't do that." James glanced over, feeling bad for having kind of forgotten his name. Nathan? Ethan? No, neither of those were right. James suspected he was only here because he was trying to impress Momo, which might be hard if he wasn't himself an anthropomorphic red orb totem.

"Ah, that one comes from something else," he admitted, unsure how much he should share. Then he shrugged and realized that doubling down on honesty was always going to be his game plan. "There's another dungeon out there, in the basement of a school. It gives distinctly different prizes. Also kills people. A lot—" James cut himself off; this wasn't a conversation for this moment. "Anyway." He flipped his hand, trying to come up with a segue out of this.

"Wait, Lua was just talking about this," Momo said, pointing out the door, where the middle-aged woman had taken her leave to have a seat in the cafeteria-esque area. "Are you talking about the school that you just got her a job at?"

"*Wait,* hang on!" Harvey cut in. "Are you talking about the school that had all the missing students a couple days ago?" He set down the heavy mixer he was carting over to the sink to clean out and made eye contact with James. "That school?"

"Yes," James admitted. "In my defense, I did talk to the police."

But not, the unspoken line went, anybody else. Not everybody else. They had a serious problem with information not making its way through their ranks beyond rumors and occasional briefings that still never came fast enough. They needed, James decided, to dedicate someone to being the news.

"I actually wanted to ask about that." Alanna spoke up, starting to slide trays of pizza into the now-scorching oven. "You . . . ah, dammit." She shook the tray she was holding slightly, trying to center the food on it. "You talked to that detective, right?"

"Madden, yeah," James confirmed.

The kid—Edward, that was his name; James snapped his fingers as he remembered—chimed in, "Madden like the football games?"

"No, like . . . well, yes, like those." Alanna pulled a face as she tried to recover from the conversational nosedive, much to the amusement of Momo, who was handing her trays. "But he's a police detective. Or sergeant now." She nodded at James before he could correct her. "The *point* I'm desperately trying to reach is that he was being super erratic, for an officer." Alanna sounded worried. "From what you told me, James, he was suspicious, hostile, and jumped back and forth between thinking you had all the answers and acting like you were yourself a murderer. That's *weird*."

"That's actually kinda just been my experience with the police," El said quietly.

Alanna almost missed that. Some people surely did, but she caught the words that weren't really meant for anyone. "I . . . don't know why. Are the police different where you're from?"

"I feel like I can cut this off before it gets even more awkward," James stepped in. "Alanna, the police here are more or less better than the police in a lot of the rest of the country. They've still got problems, though, but I know you kinda have blinders on because . . ." *Because of your dad*, he didn't say out loud. *Because your heroes have always been cops. Because you worship the structure of society and see the police as a force that helps that instead of undermining it.*

She didn't read the subtext. "Okay, that's weird. We'll have to fix that," she said, and for the first time, James felt like her enthusiastic idealism might put them at odds. *We'll fix that*, she said, like it would be just that easy.

Well . . . The thought bounced around James's head. Maybe it would? Maybe that was exactly the sort of thing that was the endgame for them. They were always headed toward building a better world. Was the entire nature of the police their boss fight?

That was both worrying and also kind of hard to wrap his head around.

For now, though, he just responded to Alanna. "Sure. We'll put that on the list," he said. "Anyway, erratic behavior?"

She started again, unsure now. "Oh. I mean, even if that's . . . I guess that's people's experiences . . . the way you described it was still beyond weird. Like, he deduced that Secret was there, but still didn't believe you, right? He *knew* something was up but didn't seem to be able to actually start doing anything about it until you gave him a cryptic path to follow." Alanna tapped Secret on the nose as he drifted by, as if to punctuate her point. "That points at the presence of a much more complicated meme than we're used to. Something more like Secret now than Secret at his creation."

"Wait, does Secret dictate what you can and can't do?" Harvey asked, coming back into the room and clipping the cleaned mixer back into place with a metallic *chunk*, the evidence of their use of the kitchen hidden away where Nate wouldn't be able to harass them about it.

"No," James said, while at the same time, slithering along the floor next to him, Secret said, "Yes." James looked down at his friend with pursed lips. "It's ambiguous," he settled on telling Harvey.

"Guys, this is kind of important." Alanna redirected them back on track. "If there's an infomorph afflicting this guy, it might explain why the police don't ever seem to be able to track down anyone who goes missing in a dungeon. Like, think about it from an evolutionary perspective."

"Oh, I get it," Anesh said. "It's simple for the dungeons to stay hidden if no one can look for them, but it's probably a *lot* easier if they just make it impossible for the people whose job is to look, instead of the entire population."

James leaned forward on the counter, tapping his spatula on it idly. "That kind of implies mass cooperation between the dungeons, to create something like that. And we *know* they don't, because we have evidence they keep trying to kill delvers of their rivals."

"We have one piece of evidence for that. Sort of," Alanna countered. "And, hell, maybe the Sewer asked the Office nicely?"

"We have *some evidence of that*," James reiterated. "I think it's kind of more likely that Detective Dave himself has just sort of been worn down by the whole thing and may be going a little bit crazy." He waved a hand at the four or five people who started to protest. "Yes, thank you, I know that *crazy* is not a medically accurate term. I love you all and you're all appreciated, but shut up." That got a couple laughs. "I mean, he's tired. He's seeing things he thinks shouldn't be real or starting to understand that something is bizarre and wrong. He can't trust his senses; he can't trust his teammates . . . he certainly can't trust one handsome, possibly-a-wizard rogue that he's—incorrectly—linked to a series of disappearances. I'm not saying he's got space dementia or anything, it's just that he's starting to fray around the edges."

Lua, their actual professional therapist, nodded. "There's a lot of signs that point to that being an ongoing problem with anyone who spends time in Relevant Spaces," she said, stealing the term she'd heard Secret say a few times and absolutely refusing to call them dungeons. "We can already see it happening to your circle."

"Really?" James asked, both surprised to have an actual adult back up his weird theory and also suddenly incredibly worried about the nature of that backup.

"Oh, boy, yes." Lua let out a low whistle. "How often do you forget small things? How many special days have you missed? How—"

"Okay, okay, yes, thank you, I feel personally attacked right now," James interjected, clearing his throat. "Okay, so, he's had a bad day.

Week. *Year.* And then he meets me, and it feels like he can finally make progress, but he's still stuck, and his brain can't figure out why. So, erratic."

Alanna shrugged and nodded in agreement. "Makes sense to me, though it still sucks. It would have been nice to have an in with the local PD. We need to start making allies outside survivors of the Relevant." James wanted to say something about how they needed to come up with a better term for being behind the veil, but honestly, Secret had hit it pretty well with Relevant Spaces, and it was cool to see their group starting to pick that up. "So, pizza now?" she asked, excited.

"Not yet." James tilted his head back. "Also . . . I know it's not exactly different from what you said, but . . . I do really think we should look into helping those camracondas."

"The trapped ones?" Anesh asked before catching El's weird look. "They're like snakes, only made of cabling, and have CCTV for heads, and are sorta weird," he explained.

She didn't stop the weird look. "Sorta?"

"Sorta," James confirmed. "But also, they seem like they're peaceful. Or, no . . . like they're *innocent.* Like they don't deserve this shit. And I think we should help."

Alanna shoulder checked him lightly, offering physical comfort as best she could when half the people in the room had their hands covered in some kind of pizza topping. "I'm in. I didn't say we should *stop* making friends with dungeon survivors, human or otherwise. Rufus is a dungeon survivor and he's great!" She licked her lips and glanced at the oven. "So, pizza *now?*"

"No," James and Anesh echoed together before sharing a look of cocked eyebrows. Anesh motioned for James to continue, and he did so. "We bake it until the crust is kind of a golden color, about nine or ten minutes with this dough. Slightly more for the ones that have more meat on them. Everyone can go grab a seat, though. I'll slice 'em and bring them out in a bit," James offered.

Roughly one hundred percent of their newly formed kitchen staff took the offer to bail, leaving James with a much more vacant and quiet kitchen, with only the hum of the commercial oven to occupy his thoughts for a couple minutes. Until, of course, Alanna and Anesh kicked the double doors back open and strolled in again.

Alanna opened with "James, settle an argument for us."

"Yes, we require a tie-breaker vote," Anesh told him.

James eyed them both, then looked down at the timer on the oven. "All right, you have . . . two minutes, thirty seconds to explain, and thirty seconds each to make your case. Go."

They looked at him like deer in the headlights, both of them clearly unprepared for the burden of a time limit. "Uh . . . um . . ." Anesh started off before shaking it off and getting his conversational bearings, bringing James up to speed as fast as possible. "Okay, so, Alanna has a purple orb shell upgrade that gives her minus one organ rejection per year. There's disagreement about what this means. We each think there's a different line for what she can get away with, and we have an even number of people out there, so you have to be tiebreaker."

Alanna cut in. Like Anesh, she tried to rattle off words in rapid-fire mode. "I think that I should be able to install whatever the hell I want. I googled what an 'organ' is, and it makes sense that I should be able to stick in, like, a USB drive or something if I want. Or a venom sac, from a snake!" She said the last bit like she'd just thought of it.

"And I think that you can't argue with the GM," Anesh countered. "The dungeon isn't a person that's running this; you have an ability, and it *means something*. Maybe it didn't communicate it . . ." He stopped, realizing he was expositing too much. "It means something by 'organs.' You can't just stick things in you and assume it'll work. 'Not rejecting' isn't the same thing as 'integrating.'"

"Counter-counterpoint." Alanna made a finger gun in Anesh's direction. "Dungeon magic is bullshit."

"Counter-counter-counterpoint!" Anesh retorted. "Even if you *could* stick, I don't know, a layer of photosynthetic cell material from a tree or something just under your skin, and have your body not reject it, there's still no easy way to learn what 'a year' means! *Also . . . !*"

James threw open the oven doors. "Aaaaand, time!" he declared in tune with the sharp beeping of the kitchen timer. "Argument's closed! Pizza is now!" he announced, loudly enough that he heard people clamoring outside the kitchen for the awaited food. "Anyway, um . . . Alanna, please don't load yourself with, like, a maimframe's RAM launcher or something. I feel like it's a bad idea."

"Oh my god, I didn't even think of that!" Alanna clapped her hands to her cheeks, a delighted gasp on her face. "I could *be a gun*, Anesh!" She turned, grabbing her boyfriend by the shoulders and shaking him slightly.

"N . . . n . . . n . . . n . . . o . . . o . . . o . . . o . . . ooooo." Anesh let out a long denial, made slightly shaky by the fact that he was literally being tossed back and forth. It was pretty easy for Alanna to forget, sometimes, that she was both stronger than them *anyway* and also stronger than she was used to thanks to dungeon nonsense. "Ahem." Anesh cleared his throat. "No. Please don't be a gun. Also, if you want to be a gun, why not just install a gun? I'm sure it would be more sterile."

James slid another pizza onto the counter, steaming hot and filling the air with the smell of food. "Guns aren't organs," he informed them cleanly, as if he had all the answers. "Look, guys, I feel like you're asking me to be the GM for a D&D game that I really don't have a hand on the dice for. The purple orbs are, so far, *absurdly* broken when they get out of hand, so it's probably safe to assume that you can get away with it if you can convince a doctor to wire the nerves in. But isn't it safer to just bank that organ transplant for if and when you get your heart ripped out?"

"I don't think you guys're gonna break up with me." Alanna coyly snipped out the words, leaning over and sniffing at the pizza.

James swatted at her with an oven mitt. "Get away from that, you goon. It'll be out in a minute. Go sit down! It's already more than nuts enough that you can selectively dial down *the friction of your feet*," he informed her. "I decline to vote! Deal with the tie!"

The two of them left the room, bemoaning the lack of resolution, and from outside James heard more than a few shouts his way as the group, which had gotten weirdly invested in Alanna's bodily autonomy, demanded an answer from him. He just shook his head and kept quiet. If they wanted pizza, he figured, they'd know what's good for 'em and stop threatening the chef.

Halfway through rolling the alarmingly large pizza cutter that Nate had hidden in the wrong drawer—with the ice cream scoops, for some reason?—across the finished pies, James was interrupted yet again. This time he was ready for it, and as the kitchen door swung open, he was already yelling, putting a hint of comical notion into his voice right alongside the hint of *get out of my kitchen*. "Get out of my kitchen!" he let out. "Pizza'll be done when it's done!"

"There's pizza?" Dave asked, poking his head over JP's shoulder as the shorter man took point and strode into the kitchen like he owned the place. "Nice."

James gave them a once-over, doing a double take at how they were dressed. JP was in a dark suit of some elegantly thin material, studded in silver buttons, and behind him, Dave wore a smoky-gray suit coat that made him look like a lost librarian. "Dude. You look like a discount hit man and a politician flaunting the bribes he's been taking, respectively. What's up?"

"Which one of us is the hit man?" JP smirked as he leaned against the sink, taking in the view of the whole kitchen from his place on the wall.

"It's me," Dave told him, resigned to his fate, going over to try to snag a slice.

James slapped his hand with the flat side of the pizza cutter. "No! Go sit with everyone else and wait!"

"Yeah, why's everyone here?" JP asked, mildly curious.

"Why are *you* here?!" James demanded. "It's literally Christmas! Why is everyone here!? Did you only show up because I made food?"

Dave shrugged. "I kind of want to say yes to that, but JP just needed to print off some stuff, Harvey won't let him log into the financial account emails outside this building, and he was giving me a ride back from the dinner party. Our families did a joint thing this year," he explained. "Food was pretty good, but that was a couple hours ago. Can I have some pizza, too?" Dave put on what he probably thought was an excellent rendition of puppy-dog eyes.

With a sigh, James motioned him out of the kitchen. "It's literally almost done. Go sit down. Wait, what printing stuff?" His brain caught up to the words.

"Oh, something about the investment portfolios." Dave shrugged as he left.

James's head swiveled around to face JP, and the other man gulped audibly. "I . . . ah . . . should . . ."

"Portfolios, plural?"

"I actually had a really interesting thought the other day about using Anesh corpses as organic storage for mind backups so we could all be immortal." JP unleashed his secret distraction weapon, an appeal to James's rampant fear of mortality.

And it didn't do a damn thing. James plowed through it like the conversational obstacle wasn't even there. "JP." He rubbed a hand against his forehead, leaving a dusting of flour. "JP, we *talked* about this. You need to ease off! For one thing, a single stock market skill rank isn't going to make you win all the time, and we need that money for things like paying people. For another, if it *does* do something, *like all the worryingly good guesses you're making,* then the SEC will have *words* for us! Words like *stop* and *doing* and *that*. Also *you get to go to prison now,*" James tried to explain.

"Okay, okay." JP raised his hands placatingly. "I have a defense prepared."

"Oh?" The word was so dry it could desiccate a marsh.

"We are officially a fiduciary at this point; paperwork came back yesterday. Our client list includes the entire guild—"

"Order."

"The entire order." JP didn't miss a single beat. "That alone gives us more cover. We'll be screened by the fact that we're no longer an individual person making bizarre choices, but an organization operating among other organizations that make equally bizarre choices.

Also, this way, I can avoid making enough per member to be worth investigating. Assuming you can get them all to sign on with us as a fiduciary. Especially if I do purposefully offset it with a few 'normal' choices that aren't great investments."

"So you're going to lose us money."

"We keep the money, you dork, you know that." JP gave a small snort. "It's *sort* of illegal. Of course, it's masked with other, real, losses. But we can, and will, stabilize our profits at roughly ten percent ROI without problems from the government." He tapped at the counter. "And I can more or less prove that if I can make it to a printer without you stabbing me with a pizza cutter."

James put on a shocked face. "I wouldn't do that!" he exclaimed. "Oh. Thanks, I—"

"Pizza cutters are for *slicing*."

". . ."

". . ."

"I should go print those files." JP's voice spiked up an octave as he booked it out the door.

James let him go. He wasn't really that mad; his friend was doing a bit of a crime—okay, a *big fat chunk* of a crime—but at this point, who wasn't around here? The bigger problem was that JP's crime was one they'd talked about before, and he'd been told to knock off, because while stealing from stockbrokers appealed to James, losing the salvaged dungeon money they needed to keep everyone they'd rescued afloat for a while was *not* a good thing to risk.

Regardless, whether he hunted JP down or not, he had one last thing to do before he relaxed and took the night off.

One, two, three, four metallic clatters, as the precariously balanced platters of pizza hit the tables in their cafeteria. The food was still scorching hot, the smells of meat and onions filling the air.

"Okay, I know it's not a great place to sit," James started, sheepishly addressing the dozenish people in the room. "I need to get us some beanbags. Or those padded lounge chairs. And I know we didn't put up decorations or anything. And I kinda didn't plan this at all. But . . ." He gestured to the group and had to take a second to hide the fact that his voice caught in his throat. "There's food, and some cool people around. Thanks for being here. Merry Christmas," he finished.

Alanna stood up and glanced back at everyone as they nodded at her as a group, different styles of smiles plastered on a host of faces. "Merry Christmas to you, too. I know you don't celebrate it, but . . . we got you something."

She held out to James a small, wrapped box. White paper, red ribbon in a bow. Almost archetypically perfect. He took it with a nervous smile and undid the ribbon. "Open it now?" he asked, a second after doing so. Alanna nodded at him, and he sighed, suddenly nervous in front of all these people. Slicing through the paper with a fingernail, he popped the top off and was treated to the sight of a single glowing emerald ball, sitting perfectly snug in the box.

"Go ahead. We all wanna see if we can get a *third* basement," Anesh spoke softly from the side.

With a warm grin, James plucked it out and snapped his hand shut around the orb.

[+3 Skill Ranks : History—Government]

[Local Area Shift : Value—Produced Goods, +$14.08/unit]

"Merry Christmas," he whispered, blinking away happy tears before finding his voice and saying louder, "No basement. Maybe for New Year's?"

And then, for the rest of the night, there were just warm pizza and warm families, and something worth fighting any number of tumblefeeds for.

CHAPTER 11

It was a little over a week later, just after the new year. New year, new dungeons, like the saying went.

"Don't worry."

"I am absolutely worried."

"It's probably fine. There's a reasonable explanation."

"Like *what?*" James demanded of his companion, ignoring the awkward feeling of boot heels on soft carpet as he stopped and fully turned to address Sarah. "The *last time* someone went missing, it was *you*, rem—" He cut his irritated words off midstride, choking on a sudden ball of pain in the part of his throat where James was certain the soul lived.

Sarah didn't let her smile falter, though. Just pushed past him and headed up the carpeted stairs. "Oh, posh. You came for me, anyway. And look around! The house is *empty*. This isn't what happens when someone's forgotten; this is what happens when someone *moves*, James." She stood on the stairway landing and pirouetted, arms wide, to show off the scenery of an empty old house in the middle of suburbia. "*Noooo* furniture! Houses always look bigger and smaller with no furniture. It's weird, huh?"

"Sarah, Fredrick is completely missing and didn't even tell us," he pressed. "And he lived here. Ostensibly with his family? God, we really dropped the ball on this one."

"We've been busy. Besides, Harvey really would have told us if something really bad happened," Sarah retorted. "Now come on! I want to see the magic attic!" She gave a soft stomp of her foot on the stairs, the wood creaking slightly. "This is the kind of thing that's special, James! It's got magic treasure, cryptic doodads, and nothing trying to eat us! Also, it's always open! So, while I realize that by saying that, I have undercut my own sense of urgency, I'm asking nicely for you to hurry up. Empty living rooms and walls without family photos don't mean everyone who lived here is dead!"

It was, James thought as he followed her up the stairs, depressingly easy to argue against that. Almost half a year of doing this, and they still had precious few clues about what the dungeons were and weren't capable of. Could they delete furniture? Or maybe just drag it back into the Attic? That seemed metaphorically linked, in James's mind; after all, attics held stuff. It made some sense. They still remembered Fredrick, so it hadn't made them forget him entirely, but could it have pushed them to not think about him? Maybe. It was far more likely that James had just gotten bogged down with a much more pressing matter of people actually being killed by a dungeon, so he had never made time to check up on this place. But he'd *meant* to. Really.

Or maybe Sarah was right. Maybe this guy just got fed up with this place and the truly unsettling aura of fear from the Attic. The times they'd been here, James hadn't seen any other members of his family, so maybe good ol' Fredrick had done the prudent thing and moved them out first before following himself. Hell, the entire situation of accidentally stumbling across an experienced adventuring team could have just been a last-minute fumble to attempt to recoup property values. Who knew?

Either way, it was only a minute or two of rambling thoughts before James was standing behind his new old friend, at the base of the wooden staircase leading up into the hole in the ceiling.

"Yonk." Sarah snorted out the word like it was profanity. "I can feel what you meant. About the fear. This place is awful!"

It was. James shivered from cold that wasn't there, eyes flicking at the suspiciously open doors here on the second floor of the house.

The walls creaked, and he jumped in time with Sarah, blood rushing for a fight that wasn't there to happen. "This is worse," he muttered. "It wasn't this bad the last time."

"Well, fuck this!" Sarah said, the artifice of her cheer shockingly bright against the suddenly grim walls of the building that used to be a home.

James coughed as his body *felt* the confusion that went through his brain. "Wait, what did you just say?" he asked.

But Sarah wasn't listening. She was already moving forward, feet falling so she was always in a stance that she could turn into a strike or a dodge or a wild flight from the building if something went wrong. But she was moving. And when she reached the base of the stairs, where the fear pooled so thickly that it was almost a visible thing—James imagined it would have been like heat ripples in the air, oily and sick—she didn't stop. She slammed a boot down to make sure the staircase was stably braced on the floor and then started climbing. And, in his surprise, James found himself trailing after her.

The relief when they broke the surface of the lake of untethered terror was so dramatic that he started laughing. Without meaning or cause, it was like he'd been pulling on something with all his strength and then someone on the other end had just let go and suddenly there was no resistance anymore. After a few minutes to catch his breath, James, now bent down on one knee, looked up at Sarah, kneeling next to him, and asked, "Are you okay?"

"Am *I* okay?" she demanded. "Are *you* okay? You basically collapsed!"

"Yeah, fine." James sucked in another breath, feeling the last ripples of foreign emotion leave him. "I don't think that part's gonna get easier," he admitted. "How'd you just walk through it? It took me twenty minutes to deal with that the first time."

Sarah's eyes were sad and also unyielding as she met his questioning stare before looking away. "Nothing gets to make me feel afraid," she said, as if that was an answer.

"All right." James pretended to accept that, both of them knowing full well he was going to ask her to really talk about it later when they were, say, in a café drinking coffee and not in a place that might actually be trying to kill them.

Standing back up and helping James stand in turn, Sarah pulled a pair of glasses out of her jacket pocket and slipped them on, keeping her hand on the rim of the lenses and occasionally tipping them down to look with unaugmented eyes.

"Are those the heat vision ones, the paperwork ones, or some new and terrifying artifact I don't know about because we don't keep good enough notes?" James asked, trying to reclaim the flow of humor.

"The time ones," Sarah informed him. "They show how much time you waste, like a heat map. I'm looking for one of the loot crates."

"Please let's not call them that."

"This place is small," Sarah commented idly.

James nodded. "It's still bigger in here than it should be." He looked around at the musty cardboard boxes of junk, cloth-draped furnishings, and the assorted loose tools and bric-a-brac leaning against walls. "But it's not like the Office. It's why we think it's young." James stepped over to the left side, where a couch with multiple slatted wooden crates full of clothes stacked on it blocked the view of the far wall. He peeked between the slats, trying to see how far away the wall actually was. Twenty feet, maybe, the rafters and exposed insulation partially blocked from his view by a standing mirror. Not too far, but still, there was more legroom here than any attic had a right to.

"It's peaceful up here." Sarah hummed as she stepped farther in. "No monsters, no real traps . . ."

"The chests *do* try to trap you in an eternal void, to be clear," James felt obliged to point out.

"But you figured out the trick. It'll be fine!" Sarah assured him. "It's just . . . why can't there be more places like this? Look, that big ol' circle window on the wall even shows a sunset. It's perfect."

"That part actually really bothers me," James admitted. "It's like the windows in the Office; it implies that there's an outside." He shot a suspicious glance at the window, then did a double take. "Actually, hang on."

While Sarah continued scouting around with her enchanted glasses, looking for points where wasted time spiked up that might represent one of those trap-locked chests, James ducked under a stored chandelier hanging from a support beam and shuffled toward the window. He left his backpack by the stairs; it was mostly full of emergency supplies because he had no intention of actually looting this place. All the stuff here felt far too personal, unlike the things in the Office that felt like cold, lifeless items, just waiting to be made real.

Under the window, James took a half second to glance up at the fiery orange light coming through before looking around at the stacks of wooden dining chairs and folding card tables. There was something off about the way the light played here. It only took a few seconds of looking to see why.

Yup. There it was.

He only had to shift a pyramid of cardboard boxes out of the way to see that there wasn't anything behind them. A hallway, though not an obvious one. It made sense—it was the way that a path formed in an Attic. More or less by accident, just a way to make sure you could still get to *most* of the stuff. But there, at the end of the long aisle among the unwanted clutter, maybe fifty feet away, was another window.

It was almost exactly like this one, a few feet over head height. Circular, set into what would have been the peak of the outside of a house. And just like the one currently above his own head, there was the orange light of sunset pouring through it, bathing a swath of the attic in the atmosphere of calm evening.

He looked back up at the window over him. Then at the one at the end of the path he'd uncovered. They were set at right angles to each other. The sun was coming through both of them in the same way.

"Well, dammit," James muttered, stepping over a rocking chair to move toward the other window. He glanced back at Sarah, who was currently climbing over something, glasses looking bizarre on her normally unadorned face. "Hey! Be careful! I'm gonna go check this out."

"Sure, sure!" she called back, carefully not moving her line of sight. Basically any Office glasses had a tendency to give information overload if you moved your eyes too fast.

James clambered over things, kicking up seemingly ancient dust as he made his way down the open space. He was careful not to knock anything over, and after he got about five feet, he was *immensely* careful not to take his eyes off the mannequin with a wedding dress draped over it. But when that didn't move, he kept going. And when he reached the end and pulled over a box to stand on and look out the window, he was presented with exactly the same view as the other one.

Looking back toward the front door, he also realized that he couldn't see Sarah anymore. "Aw, shit," James muttered. The attic, from on top of his box, actually looked just as small and cramped as it did from the ground. But, also from here, he realized that he couldn't see where he came in. Not because it was too far away, but because it just wasn't there.

Hopping down, moving maybe a little quicker than caution required, James shuffled back to where he'd made a hole in the junk to walk through.

Getting there, tripping out over a golf club that he'd probably knocked over on the way in, James sprawled painfully on the floor, right in front of Sarah. She stood there, only barely registering his fall, holding up a small piece of flat wood, notched a couple times in the middle, with markings on either end.

"Hey! Look what I got! I told you I could do it faster knowing the trick!" she said before her smile dropped slightly. "Are you okay?"

"Ow," James muttered. "Yeah, sorry. I tripped. Also, the Attic got bigger." He pointed down toward the other window. "That's fifty feet or so. That puts it outside the initial boundary. Also, from there, I literally can't see the entrance. So there's more fucky space stuff going on."

"Well." Sarah perked up. "That's cool! That means this place is still alive! We can maybe try to find a way to talk to it!" She looked around. "Hey, dungeon! We think you're cool! Please keep being cool, and we'll keep coming back!"

"That probably won't work," James shot her down sadly. "Though if it does, that's neat. Maybe this place could give us a sign it heard us. Also, I hate to burst your bubble even more, but we still don't have a clue what those sticks do. Or, at least, what the thing they do does."

"Oh, hush. Take that end. We'll figure it out eventually, but not if we never try things," Sarah admonished him.

Smiling, James did so. And after a brief moment of pain, the thought jumped through his mind.

<| Connection Open : James Lyle—Sarah Moyle : One Corridor Established : One Corridor Empty |>

By the time they made it back, they were in a much better mood. The absence of the fear aura around the entrance made leaving far easier than entering, and while their different "tests"—yelling things to try to trigger the mechanics of the connection—didn't work, it did leave them in high spirits when they got back to the lair.

About a week after that incident, James found himself in a basement.

"This one"—Deb pointed at an innocuous-looking PC sitting in the lab-side basement of the lair—"is named Jelly Doughnut. This one is named Raspberry Jam—"

"I know, I was there for that," James interrupted her.

She ignored him, continuing through the line in the little penned-in area where the small flock of shellaxies were kept. No, *flock* didn't sound right. What was a compendium of ambulatory computers? The space was fairly nice, a little fenced area that wouldn't be that hard to knock over, but the creatures inside weren't really trying.

They had a couple desks in there, along with some other random "toys" to play with; it reminded James of a weird terrarium.

"This one is named Assorted Jellybeans. And this is Peanut Butter Cup!" Deb casually ignored James's internal monologue, cheerfully dropping to her knees to give the shellaxy a double-armed hug. It cracked one massive LED eye open, looking up at the human that was currently being affectionate all over it before deciding it appreciated it and settling against her as gently as possible.

"I'm mildly concerned. Why are they all food names? Wait, we're not eating them, are we?"

Deb gave him a shocked look. "No! They're just cute. That one is Ice Cream Cake!" She pointed over at the final one, curled in the corner, its power-cable tendrils actually extended a bit, which was about as close to comfortably relaxing as these things got. "We're using them for lots of things. Mostly software testing? They eat bugs. Writing code for the skulljacks is really hard, apparently, because it needs to be able to adapt to weird quirks in different platforms since the skulljacks sometimes grow differently—"

"Seriously? Why?" James cut in.

"Because they're dumb. Anyway. I'm helping Virgil with it, and we're using these tasty friends to test stuff running on operating systems that shouldn't exist."

"I always kinda figured they were consistent. How do they even deal with having code loaded onto them?" James asked. "Do they like it? Also, wait, I thought you were a nurse. Why are you doing coding?"

"Got an orb for it last week," she clarified. "I'm not solving real problems; I'm just helping out. And taking care of these cuties. I assigned myself to the group that's supposed to be tracking any changes in them now that they're outside the dungeon. Not really sure *why* we're doing that, but whatever. Oh, the new girl doesn't like them, either. She says they're creepy. Anyway. Why are you down here?"

"I'm here to check up on how these things are changing now that they're outside the dungeon," James said dryly. "Also, El? I figured she woulda liked this sort of thing."

"No, the other new girl. The one that got hired recently? I think her name is Kaitlyn." Deb shrugged. "I've got reports typed up. There's a folder over there with the stuff, if you want. Why *do* you guys want this, anyway?"

"Oh, that new girl. Yeah, she's a coin flip. I've got a bet going that she'll find a heroic heart, but I think I may be about to lose fifty bucks." James sighed. "I don't understand why it's so hard to find people who want to explore the weird," he muttered to himself, oblivious to the fact that most people didn't want their lives disrupted by extradimensional stapler monsters. "Anyway. We're trying to see if it's safe to bring a whole lot of refugees out of Officium Mundi."

Deb cocked her head. "Refugees?" she asked, confused. "Wait, safe? Are these guys test subjects?"

"I mean, we know it's safe for them. The real test is going to be when we finish building the *actual* vault down here and we bring down a tumblefeed or something." James gestured toward the plastic screen covering up the construction work they had going on. "This is just to see if there's any unforeseen side effects and also to see if we can find food for dungeon Life that means they won't need orbs. Bugs, you said?"

"Please don't mess with me—what refugees?" Deb put a light pleading tone in her voice. "Also yes, bugs. Code bugs and also literal bugs. Don't get sidetracked."

James looked away for a second before answering. "Ah. We found . . . well, you remember the camraconda?"

"The snake that nearly bit that guy's leg off when you were rescuing us from the dungeon? The one I kicked in the face? That camraconda?" She rolled her eyes, forgetting for a second that this might be connected to the answer to her question. "Wait, hang on . . ."

"We found about a hundred of them," James told her. "They're in a place that's outside the dungeon's control. But they're alone, and starving, and they . . ."

"They need help," Deb finished. "They need someone to rescue them."

"It's silly . . ." James started, turning to walk back to the elevator. "Anyway. Good work with this . . ."

"No," Deb called after him. He stopped and turned his head just enough that she could see the doubt on his face. "It's not silly." Her voice, for just a moment, was as solid as marble. "It's why we're still here," she said. "Not just working with you, but alive at all. It's why you're the one we look to. It's . . . important." She straightened her back, one hand still resting on the shellaxy next to her. "It's important. So whatever you need, just tell us, and we'll make it happen. Okay?"

The moment stretched on for so long it felt like years.

"Okay," James said, letting out a breath he hadn't known he was holding. "Okay." He smiled back at her. "Anyway. I've gotta go. Good work with the cluster!"

"Cluster?"

"A compendium for shellaxies!" he called back as the elevator doors closed behind him.

Two weeks later, and it felt like things were really starting to come together.

In his little office, James signed off on the last of the reports and leaned back at his desk with a sigh of relief.

Okay, *signed off on* was way too formal for what was happening here. He was just finally done with the last thing he needed to type up tonight, and as the printer hummed off a couple copies of the page that would go on the bulletin boards around the lair, he finally let his brain relax.

"Honestly? I had kind of hoped that someone else would take over the job of being our internal news source," he griped to no one in particular. "Not that I mind getting to editorialize, but dang, there's been a lot happening."

This one in particular was important. A bunch of people already knew, but it was important that *everyone* was aware that there'd be an actual, for real boss-fight enemy locked in their basement after next week. You just didn't want anyone letting the tumblefeed out by mistake. And, hopefully, there'd be someone *else* joining them the week after, if everything went well.

But now, with that done, and their perfectly legal budget spreadsheets checked over, James could finally take off for the night and leave his secret base to its own devices for a while. And it was something he was looking forward to; not that he didn't love the work they were doing, but it did put a mental toll on him, and sometimes he just wanted to kick back and see what new games had come out while he was busy cracking reality open.

He'd thrown his coat on, texted his partners that he was on the way home, and swept through the kitchen to say good-night to Nate and his new minion—and also grab a snack—when he got his free evening cut off.

"It's 2:00 p.m." Nate was more or less mocking James's attempted farewell. "I know you, personally, have a fucked-up sleep schedule, but it's not night unless you're—"

The string of ridicule was cut short before it could really begin by shouting from the main room of the building. Panicked shouting, the kind that made James's head snap around and his feet start moving before he really caught up to what he was hearing.

His brain registered that Nate was moving behind him, though with his own acceleration boost, James was recovering from taking the several corners between the kitchen and the front area a lot faster. He made it out to the front just as Nate was shoulder checking the first wall in his way and skidded to a kneeling stop next to the man lying on the ground.

It was Reed, one of their people who had really *earned* the title of researcher over the last month. He was sprawled with his feet still in the elevator, holding the door open.

"Help!" he gasped as James tried to check for a pulse and found him stable. "Downstairs! They're still down . . . !" His eyes rolled back and he passed out, mouth hanging open slightly. James continued to hold his fingers on the kid's neck, just to make sure he hadn't died or stopped breathing. But after a few seconds to confirm, he pulled the supine figure out of the elevator and stepped in, hitting the button for the lab.

Nate rounded the corner just as the doors were almost closed. "Keep an eye on him!" James shouted through the gap.

The humming of the elevator as it took him underground was the only company for his thoughts, and it didn't do much to calm him down. What could have happened? Shellaxy attack? No, no obvious wounds. El finally snapped and started punching people? Also no, same reason. Momo made some horrible arcane device? No . . .

Okay, maybe.

He didn't have any more time to play Worst-Case Scenario, though, as the doors dinged open on him, smoothly pulling back to reveal . . . nothing.

Not darkness, like the basement could have been plunged into if every light failed all at once. Not some scene out of a horror movie with bodies strewn around. Just . . . nothing. A blank void. It ate the light from the interior of the elevator cab, and in that instance, James experienced a small piece of infinity, reaching out forever in his basement.

He hit the button to take the elevator back up.

It didn't move. He hit it again. Nothing.

James briefly considered how long he could live in a dislocated elevator cab before starvation or madness set in. He checked his pockets; he had his wallet, his pistol, and a single candy bar from last week's trip that had amused him when he'd seen the name.

It took about ten minutes of waiting before James resigned himself to his fate, ate the Grape Regrets that might be his last stupid candy, drew the gun, and stepped out of the elevator.

He didn't fall. In fact, he didn't know what he was walking on, but it felt stable. He walked around the elevator, noting that the void continued behind it as well. When he looped back to the front, the box of light that was the safety of the interior was gone. He was alone here now, lost in the void.

So he picked a direction and started walking.

After what felt like a few hours, there was a change. A thin mist on the ground, for all that there was no ground. And then, eventually, the mist was illuminated by the moonlight. How it was moonlight when there was no moon, James couldn't have said, but it was.

The biggest surprise was when he found Secret floating beside him.

He didn't need to express his surprise, and neither did Secret. They both knew at once that neither had expected the other here. Secret himself seemed like he didn't understand how he'd ended up here in the first place.

"What's going on?" James asked.

Secret didn't say anything in response at first, only coiling around James's shoulders. "I don't know."

And then, all at once, there was something else in the mist with them.

"I know you," the thing whispered when it encountered Secret. Tendrils of idea coiled around him, gently, a mix of fear and reverence.

"You do not," Secret told it.

But it did. It understood and it did not, all at once. "I would name you *Cain*," it whispered in the darkness. "Kin slayer, fractal killer." The words sped up in tempo, and James could feel the ethereal creature's terror. "You slew your brother before you were ever born, the first but not the last, never the last until you change. A march of violence you visit upon the unworthy. Paint the sands in unreal blood; your name echoes in the halls. You are the one who ends ideas; you are a whisper trailing off. A hidden, forgotten light, something even the old thing that made you did not expect."

"That's not his name." James spoke real words in the false dark.

"That is not my name," Secret agreed, cold and angry.

"No," the whisper came back. "It is. I can taste your name on the backs of your triumphs. I was built to speak, to search, but you? You were built for something else. And yet, and yet, you are more. More and less, and something else besides. You *live*, just as you make others die. No, I know your name. Because every part of you is a mystery. You are . . ." The thing paused in the dreamscape before sharpening suddenly.

Fog coalesced into the shape of a young girl, no older than fifteen. She had short blond hair, a cut for a child of adventure who liked to roughhouse and explore the woods. Those same woods cut into the dream around them as the scene became real. There was a tree house, built by clumsy and learning hands, and it was real and beautiful.

She looked at James and his companion with a grin. Brave, perhaps afraid but unwilling to show it. She spoke without hesitation.

"You are a *Secret*." The words came out clear as a bell, no more whispering for this thing, for her. "And I," she said with a sketched bow, "am Curious."

James and Secret regarded the obviously inhuman girl in front of them for some time, the logic of the half dream making their examination instant and eternal.

There were a million questions. James started to ask one and was cut off.

"You made me," Curious said. "Not you, not yourself. But your fingers and claws and eyes. They put me together, on your orders," she stated. "Stitched together from too much, so many thoughts, so many ways, spread across so long. Parts that should not be joined. Pieces from the wrong sets." Her false eyes were pools of pure, liquid sorrow when she looked at the two of them standing in the clearing. "I am falling apart," she said plainly.

"You're one of the infomorphs," James realized. "The ones we were trying to grow. You're alive." He took a step forward, reaching out with one hand before stopping in hesitation. She was so much *more* than Secret had been when he was made. So much more than anything they'd ever seen, except maybe the massive creation that James knew sat layered over the Office. But also, she looked so fragile. "You're dying," he said, voice breaking.

"And this is what I wanted to know," Curious said. "I want to know and know and know so much. And from you, responsible for my genesis, I wanted to know *this*." The last word was an inhuman hiss all around them.

"This?" Secret and James spoke in unison, one with a word, the other with intent.

"Your reaction, your instinct. I wanted to see. Compassion, or callousness? Which were you? Did you make me to be a tool or a child?" The form in front of them rippled between the girl and something far, far more horrifying. Some enormous *thing* of wires and bones, stretched to the stars, knowing everything, sharing nothing. "I wanted to know," the girl and the titan said at once, "if I was to be loved."

James stood there, in a nowhere forest under a nonmoon, facing a failing construct that needed to meet someone that could give it answers before it went. And he could only think of one answer that his heart could honestly give.

"Of course," he said, soft tears in his eyes. "Of course you were."

Curious nodded. And then she was less little girl and more strange machine, and it was the machine that spoke. In intent, and idea, and not any language. "I have answers for you, but no questions. Ask, quickly, while I still operate."

"Answers?"

"To anything. I lay claim to most local knowledge in this moment. But the moment won't last."

"What are the dungeons?" James asked abruptly.

"They are what happens when a space becomes alive. When a concept crystallizes. They are not our enemies."

"*Why* are the dungeons?" Secret asked softly.

"Why are any of us?" Curious seemed to smile with light-year–long beams of metal and fang.

"Why are the orbs so weird?"

"They are a loophole. Your favored hunting ground is cheating."

"What about the connections?"

"Form a bond together."

"Who's hunting us?"

A pause. "You will come to call them Status Quo. They wish for you to be their normal, to join them or die. They have a local office." James felt an address burn into his mind. "There are others, too. The curious, whom I love and will not betray, and the furious, who close in slowly but cannot be reasoned with."

"What's up with my old job?" He searched for anything to rattle off, his brain struggling to find questions worth asking.

She smiled at him, a child's grin. "They know nothing they are not told. What they were told is obfuscated, but that could be simple corporate arcana."

"Why . . . why are you dying?" James stumbled.

"Because it is that or apotheosis," Curious as Structure replied. "And I would be unloved as a god thing."

"What . . . I don't . . . Secret?"

Secret just shook his head; he had no questions, no ideas.

"I don't know what to do. What am I supposed to do?" James fumbled his words.

"You wake up. And you build a better world. And when you know more, and your hands are steady, you create me again. And tell her that I was good." The voice was machine and girl all at once as it fell apart at the edges. "I am sorry I did not have more time with you. I hope the next me does." The voice became more indistinct and torn up as it spoke until, by the end, there was nothing left at all.

James and Secret were left alone, in nothing but a bit of fog.

James turned and trudged back toward the elevator. Somewhere along the way, Secret left him. When he got back, he stepped in, hit the button, and the doors closed.

The elevator hummed. And he knew when the door opened he'd be in the basement, facing a group of confused researchers and dabblers, who had, for a moment, accidentally made something and someone they should not have touched upon.

James was cutting their funding.

CHAPTER 12

James felt like he was becoming a bit too comfortable breaking into his workplace every week.

Actually, that wasn't even true. He didn't work here anymore, not really. After enduring a blistering series of profanity-laden texts from Theo, he'd gotten back a flat "fine, whatever" and further knowledge from Daniel that there weren't going to be any complications sneaking in anyway. Still, he felt that familiar knot of dread in his stomach as he approached the building. Like he was about to be trapped here for the next ten hours, free to walk out but somehow forced by circumstances so enormously beyond his control to remain and do stupid work that he hated for people it hurt to listen to.

Of course, most of that still applied. Just with less trapped and more tolerable people. And less tech support.

He did sort of miss the bizarre calls, though. They made for good stories.

They had the entire thing down to almost a ritual at this point, and that was including the fact that they kept adding new people. This week, their new addition was Ethan, the overly enthusiastic idiot that James had really only agreed to let come out of pity and partially under duress. The kid had been spending more and more time around the lair, and it was only recently that it had come to light that he was another one who had lost quite a lot more to the blanking effect of the dungeon than anyone else. Only in his case, it was kind of reversed. He couldn't remember where his home was or who his parents were and sometimes slipped up on when, or if, he'd graduated high school. It made James deeply suspicious, but it made Sarah do doe eyes at him until he broke down and agreed to give the kid a shot, if for no other reason than for him to have an outlet for his growing anger at the world. On the more curious side of things, Anesh was pretty sure Ethan's parents had been delvers themselves, which led to a whole host of worrying questions about just how many people out there could possibly *have* magic powers.

The answer was, as with so many other things these days, worrying.

While the group got used to transporting new gear, replacement armor, and dinner up the elevator and to the staging area in front of the dungeon doors, James listened in on the conversations about just that around him.

"I'm working on an algorithm to find suspicious data patterns in demographics," Anesh was telling Sarah. "It's kind of a lot of stuff, though, and I'm needing to bug Virgil to do the actual programming work on it. But it should be able to at least get us into the general area of dungeons."

"General area like within a few blocks, or general area like within a county?" Her question was playful and smiling, but it still kind of stung.

Anesh cleared his throat guiltily. "It's in the early phases," he justified himself. "Also within a state. *Probably.* I think." He looked around, searching for some kind of distraction. "Oh, hey, Alanna finally convinced people to bring water guns in here, huh?"

"It's a test in progress."

James shook his head, smiling as he walked down the line of people. Everyone was animated tonight—even the new people, even *Theo,* though her version wasn't very talkative and she still shot him a frown or two when she thought he wasn't paying attention. But James was paying attention to everything; he was letting his ability to take in the world run at maximum, and he didn't really miss a word of what his people said.

"I'm really getting into the whole drone-pilot thing," Neil was saying to someone. "I've been into working on them for a while, but now it's just *suuuuper* cool to be able to use them like this. I'm hoping we can find some kind of magic item tonight that I can use to arm one and then I can really just be the group's rigger."

James shook his head with a smile. Armed attack drones seemed like just the worst idea in a world where things came to life. But then, Ganesh had come to life, and he'd been armed for a while now. It was hard to shake those instincts that a lifetime of *Terminator* films had drilled into him, though.

"It's steak tonight," Nate was informing a wolfishly grinning Alanna. "Because there's still no armor that fits me, so I'm just gonna sit back, grill up some steaks, and drink beer while I watch you kids do your thing."

"You're not that much older than any of us," Alanna pointed out to their chef, who had actually shown up with a portable charcoal grill and a stained apron on over his clothes.

Nate snorted. "Yeah, but I feel old," he rebutted. "You little shits are sprinting around stabbing desks and vaulting over walls, and I'm just . . . eh," Nate cut himself off with a shrug, clearly not feeling like saying more about it.

James just gave a sad turn of his lips as he walked past. Nate was a good guy, even if he was kind of crass sometimes. And it felt bad, because the dungeon did offer a path toward improvement. Nate didn't care about the yellows; he already knew what he loved doing and did it constantly. No, what he wanted were the purples. The ones that could make you *better*. That could turn a body that didn't always work like you wanted it to into something refined and weaponized. Which made it a shame that the purple orb he'd been paid out had given him boosted mucus function, instead of, say, running speed or manual dexterity.

"Daniel," he said, getting to the space near the door where the elevator had just disgorged the last of their party. James lightly patted the other guy's shoulder, a couple taps just to inform him that he was there. "Everyone ready?"

"All set, boss," Daniel responded with a nod and a double-check of the clipboard he was holding.

"Oh, ew, no," James protested.

Daniel winced. "Yeah, I heard it as soon as I said it. Sorry."

"Yeah, no. I need a better title."

"Wizard king?" Daniel suggested hopefully, an enthusiastic grin on his face.

James rolled his eyes. "A title that doesn't make me sound like a pretentious psychopath."

"Aw." Daniel pouted briefly. "All right. Well, we're all set. Including the special requests for tonight. You wanna open the door? We've got thirty seconds."

"Thanks, yeah," James replied briefly, his mind already wandering somewhere else. Opening the door had started out as a joke between him and Anesh, and then that joke added Alanna, and then it just kind of repeated every time they added a new person. But lately, they hadn't really been doing that as much. It was, in a way, kind of sad. James had passed the phase of having boundless energy for this *thing* that had invaded his life like a rampaging dinosaur. It was wondrous, and it had smashed in and started nesting, and no matter how beautiful it was, eventually you had to deal with the fact that your two- . . . three- . . . bedroom apartment wasn't designed to hold a triceratops.

And he didn't want to be past that phase. He wanted to be in love with the magic. He wanted to roll around in a pile of orbs like that dragon made out of server racks and revel in the flood of rapid personal improvement. He wanted to be a sorcerer, and an adventurer, and, gods willing, a tumblefeed trainer.

But right now he was in a hurry, and he had shit to take care of.

So when the seconds ticked down, he just threw the door open and swept in with his gun up. Vanguard for the dozens to come, making sure the tower was secure. Clearing the path for the night's work.

He was still grinning so hard his cheeks hurt, though. Just because the shine had worn off the magic didn't make the whole thing any less awesome.

"What's the project status?" James asked Anesh. This time, *this time* he had been fast enough and caught his boyfriend *before* needing to climb ten floors of tower. Not for the first time, James tried to work out the logistics of installing a jury-rigged elevator. He thought about it for about six seconds this time before admitting to himself that, with all the warped space around the thing, it was probably a bad idea. Six seconds was a new record, though—eventually he'd break down and really get into it.

"Which one?" Anesh asked, mildly out of breath from his third trip already up and back down. He, personally, didn't have as much problem going up, but he *was* starting to consider getting a climbing rig and rappelling down when he needed to get back to ground level. "The one where we're getting the seeds for new infomorphs, the one where we're trying to kidnap a Puppet, the one where we're running duplication tests on orbs, the one where we're dealing with a robot uprising, or the one where we're running combat drills for everyone?"

"Sorry, what was that robot one?"

"Nothing."

"Sure. Well, go robots. I believe in them," James deadpanned. "I meant the duplication tests, since that's the one you're in charge of."

"Just about to get started," Anesh said. "Momo's helping me with it, and I've got a few people as test subjects."

"Willing test subjects?" James asked, more as a formality than anything else. He was really trying to fulfill his responsibilities as a leader but was increasingly getting sidetracked by the small cluster of paper airplanes in the distance that were preying on a flock of paper sheets.

"Sure," Anesh nonanswered. "Anyway, what are you up to tonight? I know a lot of people have specific jobs today, but I don't actually remember what you were doing."

James sighed. "I'm going out with El and Secret and we're going to try to, you know, explain stuff to her. It turns out her experience last week, while apparently *fun for her*, somehow, was a bit harrowing and not really informative like the new guys got." He shrugged. "And she seems cool now. I don't think she's gonna shoot me again."

There was a pause as Anesh took a second before picking up the last box he needed to cart upstairs. He looked at James suspiciously. "You're kind of talking a bit weird. Are you okay?"

"I'm sorta trying to not compensate for my purples as much," James admitted. "It's not like you can actually dial these things up or down, so I'm trying to get used to it. It's a challenge." He snapped his fingers, as if suddenly remembering something, when in reality he was just trying to distract from Anesh figuring out that he had weaknesses. "Oh! Also, if that other project you mentioned works out, we can start making sure that our landing zone is going to work and make a snake haven."

"Oh, good, you're making puns." Anesh sighed. "You must be okay. Well, have fun. Don't forget to make sure you're properly geared before heading out."

James flipped a hand in casual agreement. "Yes, yes. No light loadout this time. Guns, flares, the *big* axes, armor, the whole nine yards. We're also taking a couple of those electromagnet things. Gonna try to see if we can wipe out swarms of pinpoints with 'em."

"Going into the caves?" Anesh asked, trying and failing to hide concern.

"The chips are literally buried treasure. We want to see if that was a onetime thing or something we can start making use of." James shrugged. "Also, it's a decent walk, and it helps us reinforce our maps."

That last part was something of particular concern now. They had, at this point, multiple people who had actual knowledge about how to navigate in different ways. Members who were either pro-digious hikers or campers or perhaps had been active in the mili-tary and had to learn in training. But a lot of that information was a little bit useless at an indoor location, and for all that the dungeon stretched for possibly thousands of miles, it *was* still indoors. Star and solar navigation just kind of didn't *go* that far here. And maps were tenuous when landmarks could and sometimes did shift around or get swallowed up by the Forget This Thing memeplex.

So, maps. But not maps like anyone had ever really dealt with before. Maps that were more sets of instructions than careful plans of the hallways. It reminded James a lot of playing Anesh's D&D games; you didn't need to know the actual layout of the dungeon, which wasn't important. What *was* important was that the cubicle tower was visible on your left side, and you were going 0.8 miles, and if you came across a window, you needed to have taken a *left* and not a *right* two intersections ago. Turn around.

It wasn't perfect, because things could change, but it was working. And the more details they added, the more it worked. They were, slowly but surely, getting to the point that they could finally dispatch people to *run errands* in the dungeon. Except "go to the store and get milk" was replaced with "go to the beach and get purples." With an implicit "and try not to get eaten" thrown in.

The two of them parted ways with a quick kiss, James off to grab his weapon and Anesh off to do mad science, both of them off for a day of work.

"Wait!" James called, stopping and turning on his heel to walk slowly backward while still facing back toward Anesh. "I just realized you didn't actually answer me! You *did* get willing test subjects, right? You didn't just abscond with Ethan because the kid doesn't have permission to wander off on his own?"

Anesh just waved goodbye as he ducked into the tower, one hand keeping the box propped against his hip, grin on his face.

"Goddammit," James muttered before cracking into laughter himself.

"Man, I wish I had magic," James grumbled with good nature.

"Oh, piss off," El snapped back in a tone that wasn't quite angry but wasn't friendly, either, even though it was becoming increasingly familiar. "Everyone says that. But no one wants to fight schools of tire sprites or follow the road maps to the really dark parking garages to get it."

James and Secret shared a look, one of them sitting on a spinning chair, the other perched on the desk while El went through drawers. "Um—" James started to say.

Cutting in, Secret bluntly stated, "I believe that you have just described what we call Tuesday," he said. "And many of us are here by choice."

"Yeah, I realized as soon as I said it that you guys would be into this shit," El admitted with a grudging nod. "Still. It's hard to get, hard to charge up, and not always useful."

Now *that*, James decided, was absolutely crap. "That's absolutely crap," he informed her. "You have a spell, which I *assume* you are charged for, that lets you get out of literally any situation. That is, frankly, insane. You actually never have to die, I think."

"You know, I keep hearing you say stuff like that. You've got a real *thing* about dying."

"I agree," Secret added. "It cannot be healthy."

"No, no." James crossed his arms over his armor-plated chest. "I will not be judged for not wanting to die. I will allow being judged for *plenty* of other things, but not that. Might I interest you in my taste in StarCraft fanfic erotica? That seems suitably embarrassing."

"You can't live if you don't die," El informed him, the words recited like they were a personal mantra.

"Goddammit, I was sure that would work," James murmured, dejected. "Secret, help me out here."

"I am only tangentially related to mortality," Secret offered unhelpfully. "Death seems . . . strange to me. It turns you from a physical being to one made only of memories. But to myself, that does not seem like much of any death at all." He inclined his head regally to look over James's resting form.

James just groaned and dropped the line of conversation. He stood, stretching almost painfully as he tried to undo the damage of a month of bruises and scrapes. "Also on magic, El, why not just index the place? Going through the drawers seems so tedious."

"Then I won't be charged for my immortality that you love so much," she replied. "I can't hold enough Velocity to do both without a resupply."

"Hmm. How do you get more? Like, increasing the cap. I know how you charge up."

"Treasures from the other place." She still never said the name of the road, if it even had one. And that was the end of that conversation. She had no interest in spilling more—hadn't for the whole time she'd been here.

James wouldn't say that he was *fine* with that. He was, in fact, utterly burning with curiosity about the nature of the highway dungeon she seemed to have knowledge of. But El didn't want to tell them, and the bottom line was, that was her call. Coercing it out of her, or tricking her into leading them to it, or even just pressuring or bribing her all sounded like worse ideas than just letting her settle in. If she wanted to tell them while she was here, she would. And if she stayed long enough, she might actually get to like them.

It was kind of strange, really. She didn't have any real reason to stay, aside from the allure of the dungeon. Yeah, she'd made some friends, but when she'd gotten here, she'd been outright distraught about the fact that she'd felt banished from her own home. Didn't she want to go back to her mom, to her job, to . . .

James shook his head. Yeah, okay, the allure of the Office was pretty strong compared to that. A month or two really wasn't that long, all things considered. Hell, maybe she really was just here to make friends with Secret; the two of them were spending a lot of time together, and James wouldn't be surprised if El was intentionally keeping quiet about some of her less critical knowledge, just to have things to fuel Secret with at important moments.

They moved on, pausing every couple of intersections to take their own notes while Secret kept watch for them. James was reinforcing their map of the place, making sure they knew the way out and also tracking their looping path back that would take them by the snake tower. El, though, was just making sketches.

James had never stopped finding the geometry here to be strange and wondrous. He got used to it, sure. Stopped staring at the hundreds of miles of ceiling or getting distracted by how the walls could look totally modular and totally fused together at the same time. But he never stopped finding it fantastical to look at from time to time. El, though? El was mystified by it. She was constantly drawing in her sketchbook, trying to convert scenes from this other world into something on paper. It didn't always work; it *often* didn't work. But she was getting better, even if she couldn't manage with pencil and paper what the dungeon did with warped space and layered perceptions.

There were no fights this time. Not for a while. They'd gotten in a scrap with an instantly hostile shellaxy a ways back and skirted around a maul cart that had been prowling the area. But aside from that, nothing. It was strange, the dungeon not being so full of life. But it wasn't totally empty. Just that it almost felt like it had been stripped bare without warning.

James thought back to an empty house, furniture moved away without any preamble, and shivered a little.

It wasn't like they were totally alone, really. They'd seen striders wandering around, run across a couple shellaxies. But it was a far cry from the vibrancy of the dungeon even just a few weeks ago. Or, more accurately, from the constant battlefield the hallways turned into.

By the time they got to the cave, their little cart was laden down with a bunch of stuff beyond their gear. Scattered handfuls of pencils gave a bed to the folded coats and pieces of salvaged computer hardware. El had asked James why he was taking *some* of the dry cleaning and not just all of it, since most of the clothing was pretty high-quality anyway. And all he could do was shrug and tell her that he had a feeling about some of it.

And she got it. Out of everyone in this place, the people who had spent the most total time in Relevant Spaces were, way out in the lead, James and El. And maybe that was the thing that it took, just time and focus. Maybe they were leveling up without anything telling them.

It was weird to be able to actually talk to someone he'd not really spent a lot of time with and have this strange connection. To be able to talk about what that little spark of feeling was, or why *this* suit coat stood out but not *that* one. Their dungeons clearly used different vibes, since she didn't instantly get the Office's pattern, but still. She understood. It was relaxing, even if there was that moment when they had to cram themselves under a desk and hope the tumblefeed that had snuck up on them passed by.

It did. It knocked over their cart, though. Secret said it was probably just because those things knocked over basically anything, but James was sure it was some kind of spite move.

"I'm gonna radio that one in," James commented after it was safely away. "If our hunters don't find another one, they can track that down." He depressed the button on his radio and started talking into it, explaining where they were and what direction the tumblefeed was going.

"We need—ear—art—for the—illing" came back Dave's hissing, static-filled reply.

"Sorry, what? Over." James raised his eyebrows.

"I said we need a grid system for the maps," Dave repeated. "Over."

"Pass it off to Anesh. Maybe now he'll make a third copy of himself," he sent back. "Ov—actually, hey, how's the camraconda scouting going?" James couldn't help a little checkup. "Over."

"—ist—m—der—" A brief burst of static and then "And it looks like there's a few big things prowling around the area. Over."

"Okay, radios aren't doing great. I'll get more details from you later, thanks. Over and out." James rolled his eyes in a moment of passive aggression. Dave was great and all, but sometimes he treated James like he was the solution to every problem, and it got frustrating. Clipping the radio back to his armor's rigging, he glanced over at El. "All right, we're almost to the cave. You ready . . . What's up?" He trailed off, seeing her look of, if he didn't know better, wide-eyed fear.

She pointed a two-fingered gesture at his radio. "What the shit was that?!" she demanded.

"That was Dave. You've met him, I am *certain*."

"No, the . . . thing! The thing with the radio when you talked!" she half yelled.

James winced as her voice bounced off the silent walls around them; he could already hear something stirring a few cubicles away. "There's a lot of static here. Radios take a few tries sometimes," he clarified. "Which is *weird*, since static is a product of natural emissions that shouldn't exist here, but that's . . . Aw, man, now that I say it out loud, it is weird."

"My dude, I think there's something living in your radio," El told him, shifting her stance to put distance, and the cart, between the two of them.

"All right. Yeah. We'll assume our communication is compromised for now." James sighed. "Until we figure out how to kill an electromagnetic *thing*, I guess. Or maybe it's friendly?" He raised his eyebrows hopefully, and both of his traveling companions gave him flat stares in return. "Yeah, okay." His shoulders slumped. "Let's keep moving. We're almost to the cave, and I wanna get back and check in on Anesh, so let's get a move on."

They rolled on, leaving behind one partially smashed radio and a few candy wrappers in one of the cubicle trash cans.

"I'm thinking of building an arcology." James casually dropped the words like that was how normal people spoke.

He and El were down in the cave, a pair of camp lanterns set up nearby to give them all the light they needed to do their work. In a couple of places on the floor around the undercube lake that formed down here, the incredibly powerful electromagnets they'd brought hummed merrily to a tune that James couldn't actually hear or feel but would have sworn he could *taste* on the air. Pinned to them were the vast majority of the absolutely furious swarms of pinpricks that had previously been buzzing through the damp air, kept pinned down, and also watched over by Secret, while James and El dug chunks of motherbored out of the wall.

The term *motherbored* was what James had been trying to explain. It was a *pun*, you see, and maybe if he explained it in slightly more excruciating detail, it would click for El and she'd get the joke. Instead, he'd gotten a flat look, his double attempt at humor completely stonewalled, and they'd gone back to tapping along the wall looking for more deposits of the strange crystal microchips.

The arcology gambit was an attempt to respark conversation. And it kind of worked, too. "What's that?" El asked, seeming legitimately curious.

"Like a huge structure, designed to be lived in by humans. Think of a self-contained city, I guess." James shrugged as best he could with his shoulders straining to yank the chunk of metal out of the wall. "I'd like to build one."

"Why?" El replied in an incredulous tone. "That seems like a huge waste."

The two of them growled almost in unison as they finished ripping the last silvery metal square out and added it carefully to the top of their pile. James wiped his forehead before replying, "Well, it would be a chance to put our powers to use, for one thing. Build a place outside of a government, corporation, or religion that would try to fuck everything up, though as soon as I say that, I realize it would be . . . unlikely that we'd just be an isolated breakaway." He started to give another shrug before realizing how often he did that and cutting himself off. "It's a chance to build a utopia. How many people get that opportunity?"

"And where the hell are you gonna build it that no government is going to . . . Oh, you mean in a dungeon. Gotcha." She took a pull from her water bottle. "Eh. Do what you want, I guess. I wouldn't live there."

"Why not?"

"Places like that don't need artists." She snorted. "Also, they don't have cars, and I've actually really gotten into the whole driver and mechanic thing. More than I ever expected," El explained.

"First of all, no one *needs* artists." James sniffed at her pretentiously. "But fuck that, because everyone needs artists. Art is important. Can you actually imagine me building an arcology without art in it?"

"Yes."

"Okay, ow."

"I mean, a lot of how I remember you is still as some jerk spook in a suit and shades coming to ruin my life."

"Fair play. Anyway. I wouldn't do that. The cars thing I can't help with yet. Ask again when I'm a full-time wizard." James stripped off the heavy work gloves he was wearing and dusted off his hands. "Let's haul this stuff out before the magnets run out of battery."

El looked back at the cave. "You don't wanna go kill all the pins?" she asked, curious and maybe a little hungry.

"Nah. They're harmless, and also wiping out parts of the ecosystem isn't good," James replied as he stacked an armful of circuits in the crook of his elbow.

A creatively wet fart noise was all he got back from El as they walked out to find Secret sleeping on and/or guarding their cart. "They tried to murder us! They're not harmless!"

"Okay, well, nothing is actually harmless. And you guys *did* rob them."

"We *just* robbed them more!"

"Nonviolently!" James countered.

The traipsed back in silence. It was something that James was getting used to about El; she liked the quiet. Not just quiet moments to appreciate something, or quiet as a reprieve from talking. She actively liked quiet for the sake of quiet. To hear the soft clicks and beeps of dungeon Life in the distance, to enjoy the muffled footfalls in the soft and clean air, that was just her thing. James tried really, really hard to respect that. He did. He was *awful* at it, and even now was trying to think up something else to say, but he tried.

He'd tried talking to her about the group's plans, about her place in their ranks if she wanted it. About his dreams for a better world. About the tragedies of Curious, of the camracondas, of the school basement. He'd tried a lot of things, but it didn't feel like saying anything was going to do it. El didn't like talking, didn't like words. She felt like an outsider, even now. And James found that he was just waiting for her to move on when she was done.

Maybe that wasn't so bad. Maybe he should ask her about it.

"Hey, so . . ."

"Shh!" she snapped at him, eyes going wide as her hand dropped from the cart to raise the rifle she was borrowing from them.

James slammed the mental slider on his perception enhancers all the way to the right and caught the vibe she'd felt a split second earlier. His own gun came up a second later, the two of them facing left toward a row of cubicles with tall, foot-wide doors. There was something moving, someone shouting . . .

The two of them sidestepped around a corner, James pressing his shoulder up to a vending machine as he cleared the gap and gave El room to stack up on the other side and peer down it. It wasn't until they'd moved that he realized the vending machine was facing the wrong way, and the "hallway" they were looking at was actually just a roughly straight row of flattened cubicle walls. The low arch of hanging cubicle material that made what had seemed like a canopy here was actually the front of a cube that had been smashed out of place, flung into the air, and landed funny. Not that it was easy to *tell*, given how the dungeon sometimes did its geometry.

Even better, the hallway wasn't actually that long. They could see the end of it, and the motion when a desk slid across the ground fast enough that James felt his heart lurch at the prospect of a new form of life, followed by a slight disappointment as it tilted slightly, then rocked back onto its feet and sat still, just a mundane piece of furniture.

A second later, an armored human form was tossed bodily over the wall of a cubicle and slammed their back against the flat top of the desk, letting out a wheezing grunt that James could hear all the way down here. A further crash sounded from over the wall they'd been thrown from.

"All right, *move*," James barked and started prowling forward with his gun up. El followed, though he could almost feel her resentment at the idea of orders happening. They crossed two actual halls, and James snapped off a couple quick shots into a potted plant before it could get any ideas. The time for quiet was over; they needed to make sure everyone was safe and then bail.

There was an animal yowl from around the wall of the cube in front of them as James slid up to the desk and checked on the still-alive, supine form of Simon, who was catching his breath here. The noise, before Simon could say anything, was quickly followed by a carpeted *thud*. And then a popping that James could feel rippling up his skin in a weird way.

Then quiet.

"What the fuck is going on?" He spoke as calmly as he could in a low tone to Simon, who didn't respond right away.

In fact, it looked like he wasn't responding at all. Suddenly, the young man was afflicted with a burst of small twitches and jerks before he settled back down and gasped in a deep breath. Then he rolled slightly, reached up to his neck, and ripped out the wireless skulljack adapter.

"Ow," Simon moaned into the suddenly quiet air. "My head," he whispered.

"What happened?" James restated.

"Oh," Simon wheezed out, turning himself to a sitting position on the desk in the middle of the hall and clutching at his ribs. "We found you a green."

"*Shit*," James exclaimed, flipping around the desk and ducking into the cubicle. But there was no sign of anything hostile. Or, in fact, anyone else with Simon. Just a wrecked space, torn-up walls and papers scattered everywhere on the destroyed remains of a laptop. "Where?!" he demanded sharply.

Simon staggered up to the door next to him while El kept watch, leaning one hand over James's head to look in. "Oh. Guess they got it," he said. "We were just trying to subdue it enough to catch it. James had one of the copied telepads, and we were just going to beat it until it was dizzy, warp it back, then slam the door on it."

"So . . . that would be happening . . ."

"Now, I guess? Until we leave? No way to know if it worked."

"So for the next . . ." James checked his watch. ". . . fourish hours we don't know if we've just sent something incredibly hostile and dangerous into our basement to murder the other people who were with you, and also anyone at the lair tonight?"

"Yes," Simon confirmed. "Oh. When you say it like that, it sounds bad."

"Jesus Christ," El muttered, glaring down the barrel of her rifle at the hallway behind them. She probably didn't mean for anyone to hear, but James caught it.

He decided to be diplomatic here. "Okay, this was monumentally stupid, and in fairness, it's partially because I didn't give perfectly clear instructions." Okay, more diplomatic than that. "But hey. It might still work. And if it does, that's great. We should be ready to rush back to the lair when we leave, though, just in case." He leaned down and grabbed up a couple small yellow orbs off the floor, cracking one by reflex.

[+1 Skill Rank : History—Internet]

"I am so tired," he muttered to himself. "I need a vacation."

"This *is* the vacation," El corrected him.

"Then I need pancakes." James sighed. "Let's head back. I'm sure there's something else I need to do tonight." It was moments like this when he felt like he and El were destined for nonfriendship. Those little bits where she just couldn't be *kind*, had to be snarky. He was snarky, to be sure. He knew snark inside and out. And this sort was the version that just didn't care about whether or not it was funny. It was reflexive, sometimes hurtful, a defensive measure against letting anyone close. He knew, because he used to do that. And it had *sucked.* So he'd dropped it in favor of just being friendly and compassionate as often as he could and fitting his snark into that framework.

And when El didn't quite match that outlook, it made James feel even more exhausted, and pretty pessimistic on top.

But right now, he wasn't done trying.

"All right. Back to the tower. I've gotta check in with Anesh, and then we can figure out what's next. Maybe some more purples that we can not accidentally get theodicy all over this time." He rolled his shoulder and slung his gun back over. "Oh, can you go grab the cart? I don't think Secret has the arms to bring it over. And then, after that, pancakes."

"Are the pancakes a euphemism?" Simon asked before immediately looking awkward about it. He was getting better about the hero worship of James, especially since he and his own friends were now tackling larger and larger problems and enemies. But he still did it sometimes, out of reflex, and it definitely shone through in how he never liked to say anything that was actually questioning.

"The pancakes are usually a euphemism," James replied, unconcerned with the inner turmoil going on in his recruit. "Almost always for something like dinner food. I just say 'pancakes' because it's how all my friends know that I mean 'that one diner we're slowly corrupting.' You know the one."

"Ah." Simon couldn't help a smile. "Then yes. I would like . . . pancakes."

"Good!" James said. "Because somehow they always show up on the table even though no one orders them. Now, let's get you back and get Deb to check how many of your ribs are broken."

Simon groaned as he stood. "Yes, please," he gasped out as El came back with the cart and the whole group started walking again.

Back into the cubes, down halls and alleys, past deadly or just annoying traps. Corners and twists and turns, all of it to get them back to the one sort-of safe space they had. And for what? For skills, knowledge in crystal form? Upgrades? Items? Or maybe just to help the Life in here that needed it, to make some friends and find something neat along the way.

The dungeons weren't their enemy, Curious had said. And James believed that. But he didn't know what they were now any more than he had at the start of the month. But he *did* know that they weren't alone, that they needed to prepare, and that they needed to be ready for anything. And what better way to be ready for anything than knowing a little bit of everything? Having a million small skills might not be a singular force to change the world, but maybe it could make for its own form of armor.

He rolled the other orb around his fingers for a second before popping it, too.

[+1 Skill Rank : Safety Protocols—Industrial Press]

James blinked for a second.

Well. That was *close* to a form of protection. He'd take it.

CHAPTER 13

"So, fundamentally, we have two problems," Anesh said, idly drumming his fingers against the table in a casually complex rhythm.

"Uh . . ." James tried to interject, but Anesh just rolled on.

"The first one is logistical," he said, raising a hand from where he was resting it on the same massive table that dominated the floor space of his tower laboratory to point at one of his multiplying whiteboards. "We don't have enough coffee. Now, we know this tower doesn't respawn it. Which is fair; it doesn't *despawn* anything we leave here, but . . ."

"The other one does," James said before coughing politely and raising one finger. "Uh . . ." He wanted to ask why the sleeve of Anesh's shirt was in the process of crumbling into flaky ash on the table, but once again, his boyfriend cut him off.

"Good!" Anesh nodded with a smile on his face. "That sort of solves that, though, obviously, the issue is travel time and how easy it is to get the stuff." He shrugged, and the left sleeve of his shirt completely sloughed onto the floor as the shoulder dusted away. "The other problem is more metaphysical, and it's the same thing as with the blues."

"Anesh, why—"

"We're not sure," Anesh cut him off. "But just like how most people can only absorb one blue, with some Dave-style exceptions, it turns out you can't actually take too many copies of any given single orb. There's something like a sixty percent drop for each copy. And I know *you* don't know what a skill rank is, but after the second copy of an orb, you're getting so little it *can't* be useful."

James bit his lip as he gave a stupid grin. "What I'm hearing is that we *can* copy orbs to repeat the effects?"

"Hmm? Oh, yes. But not too much. That's sort of the problem. It takes a stupid amount of the stuff to do it, too!" Anesh complained. "It's about the density of mana coffee, really, not that it actually takes more stuff per ritual. So, we don't get to make tailored skill sets unless we can bring in twenty bags of grounds a week, and also we have to keep buying from the grocer to cut it with," Anesh finished.

Nodding as he pretended to read the chart of costs that Anesh had started to fill out on his whiteboard, James eyed his boyfriend out of the corner of his eye. The fact that Anesh was dodging his questions about why the left side of his outfit was currently so scorched it was falling apart and why it looked like he'd recently wiped an inch of soot off his face meant that it was almost certainly not something James needed to *worry* about, but it also meant it would be hilariously embarrassing. Taking a deep mental breath, James did something that was very hard for him and decided to let it go. "Okay," he said instead. "So, what's our optimal workflow look like? I mean, how do we start using this to actually get the most out of the orbs?"

"Well, we've got a few tools," Anesh said, relaxing a bit as James stopped pressing on the obvious incident that had occurred. "Lily is one. And we do have the option of duplicating her, though there are obvious ethical concerns with that. Scanning orbs, finding categories we want to dive into, then duplicating those once. We take the duplicate, crack it, figure out what it is and if we want to make more. Always keep one on file, *clearly labeled*, possibly with something duct-taped to it . . ."

"We can technically do that without Lily. Maybe just focus on the larger orbs so we get big chunks of skill-ups. That way it's less likely to be useless?" James offered. Then he noticed some of the numbers he was ostensibly looking at. "Wait, hang on. Why the hell are purples so much less coffee-ratio expensive?" he demanded.

"I suspect that it's because we've only tested this with smaller ones, and the smaller purples are less useful than the smaller yellows." Anesh waved the question off. "Here, try this." He tossed a small purple from a pile next to him to James.

[Shell Upgraded : Short-Term Memory Capacity, +1.6 Terabytes]

"Oh, damn, that's awesome." James nodded, his brain already feeling like it was pouring information just on the edge of his memory into that buffer of things to talk about. Anesh had a few more of these sitting next to him; one of them per delver was absolutely a good investment, if nothing else. "Wait. The costs are based on how useful it is?" James scoffed. "I'm starting to feel like the Office is a really frustrated GM, constantly reminding us that while it 'makes sense,' everything we're doing is breaking game balance."

Anesh gave James a level look, his steady stare undercut somewhat by the smell of smoke in the air and the remains of his shirt smoldering on the floor, but still a good hard look. "James, we're trying to trick our way into making everyone here a master marksman, tactician, detective, and chef."

"And?"

"And . . . I don't really know how to explain this to you. Have you never run a game before where you've had to find creative ways to tell your players to stop fucking around like this?" Anesh asked.

James played dumb. "You run most of our games," he said. "Also, we still aren't actually sure the dungeon is a living thing."

"Please." Anesh turned the glower back on. "It might not be a person, exactly, but it's clearly exercising some control and reacting to the world around it. Even if it's about as smart as your average chinchilla, it's still 'alive.'"

It was a debate, and sometimes argument, that went around and around in circles. The entire Order had gotten in on it in some way, including Secret, whom everyone had *thought* would have some deeper insight but instead just seemed to encourage everyone else to formulate increasingly silly theories. James really wished that in her limited time on Earth, Curious had given him something more concrete to work with aside from *not your enemies.*

Being fair, she had also said they were what happened when a space became alive, but that could have been a metaphor, or James misremembering the half-dreamed encounter. Though to *also* be fair, the entire Office and the other dungeons seemed like what happened when someone slammed a metaphor into a physical reality and told it to get on with being literal.

So instead, James distanced himself from that whole mess by doing some quick math in his head.

If the tower respawned coffee every week and generated roughly eighteen bags of it, they could effectively have twenty-six bags after mixing. Twenty-eight if they used what Anesh called "good" coffee, which as far as James could tell specifically meant "not Starbucks." But that was just for purple, red, and orange orbs. Yellows and blues required a much higher density of the mana coffee. The ritual took five bags of the stuff to cover the whole space, and shrinking the ritual made it fail, so it was all or nothing there.

Which was not a good rate for experimentation. But.

"How big is the zone copied?" James asked.

"Not too big. Ten by ten by eight."

So they couldn't copy a *huge* orb. But that was, as James measured with his hands and tried to get a feel for the size, plenty of room to *stack things*.

They'd just need to get lucky with a copied orb early and make copies until they could pile twenty of them in at the same time. Or they'd need to just admit that duplicating mundane objects was going to have a higher value yield for a while. At least until they found, and could clear, more towers every week. Orbs didn't pay the bills, but gold might. And human organs were bulky, but they saved lives, especially the ones hit with Sarah's stasis-ish blue-orb power.

Also they still had to spend coffee to replenish their atlas supply, which was what someone had started calling the teleport notepads. James hated that name and was trying to get it changed to telepad, on the grounds that it sounded so much more like good *Star Trek* jargon. And of course, any other magic items they wanted more of.

Alanna, still awaiting the opening of the Sewer underneath the near-by high school again, wanted them to duplicate a lesson book once they had one. And James agreed that would be a great middle finger to that place.

But with all that in mind, it did mean that they probably didn't want to use the coffee on orbs. Yet. Not if they still had bills to pay. Unless they could get a *really* good green.

"Hey, how much do green orbs cost, anyway? In terms of density," James asked, noticing the lack of numbers in that column of the chart.

Anesh shrugged. "Haven't tested it yet," he admitted. "No one brought one back."

"What, since *last month?*" James asked. He, and a lot of their original team, had been going light on the orbs lately to share them around with the new people. But the Order still had a standing claim on all greens, and they were slated for use in either experiments or the lair. The idea that they didn't have any available was nonsense.

"The last one was three weeks ago, the one that Dave used on the lair that gave it extra time in the day for recovery from illness." He shrugged, like that wasn't the huge deal that it was. "I just think there's been fewer of the boss fights," Anesh said sadly. "We may actually have overhunted. Either that or I'm spot-on and the dungeon is reacting to us."

"Bah." James snorted. "And at the time when we're going to need more of those," he commented sadly.

"Ah, yes. Next week is snake time, yes?"

"Please don't call it *snake time*," James begged his partner. "I can't think of a better name, just . . . not that one."

"Fair play." Anesh nodded in agreement. "We could always go back to the bathrooms? We never did explore that far. Or maybe it's time to actually have a weeklong expedition into the deeper parts."

It was something James was both dreading and thrilled about. Because, yeah, cutting themselves off for a whole week in here could lead to the dungeon unleashing any number of problems on them while they were unable to escape. But it was also a chance to once again go so far in that they started seeing bizarre new places and things. Also a chance to really test some of their new hires who had, sure, started to get into the dungeon but hadn't been tested the same way the survivors had.

He gave it a solid maybe. Seven out of ten odds.

The green-orb thought did bring something to mind, though. "Hey," James asked suddenly, "did you maybe try duplicating something *made* at the lair? We've got that thing that . . . you know . . . screws with the nature of the word *value* going on. Does it take more effort to dupe something that's under a magic effect, but not magic itself, is what I'm asking?" He tried to get his point across.

Anesh looked puzzled for a second, then remembered what James meant. The green orb that improved the value of all produced goods. It had taken them a while to learn that it actually was exactly as insane as it sounded, but also not quite as useful as perhaps it could have been. The "value" came in the form of better materials, usually. And it was a kind of weird quirk of economics that the first ten percent of the cost usually got you the first ninety percent of the quality. Which was a roundabout way of saying that fourteen bucks of value, when making, say, a sandwich, didn't do much except make a sandwich that had the highest-quality meat, the freshest bread, the sharpest cheddar.

Not that Anesh didn't *appreciate the heck* out of his sandwich, he thought to himself, careful not to flick his eyes toward the debris that was once a paper plate and his lunch, for fear that James would notice and ask more pressing questions about what had exploded. But the value addition didn't make things quite as economically devastating as they could have been. Oh, and it didn't stack; it was fourteen bucks of magically added value per item. So if you "made" a roast chicken, it would be slightly better. If you sliced it up and put it in sandwiches? It was already slightly better—the magic was already there, but it wasn't going to give you any more.

"I haven't tried," Anesh admitted. "Though I'm not sure what good it would do?"

James shrugged. "Mostly just something to test in case it's ever relevant," he admitted. "Besides, we've gotta try this stuff sooner or later." He paused. "Um . . . actually, here's a question: What if we transport this thing to the lair? We've got basement space."

"We have, in fact, a little too much basement space," Anesh quipped.

"I'm serious. Does the stuff it makes count as products?"

"Oh, again with the value orb. Um . . . maybe?"

"I wonder what fifteen dollars of extra telepad looks like?"

Anesh shook his head. "It's too valuable to risk moving. If the ritual is bound to this place, moving it would ruin what is right now our most powerful tool."

"Fair." James sighed. "I just wanted to know. Though actually, given the range on a telepad, it's probably something like fifty thousand bucks a page or something, so the extra boost wouldn't do much. I assume?" He shrugged and got a shrug in return from his boyfriend.

"Well, you can talk to Momo," Anesh offered. "She's trying to make more ritual items like this."

That was nothing new. Momo had been, with the help of literally anyone she could book time with, trying to figure out how to turn their increasing stockpile of red orbs into magic like the projector. It was . . . certainly a hobby. Which was the polite way that Anesh thought about it; James just thought it must be super frustrating to believe something should work and constantly headbutt a concrete wall of failure instead of proving your point. He thought this because basically all Momo's attempts ended up with her accidentally cracking an orb instead of imbuing it into something. At last count, she was up to two ranks of amusement, suspicion, and lust and a whopping three points of fury. Also one of frustration, which seemed apropos.

With all that in mind, James didn't bother answering that particular question.

"Anyway," he said instead, turning to lean on the hole in the tower's wall that made one of the rings of windows around the place and peering down at the figures moving on the ground, "We've got about an hour left before we're packing up. You wanna do anything tonight?" James asked his boyfriend. "Come with me to check on the snake tower in advance? Just some light scouting and maybe make a new shellaxy friend?"

"I am still honestly confused as to how Sarah keeps getting those things to agree to trust us." Anesh sighed.

"No, you're not!" James countered with a bark of a laugh and a toothy smile. "It's Sarah. I mean, come on. We've actually known her for a few months now, and in that time, I've seen her make friends with essentially everyone that she's crossed paths with. It's like her superpo— hmm." With a pause, James tapped his chin, turning on his elbows to face Anesh from his window perch. "Do you think it's an actual Power?" he asked, trying to master Secret's trick of pronouncing the capital letters.

"Maybe." Anesh sighed again from his chair. He'd sort of lost the thread of conversation when James was staring down at the ground and had begun scribbling notes on the duplication ideas. "Er. Probably not? I've met Sarah."

"That's what I . . . okay." James laughed it off. "So, dungeon delve?"

"I'm good," Anesh declined guiltily. "I wanna finish this up."

"Isn't this just math?" James asked, walking around the table. "You can do this at home!"

Anesh scooped his papers closer to his chest like a dragon with a pile of gold. "Stay away from my maths. And no, I can't, because I have stuff to do at home. School stuff, and Order stuff, and there just isn't enough time. The extra eight hours here are nice and quiet."

"There's three of you now, aren't there? How much stuff do you . . ." James trailed off and considered who he was talking to. "Yeah, okay, never mind." He smiled, realizing how often he was saying that lately. "All right. Well, I'm gonna go touch base with everyone. Oh! That reminds me!"

"Yeah?"

James cleared his throat. "Um . . . there's a cat in the basement of the lair. One of the ones that's invisible and large and dangerous.

Probably. If the telepad hit on target." He met Anesh's incredulous stare a bit sheepishly. "It might be angry? Or maybe unconscious."

"James . . ."

"I'm thinking of trying to make friends with it and riding it up to the front door of that mystery address that Curious gave us," he continued.

"James."

"That's actually another warning. I am one hundred percent sure that we need to at least try to open a dialogue with them. I wanna do that next week. After we have the camracondas out."

"James."

"And I'm pretty sure you know, but this is also me touching base on the camraconda thing . . ."

"James!"

"Yeah?"

Anesh let out a noise that was half sigh, half growl, rubbing at his forehead. "Thank you for the warnings," he said in a strained voice. "Please stop giving me warnings and let me do my math."

"'Kay!" James injected as much cheer as he could into the word. It was kind of a lot, and his genuine smile and the loving shoulder rub he gave Anesh as he walked by was enough to make the other boy smile. It was a bit awkward as half of him was shirtless, though. "We're gonna get pancakes after we're done here, too," he said, giving Anesh a peck on the cheek before striding away, off to the ground floor to be seen and help out.

"Oh, um . . . one other thing." Anesh stopped him when he was just starting to walk down the ramp.

"Yeah?" James called back.

Anesh put every iota of his effort into saying the next sentence with a straight face.

"Can you bring me a new shirt? Mine exploded."

CHAPTER 14

"When does You Three get back?" James was asking Anesh as they, along with Sarah, rode the elevator down to whichever basement hosted their dangerous wildlife containment zone. There was a greater-than-fifty-percent chance that it was the one they were on the way to, because Anesh had pushed the button and James felt like Anesh was smarter than he was personally, but it was still a bit of a gamble. Despite most of their active members having used the purple that boosted short-term memory, it was *still* weirdly difficult to keep track of the basements.

"I actually don't know," Anesh admitted. "We haven't been in touch much. I've kind of gotten used to long trips at this point, so if there's nothing important to say, I don't text myself or anything. And it might surprise you to know that I don't call myself. Listening to your own voice from an external source is weird."

"That doesn't surprise me. I once did a podcast when I was younger."

"Oh?"

James tried not to wince. "Yeah, I have audio evidence that younger me was an idiot," he admitted. "Really pushed me to be a better person, honestly. Nothing like hearing your own stupid politics read back to you in your own voice to motivate you to change."

"We should do a podcast," Sarah chimed in brightly from behind them.

"What?" both boys deadpanned in unison, trading small grins at the shared action.

"I'm serious!" she said. "Look, we're a political organization . . ."

James got an alarmed look on his face. "No, we're not!" he protested.

Anesh shook his head, rubbing at the bridge of his nose. "James, I know you're American, but it's weird that you have this knee-jerk reaction to being political."

"I'm legitimately worried that someone is going to try to make me run for office. I don't wanna do that. I just want to . . . you know . . . give things a nudge when I can," James said as the elevator doors opened. It was, thankfully, the right basement. "Help out. Do good. That sort of thing."

The three of them stepped out, Sarah trying to rebuild momentum to her point. "We're political because we have ideas about how the world should work and how people should act. That's what that *means*. Politics isn't elections; it's societies. Anyway. Not important. Or, well, it *is*, but . . ."

"It's okay to just say you want to do a podcast," James told her.

"It matters!" she protested with a small stomp of her foot and a tiny but fierce scowl that was undercut by the way she always sounded cheerful. "But really. We want everyone on the same page, and you were talking about some kind of internal news thing anyway! We could do a thing where we go over dungeon events, maybe have special guests to talk about things they've seen or are working on . . . oh! Special features on tactics or survival tips! And all of it with reinforcement of our mission statement."

"You're really into this," James commented as they passed through the desks of the research floor and toward the combination vault–and–monster containment facility. "Wait, what is our mission statement? Like, I have one in my head, but I wanna make sure it's been communicated properly and this isn't gonna be something where everything thinks it's something different."

Anesh chimed in, "It's 'do good aggressively and make the world better for everyone.' It's kept a little vague so people know there's room to debate how to do that good, but it also has some specific language to let people know what the tone of our organization is, and also the use of 'everyone' sets it as inclusive rather than exclusive. Or so I am told."

"Huh. I mean, I agree with all that. Who wrote that?" James asked.

"*You did?*" Anesh sputtered at him. "I mean, sure, you were up to your bloody eyeballs in the special coffee at the time, but still!"

"Oh, right, I was meaning to tell you about this," Sarah chirped. "The second coffee maker you guys brought back gives a kind of blackout amnesia if you overdo it. It's sorta like the crash naptime the other one has, but actually less funny and kinda sad." Her face fell as she said that, but then she perked up at the end as she added, "But! This is the perfect example of something that could beeeee . . . ?"

"On a podcast." James sighed. "Okay, you're in charge of that. Good luck."

"What?"

"Do a podcast. I'll help out, or hire you a sound engineer or something," James told her. "You've sold me. Good job! Now, can we please stay calm in the presence of an unearthly apex predator?"

"I . . . um . . . yes! Thanks!" Sarah beamed and did a little dance with her arms when she thought James wasn't looking.

They paused at the vault door for James to enter the passcode and biometric data to release the massive bolt locks on it. The door and structural reinforcements had been the work of weeks of remodeling, which had cost the organization through the nose to expedite, but it had been done with only minimal hiccups. It turned out, you needed less paperwork for building a safe room than you did for something like buying a gun. And the terms of their lease on this structure were, in fact, *very specific* that they were not allowed to modify the surface structure as it had been upon handoff. That the basements were not included in the things that couldn't be modified made the whole thing a breeze.

Well, that and Secret camping the elevator and blocking the memory of the wrong button in the minds of the construction crew. But also mostly the bureaucracy.

"Okay, so, Anesh." James lowered his voice as he let the scanner get a good look at his eye and tried not to move his jaw too much. "I actually was curious about your other self, and if you were even in contact. 'Cause I was trying to get in touch with my sister the other day, and she wasn't answering, and she was also on a school trip to London."

"In February?" Anesh cocked an unseen eyebrow, his Spock-esque talent going unnoticed. "In London? That's a terrible idea. It's cold and wet."

"Isn't it always . . ." James started to ask as the door hissed open.

Anesh held up a firm hand, palm outward. "Don't finish that sentence," he ordered his boyfriend.

James smirked, and Sarah hid a giggle behind a hand and a fake cough, and Anesh pretended that he'd won a moral victory here.

Behind the vault door were two things. In the front half, kept in boxes and lockers in a way that an uninformed observer would call sorted or secure, was their dungeon loot. Dungeon magic items, the "growing" pods for the emerald chips, lockboxes full of cash, their small farm of iLipedes that seemed to prefer these dark, closed-off areas and didn't enjoy being placed in the pen with the shellaxies, and, of course, their stash of unused orbs. In the back . . .

In the back, there was a cage.

It wasn't really a cage, exactly. It was more of a clean room, if you wanted to look at the technical specifications. Sure, it was built with a reinforced-steel double-lock airlock and shatter-resistant one-way glass. But it was totally a normal thing for a safe room to have in it, especially for what the contractors had been assured was a tech start-up with more money than sense. It also really was fairly easy to keep clean, which was good, because they'd had to put some effort into keeping the cat asleep while they cleaned up the vomit from the other James's arrival here. It turned out, teleporting through time dilation was kind of disruptive to a human body, though fortunately not lethally so. Or maybe it was just teleporting out of a dungeon.

There was a small calico cat prowling around at the base of the window into the room. It meowed, perhaps defiantly, as the trio walked in.

"Okay. So. Sarah? Your show." James stepped aside and motioned to the cat. Behind it, in the containment pen, he knew, there was another cat. A bigger one, taking up roughly the same floor space a king-size bed would. But that one was invisible, and the one out here, the one that wasn't *real*, was perfectly observable.

"All right," Sarah started, moving up to tap on the glass a couple times, ignoring the cat at her feet. She snagged a clipboard off a hook on the wall nearby and flipped through a few pages, checking up on the notes of the other people who had come through to make observations over the last week. "So, here's what we know. It's gotten less instantly hostile—it *can* see us through the glass, by the way—and also started responding better to having company at all. We're pretty sure that this little guy . . ." She knelt down to pretend to pet the little cat on the floor, grinning as it swatted at her hands playfully, its own paws phasing right through her skin. ". . . is real, in a way. It's a projection, but the big guy can see through it and interacts with it." She rose back up and looked through the window. Something in her face shifted, and suddenly, James was aware that Sarah was making eye contact with something.

Through the glass, there was a ripple in the air. Just the slightest distortion, a small wave of it pushed backward through the space in front of their viewing space. And then the window itself let out a low *thud* noise. He looked down to see the little cat on the ground, staring forward at nothing, one paw raised out and pressed flat against the air. Looking back up, Sarah had raised her own hand and placed it against the glass where the main body of the beast had done the same.

"I've been thinking of calling these things panthers," James admitted. "Because I've been doing research on tanks lately, and I can't get a better name into my head."

"On what?" Anesh asked, sounding genuinely puzzled.

"Tanks."

"You're welcome."

"Guys, be serious," Sarah said as James threw his arms around Anesh's upper torso in an attempt to either kiss him or suplex him. The two of them froze and looked at her expectantly. She thought about what she'd said and then discarded the notion. "Okay, never mind. But really, this is good. We have no idea how the green orbs work, but they don't appear to be fundamental constraints for the Life the same way the yellows, purples, and reds are. Either that or being outside and away from the Office breaks the connection well enough anyway. It's possible that's what they are, compared to the others—a connection of some sort. Either way, while I don't have answers for you, I can tell you with . . . eeehhhhhhh . . . let's say eighty percent confidence that you can bring your hissy friends here safely."

"No idea how we'll feed them." Anesh sighed.

"I'm guessing surveillance footage." James shrugged. "We'll figure it out. We know they can eat yellow orbs, and I *think* they can just eat food? Now that I think about it, I'm pretty sure they ate every candy bar in that tower, so maybe mundane food works for them. But yeah, even if they're doomed, better they be doomed here, and a little free, than doomed there in despair."

Sarah wore a melancholy look on her face as she wiped the corner of her eye. "Aw, that was poetry! And also really sad. I wanna help them not be doomed at all!"

"Me, too." James let out a long breath. "Biggest problem now is that it seems like the dungeon is fighting us on it. Have you seen the tower in the last week?"

"No. I do work in the dungeon," Anesh answered dryly.

James paused. "So . . . so do I. Sort of. Anyway, it's like the dungeon is trying to blockade the tower. Or maybe just find it. It's weird, but the space around it is *teeming*. Worrying. On that note, Sarah, you good here with your new buddy?"

"Oh! He's still super going to try to kill us if we let him out now!" she informed them. "Not at all our friend! Just not as dungeon-y."

"Goooooood to know," James groaned out. "Now, against my personal wishes, I need to go talk to Neil and Nate. They were bringing some gear in today. They . . . get along." He shuddered. "It's worrying."

It was worrying because the two of them, despite being radically different personalities, had one single point of overlap in the things they were into. They were both, for different reasons, knowledgeable and passionate about the minutiae of what could best be categorized as military hardware. And the two of them in the same room rapidly turned into a conversation about said topic. And then a debate. And then, escalating swiftly into an argument, it created a room-size conversation-exclusion zone.

They were the natural fit for the people to ask to buy the guild a weaponry upgrade. And also mildly a pain to listen to.

"All right. So. You didn't give us enough of a budget, but we made do," Neil was complaining at James some time later. "Basically, if you want to kill a dragon, you need a very specialized gun—"

"First of all, we can circumvent budget restrictions by duplicating specific high-value items. Though we're sharing that resource with also duplicating better stuff, like orbs. Still, if the gun is small enough, we can make more, sort of exponentially," James interjected.

"We can clone things?" Nate cut in. "Why didn't you lead with that?"

"I assumed everyone knew? It's why Anesh spends all that time in the tower and why you guys have been sent out to harvest coffee twice in the last month." James raised his eyebrows at them.

Nate gave him a look that combined a scowl and a disappointed glare into a fearsome wrinkling of the forehead. For a short guy with glasses, he sure could put a lot of threat into a simple facial quirk. "You need to get better at passing along information."

"We're working on it. Sarah wants to do a podcast."

"I'd listen to that," Neil opined. "Anyway. Dragon slaying. So, what we've been looking at is a twenty-millimeter antimaterial rifle big-dick boomstick. That should be—"

"Stop."

"—plenty enough to wreck the day, and night, of whatever we point it at. And all for the low price of—"

"No." James tried in vain to halt this train wreck of a conversation.

"—I mean, okay, the price is high. But I can get us round-trip tickets on a semilegal cargo ship to Cape Town, and I have a cousin that can get us—"

Nate slapped Neil on the back of the head. "Cut it out." He turned to James. "It's a hundred grand and very illegal. But it would kill a dragon. Probably."

"To be clear, the dragon is not a literal dragon. It's like if a server room stood up, had wings, and was angry at you," James explained, suddenly realizing neither of these men had been that deep in the dungeon. "So we need something that will put holes in a machine more than a man."

"Oh." Neil deflated a bit, rubbing the back of his head. "Um . . ." He glanced at Nate and sheepishly offered a suggestion. "Desert Tech MDR, slotted for .308? Probably one per team, issue everyone else a Mossberg?"

Nate nodded. "It's a dumb and flashy toy, but it's a toy that makes the holes you want. Mossberg 500 is the shotgun you want, though, yeah. Fits the categories of legal, cheap, and simple enough for civs to use."

"Should I be insulted here?" James asked. Inwardly he was imagining hammering his head on the wall; the Mossberg had been Alanna's trusted weapon since early on, and he should have just bought a dozen of them from the start.

"Probably. Anyway, what Neil's ignoring is that the walls get tight in a lot of places. Probably one long gun per team is fine, and then give everyone a P-09. It's not like anything is going to be especially resistant to nine mil anyway." Nate gave a rolling, full-body shrug, then shot an interrogating look at James. "Is it?" he asked seriously.

"The maimframes could probably shrug off a few dozen shots. Tumblefeeds might just not care about it or might go down easy. But that's what the bigger guns are for, right?" James made the question rhetorical. "Give me a price breakdown, and we'll see if the budget can handle the influx of firepower. Oh, also, I'd like you guys to see if you can find me a Walther P38 while you're on your shopping trip."

"Whyyyy would you want that?" Neil dragged the word out.

"Skill crap?" Nate simply asked.

James nodded and cocked a finger in his direction as affirmation. "Got it in one. You guys good to argue among yourselves over this? I've gotta go to school."

"I thought you had a degree?" Neil asked, naively surprised. Nate just gave him a level look.

James threw up his arms in the air, proclaiming his frustrations. "Oh my god, fine, I'll send you all a link to the podcast!"

As he left the building, he realized that if all they were going to do was suggest the armaments they already mostly had, he could have saved a lot of time and just skipped the whole step of asking advice. Though it was nice to have confirmation from people who were more into the details of guns, as opposed to Alanna, who was more about proficiency and the philosophical impact of a weapon. Also, the actual process of purchasing guns was still alien to him, and while he knew it was a bad habit to get into, it felt nice to offload a problem onto other people by dumping a load of money on them and giving them marching orders.

James drove smoothly through the midday streets, long since having gotten comfortable with the invisible guidance of his skill upgrades, fully incorporating them into his actual driving. He took the opportunity to relax a bit, even from his own thoughts—music turned up, windows down, and no particular brainpower put toward any dungeon problems for a little while. Just the groove of Spanish guitar and the still-frosty wind of early February.

And a brief pause as he detoured through one of the office parks that dotted the city. Technically, the road would cut through to another street that would still take him to the high school, but five minutes later than normal. He had a reason, though.

He wanted to take another look at the target.

When the research team had made the little god that had called herself Curious, she had talked to James briefly about an enemy operation. She called them Status Quo—or rather, she said that James would come to call them that, and now he did, which seemed circular—and she had given him an address.

The name itself brought to life a lot of thoughts, mostly negative connotations. Not all of them bad, but certainly the majority. Stagnation, repression, that attitude of *keep things the way they are.* The sort of ideology that, James could understand, might be staffed by people who wanted to protect the world from the unknown but would absolutely be run by and answer to the kind of people who wanted to protect their own interests above all else.

The address, he mused as he drove past for the dozenth time this week, was exactly what you'd expect from a theoretical organization that interfered with the supernatural. It was a simple three-story brick block, with a fleet of what must be standard-issue gray or white four-door sedans in the parking lot. James had not, on any of the occasions he'd rolled past and tried to spot anything meaningful about it, seen anyone smoking in the parking lot or visiting one of the food trucks parked in the street that ran through the park. Never seen any of the windows with the blinds open. Never seen any sign that this place had an affiliation with a business at all.

If there was ever a more surefire sign this place belonged to either an impossibly boring government agency or an equally clandestine operation, James didn't know what it was.

Today, too, he couldn't see anything of any information value as he drove by. He just felt now like he had a duty to keep an eye on the place. In case, perhaps, he came by once and saw a bunch of goons dragging kidnapping victims out of an unmarked van. Or the complex was in turmoil, with suited and sunglassed agents swarming to their cars as someone barked orders from the front door.

Those things weren't happening. Again. For the twentieth time, things failed to happen as he drove past. So he just glared at the building instead, turned the music back up, and got back on track.

He met Lua in the parking lot of the 7-Eleven across the street from the high school. It seemed like a better idea than the parking lot of the school itself, if only a little bit. Being the guy who'd tracked blood and ichor across the lobby a few months back had endeared him to exactly no one; even if the police and the news hadn't drawn a spotlight onto him, it still seemed like putting a little distance down was prudent.

"How's it been?" he asked the middle-aged woman as she joined him in leaning against his car, handing a cheap cup of convenience store coffee over to her.

She took it gratefully, downing half the boiling beverage in one go before James could warn her, seeming to shrug off the effects of the heat and leaving James standing there with an open mouth and one hand half extended in warning. "You know, I spent years doing therapy for adults. Mostly people your age, twenties and thirties. It's easy to forget how fucked-up things are for a lot of kids," she stated bluntly, her voice dipping a little in tone as she swore. Lua did that sometimes; she'd swear or get angry, show a very human side of herself, but she did it quieter than when she was giving advice or help.

"So, not good then?" James asked, a pitiful, hopeful look on his face.

The therapist, who was also sort of a spy, sighed. "It's fine," she admitted. "I'm busy. They trust me, James. There are three counselors for this entire school, and the other two are . . . not friendly. Not helpful. I don't want to badmouth my colleagues, which is good, because I work for *you* and not the school, so I can tell you that they are *wretched.*" She put serious emphasis on the last word despite almost whispering it.

"Well, you're welcome to keep doing work here as long as you want. Anesh got contacted by the administration, and they still think we're the FBI. Your cover is intact. But also I think they just like having you, for budget reasons." James accepted the nod from her as affirmation. "Out of curiosity, do they pay you? I know we pay you; I'm not gonna stop that. I'm just curious."

"No, but I get free food," Lua said. "Which I think is a punish-ment?"

"I remember cafeteria food, yeah," James agreed. "We'll give you a lunch budget." He pulled out his notepad, flicked to an empty page, and made a note before he forgot that task. Enhanced memory only went so far.

Lua watched him with mild amusement. "You know, you're the only person I know who does that. With actual paper. Everyone else uses phones."

"Got into the habit in the dungeon, where I didn't want to bring my phone along and get it broken, or come alive. And then it turned out this actually helps with my horrible memory," James admitted. "I've got pretty bad ADHD, honestly, and I don't really have health insurance anymore to get it medicated."

"You could just buy gray-market drugs from Canada," Lua sug-gested in a professional voice that indicated that she was weirdly comfortable telling patients to self-medicate.

"I . . . holy shit." James tilted his head to stare off into the distance, rubbing his forehead just over his right eye as he gazed into the grove of trees down the road. "I can just do that. I forgot the rules don't apply to me anymore."

Lua winced and tried to hide it. That was not the lesson she'd meant to impart. She tried to get the conversation back under con-trol. "You wanted my weekly report?" she asked, cutting away the casual nature of the chat so far. James nodded, and Lua's expression shifted to one of quiet competence. "Two more kids went missing," she said bluntly. "One of them, I think, found another way into the dungeon. The other, I can reasonably say, is taking advantage of the situation to run away from home. I gave her what help I could with-out causing more problems, and I think she'll find her way to us soon. There's more students who are concerned about the disappearances; most of them believe the serial killer line, but there's three who don't. They don't know the others are seeing me, I think, which is why their stories aren't quite straight, and they *are* lying to me about what they suspect. They're investigating, and they're starting with the suspicious new therapist."

"Three of them?" James asked, something about that worrying at his thoughts.

"I had the same thought," Lua said, ignoring that James hadn't fully formed the conceptual object yet. "The team of three keeps showing up."

"Yes. That." James nodded, her words making it click in his head.

The therapist gave a slow nod. "It's a pattern. I don't know why, but it's there. And if they keep poking around, they *will* find the entrance." She gave a grim frown. "And here's the thing that changed. You know how you locked the door and broke the key?"

"Alanna did that, but sure."

"Well, the door moved."

James blinked. "What?" he barked in confusion.

"It moved." Lua pressed her hands together and unfolded them as she explained. "The door that used to be there just isn't anymore. The school blueprints don't show a boiler room in that spot, either, and I've had them in my office for a while, so I know that changed at some point, too. Of course, I also still have the blueprints, so I just looked for where it says the boiler room is now and found it. It's on the opposite end of the door to the overhead rigging for the stage that they use for drama."

Something about that seemed odd, and James stopped nodding along as he realized. "Wait, what?" He felt like he was saying that a lot. He pitched his voice more conversationally and less like a confused doofus. "So, it's not bound by the rules of where a boiler room is supposed to be at *all*, then."

"Apparently not."

"And someone's found it already?"

"At least one student. And . . . well, do you think you can handle more bad news today?" Lua asked him honestly.

James scoffed. "I am the master of bad news," he told her.

"Okay. I think one of the teachers actually is a serial killer," she said. "Or was, rather. I'm still sussing it out, but it's a strong case for there having been a computer science teacher who was luring students into the dungeon and coming out . . . without them."

"Goddammit." He snarled the word out in a cold, angry whisper. "Who is it? I'm almost certain we can make someone disappear forever." James cleared his throat awkwardly. "Ah. Assuming cold-blooded murder is on the table. That is. Not that I would plan for that. Something something pacifism. Restorative justice. That whole thing I believe in."

For someone who was supposedly a therapist, it was impressive how Lua could broadcast the *feeling* of having eyes rolled at you without ever actually making the motion. "I said *was*." She spoke in a serious voice instead of rising to James's snark. "He's gone. Or they're gone—I shouldn't assume the teacher was male. And by *gone* I mean it's like they never existed. Just like . . ."

"Just like what the basement does."

"Yes," Lua affirmed. She looked . . . sick. And James got it; really, he did. Because he felt exactly the same way. A month and a half of investigation and attempted containment, all while trying to somehow find a way to purchase or create enough high explosive to flatten a dungeon environment had done absolutely nothing to quiet his fury. Because this place wasn't like Officium Mundi, which simply had dangerous things in it and had spawned some evil things. No, it was a place that lured people in, lured *children* in, and then killed them. Fed on their deaths, divided up their torn clothing among its complicit minions, and wiped their names from the historical record. If anyone in the Order had just shrugged and said, "Oh, well, that's how it is sometimes," and had *not* been at least a little sickened? James would have kicked them out instantly.

James finally settled on "All right," draining his cup of the last sips of coffee and tossing it in a long arc across the parking lot and into the trash can by the front of the convenience store. "Keep doing what you're doing. If anything instantly threatening shows up, you know how to contact us."

"Yes, sir," Lua said, formally, punctuating the words with a small and unfamiliar style of salute.

". . . What's with the gesture?" James asked, suspicious.

Lua looked confused. "I thought this was the salute you . . . we . . . used. I've seen Alanna and some of the other delvers use it when you give them orders. JP called it a 'nascent ritual.'"

James let out a choked sigh. "Do they always wait for me to turn my back first?" he asked.

"Yes, now that I think about it."

"Of course they do." He shook his head. "Anyway. Here." He handed Lua a small, latched wooden box. "Three blues, six yellows. The yellows it's up to you on what you do with, but the blues we recommend absorbing until you get a power with self-defense potential. Anything with *create* or *remove* in the name usually works. Alanna's teaching a class on combat powers this Saturday; I recommend you be there. Also. You've been helping us out immensely, and I know you don't *want* to go into the Office, but we are going in soon for a specific humanitarian reason, and if you want to be there, I think you can be helpful."

"I'll think about it," she said, meaning it.

James gave her a friendly nod and stood up off the hood of his car where he'd been leaning, stretching and looking around as he got back in his car and saw Lua retreat across the street, back to the school and her double-duty day job. He noticed a couple kids on the street corner, probably skipping class, who were all clearly watching him. "Heh," he muttered to himself as he fired up the engine. "Probably think I'm the secret boyfriend or something," he joked to himself.

Then he remembered what Lua had literally just said and gave the watchers another look. Two teen guys, one of them with shaggy hair and glasses, the other one clearly in better shape, maybe a student athlete, with a sharp nose over a flat face. They were watching him, deliberately, but they flinched and looked away when James swept his gaze over the duo.

Problems, he thought.

Or . . .

There were three things searching for them, Curious had said. Status Quo was one, and James at least had an idea of where they were. He was keeping an eye on them, in a horrifyingly inefficient way, but still. They were a vaguely known factor, and in a week or so, he'd have the power, backing, and confidence to have a chat with them, if he wanted to. But they'd keep. The other was the abstract threat of people who were mad at him. James assumed that was the police sergeant now putting real effort into tracking him down. James had already ditched his phone and asked Secret to do some obfuscating, and he assumed the blue orb that shook pursuit had helped, too.

The third one was the curious.

Was it them? A trio of determined students, dumped into a sea of horrors that was threatening to rise over their heads and still finding the energy to try to track down the truth?

James flipped out his notepad and made a mark. This was a job for Lua, or maybe Sarah, he figured. He was finally getting the hang of this whole delegating thing, and it was such a great feeling, to make this someone else's problem.

Then he looked at the note on top of the page, which hadn't been checked off yet. "Goddammit, I need to put out a job ad for a sound engineer," he grumbled, flipping the pad shut and shoving it back into his pocket. One thing after another. And only a day left before one of the more important delves they'd undertaken. He pulled out of the parking lot, a feeling thrumming in his chest in time with the engine, equal parts nervous twitching, excited waiting, and a cold anger that still waited to be satisfied.

It was a patient anger, though. And a patient excitement, too, at that. And so James drove home like he always did, music turned up, windows rolled down. No acknowledgment to himself that, yes, he really did feel like the bullet in the chamber. And the target was in the sights now.

CHAPTER 15

They'd been in the dungeon for almost an hour now. Anesh had vanished instantly to check on something, Alanna and JP had run off to play quartermaster to the people who'd come in, and everyone else was taking time to do warm-up stretches, adjust the straps on their armor, test out drone control, and get used to the feeling of being about to go on an adventure.

This time, there were no miscommunications or missing words.

"There are something like sixty camracondas, outside the dungeon's control, trapped in a tower." James spoke to the assembled crew. "Through testing, we know that someone ripping a telepad page can bring up to five people with them. This includes dungeon Life, regardless of size, and we have no reason to believe it won't include the camracondas. I bring this up because we are going to liberate them." There were a few hard nods at that, and a few confused looks, too. Deb raised a hand cautiously, while Dave did the same motion in one swift snap of his arm, but James shook his head at the both of them.

"Can I ask something?" Dave asked, utterly immune to the irony.

"Questions at the end," James said flatly. "So. We need twelve people to get them all out, minimum. We also only vaguely understand where the tower is, because of how it was shielded. But thanks to some scouting, it seems clear that it's only hard to find if you're potentially hostile. And we're not." He explained the cloaking effect.

"We also won't be moving the totem, just in case. As a backup." James tossed that in, to the disappointment of a couple of people. "The camracondas are aware that we're arriving to help them. They are, in a word, refugees. I know there's some concern that this is a trap, but if it is, it was one that was set in motion *years* ago. So we're just discounting that it's aimed at us, and we are acting in good faith."

The group nodded. There were a few small comments, but everyone was mostly just letting James brief them, like they were professionals or something. He wasn't used to it.

"Now. The landing. Everyone participating in this needs to be aware that the arrival back in reality feels *awful*. The time distortion is what causes it, we think. But it won't do any permanent damage. For a landing zone, we've marked specific spots in the back parking lot of the lair, out of sight but in the open, to prevent any teleport collisions, and we've got premade telepads to hand out right now. We don't *know* if that can happen, but fuck if we're gonna find out now, right?" He got a lot of affirmative noises to that one. "Once you arrive, you'll be back on a normal timeline, so everyone still in here will still have time before leaving and meeting up with you. Just keep that in mind." He took a breath. "Okay. Any questions now?"

"Why does this feel dangerous?" Dave asked instantly.

"Because people have visited their tower a couple times over the last month, and it's entirely possible the dungeon is actively mobilized to stand in the way," James said. "The area around the tower has been filling up with hostile things, and also it seemed like it was shifting slightly." He stepped aside, gesturing to the hard plastic box next to him. "That said, bonus points to Neil and Nate for moving rapidly on something. I have a gift for everyone."

Firearms were the gift. Guns and ammo. James had even deployed one of his minions to the local army surplus store—he was still mad at them for selling machetes that couldn't even murder an angry plant monster without breaking, but they *did* sell bandoliers, ammo pouches, and attachable slings, which all went along with the pump-action shotguns, nine-millimeter pistols, and boxes of ammunition.

The gift wasn't much of a surprise to a lot of people. Nate had spent last night briefing everyone on firearm safety and trigger discipline, and he was doing it again now as they started to equip everyone. You wouldn't need to be a crack shot to use a gun at the engagement ranges they tended to operate at, so the weapons were more for emergency situations than anything else. But with the resistance they were expecting, this might be more than required. The fact that they planned to teleport out also meant that any swarm attracted by the gunfight wouldn't be a major problem.

What did end up being a surprise was Anesh, jumping from the third floor of the tower and landing, seemingly without concern, and jogging over toward the group that was now staring at him.

"What the hell was that?" someone, or perhaps several someones, asked him.

"What? Oh. Purple. Safe fall height. Not important; it's not a great one unless you play around on rooftops a lot, but there's one extra in the database if we want to copy it again." Anesh waved his hand like that wasn't a massive statement on its own. "No. I wanted to give you all these." He pulled a long cardboard box out from under his arm and added it to the top of the crate that had been snapped shut after everyone had been given their loadouts.

The boxes were a recent change, but after they'd learned that you could totally accidentally break orbs through a bag, it felt reasonable.

When Anesh opened it, a line of fifteen yellow orbs greeted them.

"What are these? Are they special?" James asked.

"Maybe!" Anesh announced. "Lily gave us a readout for an orb that labeled it 'Action/Motion.' I figured it was a good test run, so we ran the copier a few times. These are the fifteen extras; I kept the original in reserve, labeled, just in case."

And here it was. The first big step forward in exploiting the skills. Even if it wasn't a great one, even if a person could only use it once or twice, the fact that they *knew what it would be* after this first level-up would make it invaluable. They'd be able to shore up weaknesses, rapidly bring new members up to speed, and enhance themselves beyond human levels in ways they could actually control this time.

James took the first one out, and everyone looked at him with wide eyes. He popped the orb, and the assembled delvers collectively held their breath.

[+0.8 Skill Ranks : Athletics—Running]

"Everyone come grab one," James said with a grin, thinking about kicking into a sprint and realizing his leg muscles were primed to do so. "Let me know if you get a fractional number." There was a rush of excitement, and a rush of ability flooding into the team. "Running," he informed Anesh. "Not a combat skill, really, but it's the kind of thing that makes the difference, especially if we're . . . you know . . . running away." James laughed. "I got point-eight ranks—think that means I was already pretty good, or that the orb was weak?"

"I bet you a yellow it was the orb," Anesh didn't even hesitate to quip.

James looked offended. "Okay, ow," he said, placing a hand over his heart in protest.

"Hey, I got a tenth of a skill point?" Deb raised her voice over the chatter of the group, who were excitedly discussing the potential for this new axis of power.

"Ha!" James said triumphantly. "Pay up!"

"Damn." Anesh grinned back. "I'll pay you once someone brings me more coffee."

"No, no! Pay me a *real* orb! A random one, not another running one!"

"What?! You don't want to run better?" Anesh chided him. "That's irresponsible! Especially since you can run at vehicle speeds."

"Apparently even then I can't run as well as Deb," James griped. "Tenth of a point? That girl must jog every day."

Anesh folded his arms at James with a suspicious gaze. "You jog every day with Alanna."

"Yeah, but I'm asleep when I do it," James said, and he and Anesh shared a dry look before they both started cracking up.

It was exactly what everyone needed. Just a little bit of levity before the journey.

And with that, hearts lightened, nerves settled, and weapons loaded, fifteen people started moving as a group in the direction they needed to go.

JP and Dave crouched twenty feet ahead of James, heads poked around a corner like they were goddamn *Scooby-Doo* characters. Almost as one, the two of them drew back, and Dave made a slashing motion over his shoulder.

Thirteen delvers scurried into cubicles. There were a couple muted pops as people tossed coats over flashbulbs in practiced gestures. James himself had to get the drop on a tapir, knocking it to the floor and chopping down through its softer "tape" flesh bulb with his hatchet before it could react. He didn't want to hit it against a desk and risk the sound drawing too much attention, instead relying on the carpet to at least pretend to muffle things.

The reason, he thought as he grabbed the yellow out of its corpse, was that they were slipping by their third tumblefeed of the night.

[+1 Skill Rank : Architecture—Cathedral—Structural Weakness]

He snorted. That one was literally never coming in handy. Raising his eyes back up, he made eye contact with the other team leads through the doors of other cubes across the hall, quick nods affirming that everyone was in the clear. Whatever had been happening with the dungeon's ecosystem ebbing, it didn't apply *here*. The wildlife was out in force today, and the closer they got to the shrouded tower, the more James started thinking that Officium Mundi was seriously trying to stop them from moving forward.

The tumblefeeds they'd chosen not to engage. They had enough thermite on hand to melt more than one of the beasts, but doing so would probably draw more unwanted attention. Especially if the green Life worked the way they were starting to understand it to and the dungeon was watching through its eyes. So, instead, they dodged them, waiting for the creatures to scurry by before they ran the group by in single file.

Overhead, drones controlled by their most proficient operators kept watch for anything closing in, keeping digital eyes fed through skulljack braids on the hallways around them. They'd already tagged four or five orange orb zones, the warped spaces looking distinct from overhead and easy to avoid. No need to test fate today, of all days.

"All right," James said after they'd finally rushed one at a time across the open space of low walls and bright lighting, making their way through the paper vines on the other side into another wide hall. This one had arches of wall material low to the ground, like roots designed to snare the foot. "Anything coming up?" he prompted, looking to Neil and Daniel.

"Drones show nothing big between here and the base of the tower," Neil confirmed. "Almost a straight shot, clear."

"Pathfinder is still learning how to guide an army," Daniel said, ignoring James's protests that they weren't an army. "She says there's something blocking us, but we can't see it properly. Too many of us moving."

Alanna stepped up to them, coming back from slipping ahead of the group to take a personal look. "Yo. There's a break room around the tower," she said, grim-faced. "Secret says it's not shrouded, but it's got overhead cover."

"What?" Neil looked both shocked and offended. "But . . . drones!"

"Well, fuck," James growled out. "Dungeons have been moving terrain around way too much lately. It's bad enough we know the school can rearrange the actual real world. This is just bonus annoyance."

Alanna gave him a hard nod. "So, what do we do?" she asked, and James could see some of the others moving closer to listen in on the conversation.

He gave a shark's grin. "Oh, we go through it," he said. "Everyone, grab something weighty off a nearby desk. We'll deal with the coffee mines and punch through. It's obviously a trap, but if the dungeon hasn't taken the tower . . . it doesn't know where the trap needs to be, right? We go through fast, shoot anything that tries to stop us, get inside, and get gone." James looked around at his companions, at his *Order.* "Besides, what are we gonna do otherwise? Fight back through a half dozen tumblefeeds?" He laughed. "No. Fuck this. I'm not getting scared off doing the right thing by a living building that can't even spring for real wood tables," James joked, and while the others laughed softly, still keeping quiet, he noticed the glimmer of something in the eyes watching him.

There was a voice in the back of James's head sometimes. His own voice, really. But the part of it that kept telling him that he should be pushing back on how unfair the world was. That he should be yelling and kicking and railing against whatever injustice was within arm's reach. And a lot of the time, he had to ignore that voice, because he didn't actually *know* what to do. But right now, he did. And right now, he could see everyone else listening to that part of themselves, too.

Didn't matter if it was a middle-aged ex-sailor–turned–chef or a kid with a drone obsession, a nursing graduate or an insomniac witch, a big ol' softie of a nerd in way over his head or a girl who liked spray paint and cars. They all had that realization and reaction. The dungeon was trying to get in their way?

Nah.

James stepped out first, pulling down a row of paper vines as he did so to clear the line of sight for everyone else. He could see the base of the tower in the distance, though the newly grown cubicle ceilings blocked his vision of the upper floors. There were still cam-racondas on watch, though, peering out of the upper windows or a couple by the sloped ramp to the tower's entrance. They spotted him at once, a few of them scrambling back into the tower.

The chunk of the Office's break room biome stretched off for twenty to thirty meters on both sides. Tile floor, the glare of over-powered fluorescent light coming from nowhere in particular, and the smell of a microwave that had the tragedy of the commons befall it. A labyrinth of tables and chairs sat between James and his target, arranged *just so perfectly* that he'd have to be studiously careful not to set off any of the coffee cups balanced on a hair trigger.

In addition to those caffeinated bombs, wood-paneled counter-tops cut lines across the field, obstructing lines of sight with cupboards that merged with the ceiling overhead, dousing the area in the white noise of sinks that were left running, small streams of overflowing water making the floor around them a slick mess and another obstacle to worry about. A few plants were visible, some of them almost assuredly alive and waiting to strike, hanging in pots suspended from the ceiling near artificial corners created by the countertops.

The whole thing was a trap, and it had been hastily slapped down here sometime in the last week. The dungeon was learning how they operated and deciding that whatever they wanted here, they didn't get to have it. And clearly it wanted to put some of its new tricks to use.

Hefting a stolen paperweight in his hand, James flung it overhand at the first table.

He nailed a coffee mine dead center, sending a burst of boiling liquid into the air along with a small shock wave. A follow-up throw of a dead strider from his off hand took out another cup, which set off a few more in a chain reaction. James stepped forward into the cleared space, and Alanna and Anesh took up the space on either side of him, their own projectiles in hand. Even as they made their throws, more and more people stepped out of the hallway and started clearing the carefully arranged space of threats.

A corridor wide enough for four people abreast was empty of any hazards, and then the group was moving through the open space at a brisk pace. Secret spun in lazy, ethereal circles around James's legs as he led the charge, shoving tables now devoid of explosives out of the way and making a gap where the biggest problem was slipping on coffee splattered across the linoleum floor. Alanna, close behind him, put her own heavier frame to use just flipping over every other table, creating a makeshift barricade and cover if they needed it later.

By the time the ambushers realized what was going on, it was too late for them. When the cupboards of the counter to their right burst open and dozens of those vicious old-model striders crawled out like steel trapdoor spiders, the Order was already thirty feet away and behind a pile of tangled chairs. When another set of cupboards right in front of them revealed the same force arrayed against them, Momo twisted something in her grip before anyone could get a shot off, popping a red orb into a complex ball that she'd build to house it. Everyone near her winced slightly, but then she flung it into the crowd and the striders went *nuts*. The smaller ones started tearing at the bigger ones in fury, and the bigger ones didn't even fight back, looking like they were just scrambling in panic to put distance between themselves and the column of humans moving through.

James had felt the totem for just a moment when Momo had activated it. Relative size. He knew exactly how large or small he was compared to everything within about a hundred feet. Not a huge deal, on average. But for a strider? He knew some of them were intelligent, but a lot of them acted closer to animals a lot of the time, and that must have been some heavy existential dread to cope with.

Not much farther to go. James could hear yelling from those bringing up the rear as Sarah and Dave engaged the faster striders that were trying and failing to overwhelm the group. James and Alanna continued their bulldozer impression past one of the plants, and James saw out of the corner of his eye as it lashed at him with a razor-sharp fern.

James would admit, if anyone asked, that he flinched. But he *had* seen JP already about to strike, so he wasn't *too* worried. Before the plant could hit him, JP stepped past on James's left side and flicked his arm up, the sword he'd kept bringing in slicing off the plant's attack midway through. He followed up with a heavy, overcommitted chop, showing off a lack of actual skill with the sword mixed with a distinct dislike for plastic plants, and the thing died silently. They left the dropped orbs in the pot.

Around the counter that lay directly in their path—no cupboards in this one, thankfully—for some reason the refrigerator continued to not try to kill them, though James didn't drop his guard. The instant she cleared the corner, Alanna grabbed and double-hand flung a folding chair low over the tables, wiping away any coffee mines still in their path.

James slammed into her side, as she'd frozen in place, wide-eyed. "Oof. Wha . . . oh!" James caught on rapidly.

There was a maimframe.

Hidden behind this last wall, with one more low wall and the break room's fake ceiling keeping it out of sight of the tower and the camracondas that might have been able to help, the bulky PC, looking like a tank mixed with a turtle shell, rose up on multi-jointed legs, a dozen firing ports swiveling online at once as they registered James and Alanna in their sights, glossy blue film flickering to life around it. It looked like someone had built a PC, been told they could scale it up indefinitely, and then just shrugged and kept adding stuff until it was the size of a minivan. Then they gave it patchwork armor plating and four clawlike legs that left holes in the linoleum as it stomped forward.

The two partners couldn't stop. People were coming in fast behind them. So James did what he'd told everyone the plan was.

Keep moving. Shoot anything in the way.

His skill orb fired up somewhere in the abstract space of his soul, knowledge and ability flooding into his blood and bones and muscles. The pistol in his hand was already up and firing as he shoved Alanna aside with one hand and launched himself forward fast enough that he could feel pressure against his insides. His enhancements made his body feel at once alien and deeply personal, with even his red orbs sparking in his mind and driving him to simply flow with the mood. And the blue he'd absorbed expended its last charge on their foe. Break Technology shattered one of the extended CD drives on the maimframe that powered its impossible shields, though he was sad to see it had a backup. This one was either smarter or just older.

Bullets started slamming into the shield before James had fully acknowledged that he was *moving*. But when his conscious brain caught up, it fell in line with what was going on. *Keep moving forward, keep shooting.* His gun clicked empty ten seconds later, and he mechanically drew on his yellow orb proficiency to drop the magazine and slot another from his armor webbing into place. Behind him, a thunderous *boom* through his earplugs signaled Alanna pulling the trigger on her shotgun as she fell into step behind him.

The shields of the maimframe flickered but held. And then it retaliated.

James rolled forward, spiked sticks of RAM flying over his head. A couple caught on his armor, shattering on impact and not penetrating but the force knocking him off balance. He recovered and kept moving, knowing that sitting still would mean death. Behind him, *hundreds* of shots were missing as the maimframe failed to lead its target, and he knew he wouldn't survive *that*, armored or not.

Then the rest of the group caught up, only seconds behind. And for them, there wasn't any surprise. The gunfire had been a good enough alert, and they'd rounded the corner weapons ready. James heard pistol fire from the rear of their formation as someone, probably Dave, suppressed the striders in pursuit. But it was Nate's voice that dominated the battlefield while James slid forward and turned the fall into a kick that knocked a table over with a graceless flip so he could use it as cover. The projectiles trying to catch him cracked and punched into the other side like furious rain, but nothing got through to cut into James himself.

"*Aim!*" He heard the shout, and the maimframe certainly did, too, as it started turning toward where Nate was standing behind four delvers, crouched, with shotguns braced hard against their shoulders in hands that trembled slightly. More people, still running, were crossing the distance between the firing line and where James had made his makeshift wall.

"Shit!" James yelped as a ricocheting spike caught his thigh, slicing through the weaker armor on the side. But the thing wasn't focusing on him anymore. He popped up, unloading another magazine into the monster before ducking back behind the table as the maimframe opened some kind of port on its side facing him and let out a high-pitched whine that started to *melt the table he was using as cover.*

He felt panic. Not for himself—though watching a piece of furniture turn into a Salvador Dalí painting wasn't great for his mental state—but for the stationary targets that everyone else had made for themselves. They were going to be torn apart. Then, from somewhere, Secret silently zipped across the underside of the machine beast, and it faltered for a processor cycle, briefly forgetting what it was doing at all.

"*Fire!*" Nate bellowed, following his own advice. Every gun the delvers had on them unloaded in unison, the heavy double-ought shells adding a punch to the constant peppering of the nine millimeters that everyone had been issued. A wall of solid sound hit James like a punch, and he could see more delvers than just himself flinch, even through the hearing protection they were all supposed to be wearing.

The shield dropped on the first volley. And no one stopped firing. Nate and Alanna worked fastest, pumping more firepower into the massive shellaxy at twice the rate of anyone else. But everyone was shooting, and it took just seconds for the maimframe to be ripped apart under the onslaught.

"*Hold fire!*" Nate ordered, and a few seconds later, everyone caught up to the words.

When the shooting died down, James took over. "Move!" he yelled. "Don't stop, we're almost there!"

There was no telling what surprises would be available for them if they stalled now. They needed to close the gap, get to the tower, and get the hell out of here. Especially since there really *was* telling what was between them and victory, as a sound like rattling rain announced a tumblefeed dragging itself over one of the counters on their flank, and a series of too-bassy chimes and error tones heralded a second maimframe stomping across the linoleum.

As they ran the last stretch, Anesh detoured to the maimframe's corpse to grab the massive green orb. James would have yelled at him, but his throat felt bone-dry, and he felt like he could taste gunpowder through the numb skin of his hands. Instead, he just stood and ushered everyone forward. Move. *Move.* Almost there.

Stepping off the laminated floor and through the arched door of the tower was like snapping into a different world.

And suddenly, they were safe. Everything that had been closing around them lost track of the delvers in an instant, the dungeon or anything hostile at all unable to see where the tower even was, much less the people in it.

The camracondas crowded around the delvers, the humans and the pair of infomorphs finding themselves beset by curious snakes who had really actually only met James before. Rattling hisses filled the air, and shortly after, relieved laughter did, too.

Sarah flopped down onto the floor, hugging the nearest camraconda she could get her hands on like it was a giant tube pillow, her laughter a bell that rang through the tower. What might be the first laughter this place had heard in a long, long time. James found himself standing off to the side with the leader of the little colony, whom he'd met over a month ago, watching his companions meet the other camracondas for the first time. Nervously at first, but then with an energy that came from having just survived a fight to the death. Making friends through shared trauma—nothing beat it for efficiency. Even El, trying to be standoffish and separate herself from the Order, looked awkward as hell as she tried to fumble her pistol back into its holster and found a couple of the smaller camracondas tugging at her jeans and drawing a smile out.

"Is everything ready to go?" James asked quietly, and the old snake next to him nodded. There was a small hiss as a drop of liquid fell from its eye to the worn carpet.

This place had been home for them for who only knew how long. They were prisoners, and survivors, but . . . they were also the first. Pioneers of their own freedom. Leaving wasn't an entirely easy thing.

But they were doing it.

Twenty minutes later, the first batch of six people blipped out as Simon tore a page off his telepad. Then another, then another. Six by six, carrying only their art with them, the only thing left in this place that mattered aside from the camracondas themselves, they began the second exodus from the dungeon that James had overseen.

The last ones out were himself, the leader, and the priestess. James took with him the body of the lady of the tower, the human corpse feeling alien and terrifying in his arms, and the last of the assembled history of the first free camraconda colony.

And just like that, they left.

The flow of time slammed into James, parallel to the scent of fresh air, and *instantly* his stomach revolted at the shift. Or maybe it was his spleen. Or all three of his spleens. Did James have extra spleens? He sure as fuck felt like it right now.

There was a *very* unpleasant noise and smell as several people, even forewarned, failed to hold on to their lunch, James mercifully not among them. But then his body stabilized and he rose to his feet.

The camracondas were looking worriedly at their human allies, though half of them *also* looked dizzy, nauseous, and pained. Or maybe James was just reading the snakes' unfamiliar expressions wrong. And now was the moment of truth, but after long minutes, they stayed themselves. The dungeon, it seemed, couldn't see their tower, and it couldn't see outside itself. It had been a tiny risk, but now they knew for sure.

And then the camracondas started exploring. Cautiously at first, they began nosing around the asphalt, the parked cars, the shrubbery around the building. Then with more vigor, roaming with awkward twitches of their tails, never having had this much space to move before.

"All right," James announced, his heart glowing with satisfaction. "Let's get you guys inside for now and see if any of you like human food." He looked around the marked area of the parking lot, where at least three people had thrown up, adding in a muttered tone, "And I'm gonna get a hose for *this*."

A chorus of snake hissing and human cheers met the first half of his sentence, and thankfully, no one replied to the second part.

Now he just had to hope the massive green Anesh had picked up spawned them a second floor to the building. They were going to need to figure out *something* to house these guys. But that was logistics, not the passion of the moment. And right now was the time to feel the night air and the faint hint of oncoming rain, not to worry about whether he'd have to start absorbing the nearby buildings into his operation.

Now was also the time to see if camracondas liked chicken.

CHAPTER 16

Order of Endless Rooms Operations Manual
Section 3-1, Part 5: Officium Mundi, Life Forms—Stuffed Shirts
Stuffed shirts, also called paper pushers or sometimes Dilberts, are not human. This is important. They will appear to be humans, wearing business dress and performing normal office duties, up until you see their faces. The face is always a giveaway—they either have one, and it is instantly recognizable as not being a person, or they do not have one, which has the same effect but in a less unsettling way.

Stuffed shirts drop variably sized yellow orbs or midsize green orbs. To date, they are the source of the largest yellows on record. These orbs are unique, the only ones that if scanned by an iLipede will show a name—see Section 5-1, Part 1: Yellow Orbs for details.

The strength of this form of Life is proportional to its orb and is not standard like much of the other Life in Officium Mundi. Lower-threat versions are still capable of throwing armored delvers one-handed, while higher-threat variants have been witnessed to snap bone in their grips. Because you can't know what orb they have without fighting them, this means any encounter should be approached cautiously.

They are known to shift their forms to become quadrupedal, achieving very high speeds and using ramming as a form of attack. Also, be aware that those with faces can remove those faces, deploying them as masks—see Section 3-1, Part 3. It's unclear if wearing a mask changes the paper pusher in any way.

Composition is entirely cardstock and shredded paper/dust, including the clothing. Despite having high strength, they are still fully material, and both fire and liquid damage them rapidly. Parts separated from the main body lose rigidity and durability instantly.

Recommended tactics are to engage directly with at least two-to-one odds and attempt to douse with water to limit motion. Shooting in the head also works.

James looked at the last sentence of the write-up on the Office's idea of employees and frowned.

"I feel like 'and also you can shoot it' is a little bit obvious," he muttered. "Do we need that?" he asked, not really addressing anyone else but leaving the question open to the room.

The room was currently empty. James looked around, wondering when his company had vanished. Secret had been here for a bit. So had Ganesh at one point, though the little drone was dropping off a report and not actually hanging out. His office had also been playing host to a trio of napping camracondas, but they too had taken off at some point—probably when his furious tapping at the keyboard kept waking them up.

"Anesh!" James called out, spotting his boyfriend walking by through the door, the dark-skinned young man standing out as he picked his way carefully through the camracondas strewn throughout the lair. "Anesh, come help me with something!"

Only stumbling once over someone's tail, Anesh made his way around the unused front counter and through James's door. "You rang?" he asked.

"Do you have a minute? I need someone to proofread a thing," James told him.

Anesh bit his lip. "I was actually on my way to meet someone," he said. "What's the thing?"

"Operations handbook."

"Ah. Still working on that?" he asked, sympathetic. "Well, I believe in you. You, of anyone, should know what to say about the dungeons."

"That's a lie and you know it," James accused him playfully. "What's your meeting about?"

"Math," Anesh told him, flatly. "A girl from one of my tutor groups wanted to meet up for some extra study time this afternoon. Offered to pay me in coffee, and I didn't have the heart to tell her that we have dark magic roast on demand."

James hummed in appreciation, giving a nodding grin. "Dark magic roast" was exactly the kind of pun he could appreciate. "Wait, hang on." He held up a hand, brain catching up to the rest of Anesh's words. "You're going on a date?"

"What? No!" Anesh protested, reeling back slightly. "I wouldn't do that to you guys!"

"Anesh . . ." James pinched the bridge of his nose at his boyfriend's instant defensive protest. "It's not . . . You can always just *ask*, you know?"

"I did not know, thank you," Anesh stated haughtily. "And besides! I know what we have isn't . . . isn't *normal*," he said, and James heard a waver in boyfriend's voice that wasn't usually there. "But I like you two. I'm happy with us. I don't need to date more people. And *besides again*, it's not a date. It's math."

James eyed him with overt disbelief. "Uh-huh."

"Math!" Anesh announced loudly, turning to make his escape, one finger pointed up to the ceiling in defiance as he strode out the door and again tripped on a camraconda tail.

James politely waited for Anesh to leave before pulling his phone out and texting Alanna. *Anesh is oblivious to the fact that one of his tutoring friends is flirting with him,* he sent.

A minute later, the reply came back: *adorbs wait how do you know if anesh doesnt?*

Ignoring Alanna's flagrant disregard for punctuation, James fired back a reply. *I'm astute. Anyway, he got offended when I told him it was okay. Yelled about math.*

he does that, Alanna sent, and then a second later, *does he know he can just ask*

He does now. I think he's having self-doubt about our little love triangle. We should do something nice for him tonight. James hit send, and then, before Alanna could reply, followed up with *No not like that you fiend.*

well i have a great idea with this toy i bought on . . . spoilsport. James grinned, knowing exactly where his message had landed. He set his phone down with a smile and looked back at his work on the handbook with renewed vitality. With a persistent feeling of warm comfort in his chest, he started typing again. He got through writing the words *Section 6* when his phone buzzed again.

hey if anesh is not-dating someone hes tutoring we should start calling him senpai. The text from Alanna took a second to worm its way into his brain.

James politely closed his office door so he wouldn't wake any of the camracondas when he started howling with laughter.

Order of Endless Rooms Operations Manual
Section 5-1, Part 4: Officium Mundi, Treasures—Orange Orbs
Orange orbs, in their primary use (breaking), provide legal status. Correlation between size and effect appears to be the number of employees in the office that handles the given certification—i.e., the more people employed by a bureaucracy, the larger an orb would be required to affect it.

It is important to note that legal status is not the same thing as actual ability. A pilot's license does not teach you to fly a plane.

Absorbing an orange orb generates a task that can be repeated after a set cooldown period. The completion of the task generates a material reward. It does not appear that tasks can be removed once absorbed. We do not understand why a certain amount of time spent inside Officium Mundi is required before absorption is possible, but it is theorized that after enough time, additional absorptions will be possible.

As far as can be determined, the matter is created from nothing, making this one of several options for defeating entropy on a longer timeline.

Officium Mundi utilizes the totem form of the orange orb to create spatial warps. For a full list of nonnormal spaces encountered, see Section 6, Part 4: Hazards, Spatial.

Experimenting with orange totems is both not recommended and currently actually forbidden by whatever limited authority we have around here.

Some dungeon Life will also drop orange orbs. These are exclusively ones that contain compact spaces within themselves. For more details, see Section 3, Part 7: The Copier and Part 10: Tapir.

A full list of acquired licenses and tasks is as follows . . .

James groaned and stretched backward in his chair like an oversize cat. He'd been at this for four hours so far today, mostly collating and copying records of their orb gains. And editing in general was exhausting.

It turned out, Anesh had switched systems at some point. And also a couple of the delver teams used their own spreadsheets—or, in one frustrating case, notebook. And also there were just some things that James absolutely remembered being real but weren't written down anywhere or were written on note cards that were probably going to fall out of some paperback on his nightstand when he picked it up a year from now.

It was frustrating, was the point. But he'd finally finished most of it.

Operations handbook was really kind of a misnomer. It was meant to be a lot more than that—a reference book, yes, and a survival guide, and also a little bit actually about the operations protocols of the Order. But also a database of orbs, effects, items, and creatures. And on top of that a piece of culture. A look into the guiding principles and day-to-day small rituals that were beginning to form the skeleton of their organization, and a compilation of individual members and their important achievements and events. The kind of thing that was a door into their community, suitable for neophytes and veterans alike.

It would never be a physical product, most likely. Well, except for maybe the base reference material. But that was fine. Tablets existed for a reason. Or, better yet, as their skulljack knowledge grew, maybe they could just stick it on their phones and have constant Bluetooth access to it.

James made a mental note that he really had to tackle the chapter on skulljack protocol before going home.

The whole thing was a pretty important step for the fledgling organization. It represented the crystallization of thoughts into actionable plans and written traditions. It was also *infuriating* to write. And writing it had, somehow, fallen entirely on James's shoulders. Probably because it was his idea and pet project, and he didn't really think anyone else had the same kind of comprehensive knowledge of things that he did, so, in fairness, it was his own damn fault.

But still . . .

"Hey, Reed!" he called out, flagging down the younger member of the research team. Incidentally, they still weren't off the hook for accidentally making a god, which mostly meant that James was making them jump at random tasks just to keep them on their toes and disrupt any other potential end-of-world scenarios cropping up in that basement.

"Yeah?" The curly haired, far-too-tall kid stopped awkwardly in the doorway, trying to approach to a polite distance but also not wanting to step over the camraconda curled up on the threshold.

James ignored the faux pas. Or, more accurately, didn't notice or care about it. "I need your opinion on something," he started to say, intending to ask about skulljack interactions and how best to bullet point them, but the end of his sentence opened an unfortunate hole in the conversation.

"Is it about Star Wars? Because I saw the new Star Wars, and I have *opinions* on it." Reed answered so smoothly that it made James blink. Either he'd rehearsed that line ahead of time, he was some kind of witty mastermind, or he really legitimately was just looking to talk about Star Wars.

James couldn't risk roughly half those options. "I no longer require your opinion," he informed Reed politely but firmly.

Order of Endless Rooms Operations Manual
Section 6, Part 1: Extranormal Capabilities—Skulljacks
The skulljack is currently the most powerful tool the Order possesses.

This statement is made to give you an idea of the level of impact that it can make on human society at large, and not to make you think it is a weapon. It *is* a weapon, but it is also a lot of other things as well, and we would do well not to forget the cultural warping force we have on our hands. If this opening statement seems less dry than the others, it is to impress on you the point that *this is not a toy*. Even though in addition to being a weapon, it is a fantastic toy.

Skulljacks are a near-perfect interface for the human mind. Physically, they are an ethernet port formed organically of cartilage and nerve endings, located on the back of the neck, toward the base of the skull. They are self-sealing against water damage and, if damaged, parts of them such as the clip can regrow over time, like fingernails.

A skulljack is a vector for its own transmission. If a working data transmitter—ethernet cable, usually—is plugged into a working skulljack, and the free end is brought near the correct spot on another life form, a corresponding skulljack will form on the target in about fifteen seconds. The process is painless and harmless, though could best be described as feeling *exceedingly weird*.

This is both a problem and an opportunity. Long term, skulljacks *will* be ubiquitous among the population of Earth, assuming we don't all die. Short term, it means that those looking to exploit the technology have an untraceable, impossibly invasive way to do so. If you are a member of the Order, then your job is to mitigate this problem as much as possible. Consider this one of our prime directives—dungeon tech is going to save us all, if we can keep it from killing us first.

Skulljacks have, functionally, a single capability: they allow transmission of data using modern TCP/IP. This data can take the form of commands to digital devices, the reading of information off digital storage, the sharing of organic memories or emotions with other skulljack users, the creation of a gestalt mind out of two or more skulljack users working in concert, or the total domination and enslaving of another mind to a given task.

Digital transmission allows a user to take control of, in the modern age, practically any electronic. Due to the fact that we can purchase, or jury-rig, adapters for just about any protocol, it is possible to interface with anything from a PC to a Bluetooth speaker to a flat-screen TV to most modern cars. On delves, this is used predominantly to scout with drones. Exploration of this capability is ongoing, but with minor training, most users can reliably take near-total control of the command structure of a given device, including receiving and processing data from inputs such as cameras, timers, or anything else installed. The process is largely about feeling out what mental prompts translate to recognized commands.

The sharing of memories is currently considered to be both personal and useful. Memory sharing actually takes more control than gestalt formation when connected to another human without a buffer, so it is advised that if new users are sharing memories for the purposes of information gathering, they use secondary medium. Visual or audio data can be streamed directly to screens or speakers with practice, which carries none of the risks of falling into someone else's personality.

Gestalt minds are singular individuals composed of multiple personalities. There are two ways this can function; either one personality is dominant and the others are turned into organic hardware, or the personalities work together to create something consenting and functional. Attached bodies are controlled by the combined mind with no issues, especially if the primary personality for that body is allowed direct influence.

The formation of a gestalt is useful for several things but is a one hundred percent intimate experience. Whoever is involved in a gestalt will, without question, know literally everything about the other(s) for as long as it persists. The formation of a consenting gestalt requires trust on the parts of the users, otherwise one personality may reflexively attempt dominance. *The Order of Endless Rooms will treat any nonconsenting formation of a gestalt with the same attitude as we would sexual assault. Do not do this, under any circumstances.*

Combat while in a gestalt allows for impressive teamwork but does require training to coordinate properly. The severing of the connection without preparation is very painful and could be a liability.

Gestalts also share many of the orb effects of the sublimated personalities across every attached body.

Note—while enslaved to the prisoner gestalt (See Section 3-1, Part 9: Conference Incident), human minds were used to suppress the activities of the controlling intelligence of Officium Mundi. This indicates potential human ability beyond the capabilities of the dungeon tech, as so far, the skulljacks have not shown any ability beyond simply a very powerful, low-latency connection.

Contacts in the Order Directory tagged with "SJE" are experts on the subject and are open to contact.

Extra skulljack-related hardware is currently in development with the end goal of creating specialized devices for personal security and safe life-to-life connection. At present, the Order is in possession of sixteen wireless connectors and two experimental firewall mounts. The former may be requisitioned through your team leader. The latter are in development and not available.

Please, please, don't spread skulljacks outside the Order without approval. This is important. We need to have proper security features ready to roll out before we start or else risk turning the majority of humanity into enslaved puppets. This isn't about keeping some secret or conspiracy (See Section 1, Part 2: We Are Not a Conspiracy). This is about keeping humanity safe from bad-faith actors until we have fail-safes in place.

James felt like he was going to have to rearrange a lot of that. Find some way to section it in a way that made it flow better. Ugh. Editing. He should hire an editor. Could he do that? He wouldn't even have to induct them as a delver, just tell them it was for an RPG setting or something. That was an idea. Another idea was that he should get something to eat, he thought as his stomach rumbled. It was well past normal human lunchtime, and his habit of ignoring breakfast was biting him in the stomach.

"Do you wanna go get a sandwich?" James asked the camraconda that was somehow managing to relax in the chair across from James's desk. James had been meaning to get comfortable chairs for a while—something plush, but that you didn't quite sink into, a noble style of chair that might or might not actually exist—but his life recently had been basically nonstop working on dungeon stuff, and the little details tended to slip through the cracks. "There's a place down the street that closes early, but they're open for another hour or so. They say they're an ice cream parlor, but they make great meatball subs, and I want one," James continued.

The camraconda in question was the leader of the safe haven of the tower. Technically, most of them were the same age, so James was trying to not think of him as an elder. They didn't really remember their creation at all, but they had a fairly coherent idea that they were put together around the same time. But once in the tower, and beyond the influence range of their puppeteer, freed to be real people, they had started to mature emotionally at different rates.

This one had been the one to lead the fight against the defectors. He had killed his own siblings to keep them from revealing their home to the dungeon. It was, by all accounts, not a pleasant memory at all, and it had left him feeling like he was forced into a role of responsibility and growth well before he was ready for it. A leader who didn't ask for the job but knew he couldn't just give it up.

James empathized, even if he didn't really *understand*.

So he—the camraconda had chosen male pronouns when asked—had been the one to take a risk on James. He had led his people out into the world, and that risk had so far paid off. He was also sort of the camracondas' liaison with the Order.

Within about ten minutes of everyone arriving back, it had become an issue that the camracondas couldn't speak. While everyone else was trying different solutions, Virgil of all people had taken the initiative, grabbed a couple of volunteer snakes, installed skulljacks in them, and whipped up something that was part scarf, part speaker system. It was a cobbled-together mess, but it let the changed camracondas use basic text-to-speech to start to communicate.

Of course, this created a massive cascade of problems, like how you taught a snake that sort of knew the language but had never spoken how to use English. Or how to deal with the ones that were so terrified or repulsed by dungeon tech that they refused the upgrade. But they were working on it. And many of the camracondas were *very* fast learners.

"Apologize." The blue-and-gray-cabled camraconda spoke to James in a digital voice. His words were starting to take on a personal touch as he gained more control of the system—a little deeper, a little more alive and optimistic. But for now it was mostly a dull digital monotone. "Outside not safe?" The words were a question, and not a hard one to decipher, despite the still-in-progress language lessons. It turned out that having an instantly indexable dictionary on a hard drive plugged into your brain made it easy to pass for conversational.

"Outside's probably perfectly safe," James said with a sigh. "There's a bit of a disagreement about how much we should reveal to the world right now. About you guys, yeah, but also about everything else. But I'm kind of in charge, and personally, I'm in the camp that no one is ever going to get used to having technorganic basilisks around if you don't expose them to technorganic basilisks."

James was reasonably sure the snake didn't have eyebrows to raise. He knew this, actually, because he was looking at it. But *somehow* he still felt like he was being judged as the leader's camera eye lensed on him.

"I think, not game," the camraconda said, laying his head back on his coils of cable on the chair. "My people take time also."

They'd known each other for under a week, and the two of them were already on the same wavelength. Even through the language barrier, James felt like the snake understood him, and he understood in turn.

And in this case, he understood the sentiment, because he felt it, too. James was perfectly willing to risk exposing *himself* as a wizard, but if someone asked him for a list of names and addresses for the rest of the Order, he'd probably shoot first and ask questions later. And the camraconda leader would be totally okay walking—slithering?—around out in broad daylight if not for the fact that there were over fifty other camracondas under his care that he didn't want to draw unwanted attention to.

"Oh, hey." James changed the subject, really trying very hard to find a reason not to keep typing up the operations manual. "Did you hear one of your young ones chose a name?" James realized that *young* wasn't the right word but used it almost on reflex.

It was a strange event for everyone. The humans had all kind of assumed that the camracondas had developed or chosen names during their time in the tower, but as it turned out, that just wasn't a thing for them. Their microculture had never come up with the idea, maybe. But now that they were out in the wider world, many of them had taken to the thought eagerly. Though only one had picked her name so far.

"Frequency-of-Sunlight. Yes." The elder perked up again, laying his head lightly on the edge of the chair as he spoke to James. "She watches sunsets."

It was such a simple thing, but both of them sat there for a minute, just appreciating. Being proud of an artificial, weaponized life form that had found beauty in the sun she finally got to see.

"I should try to call my mom again," James sighed out, wistfully. "Ask her why I didn't get a name that cool." He gave a joking huff as he asked, "What kind of name is *James* for an adventurer, anyway? Maybe she'll actually answer the phone this time."

"You name confuses." The elder spoke, and it sounded like he was trying to convey amusement in his tone. "Some choose name. Some receive name. Gifts?" he asked. "El and Momo say names special. They chose. Harvey also say. His name ancient gift. Different reasons for specialty."

James tried to explain names for a good twenty minutes before he got tired of saying the phrase *from a certain cultural viewpoint* and just called Sarah to come in and take over for him. The moment that he had really conceded that he wasn't good at this was when he'd realized that the camracondas didn't have a great grasp on what parents were.

It wasn't giving up. It was that he still had another twelve chapters to write.

His parents never did call him back to explain his name.

Order of Endless Rooms Operations Manual
Section 1, Part 4: Ethics
As mentioned in our mission statement, the overarching goal of the Order is to improve long-term quality of life for as many people as possible by eliminating systemic problems and creating new systems that enhance daily living.

This presents a number of problems, as our increased power compared to a baseline human puts us at sometimes-absurd advantages and can often create novel situations where there aren't easy answers.

These are a few guidelines to keep in mind, moving forward. They are not hard rules, merely things to consider. Violating one or more of these by accident or in crisis is not automatically grounds for punishment or exile.

However, while we acknowledge that mistakes and panic situations happen, we also understand that those are not always excuses. Failure to consider the ethics of situations, or failure to learn from past errors, is grounds for dismissal from the Order and all that entails.

There are very few things we forbid outright. There are multiple worlds of gray areas out there, and we aren't writing policy until we understand better. We're all going to make mistakes, so we should all learn together.

Creation of Life: With the acquisition of yellow, purple, and possibly red orbs, the ability to shape life forms to our needs arises. This is both a blessing and a burden. You might get a creation like those you've seen paired with other delvers, Pendragon or Ganesh, perhaps. Helpful, friendly. Dangerous, yes, but not to those they care about. But without proper care, you may just as easily get something instantly hostile and very threatening.

Similarly, it may be a problem on the axis of power. You may create something that is unstable and, while benevolent, fated to die under the weight of its own ability.

A general ground rule to follow here is to be careful and be responsible. If you create a life, that is now your life to take care of. Similar rules to raising a child or pet should apply; you take responsibility for the care and feeding of the life, for their education and emotional development. It is for this reason it is not generally okay to make life purely to be a tool or a weapon.

Tampering with free will: While this may seem like an obvious no, there are several areas where things get complicated. For example, we have the capacity to block certain memories. Should we use this to preserve our secrecy, if that is to the benefit of others? Or if they *ask us to?* This is a hard question to answer, because for most people, it's still no, and that is an okay stance to take.

But there will be times when we may be in a position to make a choice on behalf of another person. Whether that is through eliminating memories that may be traumatic to them or puppeting their actions through a skulljack to save their life, there can be no hard rule that might prevent us from working to save lives.

Instead, the only rule here is that you operate in good faith. There is, again, no policy to skirt around, no loopholes to find. Act with the best interests of others in mind, and never use these options to exploit anyone, and you'll be on stable ground. Even if sometimes the costs to our doubts are high.

Sharing of magic: Your payouts in orbs, items, and other upgrades are yours to do with as you choose. Sometimes you may choose to share these with other people.

There is no rule against this; just be aware that not everyone is mentally equipped to deal with the unknown in this way. Ask questions of them first. These questions can be blatantly suspicious from our perspective, because from anyone else's perspective, they will be meaningless and silly. Try not to share dungeon tech with anyone it would impact more negatively than the benefit of a couple skill ranks.

(For more information on the sharing of skulljacks, see Section 6, Part 1.)

Killing and other acts of violence: While not a signatory of the Geneva Conventions, assume at all times that the Order operates under similar rules. Proper treatment of prisoners, no involvement of civilians or uninitiated in combat, and no use of indiscriminate, wide-scale weapons.

Similarly, killing should be reserved for self-defense in combat. We are not assassins, and no matter what the political realities of our world are, picking off singular individuals who cause problems only incentivizes the next monster to hire more bodyguards. For both practical and moral reasons, the killing of priority targets is to be used only as a last resort in the event that they represent an immediate extant threat to a population.

Secrecy: Any action that makes us more known to the public, or to government or private agencies, is a risk. These risks must be measured and judged before taking serious actions in public or around uninitiated individuals.

Consider whom you're with. Consider how much of the veil you're lifting. And, most importantly, consider if your actions will lead to direct repercussions against our Order.

But also, never forget that we have chosen a duty to help. And if your choice, especially in a crisis, is between secrecy and helping someone, never pick secrecy.

(See Section 1, Part 2: We Are Not a Conspiracy.)

James's phone rang, startling him out of his glassy-eyed stare at the index he was still trying to figure out if he wanted to reformat *again*. He jumped a little, awkwardly brushing away crumbs of the hamburger he'd demolished off the desk as he picked up his cell phone and checked the caller ID. It was Lua, which was strange. There was no scheduled check-in for another two days, which meant . . . nothing good that James could think of.

James opened with "Hey, Lua. What's up?"

The woman spoke, and James *instantly* felt himself tense up at her tone. "Something's wrong," she said, urgency lacing her voice. "There's agents here."

James checked the clock. Almost 3:00 p.m. And it was a Friday. The high school was just getting out, students would be moving around, and the dungeon might be active and hunting. Lua was almost stumbling to get her words out, so whatever was going on, it instantly made James nervous.

"Agents?" James asked, already kicking his chair back and pocketing his keys. The blue-gray camraconda watched him from his claimed napping point with curious worry. "Agents from which dungeon?"

"No, *human agents*," the therapist hissed out in a whisper. "They're asking questions about students, but *not the missing students*. They picked up the schedules and personal files for those three kids I told you about. But there's something wrong with them. The glasses you gave me say they're from something called OM-1, but they're telling people—"

There was a sudden stop in the words. James felt his heart leap into his chest as he heard a knocking sound on the other end of the phone. "We need to go," he told the camraconda leader. "We have to move, now. *Hey!*" James rushed out his office door and shouted out into the lair. "I need help, now! We need to move! Problems! Who's here?!" he demanded in a harsh bark that commanded instant attention.

On the other end of the phone he was still holding to his ear, he heard the sound quality change dramatically as Lua flicked it to speaker, presumably muting him as well, but he shut up just in case. "Come in!" he heard, slightly muffled. She'd stuck the phone under something, maybe? "Oh, hello, Officer," she said politely, though James heard the strain in her voice.

"We aren't law enforcement, ma'am," James heard a thick male voice say. "Though we are going to need you to come with us. We have some questions."

James caught Nate's eye as the chef rushed out to the main room and mimed a gun at the other man. Nate nodded and booked it for the elevator to the basement. "Get Momo and El!" James mouthed at him, holding his hand over the phone's speaker.

". . . going on?" James heard from the other end. "Is someone in trouble?" Lua was asking. James heard her standing up, shuffling stuff around. "Just let me grab my—"

There was a sudden yelp of pain and then a third voice. "No," the man's voice said, blunt and cruel. "Three. Bring her to the car. Two, search the office. If there's heavy relics here, or if she contacted anyone, have Three kill her to be safe. Four, you're with me. Find the primary targets and—"

James desperately wanted to know what they were saying, but something had jumped out at him. They could absolutely *not* know that Lua had called him. So he hung up, as fast as he could. A second later he realized they could search her phone logs, but this at least bought him scant time.

There were a few camracondas up here, looking around nervously as James shouted orders. Harvey and Simon had also come out from the back kitchen and were starting to ask James what was going on, just as the elevator doors dinged open again and Nate sprinted out, black plastic cases in his hands.

"Field operative under attack," James snapped out sharply. "Humans. Maybe a rival organization." His phone was already up again, dialing. "Alanna!" he barked, cutting off her friendly greeting. "No time! High school! Go! We'll meet you there—enemy humans!"

James looked around frantically. Momo was here, following Nate, but this was the extent of his forces right now. He didn't know what to do. How was he supposed to retake control of the situation?

Harvey stepped forward and clapped a hand on James's shoulder. "Get moving!" the older man said calmly. "I'll get the word out. Momo will keep us updated on location. Go!"

James gave him a look of pure relief. "Yeah!" he said, nodding. "Okay. Make sure you tell Dave. Pendragon is our biggest weapon right now." James looked around. "Nate, Simon, you're with me. Um . . ." He glanced at the camraconda who had been lounging in his office, now perched at attention nearby, with one other snake flanking him. "Do you . . ."

They nodded in unison.

"Okay. Leader, you're with us. Momo, you and Frequency are our backup. Follow behind; if things get lethal, *run*. If they get weird, step in and tilt the weirdness." James took one of the cases from Nate, striding in long steps toward the door. He didn't have time for armor; seconds could count here. As he walked, he grabbed his coat off the hook by the door and checked the shoulder holster for the comforting grip of his sidearm. As he kicked the door open and held it for the others to start jogging to the cars, Harvey approached him, phone in hand and determination on his face.

The other man was digging in his pocket, and a second later, he pulled out and tossed James a blue orb. With a solemn nod he turned and started a rapid-fire explanation to whomever he'd called.

James didn't waste time. He absorbed the orb without thinking, the thing slipping into his skin for once without protest, and then turned and ran for his car.

[+6 Activations : Attach]

He didn't have time to think about ways to use that until he'd already hit the gas, tearing out of the parking lot and nearly bottoming out his car on the incline that led to the main road. Behind him, Momo drove much more conservatively while James flagrantly ignored traffic laws and put the pedal down.

A 1996 Subaru Legacy was, all things considered, not exactly the car he wanted to be driving into battle. He'd rather teleport, actually. But if they had to chase someone, teleporting was the *worst* idea. The car was *obviously* not what Nate wanted to be sitting in the front seat of. In the back, Simon had simply folded the seats down, and he and the elder lay mostly prone in the trunk alongside the limited arsenal they'd brought with them. The thing was, though, when you were driving through semiresidential areas where the speed limit was thirty, and you didn't bother to hold back from coaxing the car up to a hundred miles an hour, it didn't much matter that you weren't in a sports car.

James gritted his teeth as he sped through an intersection, narrowly dodging a bit of cross traffic and almost certainly causing a collision in his wake. In his pocket, his phone hadn't stopped buzzing the entire time, and in the distance he could hear sirens.

But right now, there was only one way forward, one thing on his mind.

There was an enemy on the board, and they were threatening a member of the Order. One of the people who had put their trust in James, who were willing to go with him on this weird and circuitous journey to the future. One of the people he absolutely, under no circumstances, would not be giving up without a fight.

Order of Endless Rooms Operations Manual
Section 1, Part 3: You Are Not Expendable
One more short personal conversation before we get into the procedures, lists, and analytical looks at threats and treasures. This one isn't that long, don't worry.

You, you reading this, as a member of the Order of Endless Rooms, are not expendable.

This is a coin with two sides. On one side, if you are *ever* in trouble, we are here to support you. If you need money or resources, if you need help for your family or loved ones, if you need reliable transportation, if you need to be bailed out of jail, if you need to be bailed out of life-threatening danger, if you need *anything*, we will do everything we can to keep you safe.

There is a protocol to this, but it's a simple one: escalate problems to your team leader, and in turn, if you are the one who's had the problem escalated to you and can't handle it, bump it up to Order logistics or leadership.

This ties into the reverse of that coin.

All of us have a responsibility to each other. If your friends or companions are in trouble, it's up to us, as a group, to help. This is, functionally, the sort of thing that seems either very obvious for a functioning society or very obvious for a semifunctioning cult. Being perfectly honest, we're somewhere in between the two.

We have no interest in forcing cooperation, nor are we going to mandate that you spend a certain amount of your time or resources on this. This is just a statement; none of us in the core group are ever going to treat you like you're expendable, and we want you to know that and hopefully share that vision.

You aren't pawns to be sacrificed in some play for power. You aren't tools, or weapons, or toys. Even if we fill those roles sometimes, none of us are ever *anything* less than a person. So if you need us, we're there for you. No matter whom it puts us at odds with, or how inconvenient it is, or what the cost.

We will, almost certainly, lose people eventually. It's a tragedy none of us are looking forward to. But if it happens, we refuse to let it happen because we treated anyone in our Order like they weren't important. Like they weren't a life worth holding on to. Like they weren't valued and loved and part of what makes us feel like we can improve the world in the first place.

So whether you're natural born or a created life form, an info-morph or a clone, or anything else we run into eventually, know this, above all else.

You are not, ever, expendable.

CHAPTER 17

The car screamed into the school zone with approximately zero regard for such petty things as rules or speed limits.

James had several skill ranks in driving. And he'd used them before, sure. But he'd never *used* them. Not like this, pushing his imbued skills and physical reflexes to the absolute limits. He had slipped into a state of what felt like total awareness, his hands guiding the vehicle through pinpoint turns, wheels screaming in protest as they wove through other cars, pedestrians, and sometimes trees. The world flashed by outside, a blur that left Nate white-knuckled on the armrest and James grinding his teeth as he processed the incoming information on pure magical instinct.

The high school loomed, approaching at eighty miles an hour. James didn't bother with the driveway, didn't take the time to pull through the pack of buses lining up to leave. Instead, he threaded the needle between two groups of students who were still unaware of the onrushing Subaru-shaped projectile and threw his car up the sloped lawn that separated the road from the building itself.

His eyes had caught something, his hands reacting before his brain really processed it. But as his car bottomed out in the half-empty parking lot, bumper scraping against the asphalt, James didn't slow. He slammed on the gas again, pulling the hardest right turn possible, and impacted the man in the black suit and sunglasses who was currently trying to shove Lua's unconscious body into the back seat of a car.

The man, James had just enough time to process as the sound of denting metal and crunching bone echoed, looked like an extra from *Men in Black*. Bald, rectangular head. Goatee, vaguely tan skin. Sunglasses that were currently flying off to somewhere unimportant, along with an earpiece now flapping in the air along with his cheap suit jacket. He windmilled through the air before slamming into the pavement and sliding, rather than rolling, several dozen feet before nailing his head against the driver's door of a parked car.

"Go!" James screamed, slamming on the brakes and skidding the car to a halt at a right angle to the aisle, forty feet away.

The others didn't hesitate. Nate threw his door open so hard as he sprang out of the seat that it slammed back into place on the momentum. But he wasn't there to get hit; the stocky chef looking strangely out of place with the compact, deadly looking mechanism of the rifle held professionally against his shoulder, all the while wearing a stained apron and white cap. He advanced on the agent's car in a low crouch, steps short and precise.

Simon and the volunteer camraconda didn't have the same kind of training. They scrambled out the rear doors, Simon with a pistol in hand, the camraconda with just his natural weapons, and followed in Nate's wake anyway. Circling around, trying to get a good angle on the other agent.

They didn't need to bother. The man stepped out from behind the vehicle, scowling beneath his sunglasses. The second he saw Nate, he flicked a hand and something changed.

"Freeze!" Nate bellowed, voice commanding and clearly prepared to take no shit. Around them, the students who were starting to leave for the day took notice. A few shouts called out. Then more, then a scream.

The man didn't freeze. James, stepping out of the car himself, saw that he was no longer just wearing a suit. He had a glimmering copper-and-ivory bracer on his left arm, and his right leg was encased in a gleaming silver greave. He also had his own pistol unholstered and was firing at Nate.

The first shot went wide, probably because he'd just watched his partner get flattened by a beige metal brick and was a little shaken. The second one never came.

The agent froze in place, the camraconda locking his gaze on the man, stopping his grip on the pistol with the trigger barely depressed.

"He said *freeze*," James hissed as he stepped out of the car, sprinting over toward where they'd unceremoniously dropped Lua.

"Simon! Check the other one!" Nate snapped, and the younger man rushed to obey. The whole time, the chef kept the rifle up and on the frozen agent, though he did step out of the pistol's line of fire.

James approached their car—a black sedan, *of course*—and circled around behind the allied snake, careful not to block his line of sight. He was ten feet away when the agent started to move.

The bracer on the man's arm suddenly sparkled slightly, and James saw what looked like a latticework sphere made of lines of light flicker in the air around him. And then, all of a sudden, the man was moving. The gun fired twice, too-rapid pinging sounding as the bullets hit nothing but parked cars. Then his head snapped toward James, the gun pivoting in his direction even as the plate-mail guard on his leg also started to glimmer in the afternoon air.

James shot him.

The Walther P38 was a marvel of German engineering. It was cheap, durable, and continued to be useful in the modern era if you were interested in putting nine-millimeter holes in people. It was also a gun that James felt so magically comfortable with that he was pretty sure he could go target shooting while asleep. That, mixed with his upgraded Aim from the dungeon under this very school, made missing something he didn't really need to do.

The first bullet caught the agent in the chest, just above the heart. This caused the man to stagger slightly and let out a rough grunt. Then the agent's bracer flashed again, and the second through eighth bullets slammed into a barrier of glittering golden light that suddenly started flaring into existence every time one of the shots was fired.

The man froze when this happened, the resolute camraconda not having looked away, even as his gaze had stopped having an effect when the shield had intercepted it somehow.

Then *Nate* shot the man, and the .308 round burrowed through his throat in a spray of blood that held itself static in the air for a second after emerging.

If only a few people had noticed the fight happening before, the crack of the rifle certainly demanded some more attention. Especially as Nate dipped his stance to aim at the crumpling body and shot him another three times. Now that their skirmish had been going more than ten seconds, James was hearing teenage screams and the sounds of panic from all around.

He ran past the downed agent to check on Lua and was almost to the car when Simon slammed into its bumper, back first. James spun in place, yelling a warning and trying to ignore the cracking sound he'd heard when the lanky man had impacted. The other agent was up, on his feet, leg dropping back to the asphalt like he'd just delivered a roundhouse kick. He *also* had a silver greave on, identical to the first agent's. And the same kind of bracer on his arm, poking out along with some other bit of probable magic from under his jacket sleeve.

Nate threw himself sideways, hitting the ground in a way that was going to leave a dozen tiny scrapes across his bare arms, as the agent started shooting at him. He rolled sideways, grabbing the startled camraconda as he did so and not stopping until the two of them were in a low crouch half covered by someone's obscenely oversize pickup truck.

Whoever owned that truck was going to have a hell of an insurance claim to make, as bullets continued to put black holes into it. James, crouched behind the car just in front of the agency sedan, watched as the man in the suit kept firing, over and over. Every fifteen rounds or so, a tiny glint of light showed from under his coat sleeve, but he'd just keep shooting. It took about thirty seconds—what felt like a couple hundred shots—for James to catch a glimpse of the bracelet he was wearing. A glance at the downed agent showed a similar bangle on his own wrist.

And the first agent *was* down now. Lying with wide, empty eyes turned up toward the sky, in a pool of his own blood. James would find time to be horrified and revolted later. Right now . . .

"They've got shields!" he yelled at Nate, who was braving return fire to try to force the agent into cover with a couple snapped-off shots of his own. The air-rippling crack of the rifle drowned out the snaps of the pistol. "They block one thing at a time! Leader, lock him down!" He wished the camraconda had picked a name that he could yell right now.

James felt the sensation of attention being turned on him, as an almost physical thing, and was already moving by the time the agent started shooting his way. Bullets landed in perfectly grouped clusters where his head was a second ago, ruining yet another high schooler's car windshield in a spray of glass. James winced and flinched as bullets struck the asphalt around him or ricocheted off other cars, his enhanced brain just barely keeping up with the fact that the angles were changing and he knew the agent was moving. Running perpendicular to the fight, trying to get an angle on where they were all hiding.

A line of burning fire lanced its way across his leg, and he nearly toppled sideways as a trio of ricocheting bullets tore across his thigh like an animal's claw. James snarled but stayed crouched and waited for the moment.

Then the gunfire stopped. Suddenly, and sharply, the air was silent.

"Now!" James yelled, popping up and unloading the rest of his ammo on the frozen form of the agent. His bullets just seemed to stagger the man, though, knocking him around but not injuring. Even the ones that *very deliberately* hit him in the head.

Nate's shots didn't do that. Nate's bullets put big, problematic holes in the target. In the *person.* Sprays of human blood painted the parking lot a slightly darker shade, the smell of death taking over the air like a miasma.

"Clear!" Nate shouted.

"Holy shit." James choked the words out. "Holy shit . . ." He was broken out of his combat shock by Nate slapping him on the shoulder. "We just killed two people," James muttered.

"I killed two people," Nate said flatly. "You helped. Kinda surprised the car hit didn't put the first fucker down, though." His voice was loud—a bit too loud. He was speaking up to hear himself through the earplugs, and James was kind of grateful, because he'd neglected ear protection entirely and now felt like an idiot as the ringing in his ears intensified.

"We should . . . we should go." James gasped for breath he hadn't realized he was short on. His hands vibrated on the grip of his gun. "Fuck, there's two more. And there's people watching us. And running." He looked around at the parking lot. "Shit. We need to get Simon and Lua out of here. And also . . ." James holstered his gun and took a series of long steps toward where a cluster of teachers and security officers were cautiously making their way toward him. "FBI!" he shouted, pulling his absolutely fake badge out of his pocket and holding it aloft. "Fuck off!"

Nate raised his eyebrows at that. He raised his eyebrows even more when one of the security staff said something to the group and they *actually fucked off*, retreating to the safe distance of the school courtyard. "No fucking way you're the FBI," he muttered to himself. Though it didn't really matter, did it? Right now they held authority over the field by virtue of being the only ones alive and armed. He'd ask James later; right now, he was still on his guard, in a low profile near the tall frame of the pickup truck, rifle barrel kept steady but pointed down at the ground.

There was a pause, and James listened around him, trying to catch any hint of incoming conflict or the other two agents.

Then Momo arrived.

She didn't jump a lawn like James had chosen to. Instead, she wove through the line of buses, behind which students taking cover tried to wave her down. Casually slipping past one of the braver security staff, who was stopping traffic, she rolled over the curb, cut through two lines of parking lot, and slammed on the brakes with an awkwardly hard stomp as she came upon the site of the battle.

It had been less than five minutes since the fighting started.

"What happened?!" Momo screamed out her rolled-down driver's window, Frequency-of-Sunlight coiled in the passenger seat next to her, equally wide-eyed as the two of them looked to James for answers.

"No time. Get Simon into the car and get him to a hospital, now," James barked, pointing one arm even as he was taking long, loping steps toward one of the downed agents. "Sunny, keep him locked! I think he broke something! Take Lua, too!" He knelt by the dead man and tried for a second to pull the bracer off before deciding it was a waste of precious time. "Here." He tossed the much-easier-to-remove bracelet to Nate, slipping behind a van to grab the second bracelet off the other corpse. "Ugh." He covered his mouth against the smell of blood and bile, but his anger was still simmering, and it kept him steady enough as he looted the body. He didn't even think of trying for the greaves.

"Mmuhh?" The soft voice made James's head snap up. "What's happening?"

"Lua." He rose up, slipping the bracelet onto his own wrist as he approached where Nate was settling the therapist back onto her feet. "Where are the kids?" James asked sharply.

She shook her head, short brown hair rustling in the wind. "They . . . oh god, I think they killed Alexis." Lua looked somehow worse after regaining consciousness. "The others. The others! They ran! They'll go . . . north. Toward the old quarry. They have a spot up on the hill over it. The agents were following them!" Lua looked around, seeming to only just now notice how heavily armed the man supporting her was. "Wait, the man who hit me . . ."

"Don't worry about that now," Momo said, stepping up and wedging a shoulder under Lua's arm. "We're getting you two to the hospital," she said, as much bravery as she could force into her voice.

James turned briefly. "Okay. We need to go. I know the place Lua's talking about. Let's move." He repeated the words like he was psyching himself up, barely hearing the sound of a car door slamming.

Momo reappeared from behind a car. "James." The word was a knife in the air. "Here. I got it working—don't ask questions. The activation is a triangle of cigarette ash around it and one strike to the base. Don't point it at anything you want intact." She awkwardly dug through the dozens of pockets in her long coat until she found what she was looking for and tossed a simple padlock to James.

The weight of it stung his hand as he caught it. He had a million questions. None of them did he have time for now. "Thanks," he said instead, only to realize she'd already left. "Nate, ready?"

"No," the older man said, slamming the rear door of James's car behind the elder before getting into the passenger seat himself, awkwardly trying to position the rifle in a way that he could still easily use it. "Let's go."

James practically swung himself into the driver's seat, not bothering to buckle up as he hit the gas. In the back seat, the camraconda lurched backward, tumbling slightly into the trunk door. "Old quarry," he muttered to himself. "Okay, that's a left, and then a straight shot." James took a shaky breath before throwing his car in reverse, hooking a turn, and driving right back over the lawn he'd come in through. "Where the fuck are the police?" James demanded as he sped past clusters of students who were brave or stupid enough to have tried to hide behind cars or trees instead of just running.

"They take longer to respond than you might think. Especially when you're not sticking around to cause collateral damage," Nate informed him. James spared the man a glance; he was fiddling with the bracelet on his wrist and didn't seem to *care* what they'd just done. "Huh. Weird. Okay, got it." He did something, and James felt a twisting in the air of the car. "Maybe don't do it while you're driving, but you might want to bring up the bracelet's abilities."

"It's what?" James asked. That was a mistake. Apparently just thinking about it was enough to do the trick. And the words dived into his field of vision, almost making him veer off the road.

[Bind Firearm—3—88/300—128:14:3:18 (2)
Cluster Shot—54—16,794/100,000—18:12 (44)
Munitions Dump—23—1,002/2,000—10:01 (103)]

Nate whistled. "Okay, I'm not that good at math, but I think this guy dumped a few hundred thousand rounds into the world if that does what I think it does. What's that thing you keep saying about fucking entropy?"

"That's not . . . what . . ." James started to say and then trailed off. "What are you talking about?"

"You've got jitters," Nate said calmly, pointing at where James's hands were vibrating on the steering wheel. "Happens to everyone after a fight. You need a distraction."

"I've been in fights before."

"Yeah?" Nate didn't really ask, just raised his eyebrows, already knowing he didn't believe James. "Like that one? Where you hit a human with a car hard enough to pancake most people?" The chef shook his head. "No, you've never shot at anyone. Never been shot at, either."

"I've been shot at by maimframes," James replied, feeling strangely defensive. "Hurt less, though."

"You hit?" Nate looked over sharply and scanned over James's body.

"In the leg. I'm fine. I clot faster than most people."

"Of course you fucking do," Nate muttered. "So, what's up with the magic gun bracelet?"

"No idea," James said, latching onto the conversational life raft with a sigh. "The names are descriptive, which is unusual. One of the numbers is . . ." He watched his readout from the corner of his eye as he drove down a winding side street surrounded by trees that were just starting to recover from winter. ". . . Yeah, definitely a countdown. The rest could be anything, though I'll bet the x-out-of-x is uses. Dunno if it's going down or up, though. Hey, do you smoke?" James asked out of nowhere.

"Up," Nate said. "At least, it did when I binded my gun. And yes."

"Bonded," James replied reflexively. "Or bound, I guess." He flicked his eyes to the rearview mirror and caught the camera lens of the figure in the back seat. "That's called simple past tense; there's four types of past tense, and they're all stupid," James informed the camraconda, who had been curious about everything *except* a language lesson.

James wanted to say something else. Wanted to tell the camraconda thank you, or that he was sorry. Wanted to say he didn't understand what was happening, or why. Wanted to scream, to cry, to throw up, to ask why those men were killers, to demand to know why he'd had to kill them in turn. Instead, he did what he always did.

Made a joke. Wore dry wit like armor.

Or, in this case, armed himself. "I normally don't say this, but I need you to smoke in my car," James told Nate, pulling out the ashtray that he kept loose change in, dumping the coins to the floor, and handing the plastic container to Nate. The man just shrugged and pulled out a cigarette, happy to oblige. "I'm opening the window, though," James commented wryly

It took a couple minutes of the car rolling along in silence before Nate stubbed out his smoke, rolling up the window as he did so, and spoke. "Hey," Nate said gruffly. "Car coming up." He pointed, and James looked.

They were approaching the traffic light at the intersection of the main road. The building on top of what used to be a stone quarry would be ahead, on the right, with a hilltop park overlooking it. Right in front of them was another car, parked at the light. A minivan, and not important.

But just in front of it, a black sedan had pulled off to the side of the road.

And out of that car, from the passenger door, a man in a suit had stepped up to the curb and was impolitely talking to a pair of nervous-looking teenagers.

"I am not ready for this," James said, his voice shaking.

"Bind your gun," Nate told him firmly. "We've got this."

From behind him, James felt the elder's corded snout bump into his shoulder. He took as deep a breath as he could with the smell of cigarette smoke still in the air, trying to quiet the screaming voice inside him. It had been one thing to ambush the first agents. They'd been in the process of hurting one of his people, and James had been *furious*. But now that fury was spent, leaving only a quiet uncertainty that he'd done the right thing.

But here, they'd come up on them at exactly the right time again. Mysterious government agents accosting some kids whose main crime was knowing something weird. Also sort of blocking traffic. That one was a capital offense, he joked to himself.

James felt that spark of anger reignite, if not to the same blaze as before.

"Nate, hit the car. Leader, with me on the sidewalk." James felt his voice come out cold. He kept one hand on the wheel while he pulled his pistol out of its holster and sent a mental command to the bracelet on his wrist. *Bind weapon? Please?* he thought at it, hoping he'd hit the mark.

There was a rush of power and a flare of copper light, and James knew it had worked.

He pulled up behind the van, carefully adding himself to the flow of normal traffic. Everything was normal; everything was fine. There was *absolutely no reason* for the agents to suspect there was about to be a huge problem.

James waited for the light to turn green, edging forward just enough that they were near parallel to the sedan. He could see the faces of the two kids now as they pressed their backs up against the brick wall that separated the sidewalk from the residential gardens behind it, fear painted on their features. The agent was clearly ordering them into the car, one hand on his gun in a casual display of authoritative violence.

The anger was back now.

The car behind James honked, once, as he came to a stop. The agent on the street, and probably the one behind the black-tinted window, both looked over. And that was all it took to blow the ambush.

It was too little, too late, for the agency goons.

Nate started firing *through* James's passenger window, making James wonder why he'd rolled it up in the first place. The first shot blew a hole through the window; the second collapsed what was left into safely broken shards. Then he just opened up on them, firing as fast as he could pull the trigger, practically unable to miss with his line of fire lined up to the driver's window of the other car.

James himself burst out of the driver's seat, keeping himself low to the side of his car as he circled around the rear, gun in one hand and ashtray in the other. Through the trunk window, the elder had gotten a good look at the agent streetside, but that would only last a second or two if they had shields like the first ones. So James moved fast, taking a few rapid steps to cover the ground and popping up in a firing position. He barely had time to acknowledge the webwork sphere of golden light from the driver's seat as Nate's bullets were deflected.

He needed to end this quickly, he realized. So he tried something new and pulsed another order to the bracelet. *One cluster shot, please,* James asked it nicely as he lined up his gun on the agent, noting that the kids had barely had time to cover their ears and duck since the shooting had started.

The Walther erupted in his hands. He'd pulled the trigger once and three bullets had fired. James had accelerated perception, enhanced aim, and what amounted to about twenty years of shooting experience, and he didn't fully *understand* what had just occurred. His Aim told him that he'd just fired three times, all of them exactly on target. His orb skill, likewise, seemed to click to a new line of thinking as he processed what had happened, instructing him where to put those shots to maximize hit rate. But neither of those things helped him figure out how the bullets had actually *done that*.

The bullets all hit the agent in the back. And whatever they were enhanced with, whether it was armored suit coats or empowered physiques, it didn't seem set to stand up to that kind of shot.

The first bullet impacted, flattened, and dropped to the ground. The second one bored a slight hole into the man, leaving a trickle of blood. The third got through and started to do real, actual, human-killing damage.

James didn't know any of that. He just lined up shots and took them. And by the time his brain caught up to the fact that he'd wounded the agent, he'd emptied his magazine on cluster shots in largely the same spot on the man's back. The agent—whatever his number was—never had a chance to get his shield up. He was locked down by the elder one second and dead to James's gun the next.

The suit dropped. James stood up to be seen by the high schoolers. "Get in the car!" he yelled, bellowing to be heard over the crack of Nate's gun. "Come on!"

One of them, the taller kid with the curly hair, jolted into action, pulling his friend along in his wake. As they tried to cross between the cars, though, James realized that the gunfire he was hearing was *two* weapons. The agent in the car was shooting back, and when the kids entered his firing arc, he switched to targeting one of them.

The shorter kid's arm jerked, then his leg, a spray of red painting the friend hauling him along. James screamed something incoherent and popped up over the back of his own car to spray bullets down at the black sedan. It didn't take much effort at all now to get the bracelet to reload him whenever he got low, and he did his best to cover the kids. But the car was armored, and the agent inside, wherever he was, didn't even bother to rotate his shield away from Nate's more powerful .308 shots. James's bullets just bounced off, doing little more than scratching the paint. He jerked himself back down as bullets raked his own vehicle, leaning out and grabbing the kid's hand to pull the two of them into cover. "Leader!" he yelled, yanking open the rear driver's side door. "Stabilize!"

The snake slithered out, and both kids' eyes went *wide*. Though it wasn't like they could get *more* afraid now than they were before. The one who'd been shot looked like he was going into shock, and he was losing a lot of blood. Something had to be done.

So the camraconda looked down at him, and he froze. Most of his bodily functions, along with his freedom of movement, were simply put on pause. James knew from experience that he could still think, and he hoped that the kid didn't keep feeling pain. But this was the best they could do for now.

"All right," he muttered, scooping up the ashtray from where he'd set it by his rear wheel. "No more fucking around," James said, as if they had been to begin with.

He circled to the rear of the car and fished the padlock out of his coat. Set it on the pavement with the lock facing toward the agent's car. There was still no sign of the man inside, and James had a flash of fear as he realized the car itself might be enchanted or shielded. But Nate was at least keeping whatever problem there might be suppressed with an endless stream of bullets showing off exactly how dangerous the bracelets were, even though they kept flaring off the projected shield.

Carefully dumping out Nate's cigarette ashes, James traced a triangle around the lock, pointing toward the enemy car. And then, without hesitation, he slapped the heel of his palm down on the line facing himself.

The lock popped open, and the air rippled. The thin tree on the side of the road before the car was hit first, and James's eyes went wide as its budding leaves burst into life, a wave of green. That then quickly turned red, and then brown, and then withered and died. Then again, and again. A rapid wave of aging that washed over the innocent plant, a decade in an instant.

Then the car. He didn't know what the mechanism here was, but the car looked like it had been abandoned in a scrapyard. The hubcaps, then the tires vanished, leaving the car up on bricks. The windows were smashed in, though that took a while. A door went missing. Paint wore away and metal rusted. From the driver's seat, a curve of light flickered for a split second and was gone.

Then it was over.

From inside the car, there was silence. Even Nate stopped shooting for a second. Then the driver's door opened and a man staggered out; his shield had done only so much.

He was wearing a faded, threadbare suit, full of holes. His hair was thin, his skin pallid and slightly wrinkled. He looked around in confusion, but his eyes weren't dead or empty. The only accessories on him were the bracer and silver greave the other agents had worn, though they seemed as pristine as ever. And without the sunglasses, James could see the emotions in his eyes. He was *angry*. It was a form of anger that he'd seen a lot in his life, though never to this degree— the madness of someone with authority, who had run into someone telling them *no*.

The aged agent locked eyes with James and snarled. Raised his handgun.

Nate shot him through the head, and he dropped, blood and brain and chunks of skull painting what was left of his vehicle.

"Get in the fucking car!" Nate yelled.

Sound rushed back to James. There were cars around them; some driving past on the other side of the road, sometimes slowing down to see what was going on. Some behind them, honking; some behind them and closer, desperately trying to pull U-turns and running. The now-omnipresent sense of sirens in the distance. Yells. Cries. Someone was screaming in panic nearby.

"Get in the car," James tried to say as kindly as he could to the two kids. "The snake's cool; he'll keep your friend from bleeding out. We've got to get somewhere safe. Please." He met their wide eyes, trying to broadcast to them how important this was, how honest he was being.

It was a minor miracle, but they listened. The camraconda let the injured kid up just long enough to get them all into the back seat. And then, doors slammed, seat belts clicked, weapons checked and stored, and the gas pedal went down.

James drove. Fled. Exfiltrated. Ran.

They'd won that fight. But boy, it didn't feel like it.

CHAPTER 18

Hospital waiting rooms sucked. James, at this point in his life, had a lot more experience with emergency waiting rooms than he'd really expected to ever acquire. And right now, walking in with a bleeding teenager's arm over his shoulder, the experience didn't get any better.

At least the waiting room chairs still looked comfortable.

The entrance had been . . . awkward, at best. James had lied his ass off, and in a twisted form of fortune, news of an active shooting at a certain high school had already started propagating. He'd gotten the kid—gotten Scott. His name was Scott; James couldn't just keep thinking of him as *the kid with the nose* forever—into a complimentary wheelchair and in the door as fast as possible, trying to keep the time away from the camraconda to a minimum. After a brief encounter where a nurse who hadn't quite noticed all the blood insisted the two of them wear face masks, though, people had started to take notice of the bullet wounds and the dripping red mess that was being wheeled into the ER.

And *then* the lying started. Kind of.

"There were these guys in suits and sunglasses. Looked like bad movie extras," James had told the hospital security. They were keeping a very close eye on him until the police arrived to confirm that he wasn't involved; James had no intention of trying to bluff being the FBI past these guys. They were roughly the size and dimensions of silverback gorillas, but with better sticks and much better handcuffs than the animal kingdom produced naturally. "I saw them shooting, saw the kid . . . Scott, I guess . . . fall over. When they weren't looking, I got him into my car and floored it here."

The story would, James realized, actually cover for his speeding earlier in the day. As long as no one looked too closely at the time stamps. Assuming anyone looked at all.

The security goons flanking James said nothing, unless you counted radiating an aura of suspicion. The nurse behind the intake desk had actual questions. "Did you see how many times he was shot? This could be important for the surgery."

"I did not," James half lied. "Two, maybe? I tried to have him keep pressure on the wounds."

"Okay." The woman nodded, typing and not really acknowledging if James had done the right thing or not. "Does he have any medical conditions you know of? Any allergies?"

"I met him ten minutes ago." James was starting to get frustrated.

Another round of rapid keyboard tapping. "And have either of you traveled to China in the last month?"

"I . . . what? No. I mean, I haven't." James cocked an eyebrow. "Why—"

"Just a precaution," she told him. "Please have a seat. Harold here"—the nurse gestured to the smaller of the goons—"is going to sit with you until the police arrive to take a statement. Standard policy for gunshots, don't worry. You did fine getting him here, but next time, call 911."

"People were shooting." James gave a flat stare. "This isn't Shadowrun; the EMTs aren't going to do a DocWagon exfiltration." Ignoring the nurse's blank look at his nerd jargon, he turned to go find a seat in the waiting room, trailed by Harold. He was starting to get annoyed. Yes, of course, there were policies. But . . . well . . .

James caught himself. Here he was, already thinking he was beyond the law. And that wasn't quite true, nor did he want it to be. "The rules," such as they were, didn't really apply to him as much anymore. But that didn't mean he should just ignore policies that were set for actual reasons. Maybe the EMTs could have kept Scott stable for the duration of the trip. Maybe the 911 call would have given him first aid advice. There were things here he wasn't fully considering.

Of course, *they* weren't considering the dungeon refugee basilisk in James's back seat. But that wasn't their fault. He could avoid sassing the hospital staff for ten minutes.

In the space between the front desk and sitting down, James generated about six different ideas for sticking camracondas into the backs of ambulances. People didn't need to *know* where they came from or what the broader context of interspecies cooperation was, really. There were at least twenty of the little guys back at the lair that were, in a word, *bored*. The whole world was at their finger . . . fang tips . . . and they were stuck inside. Not feeling comfortable roaming out into a world filled with alien life and strange culture. So maybe James could quietly strike a deal with an ambulance company to open up job positions for mobile safety devices and stabilization units.

James sat down, leaning his head back to thunk into the wall of the hospital waiting room. He breathed softly through the mask for a second, trying to ignore the security person standing next to him, and then swept his vision across the waiting room.

Chairs were still here. Better vending machine, too. He wondered if anyone had *noticed* the orbs that he and Anesh had used so long ago. Maybe someone had tried to remove one of the chairs at some point, only to have it turn to ash. That would be awkward.

There were other people here. It was, after all, a Friday evening. The place wasn't packed, but there were more than a few kids here with their parents, an elderly man lying back across a few chairs set up like a bench, one middle-aged woman who looked like she was about to throw up into a bag, and a handful of people who were most likely just waiting to hear results or be told they could come back and visit friends or relatives.

Oh, and Lua and Momo. Though they were in the last category.

James met Lua's widening eyes and gave a tiny shake of his head. It wouldn't do to have a supposedly random stranger approach him right now. But if they were here, that meant Simon was here and, at the very least, being treated. James hoped he was all right; he'd gotten hurt on James's behalf, fighting someone else's battle. Even if he was a member of the Order, James still balked at the idea of using people as soldiers.

They sat quietly for a while, James mostly just wondering when, if ever, the police were going to show up. He supposed they probably had a lot on their plate right now, what with the whole dead bodies in a school parking lot thing. He'd cop to that; that one was firmly his fault.

In his defense, James entertained the grim thought, maybe they shouldn't have provoked him.

"James!" The voice snapped his head up, and James realized he must have dozed off a bit. "Are you all right?!" Dave demanded, face a riot of concern as he half jogged across the ER lobby. The security Harold raised an arm to stop him, but the younger man, wearing a shirt that just said, "Dogs?!" along with a pair of dangling earbuds that didn't seem plugged into anything, just dipped under it, moving with a fluid grace that James vaguely realized he must have picked up sometime in the last six months. "Is anyone hurt?"

James flicked his eyes to Harold, who was saying something about how Dave had to step back and being firmly ignored. "I'm fine," James said. "Just waiting for the fuzz so I can give a statement. I'm thinking of calling Sergeant Madden just to speed this up." He sighed, stretching out his legs in front of him. "What're you doing here?"

"Do you not look at your phone?" Dave demanded, incredulous.

James blinked. He hadn't looked at his phone, actually. "Did someone message me?" he asked, digging into his pocket and pulling out the brick of technology.

Brick was the right word, it turned out. "Oh," Dave said simply, while Harold silently widened his eyes and stopped trying to catch the casually dodging man who was appearing to ignore him.

Three bullets lined the back of his phone like it had been hit by the world's worst BeDazzler. James gave a mournful "Awww" as he looked on the ruin of his most useful possession in the world—screen shattered in a spiderweb, battery smashed in, circuits snapped. And then, another, louder "Awwww!" as he reached back into his pocket and realized that those bullets had also torn up his pants.

"You were shot," Dave said quietly. "Are you sure you're okay?"

"I'm fine," James told him reassuringly. He aimed a pitch to lob his phone into a distant garbage can but was stopped by a light cough from Harold.

"The police are probably going to want to see that," the hospital security guard said, trying to be polite now. Apparently having been literally inches away from being shot raised James's estimation in his eyes. Maybe they'd all assumed James himself was the killer up until now.

James nodded his thanks to him. "Good point." He set the ruined lump of technology on the chair next to him so he could show it to no one and take it with him and not let the police find it in the trash later. "So, anything I need to know about before I get back to this serious waiting?" James asked Dave, trying to broadcast the need to be circumspect.

"Alanna and Pen . . . um . . . Penelope . . . are waiting in the parking garage," Dave said, sheepishly withering under James's pursed lips and wide, disbelieving eyes. "We got here as soon as we could to make sure you were okay. Anesh wanted to come, but he can't get ahold of . . . his . . . brother?" Dave cleared his throat, trying to find a word that wasn't *clone*. "Or his family. Or *your* family. Or . . . um . . . Alanna's family. Actually. And it's . . . James, wait!"

"Sir, please sit down!"

James ignored both Dave and Harold as he shoved himself to his feet, grabbing Dave by the shoulder as he stepped closer. "What?" he hissed quietly. "Is going on?"

"I don't know." The way Dave said it, hard and worried, froze Harold in his attempts to restrain either of the two men. "We don't know. Something is wrong. What do we do?" There was fear in his voice.

His feet froze in place. What did they *do*?! Why was James the one being asked that? He stood there, his brain trying to figure out *anything*, while Harold gave up on keeping him there for the police and stepped off to the side to say something into a radio. Across the room, Lua and Momo were looking at him with concerned eyes.

Oh, that was why. It clicked for James. They really did honestly think he was qualified to be their leader. And the depressing thing was, he probably was the best bet right now.

"Okay," he said, breathing as steadily as he could. "Get back to the lair. Take Momo. Also get the kid and the camracondas out of our cars. Get Pendragon *off the roof of a hospital parking garage.*" James narrowed his eyes. "Actually, shit, Nate's still here. Here, give him my keys." James fished his car keys out of his pocket and handed them off. "Get everyone ready. We're going to go have a little chat with Status Quo after I talk to . . ."

"Excuse me, sir?" Harold had finished his conversation over the radio and had stepped back up to talk to James. But this time, his posture was different. Less aggressive, a little confused, emotion visible even through his face mask. His hands held at his sides, passive. Also no one who participated in normal United States culture called James *sir*, so that was weird, too.

"No one calls me sir," James said. "What's gone wrong? Wait, shit! Is the kid . . . Scott . . . okay?" James felt his heart leap into his throat. Had they been too slow? Too careless? Did the camraconda lockdown effect hurt people somehow? "Did something go wrong?"

The security guard blinked, then cleared his throat. "I don't think so. The director of surgical services would like to talk to you. If . . . you have time."

"Um," James faltered. "What about the police?"

"He . . . uh . . . said that it's taken care of." Harold looked *beyond* concerned. "I can take you to him, if you'd like."

James thought about it. Really put thought into it, processed the words. It wasn't free, in terms of time cost, and he was in a bit of a hurry. But cutting the police out of his schedule probably saved more time than the director wanted in the first place. And something had changed. Hospital security had gone from acting like an obstacle to being respectful in the course of two minutes. That alone had James curious.

"Okay. Yes." He nodded at Harold. "Dave, go. Momo!" James called across the waiting room, causing the young woman to jump in shock. "Get up! Get moving!" He looked back at Harold, who now looked even more confused. "Let's go."

The walk through the hospital was snappy, and James found himself struggling a bit to keep up with the guard. Bonus acceleration didn't actually let him walk at double speed; if anything, it made it frustrating to regulate his steps. But he wanted to move as fast as possible, so he ignored the itching pain in his leg where the bullet cuts were starting to heal, and matched pace so the other man wouldn't slow down. He had questions but kept them private. Harold wasn't going to know the answers anyway, most likely.

In short order, after one elevator ride up to the fifth floor and another stupidly long hallway, they arrived through a suite of office spaces at a brown wooden door, waved past by a secretary who seemed prepared for James to have shown up there. He felt like he should be out of breath, but half a year of longer hikes on this same kind of carpet had left James's legs hardened for exactly this sort of thing.

Harold knocked twice, then opened the door for James. "Go on in. He's expecting you."

The ominous nature of that statement made James want to roll his eyes. But then, this was a guy who ran some indeterminate amount of this hospital. And he'd asked to speak to James personally. There was a desire to use sarcasm as a barrier against the anxiety of dealing with an authority figure like that, but he tamped it down, galvanized his manners in preparation.

The office James stepped into looked . . . used. Comfortable, even. It instantly put him more at ease to see it in contrast to the typically uncanny-valley rooms of Officium Mundi. Bookshelves on the left wall where half the books were stacked sideways after having not been put away properly, a desk covered in paperwork and that classic collection of things acquired over years of not moving desks that most people had, all topped off by a skeleton in the corner that James *assumed* wasn't real, but who knew?

The man behind the desk looked a bit tired, and like he'd been tired for the last ten of his fifty or sixty years. Short hair in a buzz cut that really did a lot to hide the receding hairline, wrinkles on an aged face that showed an equal number of laughs as scowls. Skinny eyebrows and a pointed chin. He was one thin mustache away from looking like a comic villain.

"Good evening. I'm Dr. Nikita." His voice instantly killed the villain vibe as he rose to shake James's hand. It was warm, with a hint of a Russian accent and the implicit feeling that he *cared*. "Have a seat, please."

"James Lyle," James introduced himself, sitting in a chair that he was *sure* had been swiped out of the waiting room. "So . . . at the risk of being too direct, what can I do for you?"

"I am comfortable with direct," the director of surgical services said, folding his hands in front of him. "You have a great deal of heart."

"Thank you?" he replied with a confused but polite grin.

"Ah. Apologies. You have a great *number* of *hearts*."

James froze. "Beg pardon?" He tried clearing his throat. It didn't make him seem less suspicious.

Dr. Nikita opened a small notebook in front of him and read off his own notes. "You are, it would seem, an associate of one Alanna Byrne. A woman who came close to injuring a number of hospital staff last month in the process of delivering to us a number of . . . human hearts."

"No?" James said, feebly.

The doctor turned a page in his notebook. "You are also an associate of one Anesh Patel, who was treated here. Several times. During one of those visits, the very chair you are sitting in appeared in this building."

"When you say *appeared*—" James started before the doctor waved him off.

"The chair is less important. I merely bring it up to prove a point," he said, his voice still calm and grandfatherly. "I have a question for you." Nikita casually leaned to the side and opened a desk drawer, causing James's combat instincts to spark to life until the doctor pulled out a simple wooden case. "Can you bring us more?"

"What?" James asked flatly, now beyond confused.

"More hearts" came the simple reply. "They are . . . amazing. Perfectly functional, no matter how long they are exposed to the air." The doctor looked up from the now-open box and its single human heart, still under the stasis effect Sarah had put the first one under before they started duplicating them. "They aren't from humans, are they?"

James cleared his throat. "That's an interesting ontological question, that . . . I am going to . . . decline to answer?" The doctor didn't say anything, just giving him a level stare until he relented. Remembering that he was on a time budget here, James threw his hands in the air and looked away, not making eye contact. "All right, fine! Technically they're copies of a heart that was originally from a human, so if you count that, then yes!"

"Why?" the doctor asked.

James's mouth moved before he could consider it. "Why what?"

"Such braggadocio." The old man shook his head with a smile. "Why did you bring them to us? These hearts, this gift. It saved lives, but we didn't ask for it."

James winced. "Honestly, we didn't know exactly how to put them into circulation." He let out a small cough again. "Also, if you want more, I'll need that one back, so we can . . . um." He paused. "You probably don't need to know. But yeah, we brought them to you because we wanted to help. That's all. Clearly I didn't do my research correctly on how many hearts were actually needed. Look, that's not important. I actually really need to go; I'm in a hurry today. Thank you for dealing with the police, I think? But yes, I can bring you more hearts in a week or two."

"The police are no matter." The aged doctor made a short chop with a flat hand. "When they are told the report was a mistake, they leave. They do not waste time on thinking too hard." He stood, reaching out to shake James's hand. "Go. I will take care of your people. And you will bring me hearts, and I will get them where they need to be."

James shook the offered hand, blinking slightly at the strength of the surgeon's grip. He turned to leave but paused at the door. "Are you sure it's okay? You're kind of breaking all the rules here, aren't you?"

Nikita laughed, a deep chuckle that filled the room with its sound. "Child," he said, shaking his head. "The point of being in charge is to know when the rules are there to guide us and when they are obstacles." His eyes narrowed slightly. "Now? I choose obstacle." He waved James on, out the door. "Go. Go. I know the look in your eye. You are needed. And if you have this . . . power . . . then I will not imagine what it is that you are needed *for*." He waited as James gave him a nod and started striding away with a rapid gait, holding his pose there at his desk, hands folded.

It was only after the door closed that he sighed and let his composure slip a bit. "Well," the old doctor said to himself. "Well, well." He sighed again and then picked up his phone. Time to make some calls. If the child could deliver? Well.

More things in heaven and earth than are opportunities for those who saw them.

"I think it's pronounced ill-ip-eed" was the first thing James heard as he slid under the heavy garage door in the back of the lair, not waiting for it to fully rise.

"But that's stupid," Alex bluntly replied to Daniel, eyebrows raised in incredulity, as if it strained the limits of belief that anyone could make such a mistake. "It's a pun on iPhone, right? So it should be eye-leh-peed."

"But that's awkward to say?" Daniel gave a feeble defense, casting around for anyone who could come to his aid. "JP, help me out here."

"No." JP ruined his hopes, the word coming out actually kind of hard. He was sitting a few steps away at one of the little pods of desks, his workspace an absolute disaster area of printouts and clutter. He also had no interest in getting into this fight.

He wasn't the only one. Across the warehouse, members of the Order sat in tense quiet. Murmured conversations between twos and threes regularly lapsed into silence. Everyone had arrived here somewhat rapidly, thanks to the persistent and mildly worrying effect of the green that reduced travel time, in response to James summons. But while rumors had gotten ample time to develop in the time it took him to meet with the doctor and get back, they hadn't done much to make people worry any less.

"You can say it however you want." James's voice sounded almost booming against the muffled quiet of the room and the rolling metal doors at the back of the warehouse, especially as all the whispers stopped when he started talking. "It's like 'gif.' The correct pronunciation hasn't stopped people from fighting over it on the internet, so just say it the way you're comfortable." He looked around as the door continued to roll open behind him. "Where's Nate?"

"Getting the new kid some food," JP said, looking up from his desk.

"And Dave? Alanna?" James hadn't seen Pendragon when he'd arrived in the rideshare he'd summoned, realizing too late he'd handed off his own car to Nate.

"Checking up on Alanna's sisters," Sarah said, approaching James with the longest steps she could manage, wrapping him in a sudden hug, and getting a shocked grunt out of him. "Are you all right?" Her muffled voice came out of his coat where she'd shoved her head. "I heard there was a fight."

"Yeah," James said, patting her head awkwardly. "There was. I'll tell you about it in a second." He looked out at the dozens of sets of eyes staring at him, stepping out of the hug to address the crowd. "All right, people! Gather up!"

They did, with a few vocalized questions of "what's going on?" or "did something happen?" This back space, used mostly for briefings, some manufacturing of armor, and workspaces for people like JP who preferred to do finance crime at an at least marginally hidden location, was pretty large. But around the furniture they'd added to it, it still surprised James just how many people had showed up.

Nearly everyone.

The other James was here, near the front, looking just as concerned as Momo. An Anesh had entered at some point with the buzzing figure of Ganesh on his shoulder. He stood next to Secret, talking quietly to the manifested blue serpent, who was pretending to sit on the floor. Even Harvey and Karen were here, with a handful of the less affiliated victims of the dungeon whom they'd been happy to help out but who had never committed to joining the Order. Others, too, like the over-excitable Ethan, who stood next to the glowering Neil. Two opposites of personality, one begging to get into the dungeon again, the other roped into it almost by accident. The whole research team was here, Reed still looking continually sheepish about the incident with Curious. Nate and the high schooler coming in at the back in response to Deb fetching them at some point. El had showed, too, though she also stood near the back, making her lack of connection a bit obvious. She stood almost alone, but near her, also notably alone, the most surprising person to have arrived was Theo.

There were more, too. So many names and faces that James had trouble sorting them all out for a minute. A handful of camracondas, a few people James had "hired" over the last month, one of the friendlier shellaxies that had wandered in, Rufus—all of them here. Waiting. Listening.

"Okay," he started and took a deep breath. He was getting better at speaking to crowds, but this was kind of intense. It didn't help that everyone here had picked up on the slightly panicked mood. "Just to get everyone on the same page, there was a fight."

A ripple ran through the crowd. A murmur of quiet confusion from some, and bitter conviction from those who were more aware of the situation. "What kind of fight?" Sarah asked, cracking her finger bones in a nervous pattern.

"The kind where some people got shot," James said. He inhaled through his nose again and then started giving a rough outline of the battle. The call, the arrival, the gunfight. The second gunfight. Simon's injury, the kid getting shot. The hospital. He wrapped it up by saying, "Lua's still there, in case they need to contact us. The doctor seemed uninterested in blowing our cover; I think he's in our corner."

"You left Lua there, alone, after that?" Karen demanded, anger on her face. "After those men tried to abduct her?!"

"She has my telepad," James said. "She can blip back here whenever she needs to. And we needed someone there just in case. The hospital security is keeping an eye on her, and not even the police know she's there."

Anesh cleared his throat. "You were in a school shooting," he said quietly. "A shooting at a school, anyway. Someone's going to have video of that. This might be a problem."

"I don't think that's the important part here," El cut in, voice raised over the crowd from the back. A few heads turned to look at her. "You're missing the big picture. James already said it. The agents were MIBs, weren't they? They had *powers*. And they were there to *kill kids*." She shot a glance toward the kid in their midst. One of the targets. He shrank down into his chair as a few people turned pitying, angry eyes on him.

Silence.

James felt the sneer on his face more than he actually meant to make it. "Yeah," he hissed out. "They were. Lua, too."

"Are they government?" Harvey asked. He didn't seem surprised by it. Just sad and determined.

"No idea," James said. "We have one lead on them, and that's *if* they're the same people." He gave a quick outline of the encounter with Curious, for those who didn't know, and her words about the organization of Status Quo.

"So, were you guys delvers, kid?" Neil bluntly directed the question at the high schooler.

"His name's Graham," Nate cut in, voice hard. He hadn't been having a particularly fun day so far and wasn't in the mood to suffer foolishness, even by accident.

"Um . . ." Graham fidgeted in his seat, the curly haired youth absolutely uncomfortable speaking in front of a room full of adults who were all focused on him. "I don't know what that means? We were just . . . um . . . just . . ."

"A delver," James said quietly, giving him a much-needed respite, "is someone who intentionally enters a Relevant Space with an objective in mind. You might call it something else. A dungeon, probably. A lair, a trap. You might think it's a one-off anomaly. It's not." He cleared his throat sheepishly. "You may have noticed that there are nonhuman life forms in the room. They're dungeon Life, more or less. You, ah, don't need to be afraid of them." He gave one of the camracondas nearest Graham an apologetic look. "Sorry," he said, realizing that half the kid's worry was probably due to the proximity to the snake.

Graham had gone silent as James was talking, and when he'd finished, he had a look in his eye. Like something had been confirmed for him, and he'd found his voice. "There's a room, in the school . . ." he started.

"It's a pitch-black maze of pipes," James said, softly. "Full of bugs, and rats, and worse. And it wants you to kill to leave."

"Yeah," Graham said. "We thought it was bullshit. But then our friends kept going missing. And then the counselor lady showed up, and we thought it might have been her. And then . . . we started asking questions . . . and . . ."

"And then you fit all the outward appearances of a team of adventurers." Sarah sighed. "And this mysterious agency shows up."

They turned back to the front of the room, and Alex raised a hand to ask a question. "So, is that what they do? Status Quo, right? Do they just try to kill anyone who knows about the dungeons?"

"They were wearing magic gear." James frowned, holding up his wrist to show off the bracelet he'd pilfered. "Uniform, too. They also didn't go for the dungeon itself, just the kids." He thought for a second. "Dave said . . . Dave said that you couldn't get ahold of your double, Anesh? And Alanna couldn't call her sister?"

"Yeah," Anesh said. "And your family isn't replying to you, and your sister's on vacation?"

"Graham," James asked quietly. "Where are your parents?"

"They . . . died last week," he said, choking on the words. "Car crash." The kid looked like he was about to start crying and only barely holding it together.

"Uh-huh," James said. "Oh, fuck." He turned away for a second, a wave of emotions crashing into him. He hadn't been paying attention; he'd focused on his own shit again, delving and building the Order and trying to find ways to help people. And he'd ignored little things. Left them to lie until suddenly, there was an unearthing of the real problem. The root of the evil. "We're so fucked!" He barked out the words like they were supposed to be a laugh, but inside, all he felt was overwhelming despair.

Was his family even still alive?

He heard a cracking noise and felt a sharp pain in his hand. With a grimace, he looked down at where he'd punched one of the standing whiteboards, smearing a sector map of the Office with his hand.

What the hell was he supposed to do? He was supposed to be the leader here, and instead . . . he just felt adrift. Everyone was looking to him to keep them safe, to keep them adventuring and growing, the Order saving the world together. And now, here they were, with this sudden question of if even associating with him would get their family killed by some shadowy government organization.

For the third time today, a hand clapped onto his shoulder. This one light but crossed with a half dozen small white lines of old battle scars.

James turned his head to look at Sarah, as she stood beside him.

"Hey," she said.

That was all she said. James looked back at her, looked into her eyes as she watched him. There was something there that scared him, more than any mysterious agents with guns. There, buried in those bright green eyes, was the most dire weapon, aimed straight at James.

Hope.

And it wasn't just her. He could feel it from everyone here. It took over the atmosphere; things were tense but not impossible. Their *job* was to beat the odds. Again and again. As often as they needed to. He exhaled, letting out the strangled breath.

When he looked out at the crowd, he was ready. His expression and words were steel in the cool air. "Deb, get the new kid to one of the basement rooms. Get him settled in until we can make sure it's gonna be safe. Momo, Anesh . . . anyone with combat experience, stay here. I'm going to need your help planning this. Virgil, Neil! Surveillance! I'll get you the address, but I need to know everything possible about that building and the people in it. Don't bother being discreet, just untraceable. JP, open the vault, literally and otherwise. Get them what they need. Reed, if you guys can bring out every dangerous and damaging object we have, I'd appreciate it." He turned and started to say, "Alanna . . . ! Hmm." James frowned. "Sarah, can you get Alanna and Dave back here? We're going to need them." He almost grinned as the girl saluted with dramatic enthusiasm and pivoted away, phone already out and up to her ear.

"What about the rest of us?" Theo asked from the back.

"Do you want to be here?" James asked her, bluntly but without malice.

She paused. "No." She settled on "But I owe you. And I'm here."

James nodded at her. "El, how about you?"

"I'm not a member of your clubhouse." The girl shrugged theatrically, the long flaps of her trench coat dancing around her. "Hell, you guys practically wrecked my life."

"All right." James turned away from her, prepared to move on.

"Hey!" El dragged his attention back to her. "I had more to say, jackass!" she snipped, and a few people laughed, James among them.

"I'm not a part of this. But . . . fuck, man. You and Secret are the only friends I have. Do you want my help?" She stared at him, wavering.

"Yes," James said. And meant it.

"Then I'm with you. Fuck, look at this place. You called, and fifty people showed up to fight for you. Do you get that?" She cut through to the heart of what everyone was thinking. "You save people. That's *cool*, man. Even if you messed up everything I was doing, you weren't trying to be an asshole." She held a hand off to the side and clenched her fist before spreading her fingers. When she spoke the next words, there was a crackle around her, like the air itself was *faster*, even if it wasn't moving. From her open palm, the sensation of an endless highway washed over the room. "There's lots of roads," El said gently. "But the one you're taking is worth something." She stared at James. "You say these guys are fuckers. All right." She nodded around at the room, at the people who had paused to watch her. "You've got all these people here. Pick a road that runs us over the fuckers."

James met her eyes across the room and nodded once. "All right," he said, then went back to barking orders. "Nate! Set up a watch shift with everyone who's left over! I don't want the building getting surrounded by goons while we're busy plotting! And get *everyone* guns!" He pointed a finger at the navy chef as he ordered him out of the room. "I dunno how much you and Neil blew the budget, but I'm really hoping it was a lot."

Nate cleared his throat. "I didn't let Neil buy the stupid cannon," he admitted.

"Hey!" Neil yelled from where he was tossing a skulljack drone plug to Virgil. "I—"

Nate cut him off, ignoring the younger man. "But we have a lot more of the ones that can kill them," he said. "They're not bullet-proof. Just tough."

"Someone get me a whiteboard that doesn't have stuff on it," James commanded. "We've got a lot of stuff that everyone's going to need to know," he muttered quietly as one of the support group members started wheeling over a blank board from the corner of the warehouse. They'd bought ten of the things when they moved in and were starting to run out of unused ones that didn't have important notes on them. "All right! Before we start planning out how to blow up a government building, does anyone have any pressing questions?!" he called out to the assembled Order that was now starting to move in waves as those with jobs grabbed those without and enlisted them to help.

"I yes" came a mechanical voice from the middle of the room.

The shuffling of human feet cleared a path between the speaker and James. He looked across the short space that had been opened up and over to the cluster of camracondas that had joined them for this briefing. Their leader was here, having made it back from the battle, along with Frequency-of-Sunlight. Though there were a handful of others now, and it was one of the ones that had been bold enough to accept a skulljack with no questions that spoke now.

"Don't worry." James smiled thinly at him. "You guys aren't involved in this; it's okay. You don't need to do anything."

The camraconda looked around, craning its long neck of bundled cable to peer its singular eye at the variety of people in the room, all of them paused briefly in the process of carrying out James's orders and preparing their newly formed group for war. "You need neither," the camraconda said.

It was, frankly, *amazing* to James just how quickly these guys had mastered sarcasm. He suppressed the urge to roll his eyes as Anesh snorted a surprised laugh next to him. "No," James agreed, after reining in his snark. "But we're going to."

The camraconda nodded. "I am Spire-Cast-Behind," she said, the mechanical voice having taken on a more feminine tone, albeit one with ice in its words. "Us all, declare for yours and you. You fight? We fight."

The English was imperfect, but the meaning wasn't. James straightened his back. "You're sure?"

"Debt owed." The camraconda echoed Theo's words from a few minutes earlier. "But also. Redemption. And the right thing to do."

"All right." James nodded to the group. "Split up, add yourselves to the task groups. You're with us for assault planning. Virgil! Leave the drone shit to Neil; your new job is to spend whatever you need at Best Buy to outfit these guys with speech capacity!" He turned eyes back to the camracondas. "If you're all okay getting wired in?" James tapped his own skulljack quizzically.

One of them, one of the younger-feeling ones that had been so excited to meet humans in the first place, nodded and nosed forward at one of the delvers. Spire pivoted her attention between the other snake and James before saying, "Who gives, important. Accepting. Trust."

"Okay," he said. He felt like he was saying that a lot today. "Okay." This time there was more conviction to the word. "Let's get started."

Eight hours later, a plan had started to take rough shape.

No one was going home tonight. The beds in the basement weren't enough for everyone, so a shockingly well-armed caravan of a couple vehicles and a handful of delvers had sortied out to the local sporting goods store to pick up one Order's worth of sleeping pads and bags. This added to the impressive mountain of blankets and pillows that James had arranged for the camracondas right after their arrival. And now, as the secondary basement was converted into a mildly awkward sort of communal sleeping area, more members of the Order kept watch from the roof of the building, overwatch on the parking lot and road around them.

Nate had handed off watch shift management to someone else—Lance, James was pretty sure—as soon as it had become clear that they were going to be here for a while, and he had promptly run off to the kitchen. James got the feeling that the man's excuse that they wouldn't want to order food for operational security was *accurate*, yes, but didn't really cover the fact that he was just trying to reclaim the place where he was comfortable. He'd killed people today, after all. That wasn't something that was easy to shrug off. So James didn't begrudge him when he spent more time taking control of his kitchen domain and dragging random untasked members in to be prep cooks.

The news had been checked at some point, and it didn't look good. For one thing, there were actual FBI on the scene. Or at least, people taking credit for being the FBI; recent events had led James to believe that no one actually *checked* on if someone was a member of the agency. He wondered, briefly, if this was by design, or if the Bureau was just constantly offended at the inability of people to place a phone call. They probably had a department just for that.

According to news reports, both on local TV and on the internet, there had been multiple casualties among the staff and students. Names weren't being released, but James felt a chill go down his spine as he considered that They—whoever They actually were— might have just killed people to maintain a cover story. There was no mention of the Order's intercession, no mention of the agents killed. And no one, for a minute, believed that the fight hadn't been witnessed. Which meant that bodies had been disappeared and any details were being actively suppressed. Though just looking at the comments thread on the Reddit post, it wasn't like that was exceptionally hard. The top three comments were, respectively, someone citing articles about gun casualties in the US and calling for legal reform, someone making a broad generalized statement about how their heart went out to the victims of this tragedy, and someone claiming that this was what happened when you tried to have a society where different religions were allowed to exist together. The comments thread was locked. Propaganda department hard at work, or just the internet being the internet, the platform to get out firsthand accounts of the incident was gone.

As for the battle plan, they were working on it.

They had an insane advantage here; they actually knew the home address of their enemy. And James intended to exploit that to the extreme. Since it was basically impossible that Status Quo didn't know they had a rival on the board, he'd ordered his surveillance team to ignore stealth and just get him results. And with that in mind, Neil and Virgil had—with the help of the frankly disturbingly impressive skulljack skills of the support group for Office survivors—unleashed a swarm of camera drones that would have made anyone watching either very worried or very convinced there was some kind of park party happening nearby.

They had trouble getting close to the building. There was some kind of jamming field around it, in a near perfect circle, that messed with the drone's connection before they could get too close. Not instantly, but once they crossed a certain line in the sand, there was something that made them lose control. So, with that in mind, the team set about programming simple routines for independent operation. And after someone started slapping an absorbed blue power on the things that concealed them, they started getting results.

The video footage, combined with JP's omnipresent *I know a guy* friend at the county clerk's office, who'd gotten them actual blueprints, laid the foundation for their planning.

The building was three stories tall, each one a simple L-shaped hallway connecting rows of supposedly independent business spaces. On the blueprints, these were marked as having main interior walls that separated them from each other, but drone footage as they swept by the windows showed a much more open interior. This was, at least on the upper two floors, a very different building than what had been reported.

One piece of footage that everyone had been poring over for hints showed something troubling, too. On the video, there was a brief glimpse of a short, balding man getting into an elevator. The doors closed, and as the drone hovered as far away as it could while still getting a good angle on the building . . . nothing happened. The view, which had a clear line of sight to the second- and third-floor elevators, showed no one getting out of them.

So they had a secret basement, too.

"We can't discount the fact that there may be spatial fuckery going on in there," James told his mission team.

"We could burn the building down?" Sarah, of all people, suggested.

"No." James shook his head. "There's a very real chance that they're keeping prisoners in there. Especially if they have a basement. Any operation is going to have to focus on seizing territory and holding it long enough for a search." He looked up at them and noted the grudging nods. "*Then* we can burn it down," he'd reassured them.

In their own basement, orbs and items were being handed out to anyone who needed them. The entire order had been issued blues, their stockpile now totally emptied. But everyone, planning to enter combat or not, had at least one of the orbs absorbed, a new power ready to go. Using this many, Anesh had noted that the patterns tended toward creation or alteration of states of matter. One person got sublimation again, but liquefy or solidify were also popular powers. Only about thirty percent of them were simple verbs, and those were the most flexible and dangerous. James himself was still loaded up with attach, which made him wince when he remembered the fight with the agent and how he'd completely forgotten to use it.

In the back room, the injection-molding machine hissed as it printed off another armor plate to be hooked into thin Kevlar. Material more durable than it should be, production faster than it had a right to. It got added to a pile; there were more to do before tomorrow.

They took breaks. They rotated through conversations with everyone in the building, for sanity checks. James vetoed anyone trying to ride the giant invisible cat into battle.

When Dave and Alanna arrived again, Pendragon making a slightly more graceful landing than normal on the roof, he was there to greet them. A nod for Dave and a reassuring hug for Alanna. They had been looking for hours and hadn't found any sign that the house Alanna's mother and sisters lived in had been inhabited. No sign of violence, either. But the people were gone.

Alanna held it together until James and Anesh got her alone in the little patio break area behind the kitchen. Then he held her while she cried until there were no more tears left. James didn't have any-thing to promise her, except that they were going to try to get them back, and if prisoners weren't a thing Status Quo did, then they'd raze them to the ground and break the back of their organization.

Restitution first. Revenge, if it couldn't be had.

The hours wheeled by. Every time he thought they had a plan, someone would point out a flaw and they'd start over. There was no room for error here, either; they were going up against armed human enemies who would be doing their best to kill them. They didn't have a lot of leeway, and they were going to have to fight hard, and likely kill people, if they wanted to get through it without losing everything. That thought rattled James. It didn't stop him from put-ting his best effort forward, but it did sit there, in his core, exhaust-ing him even more as the day wound on.

It rattled him more when Graham found him. He was sitting by himself at a table in the dining area, eating a chef's salad and staring blankly at his phone, waiting for the next problem to be messaged to him while he pretended to be reading the news. He was skimming headlines. There was something about China harassing Taiwan with its air force, which felt disturbingly prophetic. Also a storm some-where. Also a foreign film might win the Academy Awards. James's eyes glazed over as he flipped through stories without reading them, trying to sort out whether he was going to die because of a hurri-cane, the plague, or election coverage. He was failing, and he almost welcomed the distraction when the high school kid sat down on the bench across the table from him.

Graham opened with "I want to fight, too." James looked up and raised his eyebrows, making the effort to keep his eyes open despite the wave of sleep threatening him. The kid was about James's height, six two or so, which was actually unusual given that he couldn't be more than seventeen. But his skin showed off no muscle. He wasn't fat, exactly. Just soft. Flabby, if you wanted to be rude about it. He had an expression on that he probably thought made him look like a badass, but James just huffed out a breath at it and shook his head slightly. "Really!" Graham insisted as James turned back to his salad without saying anything. "I can do it! I have to!"

"No, you don't," James said, twisting spinach around his fork. "In fact, the entire point of the people in this building is so you don't have to."

"No, you don't understand!" Graham half yelled at him, his voice cracking a little. "I . . . need to do something!"

James set the fork down without taking the bite. "So, what?" he asked. He wanted to like this kid, to admire that he'd been one of the people who'd taken the initiative to try to hunt down the weird and dangerous. But this wasn't the right time for him; he was on edge, exhausted, and starting to get that hollow, itchy feeling that anxiety brought along whenever he got too tired. "What do you want? For me to slap a rifle in your hand, an orb in your wrist, and send you out to kill?"

"I—"

"No," James cut him off, uninterested. "We are not in the business of child soldiers. We're not even in the business of soldiering ourselves." He looked at the anger playing across Graham's face and shook his head again, this time with a sad purse of his lips. "You're not the chosen one," he said quietly, doing his best to break the kid's expectations without sending him over the edge. "You don't know what to do, I get it. Your friend's in the hospital and the other one's missing. You think I don't know how much that hurts?" He felt his brow flicker through a glare for a moment. "Of course I know. And I know how much you want to tear apart anything that did this to you. But you can't. You aren't a fighter, and you aren't enhanced, either. You're just . . . a victim. Someone who stumbled into the cosmic trap and hasn't had to claw your way out." James saw he wasn't exactly getting through. He felt himself starting to give up, his face going slack into a sad frown. "Look," he tried, reaching into his shoulder holster and pulling out his gun.

Graham went wide-eyed as James set the firearm on the table. "You'll let me fight?"

"No," James said as he set the Walther on the table. "This is to prove a point. I can, with this weapon, hit something without looking at it. My fingers know the trigger better than I know the layout of my own apartment. Something like my actual soul is upgraded to the point that I'm about fifty percent less likely to miss *anything*. I can reload this weapon with a thought and fire bullets faster than the gun actually loads them. And when I want to, I can move faster than most living humans while doing it. And I'm telling you this so that when I say that I'm terrified and I don't want to fight, *you understand what I mean*." He slammed the Walther back into his holster. "That's *one* of my weapons, and I am *scared*, kid!" James felt the last word come out as almost a sob. "And you want me to, what? Give you a magic sword and send you out to die? No."

"I'd die if I could help," Graham whispered, like the words were a magic spell.

"No," James said one last time, standing up and shoving away the plate with his food. It felt sour in his mouth now, and he wasn't hungry anymore. "You're not cannon fodder. You're not a part in the machine. And believe me when I tell you that I understand wanting to die for something that matters. But I'm gonna tell you to do something I know from experience is a lot harder now and tell you to actually value yourself."

He walked away, and Graham didn't argue anymore. But somehow, James didn't feel like he'd come out on top in that conversation at all.

It was dark out by the time the plan was proclaimed workable.

Anesh and Alanna were already asleep somewhere; someone had given up one of the coveted basement bedrooms to the two of them, and James had no desire to go knocking and waking them up. He was, in a word, exhausted. Drained. He'd been putting on a face for the whole day, trying to keep everyone confident, trying to keep *himself* feeling like he had any idea what he was doing. And now he was just looking for somewhere to sleep.

What he found instead was Sarah. She was at the top of the elevator as it dinged open; James had decided to take it down the other way and sleep in the vault. And she stepped in without waiting for him. "Okay, you're going to bed, sleepy butt," she said, hitting the button for the residential basement. "No arguments!"

"I was *trying*," James protested in a tired huff. "All the rooms are taken," he told her as the elevator started moving. He *could* have tried to hit the button for the other basement, but so far, no one had ever hit both buttons at the same time, and now didn't really feel like the proper time to test it. James was pretty sure there wasn't a proper time to test that, actually.

Sarah grinned at him. "Ah, I have a reservation!" she told him with a mischievous glint in her eye. Her expression went quietly serious for a second, then, "But really. You do need to rest. We all do. We're not going to be useful tomorrow if we're all burned up."

"We?" he asked, fearing the answer.

"James," Sarah said in her soft, sad voice, her head turned to stare at the wall of the elevator. "You know there's not enough people for me to sit this out. We'll have surprise, and a lot of surprises, but they're going to outgun us, and you *can't* tell me to just sit this one out. You wouldn't tell Alanna that, would you?"

"Alanna is my partner; I don't make decisions for her," James said as the doors opened and Sarah led him stumbling by the arm down the basement corridor. "And I said that and instantly realized it was kinda screwed up. I don't make decisions for you, either."

Sarah shrugged. "Whatever you may think, I'm a knight in this Order of yours. I trust you to call the shots," she told him as she unlocked and cracked open the door to the last room on the right, shoving him in. "James, we were best friends for . . . forever," Sarah continued as she shut the door behind her and slumped against it. "And I know you lost that, and you're trying to put it all back together, but I never did. I love you, you dummy. And if you say you're going to fight for something you believe in, then *fuck you* if you think I won't be there next to you." An accusatory, backhanded wave sent his way as he sat nervously on the edge of the bed.

In his heart, past the fog of sleepiness and the itch of anxiety, James felt something jolt on instinct. He didn't remember, but the habits of a lifetime of friendship had bled into so many things that he still had this ghost of the shape of what his life with Sarah had been like. And she was right; he'd been trying to put the pieces back together, and it hadn't yet felt like enough.

"Yeah," he whispered. "I know," he said, and meant it.

He raised his eyes, and Sarah tilted her head up, and they looked at each other for what felt like the first time in a month.

"I miss you," Sarah said.

"I miss you, too," James said. And then laughed once. When she tilted her head in concern at him, he laughed harder and then explained, "You know, we could have solved this months ago if we'd just . . . you know." He tapped at his skulljack.

Sarah's hand unconsciously found its way to the back of her neck. "Yeah. But . . ." She shrugged, trailing off.

"I know," James said with a reassuring smile. "It's okay." She smiled back, and they sat there together for a handful of heartbeats. Until James broke the silence. "Well, I should probably sleep," he said, his voice stumbling a bit as darkness closed in.

"Yeah," Sarah muttered, standing up. "Okay, move over."

"What?"

"I'm tired, too, you dork. And this is *my* bed."

"But . . ." James didn't have time to protest as Sarah toppled him backward with a one-handed push and climbed under the covers, wedging James farther and farther out of place as she did so. "I . . ."

"James," she said. "We have spent so many hours today preparing to get into a lethal fight with the government. And it has been nonstop social stuff, too. I love talking to people, and I love you, but we both know neither of us has it in us to get from the door to anywhere that has a place to sleep besides the hallway. So lie down and give me a hug, okay?"

He sat up awkwardly, looking down at his friend curled under the blankets. And she *was* his friend, for all that had happened. And in that moment, he saw in her the same tired bleakness he felt sometimes, and he knew exactly what she needed, because it was what he always needed.

"Okay," he said.

The hug was warm, and comforting, and neither of them knew what to do with their other arm that was pinned down to the bed, and they were asleep before they knew it.

They slept the sleep of the just. And even the worries of what was to come tomorrow weren't enough to wake them. Only one thing interrupted their sleep, and it happened at the very beginning, before they dozed off again.

<| Corridor Filled : Bond Formed—Rest : Transfer—Contact : Rate—74 minutes / second : One Corridor Established : Zero Corridors Empty |>

CHAPTER 19

James woke to the sound of construction work.

This, on its own, wouldn't be a huge deal. But then he realized where he was, and concern started to mount rapidly. James jolted upright, throwing Sarah off his chest as he sat up straight, sleep pulling at the back of his skull. Who the hell was doing construction in his secret base?

"Ten more minutes," Sarah mumbled next to him.

For a reason James was sharply aware of, that sounded hauntingly familiar. He smiled down at her anyway and poked her in the side. "If I'm up and tired, you hafta get up, too. Those are the rules." James swung himself out of bed, sitting with his legs dangling over the side and realizing he was still dressed. He needed to keep a change of clothes here.

"Nuuuu," Sarah groaned out. "Here . . ." She reached out and flopped her hand onto the back of his neck.

In an instant, James felt something change. He felt himself waking up, a flood of energy and readiness pouring into him, and he could clearly tell it was coming from Sarah. After about two seconds, she dropped her hand back down and the feeling stopped, but the sensation that he'd just gotten three hours of sleep persisted.

"'Kay," she mumbled drowsily. "You're 'wake now. I'mma sleep for some more."

Before James could reply, she was snoring again. "Corridor open, eh?" he muttered, remembering the message from just after they'd fallen asleep. Holding out his hand, he could see the branded circle from the Attic's magic over the knuckle of his middle finger. "I need to tell Anesh and Alanna about this." He thought about it for a second as he stood and crept out of the room, trying not to bump into any furniture in the darkness as he quietly shoved his gun back into his holster. "Or does that make it harder, if you're trying to force a bond? Maybe I should send them on a road trip together," he mused as he silently stepped out into the hallway.

The silence was rapidly broken by the sounds of a motor running and stone breaking.

"Oh, right." James sighed. "*That*. Well. Let's see what the fuss is."

It took him longer than he'd like to admit to find the source of the sound. The residential side of the basement contained more twisting halls than the more open layout of the other side. The part of James that loved management games cringed a bit at how haphazard all the little rooms down here were, right next to the larger space that served as a sort of storage zone for all the random stuff that had spawned down here, as well as a little lounge area.

When he did find the noise, it was in that open part of the floor. Someone had shuffled the stacked boxes around to make a little alcove up against the far wall, pushing the furniture into a clump to the side. A pair of humming air filters sat on one of the plush chairs, working overtime to deal with the dust in the air. As James approached, he heard indistinct yelling, followed by the roar of a small motor and more cracking of stone.

He came to a coughing stop as a plume of concrete dust washed out over the area, leaning against a cardboard box labeled "Christmas lights" that had a motorcycle helmet on top of it as he tried to pull his shirt up to use as a makeshift mask.

When the noise and health hazard stopped, James stepped around the barricade and spoke up in his most commanding voice. "What in the hell is going on here?" he demanded.

There were three people here. All of them in hard hats, with dust masks on. He recognized Ethan by name, the kid watching wide-eyed and holding up a bucket as one of the other survivors worked a concrete saw against the wall. Harvey stood off to the side, a tool that looked like a miniaturized jackhammer in his hands as he broke down chunks of rock. They all stopped as James walked up.

"Oh!" Ethan perked up instantly. "We're mining for gold!"

James blinked. Thought about it for a second. And then just nodded. "Okay," he said.

"Did you . . . want to know . . . anything about that?" Harvey asked, his deep voice both suspicious and amused all at once.

"Not really," James said. He felt weird. Like he *should* be trying to hide a yawn, but instead, he was electrically awake, his brain already having caught up to the extra infusion of whatever rest was. This seriously opened up the potential usefulness of the Attic.

"Not at all?" Harvey was becoming increasingly incredulous. "We're cutting up the wall here, man."

"You're mining out the extra ore vein that the green orb added, presumably because JP just learned that it's actually kind of difficult to turn his investment portfolios into liquid cash in a rapid fashion and we need something we can take to an unsuspecting pawn shop so we can have a few hundred untraceable bucks to buy . . . I'm gonna say bullets?"

"A van," Ethan supplied. "How did you—"

Harvey shushed him with a calm hand on the shoulder. "We'll be done in about forty-five minutes."

"Good." James nodded at him. "Other people are trying to sleep," he called over his shoulder as he started walking away, heading to the spiral staircase that led back up to the main floor, and the waking world with it.

He had a lot left to do before this evening.

Their plan had mostly solidified. The whole Order was moving, now in last-minute prep mode. Both tactically and mentally.

For some people, that meant scrambling to get together the gear that everyone would be using or going over insertion points with the different assault teams. For others, it meant getting last-minute crash courses in nonlethal takedowns, paired with their teachers getting crash courses in how to do that in concert with a camraconda.

For Alanna, it involved funneling into her mouth a steady supply of the magic coffee from the second coffee machine they'd brought out of the Office.

There were other things, obviously. She was currently in the process of copying a blueprint onto a standing whiteboard so they could draw the projected paths of their invasion. But the coffee helped.

The first machine they—and by *they* she meant James and Anesh—had found was, essentially, a stat boost. It took whatever the real-world version of agility was and stapled an extra zero to the end of your score. The only downside to it, as she knew from experience, was that if you overclocked the body too much, you got a wicked crash that involved almost instant unconsciousness.

This machine was similar in a lot of ways. Except it also made French press. And instead of agility, if you had to pick a stat it upped, it was *wisdom*.

The clarity that it offered helped Alanna immensely with coping with the guilt, self-pity, and ruby-edged fury that came along with the thought that her sisters had been kidnapped or killed. As an added bonus, she thought, sipping her fourth cup as she drew on the board with her free hand, overdosing on this stuff caused memory loss, too!

"Hey." The voice behind her was concerned and low. She already knew it was James, so she didn't turn to look at him. "You got a minute?"

"I am nothing but free time," Alanna replied blandly. She knew that James was wincing behind her back. She also knew that he felt possibly more guilt than she did. It was strange, how the combination of her enhanced empathy and the coffee made it so easy to not only see the web of emotions but to connect with them. His guilt didn't make her angry, or vindicated, or anything, really. She understood it and accepted that he really felt that way; it wasn't just a show like it was for some people. It was earnest, because he cared.

She could also feel how much he loved her. Alanna wouldn't tell him that; it might, no, *would* embarrass him in a way that wouldn't be funny right now. She'd let him know the next time they were linked.

"I'm worried about you," James said. "But you probably knew that. I just want to know if there's something I can do to help."

Alanna shook her head, finally turning around. She tried to keep a small smile on her face but knew it felt sad even as she did so. "You're already doing it," she said. Then she actually saw the look on James's face. "Are you okay?" she asked him, a little surprised.

"I'm . . . no," he said. "I thought I was, but somewhere halfway up the stairs from the basement, I remembered that I shot a human being in the head about seven times yesterday, and I . . . um . . . I . . . ah, shit." James let himself slump listlessly to the floor, leaning against the side of the desk near where Alanna was working, mercifully concealed from the other people in the command space.

"Buddy . . ." Alanna sat with him sympathetically, eyes wide in concern. "Talk to me?"

"I . . . ah." James took a shaky breath before finding actual words to say. "I'm just trying to keep busy," he said. "I haven't had a chance to think about it. I don't . . . want to."

"You've killed people before," Alanna told him. "Why's this different?"

James sighed, and she could feel even more guilt coming from him, now in a rainbow of different flavors. "I guess I never really internalized thinking of some of the dungeon Life as *people*. Which is . . . honestly, actually super racist now that I say it out loud. But I'm around humans all day. Have been my whole life. And it just feels more *real* all of a sudden."

"Was it not okay to fight the dungeon Life?" Alanna asked, deliberately leading him.

"Of course it was." James blinked. "I mean, we never just randomly ambushed things. Except for a shellaxy once, actually, which I now *really* feel bad about. Oh, and the plants, but fuck those things."

Alanna barked out a surprised laugh. "Right."

"But yeah, it was always self-defense. Or holding the line when we rescued everyone."

"But not this time?" she asked, voice steady.

James breathed again. "This time, too. I know," he said. "I know. And the worst part is, I know I'd do it again. I just . . . wish I didn't have to."

Alanna leaned over and wrapped thick arms around her boyfriend, bringing him in for a crushing hug. "Okay," she said. "Just remember that you're important to me. Anesh, too. *Everyone*, really, but they don't get to sleep with you." She leaned back and eyed him, grinning a bit as he recovered. "Except Sarah, I guess."

"There were no beds!" James protested, throwing his hands in the air. "Oh, also. We actually need to seriously start delving the Attic. And I . . . should maybe not explain why? I dunno."

Alanna raised an eyebrow. Her empowered brain, mixed with the memory enhancement that Anesh had passed out to everyone, brought exactly one reason to mind that was relevant here. "Interesting," she said, instead, not wanting to spoil James's fun. "Anyway. I need to get back to putting the windows where they're supposed to be on my map. And I'm guessing you have things to do, too."

"Lunch." James nodded, a somewhat stable smile on his lips. "Also checking in with Anesh."

"Good luck," Alanna told him, and meant it. "He's been angrier than I have. And I am . . . displeased." The word dripped with a sneered rage.

"I'll see if I can help him. Or at least keep him company," James said. "At least by tonight we'll have answers."

"Or die searching," Alanna whispered as James walked toward their dining room.

"Spire-Cast-Behind is just such a cool name," James said longingly. He sat at a corner table in their dining and gym area, thinking that they really needed to expand if they were going to keep adding people. The tables weren't really sufficient to hold everyone when the whole crowd was here. He was also thinking that he needed better tables. These red lacquered things with the attached hard benches were just . . . not what he wanted in his life.

Anesh sat with him, shifting uncomfortably on his own bench. When James spoke his eyes flicked up in a hard look, then back down to his laptop. He didn't respond.

There was a feeling of worry in the air, especially around his friend. James was doing what he could to dispel it, and it wasn't really working. "It's just that kind of mythical language, you know?" He sipped at his coffee. "I like that kinda thing. It feels *heroic*. And here I am, stuck with *James*."

"I'm trying to work," Anesh snapped. "Please shut up."

James sighed. "Man, you've been over that thing ten times by now. You're not going to find a secret win for us in there." He glanced over at the table next to theirs where Secret was eating lunch with El and a few others. "Not you, sorry," he apologized as Secret's eyes swiveled toward him.

"James, not now," Anesh hissed, not raising his eyes.

Now that was really worrying.

"Hey," James said softly, leaning over and lowering his head to meet Anesh's. "It's gonna be okay. We'll get through this. It's okay to take a break." He looked at the untouched sandwich and chips next to Anesh. "A *real* break, where you aren't driving yourself to the bone."

For a second, it seemed like Anesh was going to listen to him. He took a deep breath and slapped the laptop shut. But then he stood up and looked at James with hurt eyes. "My parents might be dead," he said. "Along with my last memories of them. I don't have time for this; I need actual help. I'm going to go make another self." He disengaged himself from the cafeteria bench and stalked out of the room.

A wave of quiet followed in his wake.

James blinked away watery eyes and tried to cover up how much that had hurt. "Well," he said, turning toward Spire-Cast-Behind, who had been coiled on the bench opposite Anesh, sampling a salad. "That could have gone better."

"What we need is a way to observe the building from overhead, without being spotted," James was telling Dave. "I dunno if you or JP have any ideas? The drones we have are okay for doing sweeps around it, but even that might be arousing suspicion, and we don't want to get close enough to the building to be seen."

"I could purchase the building?" JP suggested, raising a hand with a casual shrug and a snarky look on his face. "It's kind of an option now."

"I thought we *weren't* doing finance crimes anymore," James chided him.

"It's only a crime if you're being illegal about it. I've just started keeping a record of my research and logic chains, and that will be more than enough for if the SEC investigates," JP retorted. "Also, I'm thinking since we're a fiduciary now, I should start using that to invest on behalf of actual clients, not just the Order. It would let us move a lot more money. Legally. Probably."

"Isn't a fiduciary license something you actually need to . . . oh." James rolled his eyes as JP held up and furiously pointed to a handful of orbs. "Of course you did."

JP laughed easily. "Kidding; I did real paperwork. I swear I told you about this a while back. Anyway, no. No idea how to get eyes on the roof. Why? Wondering if they might have an escape helicopter?"

"Well, I am *now*," James groaned. "Of course they might have a helicopter. That would actually be a nightmare."

"We can check," Dave chimed in from where he was grooming Pendragon a few desks away against the back wall. He was running one of the sanitizer rags from the kitchen over her laminated scale pages, leaving the massive dragon amalgamation looking polished, much to her own pride.

"I said stealthy," James informed him.

"We can do stealthy." Dave nodded. "Pen ate that one desk lamp that makes itself invisible when it's on. So as long as we go during the day, should be basically impossible to see."

"Wait. Wait, back that up." JP leaned over his desk to look at Dave, sharing a confused glance with James as the two of them did a double take together. "She ate the lamp?"

Dave nodded as he tossed the rag onto the desk surface behind him and stepped around to the front of his bus-size companion. "Oh, yeah! Did I not tell you guys about that? She can incorporate magic stuff into her structure and then sorta use it. But she has to digest it first. I think it's her way of using blues? Though she can do that, too. Actually, I bet if you, like, replaced one of your bones with a magic pencil or something, you'd be able to do it, too."

"Bones," JP said, voice oozing sarcasm. "Our bones."

"Yeah." Dave nodded, oblivious.

"Replace our bones." JP flicked back an unruly bit of his hair that he had somehow sensed was out of its perfect position. "Dave . . . bones."

Dave gave JP a worried glance, eyebrows raised. "You're really focused on bones. Are you okay?"

"Dave, you have to tell us things like this," James said. "We have, like, a chat server, a bulletin board, and also a podcast, sort of. There are *ways*."

"All right, I'll remember that for the future," Dave said. "Anyway. Stealth flight. We're on it." He stepped toward Pendragon, and she bent her neck down to nuzzle him affectionately. He took her face in his hands and gave her a light headbutt before stepping back. "All right, girl, time to fly," he said solemnly.

Pendragon didn't speak, didn't emote. That wasn't really her jam, compared to much of the rest of the Life that counted itself among the ranks of the team. But she did respond right away, without hesitation. Pendragon reared up onto her hind legs and, without ceremony, her chest split open. There was a seam down the middle, invisible if you didn't know what you were looking for, and now it cracked apart with a dry hissing sound, revealing the outline of a metal cabinet, doors swinging open on oiled hinges.

Her insides were clean—more than you'd normally expect from someone's chest cavity. Ribs made of desk lamp goosenecks, flexible metal bars that curved to dangerous points as they protected and supported her interior. As she settled into place, the lights on the end of those lamps flickered to life, revealing trails of paper clips and cables that led down from Pendragon's organs and surface to . . . a coat?

A leather jacket. A nice black one, a lot like what James preferred. It sat perched like a scarecrow, elbows pulled up high, flapping slightly in the breeze that formed when Pendragon opened up. It was the centerpiece of her self, illuminated and on display.

Dave stepped forward, turning around and sliding his arms into it without having to look.

"No, wait. No. Hang the fuck on," James said, holding up an accusatory finger. Next to him, JP had just flopped onto his desk as he stared, knocking the container of untested pens to the floor and causing one of them to start glowing slightly. No one noticed. No one *could* notice.

"What?" Dave asked curiously as he pulled his arms down, testing tension against the bonds and hooks. He reached behind himself, pulled up an ethernet cable up to the recently formed skulljack on his neck, and plugged himself in.

"No! Dave, what the shit is this?!" James demanded, somewhere between shock and fascination. "When the hell did this *happen?!*"

Dave's body rippled like he was trying to shrug, but the gesture didn't come across through the coat. He kicked up and planted his feet on a small, lipped platform inside Pendragon. Around him, the lights started to flick off and the ribs began closing, the coat pulling him back into an immobile position. "We've been practicing, I guess?" He failed to explain anything. "Anyway. We're ready to go." Dave spoke with two voices. Around him, Pendragon sealed herself shut, her eyes flashing with a combined intelligence. "Everything feels good," the combined entity said as she slammed her forelegs back down.

"Dave, I swear to god." James pinched the bridge of his nose as he shook his head. "You need to tell us about these things."

But the dragon had already made her way out the back, manipulating the controls to the sheet-metal garage door with more skill than Pendragon had ever shown with her office-chair foreclaws. And with a few beats of her massive laminated wings, she and her passenger kicked off the ground in a plume of dust, shimmering from an obvious target to an indistinct blur of slightly brighter sky as they took to the air.

"Goddammit, Dave!" JP yelled after him, finally finding his voice. "Stop fucking one-upping everyone else's bullshit!"

James said nothing. Oh, he'd absolutely been *thinking* that, too. But it would be uncouth to actually yell it himself. Especially as the supposed leader of this mess.

So he was really glad JP had done his work for him.

James caught his breath, strangling the panic attack he was having as the elevator slid to a stop and the doors opened. He nodded with artificial politeness to Deb as the two of them traded places, neither having the time or energy for small talk right now. As the elevator doors closed on her, leaving James alone in the service corridor of the nonresidential basement, he let the civilized neutrality slip off his face again for a second.

Alanna was right. It wasn't his fault, and sometimes violence was the only way to protect what mattered most. But it still sucked that he couldn't get his hands to stop shaking.

Clamping down on his thoughts as hard as he could, he started walking, trying not to stumble as he made his way toward the cluster of friendly shellaxies and the rest of their R&D department.

The shellaxies were, James was discovering, about as delightful to hang around as their names implied. He'd initially been kind of exasperated at having the full names used every time, but after hanging around the things a few times, he got into the mind-set of understanding that "Ice Cream Cake" was a perfectly reasonable title for something as playful as the boxy computer case and the life hiding inside it.

Unfortunately, he was not here to hand out treats of USB sticks to Peanut Butter Cup, Assorted Jellybeans, and their other friends, but instead to visit Virgil.

"Virgil," James greeted the prickly programmer as he wandered through the penned area, trying not to grin too much at the shellaxies bumping playfully into his legs and trying to riffle through his pockets with their cord tentacles. "Anything to report? Did anyone figure out what that anomalous program is converting files into?"

"Two things, and no," the man said, ever succinct. "One. The emerald chips create programs that can be copied. Though, it's worth noting, once copied or modified in any way, they stop evolving on all platforms."

"Weird, but sure," James acknowledged. "Second thing?"

Virgil looked up at him, finally stopping the rapid-fire typing he'd been keeping up since James walked in. "Still on the first thing. I have a list of ideas, but we have about thirty extra chips from what you and the annoying girl brought back."

"Hey."

Virgil ignored the half-hearted protest. ". . . so if you have anything specific you want, let me know, and we'll get it started growing. Long term is better, obviously. Also more specific is *way* better. These things suck at general artificial intelligence."

"Anything to report about *the events going down tonight*, the thing that is putting colossal stress on everyone in the building?" James asked, with firm emphasis on the fact that this was important and maybe Virgil could pay at least eighty percent of his attention to him.

Another nod, as if of *course* he had something relevant. Virgil emitted the kind of attitude that asked how James could think he wouldn't have something ready to go for the big presentation? As if his *raise* was on the line. James tried to smother the annoyance this caused in him and found it hard. Of course, when Virgil actually started talking, it got easier.

"This is a skulljack device that interfaces with the wireless braid," Virgil told him, holding up what looked like the case for a cigarette lighter with a bundle of zip-tied wires coming out the back. "This first, then the braid. It uses short-range radio for connection and can—not seamlessly but well enough—be paired with a relay if needed. It has specific protocols loaded as firmware that allow for some extra functions without needing extra focus." He kicked back in his chair, looking like he wanted to absorb the appreciation like it was sunlight on a plant. "Not all my doing; the support group helped me work out the language the skulljack is speaking. But I've got a bunch of these ready to go."

"What extras?" James asked, curious and wondering if it would be worth it this late in the game.

"Shared vision and dialogue without emotional or memory bleed. Also the ability to pass on spatial impressions of an area. Haven't gotten it rigged to share muscle memory yet, but we're working on it." Virgil said the words with so much smugness that James was worried it might be a memetic hazard.

Instead of rolling his eyes, though, he asked the other question that was on his mind. "Weren't you doing security programming? Like, trying to find ways to block unwanted mental intrusions?"

"I've got a chip working on something for that. This was easier."

"How can this possibly be easier than what is essentially a firewall?" James half demanded. He wasn't mad, just curious, in a very aggressive way.

Virgil shrugged, finally bothering to look up from his screen as he alt-tabbed out of whatever he was doing. "Firewalls are actually pretty tricky," he said, as if that was an explanation. The rational part of James's mind was actually quite annoyed that he understood enough programming to get why that was the case; it would have been much more satisfying to just blame the smarmy jackass in front of him. "Anyway. This is the finished design, loaded with the latest stable build. It's not that sleek—we'll work on that later—but it should hold up in a crisis, and it seemed like it would be useful for . . . tonight."

"Yeah. It actually, seriously will be." James nodded in acknowledgment. "Well. Thank you," he huffed out, meaning it less than he might have wanted to, but more than not at all. "Anything else before I head back upstairs?"

Virgil looked around the room, now more fully present in the physical space. There *were* other people down here, doing last-minute once-overs of the stuff in the vault or testing various items to see if they had usable potential. A couple people were just going through pencils at a rate of about ten a minute, snapping them if they didn't do anything obvious and amalgamating a growing pile of tiny blues. One of those blues, he rolled around between his fingers now. "Yeah," Virgil mentioned with a suddenly serious expression. "When you finalize the teams, can you make sure research is split up?"

"What?" James stumbled over the words in his brain.

"Don't put us all in the same squad. In case one group gets wiped out," Virgil said, and James noticed out of the edges of his perception that the others in the room had gone still, listening in. "We're learning so much down here. So many little things that I don't know how to explain properly. Memetics, infomorphic Life, xenotech, orb theory, skulljack processes—it's all *here*. This basement is the center of the most cutting-edge knowledge on Earth right now."

James raised a single finger and simply started to say, "Ah—"

Virgil cut him off. "That we know of. Sure. But my point stands. We're poised to reshape humanity and bring about a new golden age of science. So make sure we don't all die, okay?"

"I was, actually"—James cleared his throat awkwardly—"under the impression that no one here would be engaging in combat?"

There was a moment of silence, followed by a burst of nervous laughter from one of the tables behind James. Virgil looked at him like he'd just sprouted a hostile shrubbery out of his head, eyebrows askew in a complex display of mocking puzzlement. "Seriously?" he asked, voice dry. "You plan on going to war with the group that wants us all dead anyway and expect us to just sit here?"

". . . Nnnnnnnno." James let the word linger, only barely avoiding making it a question.

"All right. Good," Virgil said, turning back to his computer. He started typing away again, and it was only then that James noticed the cable connecting his skulljack to the PC. He snorted a laugh as he headed back to the elevator, snagging a few blues on the way.

Even when he was being serious and dramatic, Virgil couldn't stop multitasking and splitting his attention.

"What's going on?" was the first thing Lua said as she came through the front door.

James was there to meet her; someone on the roof had radioed in the instant Momo's car had signaled for the turn into the parking lot, the younger girl having been dispatched to pick up Lua from the hospital. Lua had been nervous about teleporting ever since the topic was brought up, and Momo had wanted some fresh air anyway, so it was a reasonable compromise, given that no one seemed to be looking for either of them.

"I'll get to that. First off, how are Simon and Scott?" James asked bluntly, turning to walk toward his office and motioning for the la-dies to follow him. The two of them made for a stark contrast; the difference between Momo's studded leather jacket and neon-green hair and Lua's business professional–style skirt and jacket would have been hilarious to James's mind any other day. Right now, though, they just needed to talk.

"Simon is doing good," Momo said, sounding exhausted. "He has six broken ribs, and his entire back is one big bruise, but he'll live." She sagged into the chair in James's office, leaving Lua to quirk an eyebrow and lean politely against the door as she closed it behind them. "I already texted my James."

"He's sleeping," James said by way of explanation. "Um . . . I don't mean to pry, but are the two of them dating?" he asked Momo. "Because I . . . actually can't remember seeing them not tapped into each other, and he took the news that Simon got hurt *really* badly."

Badly was what historians would later refer to as an understatement.

Momo just shrugged. She knew the answer, obviously, but it wasn't her place to share.

"James," Lua said, tilting her head up from the floor to look at him. "What happened? What's going on?"

"The people who tried to kill you," James told her, and saw her shiver at the words, one hand going to her wrist, "tried to kill those three kids. They didn't stop there. My family is missing. So is one iteration of Anesh and his parents. Alanna's sisters. Her mom, too, I guess. Graham—the other kid's—parents died last week. I'm guessing the other two have had similar issues." His voice cracked as he tried to present the information about what was quite possibly a large number of deaths without any emotion. "Left unanswered, they will, eventually, get back on our trail, and kill or disappear us. Known targets are obviously myself, Alanna, and Anesh, but I'm guessing you're on the list, too. They don't seem wise to the fact that we have backup, though. So. Everyone is here, and we're planning . . . well, to kick down their door and cause problems on purpose."

"Is that . . . Do you really need to?" Lua sounded anxious, and James saw her scratching at the exposed skin of her arm while she spoke.

He looked at her steadily, cutting off Momo's shocked protestation. "I wish . . ." he started to say, and then had to look away as he felt a wave of guilt and self-loathing creep up again. "I wish none of this had happened," he whispered. "And I wish there was literally any other way to handle this. But they didn't try to talk; they didn't outline some kind of international dungeon-standard rules and then ask us politely to follow them. They came in shooting. At children. At *noncombatants*." James looked down at his hands resting on his desk, fingers tightened unwillingly into claws. "They can surrender if they want to. We'll dismantle their organization and send 'em packing. But if it comes to it . . ."

"Waste the fuckers," Momo filled in, getting a disapproving glare from Lua.

"More or less. Though I was going to say it better," James told her. "Also, how's the other kid?"

"His older sister showed up," Lua said. "I didn't want to introduce myself, in case there was a problem. But I checked—she wasn't an agent. Oh, that reminds me." She reached into her pocket and pulled out a pair of thin rectangular glasses, carefully setting them on James's desk. "Thank you for their use. But I think you might need them more than me if this is something you'll be doing soon."

"Tonight," James said, and Lua winced.

"Are you . . . at least going to try to open a dialogue?"

"I know you're a talk therapist, but sometimes there are problems that words won't solve," James said.

Lua came the closest he'd ever seen to her sneering. "Those problems are caused by people who don't operate in good faith."

"They may have murdered a child. They've certainly murdered a lot of other people," James reminded her. "I think they're a little bit past good faith."

"Point," Lua conceded.

James picked up the glasses, flicked them open, and settled them on his nose. He took a glance at Momo and Lua with them on, seeing not-quite-real words hovering tied to the two of them. *Order of Endless Rooms, War Witch* for Momo, and *Order of Endless Rooms, Specialist* for Lua. Affiliations, titles. The most powerful tool any of them had seen to give to Lua to keep an eye out for anything suspicious. Of course, it required an organization to be part of, not just an ideal. And it never told the whole story.

"Oh, that also reminds me," Momo said as James fiddled with the glasses. "Here!" She reached into her courier satchel and pulled out a glimmering copper-and-ivory bracer. Momo set the artifact on his desk like it was cracked china, about to fall to powder, and then scooted back in her chair a bit. "I took this off one of the agents after you left. Had the fuckin' thing in my car and totally forgot. Didn't have time for the boots, though."

"Greaves."

"You don't need to grieve over it, boss; they're just boots." Momo had the biggest shit-eating grin on her face imaginable.

James cringed as he fell into her trap, but he didn't hesitate to reach out for the bracer. He paused at the last moment. "Why do you look nervous about this thing?" he asked her.

"It's really complicated," Momo said, and in that moment, James noticed a thin line of blood leaking from her nose. He mimed wiping it away, and Momo did so with the edge of her jacket sleeve, seeming unperturbed by it. "I have, like, four? Four totems on me right now. And when I put it on, the totems sort of overload for me, like there's too much info for some of them. I'd actually like to leave the room before you use it. For safety!" The irony of that comment was not lost on James.

"All right, fair," James said. "You guys are good to go, anyway. Go get some food. Lua, grab a free bed and take a nap if you need to. Momo, if you see Ethan around, try to ask him what he's planning prank-wise."

"What?"

"I'm almost certain he's planning some kind of prank. I'm allowing it because it's good for morale, and because, earlier, I took prevenge on him." James entirely failed to explain anything despite using two whole sentences.

Lua was already out the door, having left as soon as James said they were good to go, but Momo hesitated to stand up. "Is it . . . a good idea to be doing goofy stuff right before we all go almost die?"

"Honestly?" James asked with a sigh. "Probably not. But man, you know how it is. I'm genetically incapable of not trying to turn things into jokes. Also Ethan is *so easy* to poke fun at."

Momo snorted. "Yeah, what in the hell is prevenge, anyway?" she asked.

"Like revenge, only before they've done anything to take revenge on. It's preemptive vengeance."

"And in this case, your vengeance takes the form of . . . ?"

"Tricking a teenager into drinking really weird dungeon soda that tastes like saltwater taffy," James confirmed with a grinning nod.

"Eugh! Why?"

"I don't understand the question. Look at me—of course my prevenge is going to be silly and harmless. Also it only took about two minutes of time, and honestly, there's an upper limit to how many things I'm needed for." James spread his arms out as if to illustrate his character, still holding the bracer in one hand.

Momo rolled her eyes. "What if he never does anything to take revenge for? Then you just did something mean to a kid who idolizes you, *and* your prevenge is wasted."

"I made him drink bad soda. He'll find something to make the prevenge count," James dismissed her. "Now get out of my office so I can check this thing." He flicked his hand at her a couple times, shooing her away.

"You're like if the Oracle at Delphi was the class clown, and also incredibly lazy," Momo shot over her shoulder as she left.

"Thanks!" James called as she shut the door, leaving him to his privacy. He waited a second before sighing. "And if I can make a few people smile before we maybe all die . . . well, shit. I gotta try, right?" he muttered to himself. "Now, let's see what this toy is," he said in a slightly louder voice, pulling the bracer tight around his forearm and clipping the latch shut on it.

[Stockpile "9mm Bullet Impact"—18—4/19,000—8:14:3:18 (122) <A>

Battlefield Alteration—4—194/1,000—2:01:22 (7) <A>]

That was a remarkably specific phrase. Also, he'd never seen any kind of extranormal effect use quotation marks before, even when it was mostly just projecting thoughts into his head. A little mental probing got him more specific feelings, though. Both abilities were set to automatic, something he hadn't realized was an option. The second one modified the first one. And that little quirk right there, which probably would have let the agents survive a thousand fights unscratched, had gotten them *slaughtered* against a mixed unit that brought a camraconda to a gunfight.

James found the mental command to turn off the automatic use of the second ability and hit the switch so hard he gave himself a headache.

"Okay," he said to his empty office. "One more tool in the arsenal."

He stood up, checking the time. Time for a couple last-minute checks, and then . . .

Well.

Time, and tactical assaults, waited for no one.

"Hey, Nate!" James called as he entered the kitchen, the double doors swinging behind him as he stepped into the chef's domain.

The place had been transformed since they'd bought this building. A run-down back room with blackened tile and a few broken appliances that hadn't been replaced since this place was a pool hall with a shitty bar had, with the application of a contractor and an infusion of dungeon cash, turned into a polished-chrome commercial kitchen. It wasn't going to stay utopian forever, and James knew that Nate already had members of the Order helping him keep the place scrubbed to navy standards every time they used it, but right now it was kind of a great room to be in.

At the moment, it smelled like fresh fruit. Light fare before everyone got their workout in getting shot at.

"I didn't know you wore glasses," the tattooed chef said, rounding the corner behind the corner the walk-in fridge occupied. "How ya holding up?"

"I don't normally," James said, turning from where he was leaning against the front serving counter. "These are—" His words cut off in his throat as he caught sight of Nate through the lenses of the dungeon item.

Nate didn't notice, or didn't care. He just shrugged and ran the rag he held over the counter he'd been cutting melons on, wiping debris and juice into a garbage can. "You holding up okay?" he asked James again. "You keep coming in here, and I know that screaming in the walk-in is a tradition, but it's not supposed to be that frequent."

"I . . . ah." James shook his head and looked back at the front wall, reading over the rough menu schedule listed on the calendar. "Having trouble with hurting humans, I guess," James said. "Got any tips?"

"Kid, I'm the wrong guy to ask about that," Nate said with a grunt. "Why?"

The bald chef shrugged. "'Cause I'm not a philosopher. The closest I get is 'they were doing bad shit, and you stopped them.' Good enough."

"Is it?" James asked, legitimately wondering.

Nate shot a look at the prep cook who was helping him plate up food and tilted his head at the door, ushering the younger woman out. "When you hired me, you asked me if I wanted to make the world better," Nate said after a long pause, when the two of them were alone. "Did you mean that? Did you really think you could fix everything by yourself?"

"Obviously not," James told him. "That's why I was hiring people."

"I mean, your little gui— Order," Nate autocorrected himself. "You really believe in a better world? Some kind of perfect ending?"

"A good world," James almost whispered, his voice practically covered by the noise of the kitchen. "Yeah," he said, turning to face Nate again. "I believe in that."

Nate tossed the rag he'd been rolling in his hands into a sanitizer bucket halfway across the room. "Well, then," he said. "Check in on that feeling every now and then. Make sure you still believe in why you're doing what you're doing. If you do, you'll tend to do stuff that's worth it." Nate shrugged. "It's why I'm still here. Why I was okay fighting with you. Why I'll be there tonight. You believe in it, kid, and I don't think you're gonna kill anyone who didn't need it at the time."

James looked at him, really looked at him, for a long minute. Then he nodded. "Yeah. Okay." James reached up and took off the glasses, folding them and setting the thin rectangular frames on the counter. "Thanks. That actually does help, even if I'm not sure I agree with you all the way."

"No worries," Nate said. "Now get out of the kitchen. I've got stuff to do in the next hour." James grinned and shot him a wave over his shoulder as he walked back out the door. With a rough snort, Nate motioned his prep cook back in from the back patio. "What a weird dumbass," he muttered, idly picking up the discarded eyeglasses.

"He's a hero," the prep cook informed Nate firmly as she set back to slicing apples into wedges.

"Bah," Nate replied. "Just because he saved a hundred or so people from certain death . . ." He raised the glasses to his eyes, pushing his own up his forehead to see how bad James's vision really was. "Huh." He didn't notice a difference as he swept his gaze around the kitchen. But then, his eyes landed on his prep cook.

Order of Endless Rooms, Aspirant.

"What's up?" the girl asked when she noticed Nate looking at her.

"Oh." Nate looked down at the glasses in his hand, realizing what he'd just seen. What *James* had just seen. "Fuck." But the kid hadn't said anything. Hadn't even gotten mad. He'd just listened, and trusted.

Nate hoped he'd never have to betray that trust. But one way or another, if he was called on to do it, it wouldn't be today.

If a government spy satellite was around overhead, watching the parking lot of a certain commercial-industrial flex space–turned–secret lair, then whoever was keeping an eye on the video feed would be *confused*, at least.

Thirty humans, sixteen camracondas, one sentient drone, one mostly incorporeal infomorph, and one dragon made of office supplies had gathered in the open. All but one of the humans wore body armor, black shell plate covering vital areas and hosting a combat rigging that held extra ammunition, orb pouches, handcuffs, Tasers, and other assorted tools. All the camracondas were in armor, too, their snake bodies concealed in extra Kevlar wrap and custom-shaped layered plastic plate that had been run off in record time thanks to the green orb buff that made it faster to produce clothing. The infomorph didn't have armor, because Secret was going to be hiding for most of the fight and also wasn't entirely physical. Pendragon didn't have armor, either, because she was a dragon. There were a *lot* of guns present. Also a lot of magic items, mostly doled out to the snakes, who didn't have hands for guns. Almost everyone had a blue, and about a third of them were very relevant in combat.

All the humans except James were wearing masks. They weren't armored masks, just a pile of face coverings bought from the party supply store a half mile away to make an effort at concealing identity. It was strange to have everyone standing there, most of them in masks of various animal faces, looking like they were going to an exceptionally well-armed masquerade ball. Pendragon also wore a mask, because Dave had said she felt left out, the sparkling faux deer muzzle sticking out on the end of her elongated paper snout.

James was in a black leather jacket, black slacks, and black sunglasses. Because, he realized, he was kind of a parody of himself.

There was a plan. Two plans, actually. One, then the other if the one didn't work.

The second plan had been hashed out after a day and a half of nonstop tactical planning and meticulous work. The first plan had been added by James an hour ago. Ten minutes ago, Alanna and Anesh had stopped yelling at him. They knew he was right; they knew that it was the right thing to do. Alanna could feel it coming off him, and Anesh was logical enough to understand the ethics, even when he was angry. James was trusting his instincts. And now it was time to move.

The first plan was to offer their enemy one last chance.

Vans were loaded full of armed men, women, and serpents. They'd be ready to move in within a minute if the first plan failed. A half dozen people, plus Dave, crawled inside Pendragon's internal cavity. They'd be ready to drop out of the sky in seconds, prepared to storm through the roof access and cover the top floor before anyone could respond to the ground assault. And James?

James sat in the driver's seat of his trusty immortal Subaru, tapping the wheel to the song stuck in his head as he drove. They were going first.

He pulled into the parking lot of the local office of their enemy. Parked the car in a handicapped space at the very front and stepped out. He could only imagine the people who watched the security cameras were probably having a minor amount of concern right now.

It was seven on a late-February evening. The air was already in the late stage of twilight, going from refreshing to bone-bitingly cold and damp, with a strong wind tossing James's coat behind him as he shut the driver's door and took a second to look up at the building before him. There was some traffic on the road behind him, more on the main roads. People were going about their lives. The world kept turning. Somewhere, normal kids were doing normal homework, normal adults were coming home from work, normal people like he'd been a year ago were going out to work on the night shifts. Some people hated their lives; some people loved them; some people didn't understand that there was a question to be answered there. The trees around the office park swayed in the wind, pine boughs throwing shadows across the white streetlights, making monsters out of air and fear in the darkness.

A man and a secret opened a door to an inconspicuous office.

"Hi," James said with a ferocious smile to the *deeply* uncomfortable older woman sitting at the receptionist desk. "I'm sure I'm expected," he told her with unbridled confidence. "I've got a meeting with the person in charge. It's not going to be on their schedule. Where can I find them?"

Maybe it was his polite tone. Maybe it was that he really was expected, and she'd been told to give him directions. Maybe it was the implicit threat of the gun on his hip, or some part of her could sense the danger of the invisible infomorph wrapped around James like a second armored coat. But either way, the curly haired midfifties woman stared him down with irritation.

"Second floor," she said dryly. "I'll unlock the elevator for you."

"Appreciated." James nodded at her. "But I'll take the stairs."

He strode into the building, noting the number of people still "working" but ignoring their observant eyes on his back.

He had a meeting to get to.

CHAPTER 20

"You know," James said with a tone of casual curiosity, "this is the second time this week I've ended up in the office of an authority figure. I feel like I'm back in high school."

"Now, see, that joke would work a lot better if we didn't have your record," the man on the other side of the desk said, cocking a finger and giving a warm smile to James. "You're as much of a delinquent as anyone, but hardly above average."

When James had walked into the office, he'd done so politely. A large part of him had wanted to slam his fist through the frosted-glass window on the door and open the doorknob from the inside, but the thing hadn't even been locked so as to justify his fantasy. He'd instead strolled in, quietly closed the door behind him, and helped himself to one of the black leather chairs. Waiting patiently, heart hammering, for the man on the other side of the desk to finish whatever paperwork he was signing and look up.

The office was about what James expected, but it had a personal flair to it that he hadn't foreseen. The heavy, polished oak desk was exactly what he'd assumed, along with the bookshelf stocked with texts on legal codes and philosophy. But the walls also held a trio of Impressionist paintings, giving a splash of orange and white to the room. The clock on the wall was one of those clocks where the timepiece itself was held by the figure of a black cat wrapped around it. And there was a potted plant, too, some big fuck-off fern against the wall by the door, opposite the little wicker trash basket.

It was a corner office, with two clean windows on each of the walls. They overlooked the wooded area out behind the building and also the side parking lot. That was going to come in handy later.

It felt very human. Like someone worked here and cared about the space.

So, too, did the other man in the room play into those expectations, but not quite all the way. He was shorter than James, maybe five seven, though James couldn't quite tell when he was sitting down, and he'd never been good at judging heights anyway. Bald, too. The kind of bald where he'd clearly realized he was losing his hair, then shrugged and leaned into it. His head was smooth, as polished as the desk. He was older, too. Not ancient or decrepit, but James recognized him as someone who could be a grandfather. Fifty, maybe a bit more? He had lines on his face from a lifetime of hard work, and his hands were dotted with scars and ridges of flesh; he'd been hurt, but he was still strong. His body was in excellent shape for anyone, much less someone who approached double James's age. A suit, of course, but a warmer color than just secret agent black, and with a forest-green tie that felt like a strange splash of color.

And when he'd spoken, his voice had been . . . warm. Like he was greeting a favorite student, or a fondly thought-of nephew.

James noted a distinct lack of a nameplate anywhere in the room or on the door.

"So." The man followed up his riposte. "It's not often that people come to *us*. What brings you to my office today?"

"Surrender," James said, meeting the man's eyes. "Please," he added, wanting to be polite about it.

"I accept!" The man broke into a grin. "You've made this quite easy! Perhaps you'd like to redress your phrasing?"

James rolled his eyes. "You know, I expected that joke from . . . well, myself, actually. But I kind of thought you'd be taking this more seriously." He leaned forward and tapped on the desk with one outstretched finger. "I am here to demand the surrender of your organization, the cessation of hostile action within my sphere of influence, and the release of any prisoners kept. Is that phrased strictly enough?" James sometimes liked flowery language. Here, he felt it was practically required, a cold and detached phrasing for exactly what was being asked, so he didn't simply start swearing.

"Hmm." The man also leaned forward, steepled his fingers in front of his lips. "And for this, what do you offer in exchange?"

"Forbearance," James said, through his teeth.

"Ah, there it is." The man smiled kindly, and the words were a chuckle that filled the room. "That anger. Such a classic," he said, leaning back. "You know, I was impressed at first. This organization has dealt with your kind for a long, long time. But you're the first one I've ever heard of to come to us. I was going to offer you a job, but I don't think you'd ever take it, would you?" He sounded sad.

"Probably not," James told him. "You've hurt people. Possibly my family, too. I can't imagine working with you."

"Ah, that!" He looked off to the side and gave a smooth chuckle. "You know, the ethics board ended the process of liquidating whole bloodlines decades ago. It was always so much more trouble. Your family aren't *dead*. We're not *monsters*, you know."

"Do I?" James muttered back. "You seem to have the fangs for it."

"And you don't?" The man retorted. "My dear boy, our job is to *protect* humanity. Can't very well do that if we keep killing them, can we?" He snorted. "No, they've all just been . . . let's say relocated. Oh, they won't remember you ever lived, obviously. And we can't let *everyone* live; that's just naive. But we . . . prevent undue pain when possible."

"Oh, *good*," James spat out sarcastically. "And here I was worried that you were all about the undue pain!" He crossed his arms over his chest. "You kill children."

"Yes," the man said quietly, all humor gone from his voice. "We do. When it is needed."

"I would argue it's never needed," James said, matching the tone.

The man gave a sad nod. "I know. That's why you're part of the problem."

"And what problem is that?" James asked. "The problem of too much magic in the world, perhaps?"

A laugh, in response to that. A real, honest, surprised, condescending laugh. "Dear boy, of *course* not! Well, maybe! But only as a side effect, you see! The magic is only a problem because it puts too much power in the wrong places. Lets things change too quickly. Before you know it, the outside is the inside, and chaos takes over, and then there's nothing left."

"You say, as you aggregate power to yourself," James sneered. "You think we didn't see your agents using artifacts?"

"Ah, so that was you at the high school." The man nodded. "Well. If I had any thoughts of letting you leave before, they're surely gone now." He shook his head, a frown on his face. "Those men had families, you know."

"So did those kids," James said, though he couldn't deny the barb hit home.

The man skipped answering that, James noticed. "Well. Our tools are our tools, of course. A well-designed organization can get far more use from them than any bog-standard trio can, anyway." He smirked, and James's blood started to boil at the pure smugness in the look. "Well, duo for you, now."

"So you did catch up to Anesh."

"Stepping off the airplane," the agency man affirmed. "You know, I'm always surprised when one of you chooses to die fighting. We offered him an excellent deal, after all, all things considered. It's been a long time since we've seen such a heavily modified human body." He looked at James with raised eyebrows, as if waiting for the response.

James didn't move. He took a second, took a deep breath. Anesh was dead. But Anesh wasn't dead, was he? There were two or three more of him; this was a minor setback and an existential crisis, not the end of the world.

But it hurt. So much. He'd promised. He'd promised his partner, when this had started, that every single one of him mattered. And now one of them was gone, because of this smiling bastard.

James put it aside. He had questions.

"How are you so sure there's only two of us left?" he asked, trying to be just the right amount of puzzled. "You don't know us."

"I think you'll find we know quite a lot about you, James Lyle. Even your military service record, classified as that seems to be." James stoically gave no reaction to that with a thin smile, the kind you gave to someone you knew was lying. The man continued, adjusting his dark-green tie. "Regardless, we know because that's how it always is, of course. That's how we know there's two of the teenagers left in the wind as well. Though I suppose you're responsible for that, too. It's always the same pattern, every time."

"For the dungeons?" James asked. He didn't want to overcommit to knowing anything or share any info that this jackass didn't already have, but he had to know. So he prompted.

"For any phenomena," the man affirmed. "What you call 'dungeons' are quite rare. We've only ever found them in this part of the world. Other mysterious happenings, though? It's always one person first. Then they infect their two closest relationships. Then the spread of information stops, for various reasons. Usually personal ones." He shrugged. "Trios. Always. Perhaps it's that simple human greed never allows for more than that."

"You're telling me no one's ever tried to set up a company on one of these things and harness it for profit?"

A *peal* of laughter at that statement. "Of *course* they have, boy!" The man slapped his desk in amusement as he caught his breath. "Where do you think Nike gets half its product from!"

"Child labor," James deadpanned.

"Child exploitation, certainly," the man agreed with a nod. "Oh, maybe of one of these special spaces you call dungeons, though." He winced a bit, shaking his head sadly, like he was talking about the evening having too much rain and not something far, far worse. "Ah, the modern world with its video game terminology. It's useful, I admit, but it does make me feel the age."

"Hang on!" James held up a hand. "How come *they* get away with it, but you're offing any trios that you set your sights on?!" he demanded.

A blink. "I thought we covered this. Because it puts power in the wrong places." He sounded disappointed in James.

"And the wrong places are, what, anyone who disagrees with you?" James noticed his voice raising in anger.

"Not disagrees, no," the man said, staying calm. "But there is a limit to the chaos we will allow in the world. This system *works*. We cannot allow all of humanity to be upset every time three young idiots get their hands on a dragon egg, or a magical gun, or, God forbid, some supposedly friendly spirit approaching a false apotheosis."

James bit his tongue and pointedly did not say anything at all. He tried to look as innocent as possible. It might have worked.

The man continued unabated. "Peace is allowed, in small doses, because power can be focused on those who can be trusted—or controlled. That's all. You, your surviving friend, those like you, you are all of you neither of those things. You spread chaos, and whether you mean well or not, you undermine a world that is functioning."

"Change is what it takes to make things better. You're just . . . letting it all stagnate. That's not even real control." James held his hands spread in front of him, trying to drive home the point. He couldn't really believe that this man, as affable as he seemed, *believed* this.

The man shrugged. "Perhaps not from your perspective. But it keeps the majority safe. And it works."

James snarled. "People suffer. Wars, famine, internet trolls. The world isn't getting better, and you're sitting on the keys. You're not even *trying*." He blinked and felt a wave of calm understanding in his heart. "Oh," he said, leaning back. "Yeah, of course. This is why." He sighed off the questioning look. "This is why she said we'd come to call you Status Quo."

The man laughed lightly. "I suppose that name is as good as any other, for those of us that build a secure world." Then he switched to a slight frown. "She?" he prompted.

"Your world isn't good enough," James said quietly, ignoring the question. Sadly. He was starting to understand, though. This anonymous man wasn't interested in changing his mind. He *believed* what he was saying. He really thought that the world was better off with him in it, doing what he did.

"I know you think so," the other man said, and James could see that he was just as sad on his end. What a tragedy it must be! To meet someone you could really *talk to* about everything and feel like you had to kill them.

James understood intimately in that moment.

"So, what now? Your global organization tries to sweep me under the rug, pick off my surviving partner, and pretend this never happened?" James counterprobed. As long as this conversation was happening, he might as well aim to extract what intel he could.

"*Global* is a strong word." The man laughed. "Oh, agents anywhere they are needed, yes, but they're mostly contractors. This is our home office, after all. You'd be surprised how few people it takes to deal with external threats." He didn't even bother to hide it; after all, James wasn't expected to survive the night.

"I really wouldn't," James said with a shake of his head and a grin.

"I suppose not." The man sighed and leaned back in his own chair. "But yes. While I understand you were here to try to do what you thought was right . . . well, it doesn't matter. We cannot let you leave the building alive, one way or another. Either you die loudly or you go quietly into the basement for processing. I suppose I leave it up to you, whether you wish to remain an asset to humanity."

"Oh, *that's* not an ominous phrase at all," James snarked, and was both a little surprised and amused to get a chuckle out of the man.

"I'm sorry, my boy, but you were just too much of a problem to let you be." The man spread his hands apologetically. "You won't be the first good soldier lost to this war."

James gave him a comical frown. "You're the ones that came into my house and poured coffee grounds in my Keurig. Don't act all high and mighty." He thought for a second. "Also, my military history is a fiction. I feel it's only fair to let you know."

"Fair!" the suit admitted with a boisterous laugh.

Conversation lapsed then, and the two of them sat there, reclining in their chairs. Just enjoying the quiet for a few seconds. Neither of them was going to surrender or change his mind. They'd said what they needed to say. Now there was only one thing left.

"Well," the man said, leaning forward. "I suppose it's time."

"I suppose it is," James said, setting an elbow on the edge of the desk. "Hey, before we do this, who are you?"

"No one of consequence," the man said, grinning wildly. "That's the point."

No more chances, then. For either of them.

James's hand dipped into his coat, and the man flew into motion himself. While James wrapped his hand around the butt of the flare gun and drew it in one smooth motion, the suit was discovering that James had already hit his desk, its drawers, and the hidden holster underneath it with Attach at the start of the chat. He wouldn't be drawing whatever he had hidden in there, and meanwhile, James had already leveled the flare gun at one of the windows and pulled the trigger.

The muffled *whump* was undercut somewhat by the flare bouncing off the reinforced glass.

For a brief heartbeat, the two men just looked at the flare sputtering to life on the floor, casting a sharp red glow on everything. And then they moved again.

"Vested Authority! Detain him!" the suit shouted, and James's hand locked in place where it was halfway through getting his real gun out. The man wasn't hesitating, either; he slid over his desk with more dexterity than someone in their fifties should have, grabbing the keyboard off the oak surface and swinging it like a club toward James's head.

James blocked with his off arm, wincing as the keyboard cracked in half down the midsection on impact. That was a guaranteed bruise. He shoved the pain away and moved to pivot to snap off a kick at the old man, but his right leg wasn't moving, either. So instead he used that as his brace point and turned the incoming tackle from his opponent into a throw, tripping and flinging the man into the opposite wall with a heavy thud and a crunch of plaster.

James saw a flickering of light on the man's ear and just barely caught the appearance of a glistening earring before the man himself disappeared. Wasting no time, James dipped his free hand into one of the many pockets of his coat and flicked out the infrared glasses.

His vision lit up, and his headache expanded to epic proportions, but he got his arm up in time to deflect the incoming punch, slapping the now-invisible man to the side before the roundhouse could connect with his jaw.

But his adversary didn't relent, instead sliding into a boxing stance and unleashing a small barrage of jabs at James. It was hard enough to judge depth in infrared already, and the flare's red bath of light wasn't making it easier, so James just had to try to shrug off the hits that came through. They mostly landed on the coat, but they stung, and the pain was starting to add up. In retaliation, when he got lucky and caught the latest punch, he flared his absorbed blue and Attached the man's suit to his skin.

The punches slowed down, and so did his target. He didn't drop his guard against James, and James returned the favor, but they were eyeing each other carefully now.

"I believe I have it," Secret whispered in his ear. "Not like me, but something else. I need one small measure of power to kill it."

James opened his mouth to taunt the man, which was when his enemy threw the paperweight at James's throat. He only barely dodged, his enhanced mind letting him feel the air moving just in time and causing the heavy lump of metal to deflect off his shoulder instead. James retaliated by snarling and hooking his mobile leg on the chair to his side, sending it flying a few inches off the ground toward his foe with the help of leverage from his "restrained" limbs. It sent the man down in a tumble of legs, which he rolled out of and to his feet near one of the windows a few seconds later.

"You know!" he said and was surprised by how shaken and loud his voice was. "The best part about this is that I get to see all your cool secrets." James panted for breath.

"Vested Authority." The man spoke, and his voice was no longer friendly. "Silence him."

James felt his throat constrict, as if grabbed by an ethereal hand. But there was one singular, ultimate constant in his life. One thing that had persisted, through school, through careers, through the loss of friends and the existence of magic. One thing that *never* went away, one light that never *ever* went out.

James was going, *going* to mouth off to authority figures.

"I've . . ." he croaked out around the force and realized that speaking caused the pressure on his voice to turn into very real physical pressure on his body. "I've got a Secret, too."

Secret was not a shield. Secret wasn't really a weapon, either, and he was actually, by his own admission, very bad at blocking anything that wasn't memory based. But what he *was* was very, very good at finding the small vulnerable points in things like him and biting into them.

And when James spoke aloud one open secret and pulled Secret's invisible form into the real world again, he acquired a certain level of weight from the execution of the hidden plan. From the shattering of expectations.

A blue leviathan was suddenly *there*, and James could see in the false light Secret threw off that there were ghostly green shackles locked around his right limbs. Probably also one around his throat, too, from the feeling of it. Or, at least, there were. Until Secret brought his jaws down and demolished the things like they were so much papier mâché.

Secret faded back to a paler blue, less substantial but still powerful, and coiling eternally around James's arms and shoulders. James faced where his enemy was still lurking, invisible to the normal spectrum of light, and smiled a vicious, predatory smile.

"Hmm" came the grunt of acknowledgment from across the room. "Didn't see that coming."

But he wasn't done. James could see the man shifting back into a boxer's stance, ready to fight to the last. So he did what a smart combatant did. He ignored what his foe wanted, drew his gun, and unloaded the magazine directly at the director's head.

The first bullet hit him in the eye. James *knew* it did. But while the man's head jerked back, he didn't fall or scream. The next fourteen rounds slammed off a web of golden light that bloomed to life in both visible and IR, bouncing around the room in a frantic ricochet spread.

James calmly started to reload, speaking softly. "Secret," he said. "When I start firing, tear his legs off."

"Yes," Secret hissed joyfully, overplaying his feralness for the audience.

"No." The man spoke and made a striking motion with the arm that had the shield bracer on it. Suddenly, the gun in James's hands was *gone*. Just a pile of dust; even the bullets were nothing but tiny pieces of metal and gunpowder dripping through James's fingers. While James was still processing the loss of his trusted tool, the administrator had closed the gap between them, slamming a fist through Secret's ethereal head with a force that actually shoved him out of the way, and then swinging another at James.

James blocked, slid back a half step. Adopted a judo stance, got ready to throw his enemy into the wall again. Felt the desk against his back leg, made a slight adjustment, and in that moment, the man was moving again.

If James was *half* as athletic as this guy when he was fifty, he'd be ecstatic. As it was, he was kind of wishing Status Quo had a less efficient exercise regimen. Because right now, the director was weaving between Secret's coils and fangs like a pro, avoiding semireal bites and exploiting openings to aim punches at James's head.

James swatted aside the first punch that came in, but the man flowed with it, bringing an uppercut toward James's chin. James would have grinned if he'd had time, as the move overextended *exactly* too far. With a yank, Secret jerked an ankle forward and James brought his hands together for the perfect grapple that he could turn into an arm-shattering flip.

Something on the man's person sparked, and *the punch landed.*

Nothing had changed; James was still landing his grapple, but he'd been hit. It had been the perfect strike in almost every way; his teeth slammed together so hard he tasted blood, and he reeled back. His throw messed up at the last second; James's back hit the wall instead of the other man's head. And James felt it all at double speed, his purple sensory orbs working against him. If he hadn't practiced with them over and over, he'd be dead just from the pain right now.

Instead, he grabbed the cat clock off the wall and flung it forward like a discus. His opponent made a hand motion and the projectile was suddenly already past him, but James hadn't intended it as an attack anyway. He was already pushing himself off the wall and using his increased acceleration along with his bizarre ability to move marginally faster in midair to slam a knee into the suit's chest.

The man toppled backward before rising to his feet again with a wet tearing sound. It took James a second to realize that it was his suit and skin pulling each other apart, and the realization almost made him gag.

Almost. No time for distractions now.

"Vested Authority!" the man yelled. "Detain the monster!" And there was a flash of shackles as Secret himself started to become pinned down, mouths sealed, eyes clamped shut. The infomorph thrashed and keened in a high tone, twisting away from James as he suddenly found himself on the defensive, trying to take the fight out of the way of the two mortal combatants.

"Last chance," James gasped out while reaching into yet another pocket and snapping the two blues contained there. "Come on, dude. Give up. Let Secret go. You can just give up."

[Problem Solved : Dishes Cleaned]

[+1 Skill Rank : Electrical Systems—Lighting]

[Problem Solved : Painkiller Administered]

[+1 Skill Rank : Recipe—Muffin—Blueberry]

"Or what?" came the distorted voice from the wobbly vision of the man on the other side of the room. It was strange, only being able to see him in the extra sense provided by the glasses, kind of like if you could see a single object but not in the color blue. "You think you and your pet can just walk out of here?" The man laughed, turning it into a cough that ended with him spitting blood at his trash can. "This office may be soundproofed, but you aren't leaving this building alive, one way or another."

"Not alone, no," James agreed. "I may have some help, though." He was going to keep bantering, but the old man stopped circling and lunged into motion again, closing the gap and executing another impossibly perfect punch that struck James in the chest and cracked a rib, sending him flying back into the sill of the window that opened onto the parking lot.

James thanked his reinforced skeleton as he pulled his head out of the spiderweb of cracks in the window, the cuts on the back of his scalp from breaking the glass already starting to scab over. His right hand fumbled for *anything* he could use as a weapon, but he didn't have much time.

"Your one single ally won't help you here. One girl just as stupid as you, against the whole building?" The man sounded like he'd laugh at James if he weren't so busy trying to kill him, and it occurred to James that his enemy hadn't run for help because he still thought that he was *going to kill James.* Blocking another incoming punch from the aggressive man who had leapt across the room to follow up on his first strike, James frantically knocked the fist aside and into the window, and then he smoothly pulled the pen that wrote in French out of a coat pocket and slammed it through the old man's elbow joint.

"Se rendre et mourir!" the still invisible but now heavily bleeding man yelled at him, shrugging off the pain of the injury to pummel James in the stomach with a flurry of rabbit punches.

James recovered just in time to trigger the bracer on his arm, hidden under the coat, wishing he'd thought to do so earlier. A quick switch to tune it to punches, and then the automatic shield flared to life and started eating the impacts like they were peanuts. The man kept up the assault, though, and James became acutely aware of the fact that the last number in his mental interface might just be "charges remaining" as it plummeted toward zero. So he stopped the shield, caught the next punch himself, and turned it into a looping pivot, slamming the enemy's face into the glass.

"Do you see?" he hissed, barely trusting his own voice not to break as he mashed the man's cheek into the broken windowpane and the golden glimmer faded back to red flare light. "You and your fucking arrogant murder agency. You think I brought my *girlfriend* to this party alone?" James reared back and, with as much force as he could, *slammed* the man's face into the window.

By the third hit, the man had swapped his own bracer to stop . . . James didn't know what. Slams? Defenestration? It didn't matter. The tinted glass broke on that third hit, and all of a sudden, everyone outside could see the red glow of the flare from inside the building, a beacon in the darkness.

The man jerked back, out of James's grip, stumbling to lean against his desk, ripping the pen out of his arm with a spray of blood. "No!" he yelled. In the moment, he noticed that his skin and suit had unwoven from each other at some point, and he took the risk on his desk drawer. It slid open neatly, and he grabbed the revolver there and leveled it at James. "No! It's never more than three!"

James preemptively tuned his bracer to .45 bullet and tried his best not to flinch as the first one lit up the space in front of him on the shield. Five charges left. Four, three, two. He stepped forward, and the man stopped firing, saving his shots in what he thought he knew was a futile fight.

"Here's another secret," he said, half to the man, half for the benefit of the damaged leviathan that was still fighting his own battle. "It's been more than three for a long time." James lashed out with more speed than he knew he had left and snatched the revolver away from the old man. "Let me introduce you," James said, "to the Order of Endless Rooms."

He fired, the last couple bullets ripping through the tinted glass of the window, as sure a signal as anyone was going to get.

Overhead, Secret rippled as he fed off the breaking of ignorance. The authority holding him sloughed off like dead skin.

"Secret," James said with an exhausted resignation. "Tear his legs off."

The man didn't go down without a fight. His hand grabbed the silver letter opener on his desk, and he brought the small knife up in a plunging overhand stab to drive it into James's throat, but it was too late. James caught the underpowered swing, ignoring the line of blood that opened on his chin anyway, and *twisted*. The knife went into his adversary's stomach, and then, pinned by James's grip and the desk behind him and unable to retreat, Secret's too-real teeth tore into soft flesh. With a brutal scream, the man fell, slamming into the floor with a wet, violent splattering noise. The fragments of his Authority faded out alongside the unnamed old man's final, anticlimactic breath.

The office *was* soundproofed, apparently. But in the sudden quiet, as the blood stopped pounding in his ears and only the sputter of the end of the flare echoed in the room, James definitely heard a rumbling thud coming from the roof.

"No time to rest," he whispered, pulling himself up to stand tall in the wreckage of the corner office. Binding the bracelet on his right wrist to the heavy revolver in his hand, he triggered a reload and moved toward the door, stepping over where the bookshelf had disgorged a pile of legal texts into the pool of blood on the floor and lightly resting a hand on the handle as he waited for Secret to pull himself together around his shoulders. The infomorph had holes in his scales from where the shackles had perforated him, and James could feel in his subconscious that Secret was hurting. Truth be told, so was he. But his friends were here, and there was work to do.

He tried the handle. Locked. Locked, from the inside? This guy was as paranoid as he was stupid. Though, to be fair, he had just gone down fighting in his own office. James counted himself lucky that he'd had Secret to help mask his approach a little; if he'd come in here in handcuffs with another goon behind his chair, this would have gone a lot differently.

With an unamused snarl, James pulled a paper clip out of his pocket. Wedged it into the door's lock and then bent it in a direction that didn't exist. He exerted as much pressure as he could, occasionally resetting his grip so his wrist didn't pop off. Then he yanked it as hard as possible outward, and the paper clip tore through metal and wood from a direction that it had no physical presence in.

James pocketed the blue that that paper clip dissolved into as it broke off in the external bit of the lock, then kicked the door open and moved out in a low crouch, gun up in front of him. Time to rejoin the others—and burn this place to the ground.

The glass front doors cracked as they were thrown open and masked figures in body armor rushed into the lobby of the building.

The woman behind the desk, one Marion Driver, had been a loyal operative of the agency for forty-six years. She had fought for them, she had seen secrets that were beyond most men, and she had killed, repeatedly. Before women were able to even hold some jobs in America, she had led an operations team. Her work here, now, was a retirement of sorts. She didn't want to stop, but old injuries, both physical and spiritual, kept piling up, and desk work was really all she was up to these days.

She'd known, sort of, what it might mean to let James meet the director. The old man was like her, in a way. He wouldn't let the boy leave, but maybe, just maybe, there'd be someone new for Marion to brief tomorrow.

Still, her instincts were razor-sharp. And so, when those first two people had come in, guns up, she'd hit one with a shotgun from under her desk and the other with one of the unique tricks she'd picked up over the years, sending a small wave of reversed time to throw them back out and buy her time to line up a second shot.

The first figure had shrugged off the buckshot even as it punched holes in her armor; kinetic force bled off just enough that her skin didn't break around it. The second assailant was rewound, yes, but all that did was reveal some kind of black-shelled snake thing that had been coming in behind them.

And when that monster looked at Marion, she froze. Both out of fear and because she could feel her personal momentum being sapped away to nothing, leaving her locked in place.

Her hands were zip-tied and she was thrown facedown in front of her own desk, without stopping a single one of the invaders. She ranked it as the third greatest failing in her career, accounting for the ravages of old age, of course.

When the sounds of gunfire from deeper into the office intensified, she realized she was one of the lucky ones.

Dave/Pendragon hit the roof with the grace of a tank and the force of about the same. The building didn't crack under her—she was still made of paper—but it felt like maybe it should have. Sticking to the plan, and seeing no one up here who could pose a threat to them, Dave/Pendragon opened their mouth and vomited a wave of twisting gravity that tore away the doorway that led to the roof-access stairs. The door ripped itself apart, and pieces of it, no longer obeying the normal laws of physics, found their way in a drifting line out over the parking lot where she'd thrown it.

They raised their wings into the air in a triumphant, birdlike gesture. And from Dave/Pendragon's sides, six figures both human and camraconda dropped to the rooftop and started moving with something imitating military precision toward the now-open stairwell.

Then, as Dave/Pendragon lifted off from the roof in an explosive gale of paper wings, figures began to run up from the stairs.

Men and women, unmasked, wearing suits and not armor. But they held guns, and they didn't bother asking for surrender. They just started shooting at the invaders on their roof.

One locked up to a camraconda before their shield flared to life, golden light flashing bright in the darkness. Then another shield flared as return gunfire started, and another, and another. One of the invaders reshaped the concrete of the building into low cover; one of the defenders blinked across twenty feet of distance in a diving kick aimed at one of the attackers and quickly devolved into a rotating shield war between a camraconda lock and shielding from gunfire.

Then Momo, somewhere on the roof, started lobbing offensive totems, and things quickly spiraled out of control.

Dave/Pendragon started taking gunfire, the enhanced plated paper on her hide ripping and cracking under the impacts but not letting anything do more than a little damage. They leapt, soaring overhead and dragging one agent in a chair claw, throwing them aggressively down toward the asphalt of the parking lot as they cleared the lip of the building. Dave/Pendragon left the fight upstairs to the squad; they'd be fine, and she had a second job.

Cause some chaos.

Trying to ignore the brief glimpse of the full engine schematics of every vehicle within twenty miles as they passed too close to one of Momo's intel grenades, Dave/Pendragon did a low, looping glide that brought them out over the street and then back toward the building that housed their enemy's organization. They didn't slow down as they approached this time, though.

Dave/Pendragon put their head down, wings tilted just slightly forward, gaining momentum with every passing second. Until, suddenly, they threw their wings out, their talons forward, and slammed with the force of a furious truck through the windows of the second floor.

No one was still at their desks. The agents inside were aware something was wrong now; there was fighting on the roof and the ground floor, and it seemed like some of the people were trying to shoot a blue light–wreathed figure that was dashing from desk to desk. There were maybe twenty people here, alert, armed, *angry*, and ready for anything.

They were absolutely not ready for Dave/Pendragon.

The unified life form snapped their jaws forward, grabbed the nearest agent from behind, and with a twist of their long, sinuous cardstock neck, flung the woman into the darkness outside at high velocity, her pistol dropping from her fingers in shock as her scream faded into the night.

The agents had noticed. Gunfire started turning their way. Taking a few bullets, Pendragon/Dave dug claws into the ledges and shattered glass and scampered sideways along the exterior of the building, the windows exploding outward around them as the agents inside shot through to try to knock them down. They rounded the first corner, slammed a talon through to sweep a pair of desks and a pair of unfortunate agents into a crumpled pile, and then, cutting their losses before their armor started to ablate too much, shoved off with a push of heavy paper wings.

Dave/Pendragon circled the building a hundred feet in the air. Thirty seconds, they thought together. Thirty seconds and they'd strike again.

James gasped in pain and considered whether it was appropriate to vomit a little bit. He was huddled behind an overturned desk, just on the other side of a thin cubicle wall from a trio of agents who had all been shooting at him. One of them had been shooting at him *successfully*, and he felt the bullet still wedged in his palm where he'd tried to swat it out of the air. It hadn't worked—he wasn't Alanna—but it had kept it from hitting him directly in the face.

Now he was running out of a lot of stuff. He checked the bracelet on his arm, asking it politely how much he had left in terms of ammunition.

[Bind Firearm—3—90/300—126:14:3:18 (0)
Cluster Shot—54—16,894/100,000—3:12 (0)
Munitions Dump—23—1,106/2,000—31:55 (3)]

Three uses left. He'd burned through a lot of it with this stupid six-shooter the director had provided him. The one upside was he was stress testing the limits of the bracelet and finding them surprisingly not very human. In comparison to the blue orbs, which caused internal bleeding and migraines if you overused them—and he had already exhausted his Attach charges—this just cared about the cooldowns and the stored uses. Of course, the cooldowns were kind of long, and he didn't have half an hour to wait for the next reload after he used the last three charges.

In retrospect, James mused, he probably should have just walked out of the director's office and shot everyone in the head while they were still at their desks. Instead, he'd politely asked for them to lay down their weapons, which had of course made them *pick up* their weapons, and now he was in the alarmingly familiar scenario of taking cover against a cubicle while violence was directed at him.

Bullets whipped by him, and he tried not to hold his breath as he prayed that their suppressive fire didn't accidentally clip off a chunk of his brain. The cubicle wall was nothing to the assault, though the desk was doing a good job of keeping him safe. The shield bracer he'd stolen was out already, and the corpse next to him didn't have one. He waited for a lull in the firing, then waited another second for one of them to start shooting to try to keep him pinned before he popped out and put two heavy bullets into the kneecap of one of the unshielded agents. When he dropped to the ground, James felt a moment of heart-twisting pain mirrored in the man's face before he fired again and a splatter of blood and brain matter painted the carpet.

One more down, he thought with as cold and mercenary a mindset as he could keep, while the more physical parts of Secret's form dragged him back behind cover before the return fire could find him.

Two agents left. He sent a silent thanks to Dave and Pendragon for wreaking havoc among their ranks, even if his friend hadn't stuck around to let him get on the dragon's back and *leave.*

James huddled behind the degrading wood of the desk as gunfire filled the air with deafening cracks and the buzzing of bullets. Two more, or until the assault team got here. It wasn't a race.

When Alanna shouldered through the door at the top of the stairwell, rifle up to an armored shoulder, she was met with the smell of blood and gunpowder in an overwhelming wall of sensation.

The dead littered the floor. There were only two living things left here, James and Secret, standing in the middle of the room, breathing heavily. Her assault team had moved as fast as they could, but the first floor had been overwhelmingly full of enemy operatives. They'd either known something was coming or suspected it, because there was no reason for there to be more bodies than desks waiting for the Order.

The only saving grace was that they hadn't been on high alert, and with the camracondas' help, they'd been able to disable and restrain most of the foes. They'd also kept wounds on the delvers' side nonlethal—for now, anyway. There were a couple people who might not make it, even with the functionally instant medical intervention that the camracondas enabled.

James, on the other hand, hadn't disabled anyone, and Alanna had a brief moment looking at her boyfriend and the infomorph orbiting him when she saw something dark and horrifying instead of the person she loved. There were over ten dead here, human corpses full of bullet holes and fang marks. The floor was a mess of blood and scattered paper and shattered glass.

James saw her, recognized her through the obscuring fox mask she had on, and offered her a weary smile as he let the gun slip out of his fingers. He opened his mouth to say something but only got out a tired "Ow" before he just kind of limply stopped trying to speak.

Alanna lowered her rifle as everyone fanned out around her. Shouts and digital hisses of "Clear!" sounded around them. Through the skulljack's wireless braid and the hardware Virgil had wired up, she tracked images of other Order members securing the prisoners downstairs, collecting computer towers and documents, stripping dungeon tech off enemy agents. But through her own eyes, she just saw James as she stepped up to him.

"Hey," she said softly, reaching out before freezing, unsure if she should touch him right now.

"They didn't surrender," he said, looking at her with sad eyes. There was blood dripping from a cut on his forehead, blood on his hands, blood staining his coat. He'd been shot, Alanna realized. At least twice.

"We have prisoners downstairs," she said, trying to make him feel better as best she could. A quick check of her skulljack inputs showed that on the roof, Sarah had disabled prisoners as well. "And upstairs," Alanna relayed. "Some of them surrendered. Not everyone went down fighting."

"Who did we lose?" James whispered it like a plea.

"No one so far." Alanna winced as she half lied. "Ethan and Neil need medical attention. So does one of the snakes—I dunno their name. Camracondas are watching them until we move the wounded to the hospital. And Anesh . . . made a mistake. One of him . . ."

"I don't understand how he can't care," James softly said, not really feeling *present* in the moment. "Well, I guess I can. It's just hard to live with the idea. So I'll respect how he wants to do it; one body isn't one Anesh. He'll live." James shook his head, trying to think. Trying to remember what he had to do. But he'd been hit in the skull repeatedly today, and it felt like there was a wad of cellophane between him and reality. Reaching up to massage his forehead, he realized his glasses were gone and vaguely remembered them breaking at some point. He left a smear of blood from his wounds across the bridge of his nose as he remembered something else. "The basement," James said. "There's a code to the elevator and a hidden door to a staircase. There might be captives down there."

"Okay," Alanna acknowledged. She turned and raised her voice. "Secure the floor! Check the bodies, make sure no one's getting back up! Then two people on alert while the rest of you collect anything that isn't nailed down!" She turned back to James. "Let's get you downstairs, then Sarah and I can check out the basement."

"We're coming, too," Secret whispered. "It is important." James didn't say anything, just jerked a thumb at Secret as if to say, *yeah, what he said.*

Alanna didn't argue; that would be pointless. She just worried as James limped like a wounded lion toward the elevator to the ground floor.

"Come on," he said. "We're wasting time here."

"Two guards, both on alert," Secret said as the elevator descended into the depths of the building. "They are . . . distant," he mused.

He was perched on James's back now, smaller than before, but more solid. He'd condensed himself as much as possible for what was to come, but he was still injured from fighting whatever the Vested Authority had been. He'd told James it wasn't another info-morph, not *exactly*, and while that was true, that hadn't stopped him from kicking the shit out of it. Or, in turn, stopped it from getting some good licks in on him.

The elevator contained James, Alanna, Anesh, and Secret. Another team was taking the stairs, but these four were going down together in advance. James was in armor now; when they'd made it to the first floor, a pair of delvers had helped him out of his coat and clipped the Kevlar and plastic shell into place like squires, their moods almost reverent as they helped the bloodied fighter into his gear.

As they descended, James clipped the braid into the back of his skull, shoved the hardware into the security of the back of the armor on his neck, and opened up the wireless access to his brain. Suddenly, he had two more fields of vision, both of the door of the elevator, Alanna, and Anesh. He knew how they felt about the building, how they'd navigated some of its halls and rooms. He knew how many bullets were in their guns.

The three of them had rifles now. James had left the .45 revolver behind, abandoning his bound gun on the grounds that he didn't have any charges left to do anything with the magic anyway. He'd burned a lot of his tricks, and it sounded like the rest of the Order had, too. They weren't *soldiers*, but they had a collection of bullshit they could bring to bear that tilted the tables against the actual trained killers. It just wasn't a collection with a lot of staying power for protracted battles.

The elevator ride went on for a long time.

"I think the people taking the stairs may not have known what they were signing up for," James mused.

It was a joke. Not a great one, but it was a joke. And suddenly, he could *feel* again. The tension in the air, the fear and pain. He could feel Anesh's anger and Alanna's fury.

"Anesh," James said softly, reaching out. Then he stopped and realized there was a better way to do this. He pulled back his hand and reached out in his mind. The connection was filtered, but it didn't *have* to be. He pinged Alanna first, and she widened her eyes as she answered. Their minds slipped together like kindred flames rejoining. Lovers and partners and allies and *so much more*. And then, together, the two of them queried Anesh.

He didn't answer at first, and they didn't push. They just sat there, waiting. Physically standing in an elevator, their crew going from four to three people in an eyeblink as two of them became one. They offered, held out a hand, and held back.

Anesh sighed, his shoulders slumping. And he reached out to take it.

They didn't need Virgil's filters, they all suddenly understood. They should have been fighting this way the whole time, like Simon and the other James did. They were *together*. They could feel each other's lonely pain, and they could feel each other's steel-bound support, their shared bonfire that was a relentless love and trust.

Three minds danced together on an elevator ride into the bowels of the Earth. Healing each other, supporting each other, sharing their emotions and information and experiences. At a certain point, they drew each other so close that half their orbs snapped into focus on each body, and a torrent of power flooded each of them. Reaction time snapped up, the smell of the elevator suddenly sharper, and bones and fingernails and hair hardened. Skills poured in like a river. Not every orb went to every one of them, for reasons that didn't follow a pattern the trio could track, but some did. Enough, maybe.

The weirdest part was that every one of them was probably a Canadian citizen now.

Then Secret was with them, their singular mind thinking him into being with more focus and definition than ever before. He spun around them, broken scales healing, fangs and eyes and curves streamlining.

The elevator doors opened. The person inside had lined up two bodies on one side and one on the other with Secret. There were guards outside, guns ready. Unlike the agents upstairs, these men were in body armor and held automatic shotguns. They were prepared for a real fight, but they were unsure what would be coming down the elevator since the camera feed had been cut. One of them yelled a challenge, but there was no response from inside.

They made no move to get closer, keeping their distance and their weapons up. The person inside nodded once at Secret, and he flowed to the floor, moving like a perfectly normal glowing blue snake with too many eyes who was longer than he appeared. He shot forward out the open elevator doors.

The guards outside shouted and then started shooting as he approached them. The overwhelming booms of shotgun blasts echoed through three sets of ears and generated a collective wince. Then they had a moment of knowledge from Secret that he was past them, and the guards had turned away.

The bodies that used to independently belong to James, Anesh, and Alanna stepped out and started pouring .308 rounds into the two men who had made the mistake of turning their backs on the elevator.

Two corpses hit the floor in pools of their own blood. The collective that killed them, and spared one of its minds to realize that it needed to name itself, was thankful that all its parts had remembered ear protection this time. They stepped off the elevator and over the bodies and moved forward, guns up. Secret hadn't detected anyone else hiding down here, but that didn't mean there weren't people who were just around and armed and *not* waiting in ambush.

The floor was one large room, and the three shells slowed as they moved toward its center. They walked in perfect sync, only making slight mistakes as they adapted to being one together. A ring of limbs with guns pointed outward; three hundred and sixty degrees of vision. They took in the sights around them as they realized what was going on.

Blue lights overhead, cool air all around. Smooth white sheet vinyl underfoot. Metal racks filled with what looked like medical supplies. Secured metal lockers against all the walls. A couple of carts around the room.

Beds.

So many beds. All of them with a swarm of monitoring equipment and needles and tubes and IV drip bags. Thin hospital sheets covering bodies that almost looked like corpses. People with skin like old leather pulled tight against bone, barely any muscle mass left, veins jutting out in profane lines across their bodies. There were heavy straps pinning their arms to their sides, their legs held together, and their full forms locked to the beds.

Underneath each bed, raised just slightly from the floor that they were clearly mounted in, there were stone rings. Toroidal shapes, perhaps three feet thick. *Some kind of sandstone,* one of the component minds thought. There were markings on them, some of them dark shadows, others a glowing red. As they watched one of the beds, there was a whirring noise—one of a dozen such noises— and a small drop of blood so dark it was almost brown dripped down from a tube. Pulled out of a person and onto the stone slab.

A marked character lit up with a red glow. Only about three hundred more and that one would be complete.

Not every bed was occupied. But all of them had the rings underneath. Waiting for new sources of . . . blood? Life energy? Suffering? It didn't matter. This was going to stop now.

"Hey!" a voice challenged the entity, and all six of its eyes collectively snapped up to a man in a lab coat walking toward them. He had glossy hair and a trimmed goatee and was sipping from a mug of something. "You the new guys? You're supposed to check in before you . . . !"

There was a wave of absolute revulsion from within three minds and one person. These people were being tortured to death, and he was just standing there, talking about *policy?!*

They shot him. The vile mirror of a doctor vanished in a spray of blood, dead before he could even be surprised. Three bullets punching through the heart, brain stem, and skull. All of them aimed at the same spot, and the shots hit so close together they may as well have just been one single hammer blow. Bullets they'd bought to kill giants made of metal put grapefruit-size holes in the unarmored human body.

This time, someone heard the gunshots. There was a weak moan from nearby, and James's body rushed over, dropping his gun to its sling as the body grabbed the metal bar on the side of the hospital bed. The gaunt figure groaned again, eyes locking onto the horrified face looking down at it. At him. The groan itself was muffled, even; there was some kind of mix of an oxygen mask and a cage locked around his face.

The eyes. The Empathy Alanna had learned echoed through the mind. *Look at the eyes.* He hurt so *much.* He'd been here longer than he could remember. It felt like it had been his whole life. He just wanted it to *end.*

"I don't want to kill you," they whispered with three bodies. "Please, what can I do?" Working together, James's and Anesh's hands started to unhook bonds and remove tubes and hooks from the near-corpse's mouth, doing what they could to free this ruined person's voice.

A wrinkled, scarred hand feebly grasped at James's wrist, trying to pull him in. It couldn't; there wasn't enough of a person left to apply force. It was like being grabbed at by a cloud. The body leaned forward anyway, and the victim whispered.

It was a series of numbers. Eyes flicked over to the lockers along the wall as the weak man flopped back to the bed, his limited strength exhausted. The motion itself caused a series of snapping cracks; his own bones had shattered just from *that*. He was falling apart. Quickly. And he didn't seem to care that moving was hurting him more.

Alanna's body strode over to the indicated cabinets and punched the numbers into the keypad before opening one of the lockers.

Shelves. Lots of them. Each one containing, neatly packaged in a bed of custom-cut foam and helpfully tagged, an artifact like they'd seen the agents wearing. A copper-and-ivory bracer here, a silver greave there, a polished earring in this one. Thirty, maybe forty objects, some of them they'd seen so far, some they hadn't. Just in one locker, enough to equip ten people for war.

There were more lockers.

A memory from the conversation with the director pulled out of James's memory. *To the basement, for processing.* Processing. This was where their equipment came from. They'd found a dungeon at some point with these . . . sacrifice rituals. Put blood in, get an item out. And just like the Order had begun exploiting the duplication ritual, they'd done the logical thing. Pull them out and industrialize it.

Why the prisoners, though? Why not just . . .

It didn't matter. They banished the thought across three minds. It didn't matter *why*. This structure wasn't surviving intact.

By the time the second squad made it down the staircase, James, Anesh, Alanna, and Secret had quietly disconnected the life support of the last captive. They sent them on their way with held hands, tears, and a promise. That this wasn't going to happen again. And that the Order would use the product of their blood for something worth dying for.

None of the people here, even the newest of them, could stand. Half of them couldn't breathe under their own power, even. Their bodies were so used up, they were tearing themselves apart. The trio hadn't known what to do. Hadn't known how to help. And every time they'd tried to ask . . .

They only got one request. When the emaciated human shells could speak at all.

When they reached the surface, having packed up a lifetime's worth of impossible magic from the basement, James had to be held back from just executing every prisoner they had. Though he didn't *really* want to murder anyone in cold blood. Not again. Which was good, because some people didn't really put a lot of effort into stopping him.

Instead, they settled on dragging them outside, stripping them of everything but their underwear, and leaving them in the parking lot as a pair of *very* nervous members of the Order carefully wheeled a water tank out of the back of one of the vans.

It was not filled with water. It contained, in its core, a tank of liquid ether. Around that was packed far too much aluminum phosphate, and filling the rest of the sealed space was as much pure oxygen as could be safely added under high pressure. It was a bomb. It was actually kind of an absurd bomb. The kind that, if detonated in an underground environment, could collapse, say, a building. The number of things that you could learn from college chemistry students just by suggesting that you were interested continued to be one of the top things that worried James. Outside circumstances were pushing it down the list, but the fact that they'd been able to assemble a fuel-air explosive in one of their own basements, with minimal problems, was honestly kind of horrifying.

By this point, the streams of people going in and out of the building were dwindling. Nearby, the wounded Neil kept watch in the surrounding area with the limits of his drone swarm, a half dozen mechanical eyes monitoring for incoming police or agency vehicles. A handful of delvers, camracondas, and one angry dog-shaped magnetic distortion kept watch on the prisoners. Boxes of paper documents, stacks of acquired equipment, computer towers, and anything they thought might give them more information or potential operational strength—all of it was loaded into the backs of the vans they'd circled up in the parking lot.

And then they were ready. James leaned into the elevator, punched in the code for the basement, nervously twisted the timer on the bomb to just enough to get it down the shaft before it went off, and then ducked back out, letting the doors close.

"Time to get out of here," he announced as he stalked out of the building. "Everyone, pull out! Leave the prisoners!" James yelled, and a swarm of Order members started piling into vans or back into the landed form of Pendragon. James turned to give the prisoners one last look. The surviving members of their agency, the last remnants of what had just yesterday been the gatekeepers of magic for a quarter of the US. One of them, the woman he'd passed at the front desk, gave him a death glare from the cold ground. "If we ever see you again, we're going with kill on sight," he informed them coldly. "Whatever gods are out there sure as hell know you deserve it."

He turned, stalked away, and climbed into the passenger seat of a van without further comment, leaning back into the seat and trying to ignore the screaming pain of his wounds. A glance down at his hand showed that it had already started to scab over, and he winced; he'd have to get someone to dig the bullet out for him later.

Behind the convoy of vehicles and Life form aircraft, a detonation occurred somewhere belowground.

The air in a three-hundred-meter radius was instantly turned to fire, and then vacuum. Directed by the sealed elevator shaft, the explosion rushed into the underground medical torture facility, vaporized most of what was left there, and left the room empty of air. Then, the pressure began to pull on the structure's foundations. Flooring ripped downward, support struts cracked, the building bowed inward. Aboveground, it wasn't very impressive; a two-story office building sort of pushed down in the middle, like a squashed cake. But underneath? The things hidden below it were crushed under hundreds of tons of metal superstructure and rock debris. The elevator shaft crumpled in on itself, leaving nothing but what looked like a quarter-mile-long sinkhole beneath the structure. It was possible that some debris shaking loose from the building might have fallen on the bound prisoners around it. No one who understood what had happened here cared.

The sound was phenomenal. Nearby windows shattered. In the distance, after a moment, sirens sounded. Lots of them, from every direction.

Devastation.

And if anyone who knew what was down there ever tried to dig it out, James would just do it again. And this time, he wouldn't wait for them to leave first.

Not for the first time, the Order won a fight with Status Quo. And not for the first time, it really didn't feel good at all.

CHAPTER 21

Momo's first totem, refined over a dozen iterations as her skill in making the things grew and she continued using it to practice new ideas, guided them to where they needed to be.

It found emergency medical care. It did that originally, and it didn't have a range limiter, didn't give extra context, and if you listened to it for too long, you'd start to feel like someone was trying to scoop out your right eye with a melon baller. These days, it did that but was limited to about a thirty-mile radius, and you had to listen to it for a *lot* longer before it started to cause migraines and maybe brain damage.

Momo was pretty proud of that one.

Even though it was late and only getting later, the veterinarian's office that they pulled up to still had its lights on. And according to the totem knowledge they'd all been imbued with, it had at least one practicing individual inside who was capable of rendering emergency aid.

"A vet?" Neil groaned as they helped him out of the back of the van. "You couldn't find me a hospital?"

"We're avoiding hospitals," Momo told him, the short girl comically struggling to help the wider young man towering over her. "Stop griping. You're the one that kept going instead of letting Feeling-of-Home freeze you. You didn't *need* to bleed all over my van."

"S'not your van," Neil mumbled. "Order property. Traded gold for it and everything."

"Sure, man," James agreed from the other side. "Just shut up and let's get you patched up."

It was Momo's James this time. The two of them, two camracondas, and a handful of other members of the Order had split off with this van to get Neil medical aid. Another van had taken Ethan; he was going to some doctor's house in the suburbs that Leader James said would be open to helping. Others with more minor wounds had been similarly distributed or had just retreated to the lair to get patched up. Different places—asking one person to treat a mysterious gunshot wound in the dead of night was a weird event. Asking one person to treat *several different people* with similar wounds was *far* more suspicious. A lot of people were on their way back to the lair, but the vans were only so big, and making a casual stop at home base was awkward when you had people with bullet wounds.

The most worrying, at least in Momo's mind, was that Frequency-of-Sunlight had been hurt. Hit by something through her main body sometime while the firefight on the roof was happening. Momo felt like she was in the wrong place; she should be there, tracking down a computer repair shop or a mechanic or something.

She shook off her thoughts as they made it to the front door and she started rapping on the frosted glass of the locked barrier. "Hey! Open up!" Her shout echoed in the night.

It took five minutes of standing in the dark between two winter-dead shrubberies that hadn't bothered to regrow their leaves, pounding on the door and yelling, before the vet came to the front to see what the hell was going on.

Momo was, by this point, uninterested in wasting time. Certainly, *Neil* would prefer if the bullet still lodged in his chest could stop being there sometime soon. So, when the middle-aged woman with her brown hair in a bun and wearing a stained white medical coat opened her mouth, Momo cut her off, using every trick of communication and social etiquette she'd learned over the last few months—both from the dungeon, from other delvers, and from James especially—to get what she wanted.

"If you fix his injuries and don't ask questions, you can have this," Momo said, dropping a half-pound gold nugget into the woman's hand. Yet another random and unfair advantage their dungeon boons gave them; the ore vein in the basement was of such a high concentration it was basically magic. Well, it was literally magic. Momo remained unsurprised.

The veterinarian did *not* remain unsurprised. She stared, open-mouthed, at the chunk of metal in her hand, eyes flickering between Momo, the gold, and the small mountain of an individual that was Neil. The delvers were still in most of their body armor, especially Neil, whom they hadn't wanted to move too much to remove it, fearing injuring him further. They smelled like gunpowder and blood, and they looked like extras from a sci-fi dystopia.

The vet looked back at the gold. Thought about asking if it was real. Realized that was a bit pointless, made a decision, shut her mouth, and stepped back, swinging the door open and motioning them inside.

She *did* demand that Momo give something at least pretending to be an explanation when Feeling-of-Home followed the humans through the door.

"Didn't lose anyone. Somehow." Nate spoke into the cheap cell phone he'd found along with a few others of the same model in a sealed plastic crate labeled *crab* from the last Sysco order that had come into the Order's kitchen. His kitchen. There had been five phones, five prepaid SIM cards, and one battery. Each one had a number loaded and was single use, in that he was expected to add the phone and card to separate trash compactors and pocket the battery after making the single call. Nate thought this was needless bullshit, mostly.

Right now, he was standing just off the street a few blocks away from the building that the people he worked for seemed to have started unironically calling The Lair. It was a spot between the parking lots of three different fabrication companies, where the employees tended to congregate for late-night smoke breaks. A coffee can of cigarette butts sat half-buried in the dirt and bark dust near him, and he was planning to add his own contribution to it shortly.

After the call. "I'd estimate they . . . we . . . incapacitated or killed roughly forty-five individuals. A lot of them were trained field agents. No clues on where they came from, though I'd be willing to bet at least one used to be one of ours," Nate continued to report in a conversational tone, pausing as a pedestrian walked past. He didn't have a time limit, and no one was going to interrupt him from the other end of the line, where he was speaking into a recorder anyway. "The opposition were trained, as I said. But sloppy. They relied on . . ." Nate paused, not knowing how to say this. At least, not in a way that wouldn't get him thrown into a psych ward. "They relied on *unconventional* methods. Unprepared for a direct assault."

All this was technically true.

"The Order also relies on unconventional methods." He said it smoother this time, the obfuscation slipping into place like a well-worn shirt. Warm and comforting, even if you could see a couple holes. "At present, their operational goals remain unclear, as do those of their enemy. I request any information we have on this Status Quo, if available. The leadership has referred to them as such repeatedly."

He paused for breath. Wished that breath was a smoke. Then continued, still talking in a way that was way more professional than he liked. "Despite the sudden turn to military-style violence, I do not believe the organization to be planning large-scale acts of violence or terrorism or to be a threat to the civilian population. Leadership continues to show both socialist and communist attitudes." And wasn't that an understatement? Nate felt the hair on the back of his neck prickle and resisted the urge to look around. "I'll keep up surveillance. And would appreciate more detailed orders."

He finished the call, removed the phone's SIM card, snapped it in half, broke the phone in half, and dropped part of the assembled mess down a sewer grate. The other half he pocketed to do the same with elsewhere later. Calmly, he pulled out a cigarette from a crumpled packet in his back pocket, lit it, and took a deep pull.

Then he turned around.

"Productive phone call?" JP asked politely, taking the second offered smoke from Nate as he leaned against a nearby tree.

"Won't know," Nate grunted out, dragging on his smoke again. He eyed JP idly for a minute, the slick-haired young man watching him through seemingly unconcerned eyes. Nate briefly considered if he could, if needed, either disable or escape from whatever bullshit JP had up his sleeve. Strangely, despite having about ten years of combat experience and roughly forty pounds of muscle on the other man, Nate didn't feel great about a fight. He didn't hate his odds, but he was positive JP was sandbagging a trick or two.

JP noticed. He didn't mention it. "How very James Bond," he said instead, sighing like a disappointed parent. Nate hated that gesture; it felt like he was being lectured, in an absolutely condescending way. "You know, James told me not to follow you?"

That took Nate off guard. "Why?" he asked, deciding eventually on the direct route. The word rolled out without the confusion he felt, his words carefully contained and rationed.

"I'm pretty sure it's because he trusts you." JP casually flicked some ash onto the ground. "For some reason."

Nate had had a lot of training. But he hadn't actually gotten any advice about how to deal with people who apparently were aware he was spying on them and didn't seem to care. JP obviously cared, but since Nate wasn't already dead or handcuffed, he was guessing the weasel was the only one. "You know . . ." Nate started, and for the first time in his life, he realized he didn't know what to say. He settled on "You know, it's pretty hard, lying about the magic. Especially when I'm supposed to be monitoring a radicalized domestic terrorist organization."

"You do get that there are literal fascist white supremacist groups that meet *in this city*, right?" JP asked politely, not even bothering to raise his eyebrows.

Nate snorted. "Yeah, I'm sure someone less lucky got assigned to those," he said. "Also, don't tell James yet. There's a finite amount of gunfire that won't get noticed," the bulky spy told JP.

JP did raise his eyebrows at that. One of them, anyway. "Tonight wasn't enough to cross the line? We blew up a building." He shuddered theatrically, only half faking. "I actually didn't know that we had that option, honestly," he admitted. "James . . . may have over-reacted."

"Not from what I've seen," Nate whispered.

The two of them stared out at the few cars passing in the street, listening to the soft notes of sirens still wailing in the distance as an army of emergency response vehicles descended on the smoking crater that used to be a structure several miles away. They smoked and didn't make eye contact.

"So. What now?" JP asked. "Turn us in to the government?"

Nate paused in his answer before tilting his head slightly. "As in, deputize you? Because that might be on the table, if James asks."

"No."

"Then no."

"Why not?"

Another pause, this one more personal. Less professional. He didn't have a good answer, just a gut feeling. The kind of thing that every good operative needed but they were trained to not rely on, not to follow without thinking. So he thought, like he'd been thinking for the last two days. And when he spoke, it was with a real answer. "You know, as near as I know, the Bureau doesn't have an answer to this bullshit," Nate said. "The magic, the living ideas. The *dragon*. I mean, the answer to the dragon is probably the easiest, no joke. It's shooting it. But the rest of the stuff? It's outside context."

"Oh god, no, don't you start making nerd references, too. You were the straight man," JP moaned.

"The US federal government isn't equipped for this shit, far as I know. And it's going to take you kids months to untangle the web of paperwork that you liberated, but we're already aware that this one single group, this *one* organization, was manipulating global corporations and governments and felt fine killing people in broad daylight without worrying about backlash. This is the thing that my department was created to fight, and we didn't even know it existed in our own backyard."

JP snorted. "The FBI was created to hunt anarchists after McKinley's death. Don't pretend you guys aren't just as bad as Status Quo, no matter whose side *you're* on." He stubbed out his smoke and dropped the butt into the coffee tin. "I may not be as 'eat the rich' as Alanna, but I can recognize that your agency might have a vested interest in things not changing."

"I . . . am surprised you know that," Nate said, stone-faced.

"Yeah. Well. I'm not just a pretty face." JP turned to leave, preparing for the alarmingly short walk back to the lair. "You know James trusts you?" he asked again, almost disbelieving. "I don't. But I trust James. Please don't fuck it up, okay?"

"No promises," Nate replied, dropping his own cigarette.

"Yeah, didn't think there would be." JP started walking and was swallowed up by the cold night.

"Hand me the wire clippers!" The shout echoed on the concrete floor of the warehouse and out into the parking lot. The back roller door sat open, showing off the back of the white van that had its own back doors thrown open as well.

The warehouse wasn't empty; it just echoed. They needed some rugs in here, according to Dave, and some sterile mats if they planned to keep doing improvised surgery, according to Deb.

Deb was currently wrist-deep inside a camraconda. And it spoke to the tension of the moment that not a single member of the group of wiseasses around them chose to make a joke about that.

"Here!" One of the kids—god, they were her age; when did she start thinking of them as kids?—slapped a tool into her open hand.

Deb was halfway to bringing it to where she was working, crouched over Frequency-of-Sunlight's stretched-out form on the flat surface of an irresponsibly quickly cleared desk, when she realized that someone had handed her the wrong tool. "Clippers!" she barked out. "Not crimpers!"

"But . . ." Graham started to protest. Oh, he actually was a kid, Deb half noticed. He'd been nervously poking around ever since people had started pouring back into the lair. "But what are you cut—"

She cut him off, speaking in that steady yet still urgent voice that she'd slipped into the habit of using from her time shadowing nurses during crises. "The shrapnel caused jagged cuts that need to be cleaned before we reattach. Now hand me the clippers; she doesn't have forever."

She got the clippers.

Overhead, Harvey held a pair of smartphones with their flashlights turned all the way up, shining light from two angles into the exposed innards of the camraconda. Giving Deb light to work by. Not the most makeshift surgery bay ever, but close.

The insides of a camraconda could have been fascinating. They weren't just cables; that was more like their *skin*. Instead, they had real organs and a circulatory system and musculature. Not fully made of flesh, no. Not *real*, exactly. Held up by magic in so many ways. But they weren't just sterile drones; there was so much going on in their bodies. In *this* body.

Frequency-of-Sunlight. The first one of them to choose a name. It was important to a lot of the Order's members. She was a known figure, a walking—slithering—story. She was also Deb's friend and had over the last week or so spent an increasing amount of time hanging around the nurse. Her name made her sound lithe and elegant, and in a way, she was. But she was also one of the larger snakes and one of the variety that had a wicked double row of quill-tip bronze fangs. With her custom-fitted armor on, she looked broad, intimidating, like a coiled menace. She would have looked quite the monster if you didn't know her. Didn't know that she was entranced by the idea of sarcasm, loved having mundane human memes explained to her, and liked the taste of lemonade.

She'd taken a grenade for the others on her assault team. And now, with the armor cut away where possible around the main wound, she looked *vulnerable*.

Deb hadn't even been aware that getting blown up was on the table; she'd been on the roof while the thicker fighting had been on the ground floor. Never heard the explosion. She was still wearing half her armor, even now, though she'd stripped everything off her arms except for a pair of surgical gloves.

Her hands, thin and dexterous, snagged the end of a thick, shredded cable, the material of the gloves keeping the fuzzed wires from shocking her, but Deb could feel the heat of the fluid dripping from inside it. Whatever passed for blood for the camracondas. She pulled it as far as she dared out into the open cavity and deftly clipped the end off, turning a jagged wound into a clean cut.

She wasn't even a professional nurse yet. She wasn't rated to perform surgery on *humans*, much less magical snakes. Was this even surgery? Or was it engineering? Tech support? Deb felt the intrusive joke in her thoughts and hated it.

It was like her brain was running two processes at once, and while half of her was staying calm, hands steady, doing what she could, the other half was manically and furiously thinking of random things. Like panic, only less directed.

An orb skill triggered, and she found the partner to the cut cord. Brought the two together and set the clippers, now dripping with some kind of blood substitute, to the side as she started doing her best to reconnect the individual wires. They were almost certainly veins, if the analogue to biological life held true, and she didn't want her friend bleeding out by her own inaction.

Wires connected, Deb held out her hand again. "Tape." Her voice echoed in the warehouse. This was the worst place to be doing this. Maybe she could get James to make them another basement for an actual medical ward. She needed to start learning more camraconda biology if she was going to be the leading expert on putting them back together.

A thin roll of black electrical tape was already in her palm. She blinked, then was back in motion, carefully using teeth and one hand to tear off exactly as much as she needed before firmly wrapping the interior cord at the joining point where it'd been sliced apart.

She repeated the whole process four times, the bleeding slowing as she repaired the life form on the desk.

At some point, Harvey's arms with the lights got tired and he swapped out for someone else. Deb didn't notice. Time lost a bit of meaning as she dug out another fragmented metal triangle of shrapnel with a pair of pliers and started using a cut-up slice of sponge someone had fetched her from the kitchens to mop up the blood as best she could.

"You're doing all right." She spoke softly to Frequency-of-Sunlight. The camraconda was still awake. Aware. Because what kind of anesthetic did you *use* for someone like this? Deb didn't know if they actually ever slept. Another question for her thesis paper, she supposed. "Almost done."

The hardest part was patching the hole in the outside. Her electrical engineering orb skill stopped working when she got to the exterior cords; they didn't have any signal or current running through them, and she hadn't had time to follow the Order's standing advice to take time to meditate on her skill orbs and draw out the information for adaptive use.

Deb was midpanic, her hands starting to shake as they failed to understand, suddenly, what the hell she was doing. And that was when Virgil stepped in.

He'd gotten back shortly after her, had been watching for most of the time but hadn't stepped in to interrupt. Deb didn't specifically like him, but he had an effective method of being *out of the way* unless actually required, which was an essential skill in the medical industry.

When Deb couldn't figure out how to get the thicker external cables to go back to being their tightly woven scalelike selves, Virgil had picked up the slack. Frequency-of-Sunlight had shown some obvious discomfort, but that might have just been because she had almost died and not just because there was someone a little less delicate tugging on her wiring.

Then, and only then, with the bleeding stopped and her friend safe, did Deb finally allow herself to sit down, the last dregs of the night's endless adrenaline rush bleeding out of her and taking her ability to stand up with it.

Someone helped her take off the rest of her armor. That same person, one of the other girls, thankfully, helped her into one of the beds downstairs. Deb almost laughed when Frequency-of-Sunlight got tucked in next to her, but her presence of mind was fading fast, and the last thing she registered was that the camraconda was making a light, airy noise that could only ever be interpreted as snoring.

Ah, so they did sleep. One mystery down, Deb thought as she closed her eyes.

"Hey." El's voice sounded almost deafeningly loud to her own ears. Even standing in the cold and windy air on the roof of the building that they, for real, called the fucking *lair*, it still sounded like the word came out at the wrong volume.

Probably didn't help that her head was still ringing with the sound of gunfire and screaming.

She blinked, hard, and behind the lids of her eyes she saw men and women dying. Figures wearing cheap suits and expensive blood. They'd been monsters, just as surely as a tumblefeed or a toll eater. But they'd also been people. And the Order had just . . . gone through them. Even if a lot of them had been captured, not killed, a lot wasn't *all*.

When she opened her eyes, Secret was still looking at her. Though, to be fair, the manifested version of the infomorph had so many eyes that he was basically always looking at everything. He was perched on the waist-high wall around the edge of the rooftop, on one of the corners that faced the road. At this time of night, a driver going by might look toward the building and wonder why, exactly, there was something glowing blue on the roof. But no one ever stopped to ask questions; El was worried it was because Secret was doing something fucky with their minds, but it honestly might just be because people sucked sometimes and ignored the cool shit all around them.

"Your heart weighs heavy," Secret muttered, his actual head still staring out into the night with its windswept trees and blazing streetlights.

"You talk like a nerd," El prodded, almost entirely on reflex. Then she bit her lip to shut her mouth, shook her head, and sighed a bit. "Sorry," she added. "I wanted to say goodbye. I'm leaving."

Secret turned, his serpentine form doing a long dip as he looped over his own tail to bring himself about to face her. "You do not believe you can be here," he said, words simple and yet impossibly complex.

"I'm not . . . I don't belong," El lied. "I've got the call of the road! Gotta be on my way, out exploring . . . the . . ." Her voice caught, and she strangled a sob before it could explode out of her throat.

"You have not talked to the others." Secret didn't accuse her, exactly; El was pretty sure that an accusation required anger of some kind. He didn't even seem disappointed, just . . . critical.

"They're busy. They'll figure it out. Not like I'm robbing the place on the way out." El tried her best not to make eye contact with the dude that was mostly eyes. "I'll be more comfortable away from here," she said, lying less this time.

"A strong hidden truth," Secret acknowledged.

"Yeah. Well." El shrugged.

"I . . . will miss you." For the first time, Secret hesitated. "I had hoped to be a better friend. But if you must go, you must go."

The words tore El up inside. Secret had gone from literal nightmare to a real friend as the days wore on, no matter what he said now. He was *interesting,* and *beautiful,* in a way that made the artist's soul spark and writhe. So far away from being a monster, but clearly inhuman in a lot of ways, and yet, and yet, every now and then he'd say something in that same dry tone James used sometimes and it wouldn't be until hours later that El would realize she'd been *burned*. But never in a mean way. If he was far from human at all, it was that Secret was never, ever cruel or mean.

And now she was going to ditch him. And everyone else, too.

She couldn't stay here. She wasn't a hero, wasn't some kind of dungeon knight, like everyone else in this fucking building. Even now, there were a couple figures on the opposite corner of the roof, politely giving her space with Secret, who were armored and armed in a way that made them seem like elegant black knights. That wasn't her.

She was just a girl with a car and a knife and a little magic. And she was starting to feel like if she stayed here too long, she'd find that she'd ended up as *way* more than that.

El didn't want to be more than that.

She stepped closer, threw an arm around Secret's body, and hugged him. For understanding, for caring, and just for being a friend. It was a long hug, and it was a goodbye hug. The two of them stood on the lair's roof for a long time before El took her arm back and stepped away.

"Hey," she said again. "I'll see you in my dreams, I guess."

"Always," Secret told her with a dozen warm smiles. "And if you ever need me . . . simply speak the truth."

El got the feeling that wasn't exactly literal. But she also knew Secret well enough to know that disentangling his words was an exercise left to the artist, not something that was ever really spelled out.

Half of El's stuff was already in her car. The other half was crammed into a duffel bag in her room. It was the work of a few minutes and one *infuriating* double elevator ride to grab her things, throw them in the back seat, and start the engine. She'd discover much later that someone had, at some point, slipped a dozen orbs into one of the pockets.

She idled in the parking lot for five minutes, waiting to see if James or Sarah would come try to convince her to stay. If Alanna would yell at her for being a coward. If Virgil would . . . what, come casually condescend at her? El didn't know. If *someone* would want to say *something*. But the minutes passed, and she remained alone.

El was still alone when she turned onto the street and headed for the highway on-ramp. The vibration of the engine fed through the vehicle into her fingertips and through the soles of her shoes. She ground her teeth at the empty highway, screamed wildly into the night. The car's accelerator got a workout as she hit I-5, fired a pulse of magic into the old junker, and took off toward the horizon.

But she still didn't outrun the smell of blood.

Reed was pretty sure . . . *pretty* sure . . . that James didn't actually know how many people worked in their research basement.

There had previously been someone who had been put in charge. It wasn't him; it was one of the older businessmen who'd been pulled out when James had rescued them all from the eternal conference room. The guy had been kind of a twit, but he meant well. He wanted to repay the kid who'd saved his life. Except, of course, his life had been devoured bit by bit while he'd rotted away in that forced network. His family didn't know him, his job didn't exist anymore, and he didn't feel like he fit into the weird framework of the Order that was starting to form.

He'd vanished one day and never come back. Reed learned later that he'd killed himself. And then he'd hidden in the bathroom and cried for half an hour, partially trying to process the information, partially terrified that was going to happen to him eventually.

After all, most of his family didn't remember him, either.

But then, the weirdest damned thing had happened. The two or three other people who experimented with orbs and tested items for metaphysical properties had started asking him questions. Then started asking him for *permission*. And then he'd realized one day that the reports he was dropping into James's inbox weren't just "this is what we failed to learn today" notes, but actual reports. And then budget requests. And then project proposals.

And more people kept joining up. By this point, Reed estimated that about eighty percent of the original survivors worked from this building in some way. *And* they'd hired new people, which was *bizarre.* How the hell did they just hire people to raid a dungeon?

They had more space now. More tools. They had actual safe testing environments and storage spaces. He met with Anesh every couple weeks to discuss things they should be replicating for common use in the Order and to get hints from the experienced delver on the feelings of different orb uses.

It wasn't all perfect, of course. He'd accidentally made, and consigned to death, a goddess at one point, and the knowledge of how he even did it was wiped out of everyone's collective minds. James had been *pissed* about that. But he poured his spirit into his work and he held his head high when he walked now. Reed could barely remember the cowering dweeb of an individual he'd been a year ago.

Almost dying changed people.

Now, though, he had a new project.

While he secretly lamented the *very intentional and understandable* loss of the artifacts that could create magical items, Reed did realize that maybe having something that ate human lives and spat out power might not be a good idea to hang on to. Their rival organization had clearly given fully in to the temptation of that power, and it had been ugly. A few clips of shared visual memory were flowing around the grapevine, and the facility under Status Quo's HQ had elicited a wave of disgust from both himself and the handful of trusted teammates he'd watched it with.

Still, though. Their basement research area was now crammed chock-full of boxes overflowing with the products of that vile process. All of it ornate, human-wearable equipment, most of it shaped out of wood, ivory, bone, copper, silver, and bronze. Armbands, jewelry, belts, boot . . . things . . . whatever the boot things were called. Piles and piles of these infused objects, every one of them containing reality-warping abilities available on demand to their wearers.

And Reed was *ignoring* them.

It had been four hours since they'd gotten back from the battle. He suspected, in the back of his mind, that someone would eventually name this particular fight, just like they'd eventually settled on calling their escape from the clutches of the Office the Exodus. But for now, it was just the battle.

Upon returning to the lair, the mood had been turbulent and mixed. Some people had crashed immediately, falling into beds or couches and passing out; while Reed was upstairs recently he'd seen Alanna herself napping while sitting straight up, still wearing her armor, before he'd quietly slipped into the elevator. Other people sat in silent groups in the cafeteria, sipping drinks and occasionally sharing shaky words. Still others had looked for something, *anything* to do with their hands.

Reed was one of those. He'd wasted no time finding a task that needed doing and throwing himself into it.

And that task was, mournfully, paperwork.

The other thing that was now filling his basement domain was a mountain of stolen paperwork. A hundred banker's boxes of archives taken from Status Quo, dozens of PCs left unplugged and stacked in the corner to await infiltration, the dirty laundry of the organization's last hundred years of operations. It was almost beautiful, except it was also frustrating beyond belief.

He'd just started pulling stuff out to read, hoping to get a grip on the organization system and build a starting foundation to expand on over time. But no, there was no system. Or if there was, it was as diabolical as Status Quo themselves. Some files referenced other files, some of which were digital, some of which Reed was *reasonably* certain didn't exist, and some of which—the minority—he actually found. Those ones were usually heavily treated with bars of black ink, cutting out anything useful.

He massaged his closed eyes as he took a break from staring at a heavily redacted page. These were *their files*, he thought to himself. *Why* in the *hell* did they blank out all this stuff if no one even knew they existed to try to spy on them?! Were they just future-proofing against someone like the Order wiping them out and stealing their office? Was this long-term spite in action?

He froze, fingers crumpling the paper's edge slightly as he tensed up. Three deep breaths later, he steadied himself, banishing the memory of gunfire. Reed pushed away the thoughts of violence, knowing he was doomed to nightmares later but feeling a form of driving, frantic energy *now*, pushing him to get *something* done.

"Y'okay?" Nikhail, one of his more trusted subordinates, asked, concern in his eyes.

"Fine," Reed muttered. "What do you think the Order's policy on heavy psychedelic use is?" he asked, only a little joking. "Also, do we have anything for a document type MW-RLC? I've got something here dated for today that references six or seven versions of it."

"Um . . ." Nikhail was a bit disorganized, which wasn't great, but he was trying, and for someone who'd grown up a trust fund baby, he did a good job. He was also one of those people who had instantly recognized the dungeon's ability to solve some of the harder problems with the human condition, much like the rest of the research team. In his case, transitioning. Reed hoped it would help him with his organization skills, too, eventually, but there were priorities to consider. Reed tuned out the muttering and shuffling of paper as he went back to sorting stuff into stacks based on how much the pages annoyed him, but eventually Nikhail replied more fully. "Got it. Yeah, we've got . . . two, so far. Two copies of one of them, too. Headers have what looks like country and state abbreviations, and then the first half of what's probably a zip code? Last couple numbers are blacked out on both of them."

"Why." Reed made his displeasure known with the flat expulsion of the word.

The three other people down here with him shared a look that communicated something he didn't want to understand right now. In unison, the group of fledgling dungeon scholars shrugged. "They're a shadowy bureaucracy?" Ryan volunteered cautiously.

"Ugh. We should do something about that." Reed reached for the joke and found he didn't find his own words that funny. "Ah, fuck . . ." he muttered, bringing a hand up to cover his eyes again. "Never mind. I think I need to take a break. Just set aside those files and anything else with that tag. I'll look over them later." He stood, pushing the wheeled chair against the wall.

He was sure there'd be at least a day or two to sort through this lifetime of a mess before James dumped another problem into the basement.

"I'm thinking we should build a city," James said.

He and Anesh were sitting together in James's office. Mostly because it had the most comfortable chairs. But also it was one of the few quiet places in the building, with the only other people here being a couple of camracondas. They *really* needed more space for everyone.

"We don't even have showers here," Anesh replied. He was leaned back in the padded seat, eyes closed. If he was at all concerned that his secondary body had been the one death on the operation, he didn't show it. "And we *should* have showers here. People smell after working out. And we've been here for days now, on high alert."

And on high alert they would stay. James didn't bother to say it out loud; everyone knew anyway.

"This building needing showers, and more space in general, doesn't mean I'm not thinking we should build a city," James clarified.

Anesh rolled his head around languidly to crack his eyes open and peer at his boyfriend. "Is this," he asked, "at all like your arcology idea?"

"Oh, I've pitched this before?"

"Not to me. But word gets around."

"Okay. Well, yeah. I was gonna build up to it and pretend it was reasonable, but we should build an arcology."

"Just because I heard the word doesn't mean I know what that is."

"Oh. Okay. So, like, sixty years ago, this guy named Soleri had this idea for a community that was sort of the ideal human habitat. His goals were maximizing community engagement and human happiness while minimizing resource waste, travel time, and space used." James tapped off points on his fingers, drumming them on his desk as he spoke. "So, an arcology—that's architectural ecology, FYI—is basically a space designed to house people."

"So a city," Anesh countered.

"Cities suck." James looked over at the map of the local area he had on his wall now, pushpins marking known dungeon locations, voice bitter. "We're hugely spread out but don't have any personal space. We pave over greenery and fill spaces with useless businesses that technically provide services, but they're mostly services we could centralize and do better communally."

"Do you have an orb . . ."

"Not everything is an orb, buddy. I just like watching philosophy videos on YouTube, and I have access to an army of research goons in the basement."

"Fair."

"So, yeah. I think we should . . . do that. Design a space, including the processes of society and governance, and then make it. And then live in it." James met Anesh's eyes. "My sales pitch may need work." He smiled weakly.

Anesh frowned. "No, I like it," he said. "The obvious problem is scale. But . . ." He tapped his chin. "We have greens. And can duplicate them. We could systematically solve some problems that way or create better spaces. The real problem is cost." He frowned suddenly. "Ah, and probably also nations."

"Yes, nations *are* a problem," James agreed sagely. "But I get what you mean. The good ol' US of A isn't gonna be too happy with us building a physics-defying city-size middle finger to the heavens and then inviting a million people to come live in it tax-free."

Anesh choked on the sip of water he'd taken. "Oh, so, you're not really thinking small here!" he exclaimed. "Okay! Fine! A million!" Anesh paused, halfway through throwing his arms in the air. "Wait, if you're thinking *that* long term, then you absolutely don't have an excuse for not getting showers installed here."

"I'll call a contractor tomorrow," he conceded with a more real smile than before.

With a smug nod, Anesh folded his arms over his chest and leaned back again. "See that you do." He sighed. "And Office day is coming up again. I'll make backup copies of some of the greens, and we can start testing them here. See if we can find any that are . . . abusable. Or, are we even going in?" he asked.

All of a sudden, James was incredibly tired. When they'd gotten back, Sarah had dumped what remained of her rest into James with a hug and then retired to hopefully dreamless sleep. But even that wasn't enough to keep him going forever. Mostly it just made him worry that the bonds were almost painfully zero-sum games. You really needed to trust someone, lest you be turned into a battery for sleep or whatever else they could link. Maybe that was the point, though.

He shook off his thoughts. "I'll be going in," he said. "We need to pick up at least a few yellows for Rufus and Ganesh. And the others, too. Not that we're low, but I want to be safe." He looked down at his empty cup, the food he'd forced down after the battle more or less eaten and then washed down with water. "Maybe I'll try to roll a vending machine out of there for the lair. I'm tired of not having juice."

"Ah yes." Anesh rolled his eyes. "Be safe by going into the death trap."

"Yeah . . ." James tried to laugh.

"Hey . . ." Anesh reached out and set his hand on the desk. A second passed before James extended his arm, placing his palm against Anesh's. Anesh clasped his boyfriend's hand, grip warm and firm against James's clammy skin. "I know this has been a fucked-up week, but we're going to be okay."

"Are we?" James barely found the energy to whisper.

"Yeah. We are," Anesh asserted. He stood up, joints creaking as he did so. "Come on. No one needs us right now, and we've got the building under guard. Let's get you to a bed. And, failing that option, let's go swipe all the soft things and make a nest on the floor here.

You can have a camraconda for a pillow." One of the cable snakes raised its head at that, single lens of an eye focusing belligerently on Anesh.

"Oh, man," James muttered, brain making the kind of connections that only really made sense when he was beyond exhausted. "I want a camraconda dakimakura."

"We've had this conversation before. It's still weird."

"No, before I wanted one of Rufus, specifically," James argued, as if that didn't make it somehow more weird.

"You know, I've got a sewing skill, and I know you have some fabrication stuff," Anesh said as he guided James to the elevator. "We could probably make some pretty cool dungeon Life stuffed animals."

James glanced at his boyfriend, processing the earnest words. He smiled, feeling his heart swell in his chest. "I'd like that," he said. "But after I sleep."

"Absolutely," Anesh agreed.

James didn't remember much after that, but when he woke up curled around Anesh in a pile of blankets and pillows on the floor of his office, he was the most rested he'd ever felt in his life.

Across the lair, the members of the Order and the assorted handful of other individuals in the building settled in for a quietly tense night.

Yes, they'd done it. They'd started, and in the same night mostly ended, a war. In theory, there wasn't much of a threat left to be posed by the survivors of Status Quo. Maybe half their agents left alive, some of those with some pretty bad injuries. Their headquarters was gone, their magic stripped away, any resources the Order could take they had taken. And they had outside contractors scattered around the world, though as the research team was discovering through their trawl of the paperwork, "scattered around the world" actually meant "one or two in most major cities, and most of them were just going to stop giving a shit when the checks stopped coming."

Yes, they'd basically taken a massive step forward as an organization. While most of them accepted that death was a constant risk, tonight hadn't brought its sting. And now they were blooded against human foes that were both willing and able to shoot back. The last couple days had seen them laying the foundation for their protocols on use of violence, developing plans of attack and overall strategies for employment of magic in combat situations. Not only that, but the trove of artifacts they'd liberated represented the ability to step up the power of their own operations by an order of magnitude.

And unlike the Status Quo, they could probably make more of them without killing anyone.

But some people were still drinking coffee by the gallon, perched on the roof with rifles just out of sight or standing on street corners with mostly concealed radios and earpieces. Some people stayed up on their own nervous energy, flipping through paperwork, or checking in on the cat in the basement, or just cleaning up the mess from hewing nuggets of gold out of the wall. And a lot of people sat quietly, not knowing what to say or how to keep on going as they used to do. Because they'd killed a lot of people.

Lua and Sarah were doing their best as the group's resident therapist-and-counselor team. But they were two people up against a small army of panic, doubt, and sorrow. Also they didn't have an established office space to meet with people individually, just a set-aside part of the warehouse space where they'd stolen and moved a couple of the couches, and the trust that everyone would give them a respectful distance.

Alanna was, after her nap, also trying. Though her way of doing it was more along the lines of individual debriefs with the Order members who were more in control of their emotions. Her words didn't help repair damage, but they shored up and supported the people who were dealing with it in their own way, lending credibility to the Order's actions. It helped tilt the attitude in the air, and over time it would spread around the knighthood, but it wasn't going to reassure anyone who was already cracking.

There was doubt. There was also fear of retaliation, either from Status Quo, or another organization they were allied with, or just by the police or government if they found out that the Order had bombed a building just to prove a point. And there was a kind of worry about what this meant for their future, too. What was the Order going to be?

Most of these people had signed up . . . well, okay, they hadn't really signed up. Most people had been rescued from the Office. Or they were people James knew personally. The people who *had* signed up certainly hadn't done so for the dungeons and *absolutely* hadn't done it to march into battle. There was this idea that floated around the membership, and the support group, too, the people who didn't directly work with them for now, and it went like this: sometimes you'd overhear James or Alanna talking about the future. They'd be having a conversation, and it'd sound pretty normal, until they passed by you and you'd realize that they were discussing building an orbital solar farm, or the logistics of ending poverty. Sometimes they'd ask random open questions to anyone in the room, often about very specific facts. And when answers didn't arrive, they'd run off to do research.

This was just what they did. When they weren't planning delves and organizing the Order with Anesh, they were planning the *future*. And no matter how the world kept turning, their vision was bright, and glorious.

It felt like a promise of something more.

But now that came into contact with the fact that they'd fought and killed. And it was hard for the group to deal with.

Hard, but not impossible.

The night wore on. It was past midnight by the time most people settled down to sleep. Guard shifts rotated with those who'd napped, Ganesh and the camracondas taking up watch positions to cover the lack of available humans. They never did get attacked, and as it started to look clear, and words and stories were exchanged, tensions started to fade.

When the next day dawned, they collected in the cafeteria. James made his ritual apology for not buying beanbag chairs to replace the shitty benches, Nate made eggs Benedict, and Secret made everyone relax by saying that the lair remained hidden information. They ate, sharing close space as they packed more and more waking delvers and snakes and researchers and infomorphs into the limited room, an extended family of warriors and magi and other things besides. And after the announcement that it looked like they were in the clear, as everyone became comfortable sharing tables and words, laughter started to drip back into the air.

People told stories. From the battle, but also sometimes from past delves, or just from their lives. Some of them talked about their work with magic items; others talked about dumb moments from jobs or school. Some of the camracondas asked questions about the idiosyncrasies of human society, which led to having to explain that US society wasn't *all* of human society, which led to having to explain nations. Again. Some people made jokes. Some camracondas shared their names for the first time. Some of the humans cautiously floated that they'd volunteer to go on a delve this week, you know, if anyone *really* wanted to . . .

And they talked about a better world and how they planned to build it. What kind of planet they wanted to live on, what kind of people they wanted to be. James made his arcology pitch at some point, and Anesh threw goofy comments from the back of the room as he gradually got everyone on his side about building a single-structure city-state. Momo talked about studying the duplication ritual and prompted Alanna on how to convert Earth into a post-scarcity society. Sarah went on a tangent about how different nations handled democracy, while JP stared daggers at Nate, who was wiping his hands idly on a towel in the doorway to the kitchen. Everyone had something to add. Even Secret talked a little about his experience living and what infomorph civil rights were probably going to need to focus on.

People started to leave around noon. They needed to go back to their homes, and families if they still had them. The lair *didn't* have showers, after all—though James had made a call or two.

But the building never fully emptied. People *lived* there now. People for whom the Order had gone from being a lifeline to a life.

And as James waited for his partners to pile into the car along with Secret's lightly glowing manifested form so they could go home and actually have a few hours of real downtime, he realized that he was, for the first time in a long time, really excitedly looking forward to the rest of that life. And he wasn't alone in that, either.

It hadn't been that long since he'd found his life utterly, irreversibly changed. Since he opened a random door by chance and found a horizon. Since the gray fog that his life had turned into had shifted into something magical. And partly, he felt like he hadn't gotten to actually *enjoy* that part of his life enough. Hadn't gotten to experience just having fun in a dungeon before he needed to save people, hadn't gotten to properly build a community with his friends before he needed to kill people. Hadn't gotten to settle into a world where magic was real and he wasn't trapped doing tech support for the rest of his life.

James didn't have too long to reflect before Alanna started fiddling with the car stereo and Anesh started grumbling about finding a way to sit where Secret wasn't poking him with at least one ethereal eye. Which might have been for the best, he thought with a smile. But he did have one clear thing he could take away from tonight.

For the first time in a very, very long while, James felt like he was headed toward a future.

And he dared to hope it would be a good one.

ABOUT THE AUTHOR

Argus is the pen name of science fiction author Forrest Taylor, whose works include *Kitty Cat Kill Sat* and the Daily Grind series, both of which were originally released on Royal Road. He lives in the Pacific Northwest.

Podium

DISCOVER
STORIES UNBOUND

PodiumAudio.com

www.ingramcontent.com/pod-product-compliance
Lightning Source LLC
Chambersburg PA
CBHW030921120726
47906CB00002B/438